ROOKERY BLUES

ROOKERY BLUES

JON HASSLER

BALLANTINE BOOKS
NEW YORK

To Maria

Jon Hassler 8-17-96

All rights reserved under International and Pan-American Copyright Conventions. Published in the United States by Ballantine Books, a division of Random House, Inc., New York, and simultaneously in Canada by Random House of Canada Limited, Toronto.

Two episodes of this novel first appeared in *Minnesota Monthly*.

Hassler, Jon.
Rookery blues / Jon Hassler.—1st ed.
p. cm.
ISBN 0-345-39356-2 (hardcover)
I. Title.
PS3558.A726R66   1995
813'.54—dc20   95-2953
CIP

Manufactured in the United States of America

First Edition: August 1995

10 9 8 7 6 5 4 3 2 1

For my daughter Elizabeth

Contents

ROOKERY BLUES

PART 1

These Foolish Things

Before they became the Icejam Quintet, they were three men setting out on a fishing trip in an old convertible with a leaky top, and another man sitting on a threadbare couch in his basement apartment feeding grapefruit sections to a woman with pretty eyes.

The three men in the car were moving along a snowy residential street in the vicinity of Rookery State College while listening to a news bulletin on the radio—the Soviet Union had sent another cosmonaut into orbit.

The man in the basement, whose name was Neil Novotny, was listening to Peggy Benoit's life story. With only one spoon between them, they were taking turns feeding each other. The grapefruit sections had been soaking in wine overnight.

"Then we weren't together a year when he left me," she said with a bitter little laugh. "He took our television and our hi-fi and half our wedding silver and some of my jewelry and he drove away in our car, leaving me without transportation."

"What a jerk," said Neil Novotny, his eyes fastened admiringly on Peggy, whose hair was a very black shade of black and whose brown Mediterranean eyes (Spanish? Italian?) were large and penetrating. She had rather large lips, and he wanted to kiss them. To-

3

day she wore a navy pea coat over her green wool dress. Her earrings were little silver keys. At twenty-nine, Dr. Peggy Benoit was the bright new star of Rookery State's music department. She directed the college choir, gave lessons in voice, assisted the band director, and taught a popular class in Music Appreciation. She was the cousin of a cousin of Neil's, related to him by marriage, not by blood.

Unlike Peggy, Neil was famously incompetent in the classroom. Students arranged their schedules to avoid his English classes. He was aware of this and didn't much care. He was a writer, preoccupied with a book he'd been working on since joining the Rookery State faculty two and a half years earlier, a novel about a man looking for his long-lost sister. Its title was "Losing Lydia," its setting Ohio in the 1870s, its style (in Peggy's opinion) turgid. In the novel, Lydia's brother had been twenty-six when he began his search, and now, on page 203, he was twenty-eight. So was Neil.

Peggy thought Neil handsome in an undernourished way. He had no more color or robustness than you'd expect of a man who'd been living nearly three years with an unfinished novel in an unfinished basement, but the paleness and shadowy lines of his face she thought endearing. She'd never known him to be anything other than gaunt, even in their childhood years when they used to meet occasionally at family get-togethers. Peggy, in those days an apple-cheeked fatso, had been intrigued by his austere face and the precocious severity in his manner of speaking. He was a nervous child, and a bit of a show-off. When he was nine and Peggy was ten, he interrupted their game of croquet to recite four complete poems by Robert Louis Stevenson. (Always a competitor, she responded by singing "I'm a Lonely Petunia in an Onion Patch," but he wasn't impressed.) At birthday parties when the fun got too intense for him, he used to remove himself to the bathroom with a stomachache.

Neil prompted her. "You must have sent the cops after him."

He looked sincere to her, sympathetic, as though he really wanted her to continue. Getting to know him again after all these years, she'd found him still boyish and nervous, still gaunt, but not severe. The years seemed to have softened him. Well, not softened him exactly, but made him less sure of himself than he'd been as a boy, and somehow less civilized. He came to campus each day wearing a fretful look and sloppy clothes. His blond hair was long and unruly. She guessed by his whiskers that he hadn't shaved for two weeks, probably since Christmas. *Urchin,* she thought whenever they met in the hallways. His chronic squint gave him a defensive aspect, like someone suspicious of a wrongdoing and at the same time guilty of it.

"No cops," she said, "because I thought good riddance. He hadn't been very nice to me, you see, and the jewelry he took was really pretty cheap. At least he didn't get the brooch my parents had given me or the gold necklace I'd inherited from my grandmother. That's Grandmother Farber, remember her? My mother's mother? No, I guess you never knew that side of my family. Well, anyhow, I always kept the best things hidden, because I didn't trust him. I always had this fear that he'd end up doing something impulsive, so as long as I was with him I kept the brooch and the necklace in a box of pancake flour."

Peggy's eyelashes were suddenly wet, but this was the only sign of her sorrow. Her face remained composed, her voice steady. "Because even when he was on his best behavior, he had a way of making you tense, and you wondered what he'd do next."

"Pancake flour?" asked Neil, hoping that by paying close attention and feeding her wine-soaked grapefruit, he might prolong her visit. For Neil, it had been love at first sight. First sight—fifteen years after their last sight—had occurred last spring, the day she'd arrived on campus to interview for the job he'd alerted her to. He'd heard through the family grapevine that Peggy was entering the job market at a poor time for music majors. *Too few jobs and too many men seeking them, women graduates not even granted interviews.* Reading this in a letter from his mother, Neil had tracked Peggy down by phone and told her that Rookery State's music department was losing to retirement a decrepit old voice teacher who doubled as the featured soprano in the Easter cantata. He said she ought to apply if she thought she could live in the boondocks. "God, anywhere!" she'd said on the phone.

What struck Neil first, the moment she stepped off the plane, was her freshness. He thought her stunning in her cream linen skirt and her blue linen jacket with the flowery silk scarf at her throat. Her first words to him were, "Quick, teach me the Rookery State fight song, I need this job bad." It was hard for him to imagine anyone this good-looking, effusive, and funny joining a faculty as stodgy as Rookery State's. Talk about a lonely petunia in an onion patch.

Having borrowed a car from his division chairman, he drove her from the airport to lunch in the student center cafeteria, where he went over the personalities she was bound to encounter—who would feel threatened by her, who would be a pushover, who would need impressing. It came down to two men, he said—the division chairman and the dean. All she'd have to do to impress the chairman, C. Mortimer Oberholtzer, would be to act charmed by him and pretend she was his daughter, for he treated his division like an extension of his family. In fact he sometimes called them that. Looking out over the room as they assembled for their monthly division meeting, the chairman sometimes welcomed them with the words, "Ah, my big happy family." Quite often at these meetings, Honey Oberholtzer, his wife, would show up to serve coffee and homemade pastry, and once in a while she'd bring a green plant to raffle off. "She's the mom," said Neil.

The dean was another matter altogether. Dean Zastrow, according to Neil, was a petty, contemptible simpleton. He'd been hired scarcely a year earlier for the purpose of firing people. Somehow the Minnesota State College Board had gotten the idea that the Rookery campus, one of four in the state, had more than its share of burnouts, and Dr. Zastrow had been brought in to clean house and carefully screen newcomers. Further, he'd acquired by default all the rights and powers of the college president, because the president, a man named Herbert Gengler, was hardly ever on campus. President Gengler, a frail man susceptible to rashes, passed a great many of his days among the rich, begging for grants and trusts, and the rest of the time treating his dermatitis with sunshine and lotions.

There was no telling what Dean Zastrow looked for in applicants, said Neil. Peggy would just have to mind her manners and hope for the best. She'd be well advised to be a little clever, but not *too* clever, because wit was easily lost on the dean. In seeking out dullards to prey on, said Neil, the dean was looking for people a lot like himself.

"Well, at least he's doing what he was hired to do," said Peggy as they left the student center. "In the long run, I mean, he might be doing the campus a favor, mightn't he? You said on the phone there's an overabundance of poor teachers."

"That's true," Neil agreed. "And I'm one of them."

Spending that day with Neil last spring, Peggy had not been equally charmed at first sight. She'd found it only vaguely interesting to renew their acquaintance and see what the abstemious, poetry-spouting boy had grown into. She'd felt nothing for him like the infatuation she sensed from his side, nor had her curiosity about his novel lasted beyond the first sleep-inducing chapters he read to her.

With time, however, she was discovering him to be one of the few members of the faculty who didn't act brain-dead. He *was* a good conversationalist, he *did* make insightful if jaded remarks about the people they worked with, and his life in this basement seemed pitifully lonely. Thus, having discovered Rookery to be terribly dull as a town and terribly far from any other outpost of civilization, she'd begun to think of Neil as her fellow misfit, and this, together with her own periodic attacks of severe loneliness, prompted her now and then to accept his invitation to drop in on her way to and from campus. Today she'd come with a bit of news to tell him, but once she embarked on her life story—wine made her talkative—the news slipped her mind.

"I kept some keepsakes hidden in the oven too, because neither of us ever cooked. Old family silver, I mean, and a few pieces of china. I think it was harder losing the apartment than it was losing Gene. We'd done a lot of decorating."

"Why did you lose it?"

"Because I couldn't afford it. Gene was the breadwinner, a news photographer, and I was in grad school. After he left, I moved back into student housing, a tiny, ghastly dump."

Like this, she might have added, casting her large brown eyes around Neil's miserable basement. The ceiling was open floor joists, with wiring and water pipes exposed. The walls were cheap paneling, ash gray and warped. Neil had converted the central piece of furniture, a Ping-Pong table, into his writing desk, covering it with stacks of manuscript pages. Under the stairway stood an upright piano with ivory missing from several of its keys. Most repellent of all, to Peggy, was the floor tile. It was a dried-blood shade of maroon with speckles of pink. His other room, where he slept and prepared his meals, was a dark little space she never dared look into. Beyond that, she guessed, was a bathroom.

"It was my dissertation year," she explained. "My brothers and their wives said I could move in with them, but I needed to be near campus. I was practically living in the library, with Jean-Philippe Rameau."

Gratified to be let in, finally, on the years she'd been so reticent about, Neil inquired, "You were married to this Benoit creep?"

"Of course we were married, what do you think—we were living in sin?" Her laugh was music to Neil. It traveled halfway up an octave and back down again. "How do you think I acquired his name?"

He shrugged. "Well, you keep avoiding the word marriage. I mean most people would say, 'all the while we were married,' instead of 'all the while we were together.' "

"That's probably my guilt coming out. We were married by a clerk in a courthouse. My family about died."

"What a tragedy. I don't see how somebody with your grace and brains and talent and looks could be married to a guy like that."

"Well, I was."

Grace, brains, talent, and looks—the words had the softening effect he'd intended. Blinking back tears, she closed her large, pretty lips around another juicy grapefruit section, then wiped her lashes and looked away, asking, "Don't you want to go fishing with your friends?"

"Friends!" he scoffed.

"I mean it won't bother me if you go. I can't stay long anyway."

"Stay, we'll eat lunch."

"Isn't that what we're eating?"

"I'll make sandwiches. I've got salami."

"No, I have to go to the library."

"Why?" he whined.

"I go every Saturday."

"Why?"

She turned back to him with an impatient smile. "Lessons. Student papers. It's a nice place to work. My apartment's depressing."

"Work here."

She laughed. "Not *this* depressing."

This wounded him. He regarded his living room, which before Rookery's housing shortage had been his landlord's recreation room. The dearth of suitable housing in Rookery was caused by a sudden increase in the college population, a considerable percentage of it being young men seeking academic deferment from the draft. His landlord, a physicist named Albert Finn who was away on a sabbatical year, had left the upstairs occupied by a steelworker and a cement worker employed in the construction of a new dormitory. Albert Finn had offered the upstairs to Neil, but he wanted too much for rent. A tiny, two-bedroom house for ninety-five dollars a month? Outrageous. Last night there'd been a raucous party overhead. Today all was silent.

"Please stay," he pleaded.

She shook her head. "Go fishing, Neil."

"No, they're out of their minds, fishing on a day this cold." He'd decided, even before Peggy came calling, not to go. Yesterday he'd accepted Leland Edwards's invitation, believing that a novelist should understand a bit of whatever he puts his characters through (Alphonse Harker, the brother in "Losing Lydia," had been a fisherman in the Old Country), but it was a belief hard to live by. Learning how to do things outdoors, besides being very cold in winter, interrupted his writing. "They're so eccentric, all three of them."

Peggy laughed again. "Victor, maybe. They say Victor's got a steel plate in his head."

"I know, he's my office mate. He's a wild man. And the other two are just as goofy in their way."

"No, they aren't. Leland's sort of sweet."

"Leland Edwards? He lives with his mother." Neil said this with disgust, wiping his mouth with the back of his hand.

"And there's nothing wrong with Connor. He's the real thing.

I tell you, if Connor weren't married . . ." She made a seductive face.

Neil, stung, shook his head. "Connor's paintings are sentimental."

"He's a genius, Neil." Her eyes flashed defiance. "You didn't go to his exhibit. You didn't see—"

"He paints slop. There's one hanging in the president's office. A woman and a little girl."

"I know. It's one of his best."

Neil's mouth dropped wide open and his tongue came out—a gesture of vomiting.

Peggy laughed and then slapped his face, medium hard. Then she kissed him. "Neil, you're horrible."

The three men were sitting in front because the backseat was missing. When the news bulletin ended, Victor Dash, at the wheel, growled, "The Russians are nobody's fools. Once they get their weapons in orbit, they'll control the sky."

"So what, we'll still control the earth," said Leland Edwards, who sat in the middle.

"Like hell!" exclaimed Victor Dash. "Whoever controls the sky controls the earth."

"How so?"

"Bombs."

"Could you turn up the heat?" asked Connor, who was pressed against the right-hand, loose-fitting window. Connor was the artist admired so intensely by Peggy Benoit. He was a large man in his midforties, bearded and reticent. In October he'd shocked the college faculty and student body by being publicly drunk for about forty-eight hours during Homecoming weekend. But despite this binge and rumors of subsequent binges, Connor had many zealous admirers. Galleries displaying his work in several midwestern cities had, in years past, done a steady business in his landscapes, and dealers were crying out these days in despair, learning that he had gone from landscapes to mother-daughter portraits.

But despite his fame in the middle of the nation, Connor was not well known in Rookery. Like Victor Dash and Peggy Benoit, he was new on the faculty this year. With his wife, Marcy, and his daughter, Laura, he'd moved to Rookery from Minneapolis, taking a secluded house a mile or so outside the city limits, and expecting the rural atmosphere to relieve his respiratory ailments and put his wife's demons to rest, as well as his own. So far, it hadn't done much for the demons, but his breathing was somewhat improved.

Victor Dash ignored his request for more heat, because the heater was faulty and nothing could be done about it. Victor had bought the car eight years ago at the behest of his wife Annie, who loved convertibles and did not understand (she being from Louisiana) how impractical they were in a northern winter. He'd planned to sell it and buy something newer and tighter a year or two later, but soon Annie began producing babies (three in five years) and Victor was out of work for a long time after his pipeline accident (rehabilitation took a year, finishing college took two more), so there was never again enough money for a car.

Victor was a compact, broad-shouldered man with a bushy mustache he was proud of. It was true (as Peggy Benoit had heard) that Victor had a small stainless-steel plate in his skull, and he was proud of that as well. Instead of growing hair long enough to conceal it, he kept the flattop he'd worn as a pipeliner, displaying the discolored square of grafted skin above his right ear. He was a loud, aggressive man. Shouting came easier to him than listening, and he seldom laughed except in triumph.

"From orbit?" asked Leland, the thin, long-legged man in the middle. "Bombs from orbit?"

"Atom bombs, H-bombs," shouted Victor Dash, pounding the steering wheel with his fist. "They'll bomb the bejesus out of us."

"Just turn up the heat," said Connor. "There's cold air coming in over here."

"You can't drop a bomb with any accuracy from orbit, for pity's sake. How could you possibly hit anything?" Leland had a prissy way of working his lips when he spoke with strong feeling.

"God almighty, Edwards, don't you read the papers? From now on, it's war from space, and bombs aren't the half of it. They'll be able to drop poison on us like rain."

"Oh, go on, where do you get this bosh?"

"I read the papers."

"So do I. I've never read that."

"That's because you read garbage like the *Rookery Morning Call*. You've got to read up-to-date papers."

"Hey, Victor, turn up the heat. I'm freezing."

"It's up as high as it'll go."

"Good Christ," mumbled Connor under his beard. "You mean we've got to ride all the way to Liberty Lake in this icebox?"

Leland asked, "What papers are the up-to-date papers, Victor? Where do you find all this bosh?"

"I get a union paper called *Pipeline*. I'll bring a copy to campus on Monday."

"Turn here," said Connor. "It's the house there on the corner."

Victor shot back, "I know where he lives, for God's sake. He's my office mate, isn't he?"

"Don't be so petulant," urged Leland petulantly. He was tempted to apologize to Connor on Victor's behalf, but of course that would have incensed Victor. Victor meant no harm, but did Connor know that? He urgently wanted these two to like each other. Though fishing was the ostensible purpose of this trip, he'd brought them together primarily because they both played musical instruments and he wanted to test their compatibility. More than once over the years Leland had tried to put together a musical trio or quartet, but they soon came apart for lack of mutual respect or friendship or whatever you called that indefinable bond that made productive committees and teams and orchestras out of people who came together as strangers.

As new members of a rather stuffy faculty, both of these men impressed Leland immensely. They were so unlike himself. Victor Dash he admired for his freshness, his audacity, his hell-bent charge through the groves and thickets of academe. About all he had in common with Victor was his age, which was thirty-five.

Connor he thought a genius. He'd been admiring Connor's paintings for years. It was at Leland's urging that Dean Zastrow and Chairman Oberholtzer had hired Connor away from Cass College in Minneapolis. It was high time, Leland had insisted, that state colleges went out and found creative talent the way private institutions did. He guessed Connor was in his midforties. This afternoon, he would bring Victor and Connor together with Neil Novotny, who claimed to be a clarinetist, and see what developed.

The stuffiness of the Rookery State faculty was something that Leland himself, a fussbudget and twelve-year veteran, did little to alleviate. In the classroom he was versatile and precise, but entirely uninspiring—the sort of instructor who specializes in conveying facts and skills and very little of himself. His specialties were written composition, history of the English language, and anything else that Chairman Oberholtzer asked him to teach. The Oberholtzers, C. Mortimer and his wife Honey, were longtime friends of Leland and his mother, who lived together in a handsome house not far from campus. Actually, Leland and his mother were close friends of all the old guard, Leland's father having been, before his untimely death by lightning, chairman of the history department and baseball coach.

The convertible came to a stop in front of a small bungalow with icicles hanging from the eaves and two mailboxes wired to the rusty wrought-iron railing leading up to the snow-covered stoop. Because Neil Novotny was notoriously late for appointments, all three fishermen made their way across the yard rather than wait in the chilly car.

"Where'll he sit?" asked Connor, trudging behind the others through the snow. "You don't have a backseat."

"He won't come," said Victor.

"But if he does."

"He won't."

"Then why are we stopping for him?"

"Because Leland asked him and he said he'd come—but see that?" Victor stopped and pointed to a red Thunderbird parked across the street. "That's Peggy Benoit's car. He's hot for Peggy Benoit."

Leland led them up onto the stoop and knocked on the door.

"But where would he sit if he *did* come?" Connor asked.

"I'd get a bucket out of the trunk."

"A bucket?"

"Turn a bucket upside down and it's a stool."

"I doubt if he'd ride all the way to Liberty Lake on a bucket."

"Then you'd have to take turns."

———

Neil saw no alternative but to invite them in for a drink. Alone, he might have turned them away, claiming to be deep in his novel, but he didn't want to appear uncivil in front of Peggy. Besides, with Connor present, she was certain to stay longer.

The three fishermen consulted briefly on the stoop before Connor urged them inside. Connor needed a drink.

Leading them down into his basement, Neil said he was sorry but one of them would have to sit on the piano stool, he was that short of furniture. Leland did so, kicking off his boots and stepping gingerly across the cold tile in his stocking feet. Removing his blue stocking cap, he said hello to Peggy Benoit, who was smiling at him from the couch. Her complexion appeared more highly colored than usual, and he wondered if she was blushing or simply wearing more makeup because it was a weekend. He wondered, as well, what a woman of intelligence and beauty was doing in this repellent basement. It pained him to imagine her romantically inclined toward someone as unformed and unprofessional as Neil Novotny.

Connor, too, removed his boots at the bottom of the stairs. He greeted Peggy and asked Neil if he had any gin. When he stepped over to the couch to shake Peggy's outstretched hand, she pulled him down to sit beside her. How lovely, he thought, studying her face in profile as she smilingly greeted Victor. How paintable. Her hair was so black it reflected colors like polished ebony. He saw intelligence and a few secrets in her eyes.

Victor, to avoid appearing overdomesticated, kept his boots on, but he did stamp his feet a time or two, shaking loose a bit of snow, before he crossed the room to Neil's typewriter on the Ping-Pong table. He sat down before it and rolled the platen so he could read the page in progress.

Neil told Victor and Leland that besides gin, he had beer, wine, and bourbon.

"Beer," said Victor. "I suppose you're not going with us."

"I'm at a crucial place in my book, I'll have to stay with it this afternoon."

"I knew it," Victor growled with disgust. He and his wife Annie had more than once invited him to dinner and been turned down.

"A beer for me too, thank you," said Leland.

Victor read aloud from the manuscript. " 'The morning frost covered the hills along the river like a white blanket.' What's so goddamn crucial about that, Novotny?"

Peggy's laugh was brief, for Neil cast a dark look in her direction. Leland, embarrassed for Neil, turned on his stool and meditatively tried out a scale on the piano. About half the keys were out of tune.

The phone rang, and Neil stepped into his tiny dark bedroom, which was also his kitchen, to answer it. He called to Leland and said it was his mother. Leland sprang from the stool and ducked his head going through the low doorway. He took the phone from Neil and said, "Mother."

"Sit down if you want to," Neil told him, indicating his narrow bed. It was carelessly made, with blankets from an army surplus store.

Leland remained on his feet, listening to his mother and looking about him at the furnishings. There was a sink at the foot of the bed. A refrigerator stood behind the headboard. There were two bedside tables, one for Neil's alarm clock and telephone, the other for his liquor supply and hot plate.

"Just having a drink, Mother. Then we're on our way."

Neil stepped into the other room and asked Peggy if she'd take a glass of wine.

"A tiny little," she said. "I've got to correct papers."

"Beer for me," Victor reminded him. He had pulled his chair up close to the typewriter and was pecking out a few additional words on the half-finished manuscript page.

"Better give Victor water, he's driving," joked Connor, who had sunk deep into the couch with his woolly stocking feet resting on an ottoman of torn red plastic. The offer of a drink had relaxed him, made him affable.

"Victor's driving?" said Peggy. "You mean you're going all the way to Liberty Lake in Victor's rattletrap?"

"Not by choice," said Connor. "Leland's mother won't let him have their car, and my wife won't let me have ours."

She was struck by the mirth in Connor's tone. Connor was not known as a humorist. For months she'd been studying him, hoping to find common ground with him, hoping that as fellow artists they might become friends. No luck so far. The man was a puzzle. She wondered how old he was. Judging by his graying beard and his round-shouldered posture, she might have taken him for fifty-five or more, but one look at his lively eyes and the nimble way he moved and she knew he couldn't be much beyond forty.

"It's always Victor in a pinch," Victor explained. "The oldest car and the biggest heart."

"Why not stay here and drink," urged Neil, hoping thereby to delay Peggy's departure.

"I'd just as soon," said Connor.

"Do," said Peggy, plucking at the sleeve of his flannel shirt. "Stay for lunch. Neil has salami."

At this, Victor cast a reproving look in the direction of the couch. "One drink and we're heading out," he ordered.

Peggy's lower lip protruded in an attractive little pout.

"You're out of your minds, fishing in this weather," Neil called from his bedroom.

Peggy asked, "Why do men go fishing anyway?"

"I'll tell you why," said Connor happily. This was one of the best things about gin, these few minutes of giddy anticipation before the drink was put in your hand. "We go fishing to get away from our wives."

"Don't give me that."

"It's true."

"Well, what about Leland, then?"

"And our mothers."

Victor continued to stare at the pair on the couch. He felt two ways about Peggy. He'd been urging Neil, his office mate, to shift his infatuation to somebody else, say Deelane Villars, secretary to the music and speech departments. Peggy Benoit was too flashy and forward for the likes of Neil. She had a lot to say at division meetings. Very ambitious. Very energetic. Neil was an everlasting boy. Rumpled shirts and pants. Socks falling down over his shoes. Spirits up and down according to how his novel was progressing. Deelane Villars was closer to Neil's speed, not so articulate, not such a great dresser, not educated beyond business college.

As for Connor, Victor could never tell what was going on in the man's head. If anything. Was he truly the hotshot artist everyone claimed he was? His landscapes looked to Victor like child's play. What if he was a fake—a drunk and nothing more?

In the bedroom, Neil took two beers from the refrigerator, opened them, and handed one to Leland at the phone. Finding two mismatched water glasses and pouring wine into one and gin into the other, he tried not to listen.

"No, we'll be fine, don't worry, Mother. If it looks like snow, we'll start home. . . . Yes, Mother . . . Well, I'm sure you're right, Mother."

Neil shuddered, imagining himself leading this man's slavish life. Neil himself had been reared, in Dayton, Ohio, by parents with this same engulfing instinct, which was a major reason he'd taken this job a thousand miles away. Luckily, Neil's parents were not in the habit of calling him on the phone, but his mother did write him weekly letters filled with advice he didn't follow. *Find yourself a nice apartment with a pleasant view. Forget writing and get out and see people—all that time alone with your book isn't healthy. Eat more vegetables.* His father, a food jobber who specialized in selling fruit to fund-raising groups, often added a postscript concerning money. *Send me your surplus and I'll invest it in apples, it looks like a good year for winesaps.* What surplus? His father assumed that all professionals, even beginning professors, were well paid. Neil's annual salary—$4700—scarcely covered his rent, groceries, and typewriter ribbons.

Beer for Victor, gin for Connor, wine for Peggy.

"Who the hell's he talking to in there?" asked Victor.

"His mother."

"God almighty! They say the only days he doesn't call his mother at lunchtime is when he goes home for lunch. What a baby."

"See, what did I tell you?" said Neil, imploring Peggy with his boyish, worried-looking eyes to accept his opinion of Leland.

"What's so odd about that?" she wanted to know. "He and his mother are very close. Connor, do you think Leland is odd?"

Connor removed his feet from the ottoman so Neil could sit, and replied, "No odder than the rest of us."

This tickled Peggy and she giggled. Connor looked at her curiously. He hadn't meant to be amusing. He honestly considered the faculty of Rookery State a very peculiar crowd, himself no less than the rest. Five months on campus had taught him that a college this remote attracted scholars running away from various things—a good many (judging by Neil and Victor and himself) running away from scholarship. Peggy and Leland alone among present company were truly dedicated to the profession. Victor, who taught Business English in a businesslike manner, was interested primarily in labor relations. Neil, Connor had heard, was in danger of being fired.

"Any man his age ought *not* to be living with his mother," Victor decreed.

Connor, savoring his first sip, went deep into himself. His first drink of the day often turned his mind inward like this, where he liked it to be. Unfortunately, this alcohol-induced mental state gave way all too quickly to other states, like drunkenness, sometimes unconsciousness. As a younger man he hadn't needed a drink in order to ask himself such questions as came to him now: What am I doing in this basement with these people I don't know well enough to call friends? Why am I living at the edge of this forgotten little city in the wilderness, surrounded in my work by academic misfits like myself? How did I end up married to a woman who hates me, and rearing a daughter who I fear is growing up sullen and perverse? Why was I born with the irresistible need to paint, but unable to find the time to do it? And why mothers and daughters of all things? Oh, why have mothers and daughters become my obsession?

"That was Mother," announced Leland, stooping through the doorway with his long fingers playing his icy bottle of beer like a musical instrument. "She said they're forecasting snow."

"Is she blind?" blurted Victor. "The sun is out."

"Well," he chuckled patiently, "she said there are clouds moving in and the radio is saying heavy snow." He sat down on the piano stool.

"Clouds!" Victor looked around for a window. "Neil, you haven't got any windows."

"Don't I know it," he called from the bedroom, where he had gone to pour a drink for himself.

"I told her we'd keep an eye on the weather. She worries when I'm out in snow."

"I love your mother," said Peggy. "She's darling." This affection was based on the briefest of meetings at faculty parties, as well as hearing her on the radio. Mrs. Edwards had her own show, called "Lolly Speaking," on KRKU.

Leland nodded pleasantly, indicating that he loved her too, while doubting whether "darling" was a suitable word for someone as large and powerful as his mother.

"Hey, Neil," Victor called out, "how can you live without windows? It's like a goddamn gopher hole down here."

Leland said proudly, "Mother's all up in arms about the Faculty Alliance. She's bringing it up on the radio this afternoon."

"Her program is so entertaining," said Peggy. "They ought to have her on every day."

"She *is* on every day," Neil told her, returning with wine in a coffee mug.

"She is?" Peggy never heard the radio on weekdays. Neil did, she guessed, because he spent his mornings at home. To accommodate his novel-writing habits, Chairman Oberholtzer had arranged for Neil's earliest class to meet at noon.

"Mother's on for fifteen minutes weekday mornings, and a half hour Saturday afternoons," said Leland. "They've asked her to go to a half hour every day, but she's not sure she wants to. She's wary of overkill."

"What's her program about?" asked Neil. He'd heard "Lolly Speaking," but paid little attention. He assumed it was recipes and other drivel.

"Recipes," said Leland proudly. "Interviews. Local news. Today it will mostly be about the Alliance."

"The Alliance is the best thing that ever happened to teachers," exclaimed Victor. "We'll never get a living wage till we strike, and we'll never strike without the Alliance."

Leland didn't agree. "Didn't you see the *Morning Call* yesterday? They had a long editorial, enumerating the dangers."

"The *Morning Call* is ass-wipe!"

This remark jarred Connor. He came up out of himself, wondering why no one else, not even Leland, ever seemed affected by this wild man's uncivil barking and spewing. As members of the same division, all of these people had apparently grown accustomed to Victor. Perhaps Connor would have too, if he'd been a more faithful member. Despite the compulsory attendance called for in the *Faculty Handbook*, Connor avoided all meetings, remaining sequestered in the art rooms on the upper floor of the industrial arts building, where he concentrated on his mothers and daughters.

In order to forestall further mention of a strike, and possibly an argument, Leland Edwards swiveled around on his stool, set his bottle on the piano, gathered up his courage, and played the opening bars of "These Foolish Things." The piano, though out of tune, had a rich, commanding tone, and Leland had a wonderfully lyrical touch.

"Wow," exclaimed Peggy, "I had no idea you played."

Nodding, his back to the room, he started over, this time with more of a flourish, "These Foolish Things" growing gradually out of a murky opening of bass notes and then rising to a long improvisation high on the treble end of the keyboard.

They all listened in amazement. This was the real thing. This was the classy sweetness of Eddie Duchin combined with the rippling cheer of Teddy Wilson. They'd all grown up listening to this kind of playing on records. The melody came tumbling down into the murky bass register again, then quickly disentangled itself once more and climbed two octaves, then three.

"Wow," Peggy breathed in Connor's ear, and Connor smiled and nodded and glanced at Victor to see if he too was affected. Apparently he was. A look of satisfied repose was displayed on the wild man's face.

Neil, beer in hand, had moved over to stand beside the piano, moving his shoulders in time with the music while keeping a nervous eye on the diminishing distance between Peggy and Connor on the couch. Four or five minutes passed before the lipstick's traces and the airline ticket to romantic places came spinning down once more into the middle octaves and were finally eaten up by the insistent drumlike beat on the low end and faded out to a silence that lingered in the room a few moments before Peggy whooped,

"Leland!" and sprang off the couch and ran to plant a kiss on the pianist's cheek.

"Wonderful," said Neil, shaking Peggy's hand instead of Leland's.

Connor, from the couch, kept a wary eye on Victor, expecting him to break the spell with a curse or an obscenity. But Victor actually seemed to have been transported.

"Pretty sweet, Victor?" Connor prompted.

"Terrific," Victor agreed, pulling thoughtfully at the bristles of his mustache.

"More," insisted Peggy, standing behind Leland and straightening his thinning hair. "Where did you learn to play like that?"

"He took lessons as a kid," said Neil, who'd learned this about Leland two years earlier, at a faculty party hosted by the Elks Club. On that occasion, Leland had been prevailed upon to play a few old numbers that the division chairman and his wife liked to dance to, and Neil, in a mood of fellowship he later regretted, had suggested they get together sometime to try out a few piano-clarinet things. But they never had. More than once Leland had invited him to his house, but Neil was too deep in his fiction to accept.

"Well, who didn't take lessons?" Peggy said. "But that didn't make artists out of us, did it?"

"It did you," said Neil, believing Peggy to have the purest soprano voice he'd ever heard. She'd organized an adult choir at Christmastime and added her own voice to certain parts of *Messiah*.

"It did me," said Victor. "I play drums."

"I'm not bad on the clarinet," Neil bragged, sorry to see Leland draining off so much of Peggy's admiration.

"Give us 'Your Feet's Too Big,' " said Victor.

"Maybe we can give you 'Nola,' " said Neil. "I'll get my clarinet." He disappeared into his bedroom.

Peggy turned to Connor, who was getting up from the couch. "What's your instrument?" Instinct told her he played at least one.

Connor joined them at the piano. "Drums and bass fiddle in high school. I haven't played since."

"Perfect," she said, brimming with excitement. "A quintet."

Victor stood up from the typewriter and came eagerly forward.

"I'm on drums," he said in a threatening tone, in case Connor intended to displace him.

Peggy laughed. "This is fantastic."

"But I don't have any drums," complained Victor.

"Don't worry, we'll find some," she promised.

"Where?"

"The department's got drums. They sit there gathering dust."

"Is there a bass fiddle?" asked Connor.

"At least two that I know of. A faculty quintet, I can't wait. We'll build it around Leland, he's so wonderful."

The pianist meanwhile sat stiffly on his stool, frowning at the carved scrollwork in front of him. This was the part of performing that he dreaded—dealing with an appreciative audience. Applause or praise caused his ears to burn. If only his listeners would ignore him. Or not ignore him exactly—he wasn't *that* modest—but just not fuss over him, just *pretend* to ignore him.

The phone rang. Neil, clarinet in hand, emerged from the bedroom and said it was Mrs. Dash, calling for Victor.

"God almighty, how did she know I was here?" He went in and picked up the phone. "What do you want, Annie?"

His wife said, "Hey, Victor, how come you're not fishing? Leland's mother called and said you were hanging around Neil's place."

Annie's voice momentarily softened him. "Coupla beers and we're on our way, Annie."

"She said it's going to snow."

"So what? It's winter, isn't it?"

"But snow hard, she said."

"We'll keep an eye out."

"It's after one, Victor. Don't you think you'd better get started?"

"Christ, Annie, stop pressing me, would you? It's my day off." He restrained himself from shouting.

"I'm just saying Leland's mother says it's an hour up and an hour back and it gets dark early."

"It gets dark at five, what's the hurry?"

"Leland's mother says four-thirty."

"Screw Leland's mother."

His wife laughed.

"Just lay off, would you, Annie? You and Leland's mother on my back, I don't need that. Five days a week I'm under the gun on campus, I need peace and quiet weekends."

"Well, just so you're home by six. We promised the kids pizza tonight."

"Make pizza at home, I don't feel like going out." He imagined his three youngsters, aged three to seven, among the Saturday night welter of gobbling children at Soren's Pizza Parlor.

"But we told the kids we'd go out, remember?"

"So tell them we changed our mind."

"Oh, Victor."

"Listen, you think I want to come home from a hard day of fishing and watch a pack of snot-nosed kids get all strung together with cheese? Think of me, for once, Annie. Think of your old Victor."

"Next week, then. How about we take them out next Saturday for sure?"

"For sure, Annie. This week's been holy hell on campus. I been getting beat up over the Alliance. Next week's got to be better. This time next week it'll be over and done with."

"Okay, Victor, have fun."

"You bet, sweetie."

"And watch the weather."

"Will do."

"Hi to Neil."

"Yep."

"Who's that singing? Is that the radio?"

"It's Peggy Benoit."

"Who?"

"Remember the Christmas party? The good-looking dame with the chest?"

"She's on the radio?"

"No, she's here."

"At Neil's? What's she doing at Neil's?"

"I think he's been trying to get her into bed, but he got her only as far as the piano."

"She sounds good. Is that 'Bewitched'?"

"She's not bad. Leland's better."

"Leland sings?"

"No, he plays the piano. He's real good."

"Okay then, good-bye, Victor."

"Say, don't go calling Connor's wife now, Annie. We'd never get out of town."

"Don't worry, I'd never call Marcy Connor. She's too moody for me."

"She's a bearcat all right."

"Good-bye, Victor."

"Okay, Annie, so long."

"That sounds like 'Bewitched.' "

"It's 'Sentimental Journey.' "

Victor found himself another beer and stood in the bedroom doorway taking in the rest of the song, Leland curling soft runs and trills around Peggy's rather understated delivery. Her voice was true, he guessed, but a little on the thin side. It didn't have the full-throated boldness or huskiness he liked in a torch singer. Her heart wasn't breaking.

When the song ended, Neil and Connor clapped, Neil much louder than Connor, and Victor asked again for "Your Feet's Too Big." Leland played the opening bars of "Yesterdays" a few times, offering Peggy a choice of keys. The phone rang again and Victor picked it up. "Your wife," he said, summoning Connor to the bedroom.

The others fell silent, unable to conceal their curiosity. Connor's was the mystery wife in this year's crop of newcomers. Only very rarely did she leave her house and enter into campus society. At the faculty dinner in September, she'd spoken to scarcely anyone. Before Christmas, she and Connor had brought their gangly, thirteen-year-old girl to the division party in the student center, but mother and daughter kept their distance from everyone, the two of them sitting furtively at a small corner table and resisting all overtures of friendliness, including Santa's. Even Chairman Oberholtzer and his wife were thwarted in their attempts to rouse Mrs. Connor out of what might have been lethargy, stupidity, or depression.

"I got a call from a Mrs. Edwards," she told Connor in her customary monotone. "She gave me this number."

"Why?" Connor asked, his stomach cramping slightly at the sound of her voice.

"She said it was dangerous to leave town with snow coming."

"These men I'm with seem to think it's safe enough." Connor was surprised whenever his wife seemed to care what became of him.

"She asked me to persuade you not to go, but suit yourself." Her words merged into an audible yawn.

His listeners in the other room were fascinated by what he said next. "Marcy, would you care if I got lost and never came home?"

She didn't answer. Coming out of her yawn, she asked, "Who was I talking to, this Mrs. Edwards?"

"Leland's mother. He brought her to the faculty dinner last fall, remember?"

"Leland? Who's Leland?"

"The man with the long face who sat next to you, the one you liked."

"I did?"

"You said you did."

"Then I did."

The music resumed in the other room, the keyboard and a few tentative toots from Neil's clarinet.

"I'll see you later, Marcy."

His wife replied, "Unless Mrs. Edwards knows what she's talking about," and hung up.

As the piano and the clarinet began to find something close to harmony, and Peggy began humming because she didn't know the words to "Yesterdays," the door opened at the top of the steps and one of the construction workers called, "Shut up!"

Immediate silence. Neil went to the foot of the stairs and looked up at the large man—the steelworker—standing above him in his underwear. He said, "Pardon me?"

"Shut up!" ordered the man. "I'm trying to take a nap." He stepped back into his part of the house and slammed the door.

Neil turned to his visitors and said, timidly, "I'm sorry."

The musicians, brought up short, looked paralyzed, Leland's hands poised over the keys, Peggy's large eyes bulging out with the notes she was holding in.

"Who is that clown?" asked Victor.

"He's on the construction crew at the new dorm."

"A union man no doubt." Victor was mollified.

"Listen, we can't let this go," insisted Peggy. "We've got to get together and play."

"Yes, we've got to," echoed Leland flatly, concealing his eagerness in case they didn't.

Neil assented, but without much spirit, his enthusiasm tempered by the rude interruption. Connor sat down heavily on the steps to lace up his boots and said he could play anytime. Victor and Leland said the same. Neil said weekend afternoons would be best because his novel took up his mornings.

Peggy, buttoning her pea coat, said, "I'll see if the band room's in use tomorrow afternoon, and I'll see what the department's got in the way of sheet music—what fun." She squeezed everyone's hand and climbed the stairs.

The eyes of the four men followed her legs up the steps, and when she was out the door, Victor murmured, "Some dish."

"Yes," said Neil deliciously.

"A superb voice," said Leland. "I thought of Ella."

"No—Sarah," corrected Victor.

Connor gazed up the stairway, as though at a departed vision. The woman, in leaving, had tugged at his heart.

Neil, seeing the fishermen out, was thanked for the drinks and chided for not coming along. He shut the door quietly, afraid of disturbing his housemates. He descended to his Ping-Pong table. Lydia Hacker's brother Alphonse wasn't a fisherman after all, he decided. Perhaps he was a schoolteacher, thus requiring no research.

Pulling his chair up to the table, he read what Victor had typed on his manuscript page. *Better change this guy's name. Alphonse sounds like a candy-ass.*

Again today, as was her Saturday habit, Peggy climbed to the third floor of the spacious new library and corrected exams at a solitary carrel next to a broad window, glancing frequently down at the neighborhood bordering the campus. This was the pretty section of town—wide yards with lots of trees—where she hoped eventually to find lodging. Her present apartment, upstairs over the JCPenney store on Division Street, was small and lonely and looked out over the garbage bins in the alley.

Looking along Sawyer Street, she saw Lolly Edwards back her enormous box of a car out of her driveway and point it downtown, doubtless on her way to KRKU radio. She saw three little children struggling without success to build a snowman with snow too cold to adhere. She saw her division chairman, C. Mortimer Ober-holtzer, and his wife Honey emerge from the side porch of their handsome Tudor and set out on a brisk walk with their dog on a leash.

This was all very attractive to Peggy Benoit, as well as unsettling. She wanted to earn tenure in the division and own a house like the Oberholtzers', surrounded by birches and pines and substantial neighbors. She wanted to be married again and have a little boy or girl making a snowman in the yard. And yet—here among the lakes and lumber mills of northern Minnesota? It was disheartening to imagine spending one's career on a campus with no reputation, located in the last jumping-off place this side of Winnipeg. As a graduate student she'd imagined herself a professor at Middlebury or Brown. She'd never heard of Rookery State.

After an hour or so at her high window, she felt a siege of loneliness coming on. Though advised by doctors to ignore such attacks as nothing more than normal periods of melancholy, she'd learned over the years to take them seriously, to seek out their antidote before the symptoms became acutely physical—quickened heartbeat, shallow breathing, aching temples. The attacks had begun when she was a teenager feeling bereft because the last of her older brothers and sisters left home. In college, where she'd spent most of her twenties, they'd been less frequent and less severe, but now, in Rookery, they were coming at her every few days. The antidote was the company of others.

Giving in to the pull of humanity, she descended to the bustle of the main floor, where she spread her work out on a table in the periodical room and allowed herself to be interrupted by gregarious students. The friendliness pervading this campus struck her as quaint. These youngsters were so unsophisticated and trusting that the college might have been an extension of the high schools in the small towns they came from. Peggy liked this about them. She'd spent her entire life in rather unfriendly neighborhoods of Boston where the young man gazing at her now in the periodical room would have been taken for a pervert or a moron, so guileless was the smile on his slack, open face.

When she returned the smile—something she'd never have done in the city—he crossed the room and sat down across the table from her.

"Hello?" she said, as though it were a question.

He said, "Hi."

She didn't remember seeing him before. His face was freckled and rather homely. His nails were dirty. He wore an open wind-breaker over a washed-out T-shirt displaying a message she couldn't read. He was one of a good many students on this campus who seemed out of their element, who handled books and papers awkwardly and moved uncertainly through the crowded hallways, looking as though pumping gas or working on an assembly line might have been more natural to them than pursuing a degree. She guessed he was twenty.

"Dr. Benoit, right?"

She nodded.

"You're my adviser."

"I am?"

He laughed happily, as though this were a trick and she'd fallen for it. A few students, lounging idly in chairs, glanced up from their magazines.

"How did you manage to register?" she asked. Spring semester had already begun. Enrollment required an adviser's signature.

"I never registered yet. I was here last year and dropped out, and now I'm coming back again." He searched the pockets of his jacket and found a green enrollment form. It was tightly folded down to the size of a cigarette pack. "I was gonna go to the Twin Cities and find a job, but my draft board says they got other plans for me." He laughed again, this time fearfully. "Says if I want a job all that bad, they can find me one in Vietnam."

"You're a little late," she told him. "Registration ended yesterday."

"Yeah, I know, I was here yesterday and they assigned me to you, but I couldn't find you. I got a permit here somewheres that says they'll still let me in if you sign it." He searched his pockets again and brought out a yellow form.

She unfolded the green form and the yellow form, brushing away the shreds of pocket lint that fell from them. The young man's name was Chuck Lucking, and he came from a town called Loomis. His list of preferred classes, though incomplete, included one of Neil Novotny's sections of Freshman English. She recalled her surprise earlier in the week when more than one of her other advisees had chosen Neil as their English teacher. She recalled, too, that this was the happy news that she'd have told him in his basement this afternoon had she not been distracted by his alcoholic grapefruit.

"You're a freshman?"

Chuck Lucking shrugged. "I don't know, I'm probably a junior, but I flunked a semester of English when I was a freshman, and I got to take it over. Some friends told me Novotny'd be good."

"Okay. And what else? Draft boards want you to take a full load."

"I know, I thought you might recommend stuff."

She pushed aside her lesson plans and drew a catalog from her briefcase. "How many of your major requirements have you taken already?"

His answer was to call up his warm, slack smile again, together with a hint of bewilderment in his eyes.

"What's your major, Mr. Lucking?"

"Haven't declared one yet."

"Well, it's high time you did. What are you interested in?"

A shrug. "What should I be?"

She studied him, trying to decide if he was a dolt. She couldn't be sure. She'd had a few students in Music Appreciation who appeared as unschooled as this one and yet who turned out to be quite teachable and astute.

"Listen, Mr. Lucking, nobody tells somebody else what to major in. Now what's your aim in life?"

A sobering question apparently, for his smile disappeared and his eyes went out of focus for a few moments while he tried to come up with an answer. Then, finding it, he beamed. "Staying a civilian, I guess."

Justine Gengler carried a cup of tea into the austere, underfurnished morning room of the president's house on the riverbank. She placed the cup on the plain Shaker table next to the stack of her husband's mail that had been delivered to the house yesterday by the dean's secretary, Mrs. Kibbee. Reading the president's mail was a duty Mrs. Gengler had taken upon herself some years earlier when her husband was discovered to be allergic to paper.

Having slit open all the envelopes, she laid down her silver opener and picked up her cup of tea. Sipping, she watched the sparrows feeding on birdseed outside her patio doors. She approved of sparrows. True, they were the least colorful of her feathered visitors, but they were in the majority and they were careful in their eating habits. They didn't kick at their food and scatter it all over the snow-covered patio the way jays and grosbeaks did. They seemed needy and appreciative, and she liked them for that.

In the next room her husband, a needy, appreciative man, was napping. She could hear him snoring. Sipping her tea, she looked beyond the feeder at the frozen Badbattle, at the campus on the opposite bank. She sighed. Fourteen years ago, when Herbert took over as president, Rookery State might have been a calendar picture. Your eye took it in as a cohesive and pleasing whole. Behind Old Main, which occupied pride of place at the edge of the water, sprawled McCall Hall with its medieval-looking turrets and its two hundred Gothic windows reflecting the color of the western sky at sundown. The handsome old stadium rose out of the oaks on the east arm of the campus, and the old library and the old gymnasium, surrounded by birch and pine, marked the western end. There was even a rather charming aspect to the power plant, with its crenellated roof line and its single enormous window in the shape of a T, particularly on winter days like this when clouds of white smoke and steam billowed from its chimneys and vents.

But the changes. Mrs. Gengler hated the changes. The birch

had been cut down to make room for the hideous new library and the utterly featureless student center, and now, worst of all, a dormitory was beginning to poke its crooked concrete walls up out of the pines at the crest of the hill. From now till the end of time, Rookery State College would display this gray, misshapen monstrosity as its crowning feature.

She put down her cup and turned back to her husband's mail. An appeal for funds from the University of Missouri, Herbert's alma mater. An appeal for business from an office furniture firm—too late, the remodeling and furnishing of Administrative Row in McCall Hall being now complete. A letter from the chancellor of the State College System concerning the dreaded Faculty Alliance of America. This silly Alliance, the next thing to a labor union, was appealing to professors throughout Minnesota, with a view to replacing the prestigious old Congress of College Professors as their bargaining agent. Barking up the wrong tree, in Justine Gengler's opinion. The old guard of Rookery State were light-years away from going union.

Next, she came to an oversized white envelope addressed simply *College President, Rookery, Minnesota*, in a rather artistic-looking hand. There was no return address. The postmark was Boston. She opened it and drew out an eight-by-ten black-and-white glossy of a naked woman—a full-length photo of a very pretty young thing wearing nothing but half a smile and looking entirely unashamed. Holding a towel in her right hand, but not concealing her parts with it, she was stepping toward the camera with water glistening on her flesh.

Mrs. Gengler was startled, but she wasn't truly shocked. You didn't spend your life on college campuses without crudeness coming to your attention now and again. Just last week there'd been that disturbing phone call from some prankster asking about the Genglers' sexual habits, the caller identifying herself as a graduate student researching her dissertation. Last spring there had been that streaker at commencement.

She was about to tear the photo in two when something about the young woman's face struck her as familiar. She studied it at length, without being able to remember where she'd seen it. Then, feeling a bit guilty, she allowed her eyes to roam over the body, admiring the woman's full, youthful breasts and her long, elegant legs. It was a very lovely body, the sort of figure Mrs. Gengler, as a girl, had wished for herself. The background had been somehow obliterated, so there was no telling if the woman was walking on a beach or stepping out of a bathtub.

She considered the unlikelihood of her husband sending for this sort of thing from a mail-order house. Herbert simply wasn't the type. Nor was he named on the envelope. It might have come from Gary Oberholtzer. Poor Honey and Mortimer were having the devil's own time with Gary. He'd been getting himself into one scrape after another. Shoplifting. Disorderly conduct. Motorcycle violations. A year or two ago, when he was nineteen, there'd been trouble of a sexual nature, something never made completely public involving a girl younger than himself. To this day (Honey Oberholtzer had recently confided to her), Gary kept bringing home magazines purported to be about motorcycles but containing pictures such as this one. In color, no less, said Honey.

However, the postmark was Boston. Mrs. Gengler was sure that Gary had never been to Boston, had never been farther away than the two colleges in the Twin Cities he'd dropped out of. But there were ways, she supposed, to mail a parcel from a place you'd never been. Perhaps he had friends in Boston. Gary was known to be devious.

Mrs. Gengler pulled open the drawer of the table, deciding to keep the photo until it came to her where she'd seen the shameless, pretty young woman. She slipped it under her monogrammed stationery, facedown.

Upstairs in the Oberholtzer Tudor on Sawyer Street, Gary lay on his bed listening to Lolly Edwards on the radio. She was taking stupid phone calls from people worked up over something stupid called the Faculty Alliance. It was a continual wonder to Gary Oberholtzer how stupid people were.

"Never heard of public servants going ahead and doing that," said a man who identified himself as Myron.

"Doing what?" asked Lolly Edwards in the cheerful voice she

used over the air. You had to know the woman as Gary Ober-holtzer did to realize how false and stupid her tone was.

"Going ahead and joining a union. Isn't there laws against it?"

"Maybe another caller can tell us that, Myron. Thank you for calling. Hello, you're on 'Lolly Speaking.' "

"Yeah, I was wondering. Don't college teachers make about fifty dollars an hour? I mean, when they're actually working? I heard they knock off after two, three hours a day."

"Your first name, please, and where are you from?"

"Gerald. I'm calling from North Siding."

"North Siding—that's wonderful. How's our signal up there?"

"Not so hot."

"Well, it's a long way."

"Yeah, we get you about half the time. A north wind'll wipe you totally out."

"Thanks for calling, Gerald."

She was giving the stupid man from North Siding the brush-off. Gary Oberholtzer, a regular listener, recognized "Thanks for listening" as her form of good-bye and good riddance. But Gerald wasn't giving up.

"Hey, what I was getting at—is it true they work only two, three hours a day?"

Gerald got this stupid remark in before she could cut him off, leaving her no choice but to be polite. She went on and on about the hard work of college professors, and how their classroom teaching wasn't the half of it. She said her husband had been a pro-fessor and now her son was, and they brought home mountains of paperwork and had to read hard books day and night—the same ar-gument Gary'd been hearing all his life from his stupid father. If his father had to read hard books day and night, what was he doing out with his stupid mother walking the stupid dog?

The next caller was Alex Bolus, the stupid fat lady who taught women's physical education and coached the tennis team. She asked if Lolly Edwards knew that women professors were paid less than men because they were women. Lolly said yes, she knew that, and the two of them went on lamenting this stupid fact until Gary thought he'd puke. This program was badly in need of a jolt before it put the whole stupid city to sleep.

He left his room and looked through the house, making sure his parents hadn't come in from their walk. In the kitchen, he picked up the phone and called KRKU. He had to wait a couple of minutes, which gave him time to practice his falsetto, and when they put him on the air, he said, "This is Lucille. I'm calling from campus."

There was a slight hesitation before Lolly said, "Hello, Lucille," a hitch of uncertainty as if she suspected trouble but couldn't very well cut him off without being sure. He pitched his voice as high as it would go and said, stifling a giggle, "Your name won't be used in my dissertation, it's all numbers—how many say yes, and how many say no—"

Lolly broke in to say she was sorry, but her Saturday show was devoted to a single topic and the topic today was the Faculty Alliance. Luckily, this interruption came when he could no longer hold in his giggle. Covering the phone with his hand, he let out a brief cry of mirth, then spoke to her quickly, before she cut him off.

"What I need to know is whether you've ever had sexual intercourse with an animal."

Did her listening audience hear the entire question? He couldn't be sure at what point the dial tone sounded in his ear.

The bait shop smelled bad. The floor was covered by a thin sheet of stagnant water. The proprietor, obviously in poor health, emitted a dry, continuous cough between puffs on his cigarette. He smelled bad too. The three professors, peering into concrete tanks that reminded Connor of burial vaults, observed various species and sizes of minnows, quite a few of them floating dead on the surface.

Victor Dash said, "Suckers are best for walleyes."

Leland Edwards pleaded, "No, Victor, the walleyes of Liberty Lake aren't attracted to suckers. I always use shiners."

"Never fish with shiners, they die too fast."

"Not when it's cold. They die fast in the summer, but not in the winter."

"Shiners die year-round," Victor barked.

They both looked to Connor for an opinion. Connor shrugged.

They looked to the bait dealer, who laughed wheezily and said to Victor, "Suckers for walleyes—are you nuts?" He scooped shiners into the bucket Leland handed him.

Victor, severely insulted, stomped a foot on the wet floor and roared, insisting that he'd caught plenty of walleyes on suckers when he worked for the pipeline in South Dakota. The trouble with Minnesota, he said, was that things weren't done here the way they were done in the rest of the world.

Leland paid for the minnows, calling the dealer by name and saying good-bye with an apologetic smile.

They went next door to the Paul Bunyan Bottle Shop. The place was crowded with college students tanking up for Saturday night. On the breast and back of several jackets and sweatshirts appeared the word BLUES, along with the Rookery State College athletic emblem, a stylized blue heron with a needle beak and a fierce scowl. One of the students, a young man with black hair and Indian eyes, greeted Leland and asked what he knew about an instructor named Novotny. He said he and a number of his friends had enrolled in Novotny's Freshman English class for spring semester.

Hearing his office mate's name, Victor broke in and said Novotny was tops. He wasn't tops, Victor knew, but he wanted Neil to maintain a healthy enrollment.

The student seemed not entirely convinced by Victor, and he pressed Leland for an answer. Leland, aware of Neil's shortcomings, replied in discreetly vague terms.

Victor broke in again and changed the subject. Peppermint schnapps, he declared, warmed you up faster than anything else on cold days. He seemed to be daring Leland to defy him as he had next door concerning minnows, but here Leland had no opinion.

Victor then challenged Connor. "I suppose you've got something fancier than schnapps in mind."

"Booze is booze," Connor replied agreeably. He disliked schnapps. Perhaps with schnapps he could hold his drinking down. Nearly three months had passed since his famous Homecoming binge. He feared he was overdue.

"Heavens," said Leland, watching Connor take down a large bottle from the shelf. "Wouldn't a pint be plenty?"

"Better safe than sorry," Connor replied, fondling the bottle.

Leland turned to Victor. "Wouldn't a pint be plenty?"

"We don't have to drink it all at once. Come on, shell out."

They gave their share to Connor, who paid for the schnapps and a handful of candy bars.

On their way out the door, the young Indian stopped them with another question for Leland. Was there anything to the rumor that the faculty was going on strike?

Leland said it was news to him.

Victor said it was high time.

Outside, a thin, gritty snow was falling. Connor asked Victor to open the trunk, into which they had stashed their overcoats along with Leland's box of fishing gear. Connor tugged on his storm coat and settled into the car with its fleecy collar turned up around his ears, the bottle standing between his thighs, the minnow bucket on the floor between his feet.

"Victor, did you ever go on strike?" he asked.

"Damn right, on the pipeline. Best experience of my life."

"What for, wages?"

"Wages and benefits."

"Did you get them?"

Victor laughed happily at the memory. "Brought the goddamn robber barons to their knees."

"What's this about the faculty striking?"

"Where the hell you been?"

"We aren't really striking, are we?"

"Certainly not," Leland put in.

"Depends on things," said Victor. "Whether we vote to join the Alliance. Whether the state comes through with raises."

"Bosh," said Leland. "I've never heard of a college faculty striking."

They sped north through the snowy forest on a narrow ribbon of bumpy pavement. Leland, positioned again in the middle, searched the dial for his mother's radio show. Connor opened the bottle and lifted it lovingly to his lips. It eased his anxiety about spending an afternoon on a frozen lake. He had accepted Leland's invitation as a reason to leave home for a few hours. Painting was his customary escape, but he was between portraits and needed time away from his easel.

It was always a relief to separate himself from Marcy—except that he fretted about Laura when he was away. Compensating for her mother's dark moods, Laura, at thirteen, was devoting a great deal of energy to being falsely cheerful, and the strain of it was apparent in her voice and her shifty eyes. Each suppertime, returning home from campus, Connor could gauge the seriousness of his wife's emotional aberrations by the height of his daughter's spirits. He sometimes wondered if gloom might be a healthier reaction on his daughter's part. No, certainly not. Gloom was *his* reaction, and it made him feel very *un*healthy. Made him physically sick, in fact. But luckily it was a sickness for which he'd discovered a cure. He put the bottle to his lips and drank thirstily.

Leland, sitting in the middle, declined a drink. Victor accepted, swallowing a tiny amount. Handing the bottle back to Connor, he asked, "Why do you suppose Novotny lives in that hole in the ground?"

"Housing is tight," said Connor. "You saw the place I'm renting." They'd picked him up this noon at a tiny, decrepit house standing beside U.S. 2. "Trucks going by make our glassware in the kitchen ring. Pictures in the rooms hang crooked."

"But a basement, for God's sake. He's had two and a half years to find something aboveground."

"Less is more," said Leland. "At least that's what he tells me."

"What the hell's that supposed to mean?"

"It means he feels he ought to keep his life simple for the sake of his novel."

"Jesus," hissed Victor, who seemed personally offended by intellectual dedication. Never mind the hours they spent in their office together, Victor had no idea what made a novelist tick. Why would an able-bodied man with no evident literary talent want to spend every spare moment toiling over a book with no guarantee of publication?

"Nothing simple about Peggy Benoit," said Connor, chuckling happily, putting the bottle to his lips once again.

"Yeah," said Victor. "I've told him to watch his step with that dame."

"Well, I suppose maybe a fellow needs a friend." Leland's tone was soft and tentative, indicating that he was no expert in this area.

Snow continued to fall very lightly. The fields and distant trees were gray-white etchings. Connor continued to nurse the bottle. (Victor matched him sip for swig.) Leland abstained. He never exceeded the one-drink limit prescribed by his mother, who believed that you must every day present to the world your unwavering, predictable self.

A discussion of Neil Novotny's novel ensued for a distance of some twenty miles, Leland and Victor telling Connor what they knew of the plot (a man's search for his sister, who had apparently run away), and what they knew of its source. Apparently it had been handed down in family lore that Neil's forebears, when coming to America from Eastern Europe, had lost track of one of their women, and there was reason to believe—although the reason was not handed down—that she'd disengaged herself from the family on purpose. She'd disappeared in a depot in Philadelphia and was never found.

Connor felt his interest quickening the way it did when he saw movies about missing persons. *The Man Who Never Was.* *The Lady Vanishes.* If only he could pack up his canvas and paint and disappear for a time from the life he was currently living.

"Think how much easier it was for her to get lost," he mused.

"Easier than what?" his companions wanted to know.

"Than now."

Leland agreed. "No fingerprints in those days. No photos sent by wire."

"Hardly any photos period, back then," said Connor longingly.

The conversation then shifted to the meagerness of Neil's talents in the classroom. Leland said he was intelligent but failed to show it. Students had very little respect for him.

Victor concurred. "They think he's a dipshit."

Leland went on, claiming that Neil failed to prepare properly for class. He came before his students each day in a kind of daze, his mind still buried in the fiction he'd stayed up most of the night working on.

"That's the nice thing about teaching," said Victor, comparing his new profession to his old. "You can fudge on your job and nobody gives a shit."

"Oh, they care all right," countered Leland. "C. Mortimer cares. Dean Zastrow cares."

"Don't you believe it," said Victor. "C. Mortimer's a softie. The dean's a cretin."

"Nope. Nonrenewal of contract, that's the word on Neil." Leland nodded knowingly as he spoke, a gesture Victor was learning not to challenge. This hometown boy, this confidant of Chairman Oberholtzer, this family friend of the absent and ailing President Gengler, was seldom wrong when it came to rumor. Fact and unfounded gossip usually sounded the same to Victor, and he repeated both with relish, but Leland Edwards, while keeping his counsel, seemed always able to distinguish between the two—a skill presumably handed down from his mother, who had her ear to the ground all over town. While Leland covered the campus, his mother covered Rookery at large. Victor harbored a secret and grudging admiration for the energetic, opinionated Lolly Edwards, a woman of large hats and billowy dresses and stones the size of lightbulbs on her fingers. She hovered over Rookery's consciousness like a blimp, advocating things on the radio Victor mostly despised, such as library teas and Republicans. How long would he have to live in Rookery before achieving Lolly's degree of power and respect?

"It's Neil's third year," Connor pointed out. "They're not accepting his application for tenure."

"You mean they're actually cutting him loose?" asked Victor. "Who told you?"

"It's general knowledge over in art."

"Oh, my goodness, that means it'll be general knowledge in English before long," said Leland regretfully. "Poor Neil will be the last to know it."

"How do *you* know it?" Victor asked him.

Leland looked pained, not wishing to say how close he was to the administration.

"The sons of bitches, they can't do that!" seethed Victor, pounding the steering wheel with both fists, sympathy welling up in his heart for his persecuted office mate. "He's turning things around this semester. His enrollment's up."

"There's nothing says the dean can't hire and fire whoever he pleases," Leland reminded him. "Neil doesn't have tenure."

"Wait'll the Alliance takes hold, so help me, the dean will be kissing Neil's ass."

Neil Novotny, meanwhile, was striking the keys with angry force as he typed the name Zastrow again and again, the letters biting into the paper, the letter *o* becoming black circles against the platen.

This was the part Neil had been fiendishly eager to write, the chapter in which a heartless, detestable courthouse clerk named Zastrow turns up in the story and misleads Alphonse Harker, who has traveled nine hundred miles by train, horseback, and riverboat in search of his missing sister. Zastrow knows where Lydia Harker is. She's been taken downriver by a well-to-do family named Flandreau to serve as their housemaid. Zastrow knows this because he more or less sold her to the Flandreaus. For a generous fee from Colonel Flandreau, he produced a document declaring falsely that Lydia Hacker, sixteen and an orphan, had been a ward of the state of Ohio and was now a ward of the Flandreaus. But of course by the time her brother arrives at the courthouse, there is no trace of her in the files, because Zastrow has falsified her name. And so Alphonse Harker's search comes to a dead end. At least for now.

Neil, now typing swiftly, left the young man standing dejectedly outside the courthouse on the riverbank while he turned his full attention to the clerk. He gave Zastrow bushy black eyebrows and a wart on the side of his nose. He dressed him in a suit too tight for his stocky, paunchy figure and had him speak in clipped nasal phrases. He was an ambitious, lewd, and narrow-minded functionary who, whenever he became nervous, covered the wart on his nose with his index finger. Except for the lewdness, all of these details about this contemptible courthouse clerk in Ohio, together with his penchant for mishandling people and causing them grief, were an exact description—as Neil knew him—of Dean Zastrow of Rookery State College, the man who for weeks had been terrorizing Neil with threats of dismissal.

Because the office Neil shared with Victor Dash was on the first floor of McCall Hall, near Administration Row, he and Dean Zastrow had met time after time in the corridor and exchanged a nod of recognition but no words beyond hello, the dean always in a hurry, Neil preoccupied with his novel. One day in December, however, as fall semester was coming to an end, the dean stopped and addressed Neil. "Say, Steinbach, I've got bad news for you. This is your third probationary year, and if your teaching doesn't improve and you don't give us more in the way of publications, your contract won't be renewed for next year."

Neil's reply—"I'm not Steinbach"—caused the little man's index finger to jump to the wart at the side of his nose. "You're not?" His red bow tie, Neil noticed, was patterned with tiny cattle brands.

"I'm Novotny. Steinbach's in history."

"You're Novotny?" The dean appeared to doubt it.

"Neil Novotny. English."

"Well, the same goes for you, Novotny."

He strode away, leaving Neil standing in the hallway, incredulous. He wanted to object, wanted to plead for a more civil and less peremptory discussion, wanted to remind him of his novel in progress. But having trained himself to think at his typewriter, Neil was not skilled at thinking on his feet (one of his several defects as a classroom teacher), and so all he could do was slump against the wall and sigh.

"Remember, class, nobody owns the oceans," came a voice from a nearby classroom.

Neil gathered himself and returned to his office to seek solace from Victor Dash, who blew his stack for him.

"That scum-sucking pig!" seethed Victor, quoting Marlon Brando in *One-Eyed Jacks*, which he and Annie had recently seen at the Paramount. He popped out of his chair and led his office mate up two flights of stairs to C. Mortimer Oberholtzer's office, grumbling all the way. Neil caught enough of what he was saying to realize that this former pipeline worker and union griever was ready to take up arms against management, and that he, Neil, was to be the beneficiary. "We had a more humane way of doing things on the pipeline, for God's sake. Just wait till we get the Alliance up and running—the dean will be kissing your ass."

Chairman Oberholtzer's office was a turret at the top of McCall Hall. His bay of windows faced the same direction as Peggy's favorite window in the library, affording him a pleasant view of the house where he and his wife had raised four sons (all but Gary were married and out on their own) and where at this hour his wife was preparing for tonight's party, to which the division's newcomers and their spouses had been invited. Every year, before Christmas, the Oberholtzers entertained the rookies.

Victor, one such rookie, led Neil, a three-year veteran, into Oberholtzer's office and found him talking on the phone. Known as the most affable chairman on campus, Oberholtzer encouraged his staff—indeed, required them—to interrupt him unannounced whenever they needed counsel. Neil had heard him referred to, behind his back, as Dr. Pollyanna. He was so earnestly cheerful that many professors found his company severely depressing. "Tremendous," "fantastic," and "A-number one" were superlatives the chairman constantly uttered. "Superlative" was another.

Holding his phone to his ear, Oberholtzer waved Victor and Neil into chairs while saying, "Honey, I imagined nothing more than radishes and carrots beforehand." He was a tall, handsome, white-haired man who kept his hands busy with his hot-burning pipe and wore shaggy tweed jackets, button-down shirts, and wide red suspenders. His neckties too were shaggy tweed, and so was the overcoat hanging on his coat tree. On the walls of his office hung photos of dogs. On the windowsills and bookcases stood a dozen little flowerpots containing weak-looking African violets.

The two men sat down and listened to their chairman's side of a discussion about artichokes, whether grocers carried artichokes in the winter, and whether, if they did carry them, they came from so far away as to be unfresh. Artichokes were nearly ruled out and cauliflower decided upon, but not quite.

"That was Honey," he said, hanging up. "Isn't this a fantastic day?" He swiveled his chair, pointing the stem of his smoking pipe out the window. Actually, it was cloudy and cold, but he was apparently referring to last night's heavy snowfall, which some people, not Neil, found picturesque.

Victor tried to rein in his chairman's happiness. "The parking lot's full of snowbanks. The blockheads who cleared the sidewalks dumped all the snow in the parking lot. You wouldn't see that if you'd hire union workers around here instead of two-bit amateurs."

"Ah, Victor, let me give you a word of advice in the spirit of friendship. You're a fantastic addition to our faculty, your popularity in Business English is unprecedented, but I have to tell you that the department is becoming a tiny bit impatient with your constant reference to unions." Dr. Oberholtzer smiled benevolently as he regarded his pipe. " 'Who cares how things were done on the pipeline?' I've heard people saying, Victor. 'Why can't the man put the pipeline behind him and accept the way we do things on a college campus?' "

"This campus is full of blockheads."

Oberholtzer smiled indulgently and said, "Now, now, Victor." He struck a match and sucked on his pipe, clouding the office with eye-smarting smoke. "Please take what I say in the spirit I say it, the spirit of friendship."

"Never mind that, we're here to talk about the prize blockhead on this campus. Five minutes ago Dean Zastrow met Neil in the hall and told him he was on the verge of being fired."

The chairman looked suddenly apprehensive.

"And he called him by the wrong name besides. Who did he think you were, Neil?"

"Steinbach."

The chairman looked relieved. "Steinbach's in history."

"But he said the same went for me," Neil mumbled sadly.

"He scared the bejesus out of him. He's all broken up about it, aren't you, Neil?"

Both men studied Neil, who did indeed look injured. Even his voice sounded damaged. "He said I had to attract bigger classes and publish more, or lose my job."

"Everybody knows Zastrow was brought in to clean house," boomed Victor. "We had a foreman like that one time on the pipeline. They wanted to get rid of some of the guys with a lot of seniority because their wages were getting too high, so they brought in this goon they thought could break us down and force us to quit, but we broke *him* down and forced *him* to quit." Victor laughed lustily at the memory.

"I won't ask you how that was accomplished," said the chairman softly.

"It wasn't pretty," Victor bragged.

"I'll bet it wasn't." Chairman Oberholtzer thanked Victor for bringing Neil's plight to his attention and reminded him that he and Annie were expected at tonight's party, where a tremendous lot of fun would be had.

Not understanding that he was being dismissed, Victor lit a cigarette and settled deeper into his chair.

"I'll have to have a word with Neil about this, Victor."

"Well, I should think so."

"Honey and I will see you and Annie tonight at eight."

Victor finally caught on. "Okay, take it from here, then. Tell the dean we've got a gem in this man." He stood up and pounded a fist into Neil's shoulder. "Ask him how many state colleges have novelists. Will you do that?"

The chairman assured him he would.

"Much appreciated."

"Close the door if you please, Victor."

He did so.

Alone with Dr. Oberholtzer, Neil found his words of sympathy anything but consoling. First the chairman admitted that, yes, Dr. Zastrow had been chosen dean because he had, among other talents, a reputation for getting rid of people who had grown tired in the profession. He had proved himself at Mayville State in North Dakota, and before that at a small college in South Dakota, easing out the older staff and hiring energetic young members. "New blood for deadwood," Oberholtzer said. "Being young yourself, Neil, you have nothing to fear."

"Well, I'm not so sure," he replied. "He mentioned publishing. I haven't published anything."

"Your novel, my boy." Oberholtzer, closing his eyes, pronounced the word "novel" lovingly, as though he were biting into something delicious. "Your fantastic novel, when it's published, will supersede the puny scribblings of all the rest of us." He opened his eyes, smiling broadly.

"But I'm nowhere near finishing, and my probationary time is running out."

"That's where I come in, my boy. I go and explain to Dr. Zastrow that novels take a long, long time."

"You'll do that?"

"You bet your life."

"That's very kind."

"What are chairmen for?"

Neil smiled amiably, trying to feel better, but his hands were trembling and he felt sweat running down inside his shirt. The kindly chairman would be no match for the dean. Oberholtzer was a big woolly sheep, Zastrow a ravenous dog.

"There's my small classes too. The dean mentioned how small my classes are."

"All three sections?"

Neil nodded.

Again the chairman looked a bit apprehensive. "How many do you have in each?"

"Eight at noon, fourteen at one o'clock, nine at two."

The chairman wrote the numbers on a pad and carefully added them up. "Thirty-one," he said. "Well, that's far short of your share, all right. Puts extra work on the others, you understand. We like to see it even out at twenty-eight per section." Puffing smoke, he swung around and looked out the window for a long time.

"Last spring I had a total of thirty-eight," said Neil, perhaps not helping his cause, the trend being downward, but needing to fill the silence.

Oberholtzer, swiveling back, set down his pipe and said he would go to bat for him nonetheless, would change the dean's mind, would take the stress out of Neil's life so that he could move ahead, unimpeded, with his novel. The word "novel" again brought a blissful look to his face. "However, in order for me to succeed, you must do one thing."

"Yes?"

"You must somehow increase your enrollment spring semester, even if it's no more than one student per section. That way I can point to the registrar's figures and say to the dean, 'Look here, Novotny's turning things around.'"

Neil stood up and submitted his hand to the chairman's iron grip. "Thank you, Dr. Oberholtzer."

"Mortimer to you, my boy."

"Thank you."

He descended slowly and dejectedly to his office and told Victor what the chairman had said. Victor told him not to worry, leave it to him, he'd figure out a method by which Neil would entice greater numbers into his sections. "It's a matter of rewards," said Victor. "On the pipeline, it was money. Promise a pipeliner time-and-a-half and he'll work through a five-day rain. Promise him double time and he'll work through a goddamn blizzard."

"I can't pay people to take my course."

"Why not?"

"On my salary?"

"Get a loan."

Neil slumped at his desk. "I came here because it wasn't Stanford, it wasn't Duke, it was a place I could settle into and teach with half my energy and write my novel with the other half. Publish or perish at Rookery State?—ridiculous, I thought. Lose this job for incompetence in the classroom?—you'd have to be a lush or a maniac. With most people it's a question of whether they can stand to live so far out in the sticks, but I knew I could stand it. Hell, I could live in the Badlands if I could just go on writing."

"Lonesome country, the Badlands," said Victor. "We laid pipe around Rapid City one summer."

A knock on the door. It was one of Victor's students, a young woman inquiring about restrictive clauses as opposed to nonrestrictive. While they conferred, Neil drew a tattered little notebook from his coat pocket and found the page of fictional names he'd been developing. He crossed out Crowninshield as the name of the courthouse clerk in Ohio and wrote the name Zastrow.

———

And now, six weeks later, he was writing at high speed, his Ping-Pong table moving glacially across the tile as he typed, following the slant of the floor in the direction of the stairway. Every few minutes he had to stop and pull his chair up close to the typewriter.

He described Zastrow descending from a riverboat in the spring sunshine and stepping onto the Flandreaus' wharf, looking about him at the lush greenery of the plantation, and then climbing the path to the house. Neil then shifted viewpoints. Lydia Harker is on the veranda with Mrs. Flandreau, her new employer, and carefully following her instructions as she cleans the brass on the front door. When they turn and see Zastrow step up onto the veranda—on the pretext of following up her case, he is quick to explain—Lydia freezes with horror, recalling the improper advances he made in a dark corridor of the courthouse.

"What the hell you doing down there, popping corn?"

So deeply was Neil absorbed in his story that a couple of moments passed before he realized the question hadn't come from one of his characters. He looked up and saw the same large man in his underwear standing halfway down the stairs and glowering at him.

"I'm typing."

"Well, Jesus, can't you do it some other time? I'm trying to sleep."

"Just five more minutes," said Neil, hunching over his typewriter and explaining to the reader that Zastrow was mad for sex and angry because Lydia had fended him off in the courthouse.

"Hey!" barked the man.

"Okay, okay," said Neil, giving up on the narrative and typing a couple of notes for later:

Stress Lydia's beauty—give her Peggy's eyes.
Put bow tie on Zastrow—red with little cattle brands.

Leaving the library, Peggy crossed the frigid campus to McCall Hall, intending to make sure the college owned the instruments they'd need. Drums were no problem; the instrument room contained all manner of drums regularly in use by the pep band, but she didn't know if any of the basses had playable strings—the college orchestra had been defunct for years. And she herself needed a saxophone. She'd left hers at her brother's house in Boston.

Because McCall Hall was locked on weekends and Dean Zastrow allowed no one without tenure a key, the younger faculty gained admittance by pounding on the heavy front door and hoping there was someone inside to hear. Peggy pounded and called out, "Please let this poor untenured wretch into her office," but apparently there was no one to let her in, although it occurred to her that the dean (who bragged about coming to work seven days a week) might be watching from behind his blinds on Administration Row. Snow was falling lightly. Daylight was dying. She gave up and was halfway down the steps when she heard a window thrown open high above her and a man's voice call to her, "Dr. Benoit, I'll be right down."

She looked up just as Professor Shea was pulling his head of white hair back into his office on the third floor. "Oh, don't bother, it's not important," she sang, hoping to spare him the trouble, yet knowing that nothing so trivial as long flights of stairs would stand in the way of this old gentleman's innate kindness. Waiting, she studied the doorway. It was one of the few classy things about Rookery State, in Peggy's opinion, an oak door with brass fittings standing at the head of a broad stone stairway and set back under a handsome arch supported by columns. It seemed to promise all who entered a substantial education.

By the time Professor Shea opened it, she was shivering and hopping from one foot to the other. He apologized for his slowness. "Hobbled by sciatica," he said. "It comes back every winter when I shovel snow." He was a retired professor of English brought back this year to help carry the heavy student load, a lean, tall man whose paleness and studious squint somehow contributed to his Irish good looks. Peggy liked the way he leaned close to her when he spoke, like a conspirator. "One of the great curiosities of this campus, not giving you young people keys."

"One of many," she said, stepping into the warm hallway.

"Yes, we could make a list, couldn't we?" He waited for the door to swing shut and the lock to click into place, as everyone had been reminded to do in the dean's recent three-part memo entitled "Weekend Procedures." The switching off of lights and the turning down of thermostats were the other two reminders. "Such a pity our campus keys can't be duplicated, otherwise I'd have one made for you."

Heading for the stairs, they walked along Administration Row, recently remodeled, the smell of new plaster and carpet glue hanging in the air.

"Did you know these offices used to house the Department of Mortuary Science?" asked Professor Shea.

"So I heard. What became of it?"

"Died," he said gleefully.

"Of what?"

"Loss of accreditation. It was a sudden, painless death." He lowered his voice. "Although some would say we've only traded old undertakers for new."

"But you wouldn't say that, surely." It was easy for her to fall into his ironic manner of speaking.

"Oh goodness no, not on your life. At least not until June would I say such a thing."

"June?" she inquired.

"I'm retiring for good in June. Then I won't feel so much like a traitor when I find fault."

"You can fault the place to me, I don't mind."

"I can do better than that by you, Dr. Benoit." He leaned close and lowered his voice. "I can leave you my key when I go."

They climbed to the second floor, where Peggy parted from the old man, thanking him, and followed a dark corridor into the music wing, an area to which she *had* been entrusted with keys. In the instrument room, she found not one but three string basses, together with four cellos and a harp. All of them were dusty, most with slack or broken strings, but one of the basses appeared to be playable. She opened a cupboard and looked over the brass. All were marked and dented by mishandling and overuse. She chose a tenor saxophone through which she was able to utter, despite its dry reed, the certain soulful notes she thought compulsory for the sort of jazzy music they would play.

In the band room, a five-sided room with violet carpet and harsh fluorescent lighting, she arranged four chairs around the Steinway grand, an instrument in perfect tune despite its great age.

She packed the saxophone back into its scuffed black case and carried it, with her briefcase, to her office farther along the dark corridor. With the swelling enrollment had come cramped accommodations: her office was actually a piano practice room from which the piano had been removed. It contained only a small desk, a small bookcase, and two straight-backed chairs. There was no ventilation, no window, no phone. Because the walls were painted the dead shade of greenish yellow she associated with public rest rooms, Peggy had papered nearly every square inch with posters. Edvard Grieg looked down from over the desk. On another wall a bewhiskered John Philip Sousa stared past the doorway at a young Bob Dylan, whose eyes were directed at a lily Georgia O'Keeffe had painted for the Santa Fe Chamber Series. Kirsten Flagstad appeared to be singing to Stan Kenton across the top of the bookcase.

Scanning the titles in this bookcase, she found the book she'd come for, *Popular Music of the Thirties and Forties*, and she slipped it into her briefcase. Then she stepped out into the dark hallway to the phone shared by the music faculty—a pay phone. She looked up numbers by the light leaking out from her office and made three calls.

She talked to Annie Dash, who assured her that Victor would love to play drums with the group on Sunday afternoon; he loved get-togethers of all kinds.

She talked to Neil, who said yes, he'd be there if it wasn't too early; he'd have to finish his daily quota of words first.

She talked to Lolly Edwards, just this minute home from her radio show and just dying (she gushed) to have Peggy in for the evening. "Come at seven and we'll talk Leland into being your pianist. He's shy about his playing, you know. He needs coaxing. I'll serve dessert and ask the Oberholtzers in." Peggy accepted—anything to be out of her dismal apartment on a Saturday night.

She'd intended to call Connor's house as well, but was restrained from doing so by an odd trepidation, as though speaking to Mrs. Connor might be discouraging or even dangerous. At the Christmas party she'd been struck by the woman's inward, anxious expression and how closely it resembled the look on her own face whenever an attack of the lonesome blues made her feel panicky and depressed.

On her way to the stairway she was glad to see Georgina

Gold's door standing ajar in the speech and theater wing. She found her at her desk, busily searching through an anthology of poetry. Georgina Gold, professor (tenured) of speech and debate, was a tall, squinty-eyed woman in her middle thirties and the closest thing to a female friend Peggy had yet found in Rookery. Georgina's only flaws as a kindred spirit were her rather reactionary political opinions and her impending marriage to a man who took up all her spare time.

"Hi, Georgina. Let's go to the student center for coffee."

"God help us," Georgina hissed, without looking up from her book. "Can you guess what this student of mine intends to recite at the speech festival next Saturday?"

"Sure, 'Tintern Abbey.'" Georgina was fond of complaining that she'd heard so many halting renditions of "Tintern Abbey" that she wanted to throw up.

"Wrong. 'Howl.' By a guy named Ginsberg."

"I don't know it."

"Thank your lucky stars." Shutting the book, she turned and squinted up at Peggy. "It's profane. The judges will crucify her."

"What about coffee?"

"Can't. Sorry. Ron is on his way to pick me up. Why don't you and Neil go out with us tonight? Movie and supper."

"Because I don't like to encourage him."

"But who else *is* there?"

"I know, but that's no reason to actually go *out* with him."

"Oh, I don't know. Neil's sort of charming in his way."

Peggy, picturing Neil's boyish, fretful face, as well as his fits of peevishness, said, "Not my type, is all."

"Somebody will snap him up," said Georgina.

"I can't imagine it."

"Somebody in next year's crop. And just in time, too. He'll be out of work."

Peggy gave her a look of disbelief.

"Haven't you heard? Nonrenewal of contract."

"Who says?"

Georgina stood up and put on her jacket. "You hear things." She locked her office and they went down the stairs together.

Peggy's friendship with Georgina Gold had been more or less

inevitable, since they were the only two women under fifty in the division. Last September, as the faculty was gathering in the auditorium to hear the ailing President Gengler deliver his dispiriting annual pep talk, Georgina Gold had flopped into the seat next to Peggy and stated flatly, "You don't know me, but I've just gotten engaged." She flashed a diamond of impressive size while maintaining an absolutely expressionless face.

"Wow, that's wonderful," was Peggy's reply.

"The wedding's next June. His name is Ron."

"Is he here?" Peggy scanned the auditorium, imagining Ron to be one of the five or six young professors who stood out so plainly in this generally older and obviously married (or, in a few cases, obviously unmarriageable) faculty.

"No, heavens no, he's probably lying behind a Frigidaire in some woman's kitchen at this very moment." Seeing Peggy's puzzlement at this, she added, "His name is Ron Hunsinger."

"Oh," said Peggy.

His full name failing to dispel the mystery, Georgina backed up and started over. "Of course. You're new. You don't know Hunsinger Appliance. I've been here so long, I've begun to think there's no world outside Rookery. Hunsinger Appliance is Ron and his father. They sell Frigidaire, Maytag, and Hotpoint."

"What else *is* there?" said Peggy, meaning she was impressed.

"Whirlpool." Georgina Gold said this (as she said nearly everything) with a straight, unreadable face, and it was only later—days later—that Peggy realized she must have intended it to be funny, for behind the unsmiling, almost sour, expression on this woman's long, almost homely, face were the sort of derisive, irreverent attitudes she'd learned to enjoy in Neil Novotny, along with the fearless frankness she found a bit less enjoyable in Victor Dash. But if her manner was that of Neil and Victor combined, she was without the dark side of either. Whereas Neil tried to seduce you in his airless cellar and Victor tried lecturing you to death on the overthrow of the ruling class, Georgina simply kept you amused.

Or at least she kept Peggy amused. Not everyone was quite so impressed. You could tell by the way Leland Edwards stiffened in Georgina's presence that he found her scoffing manner distasteful. (Georgina, accordingly, considered Leland a stuffed shirt.)

As for C. Mortimer Oberholtzer, it was obvious that the chairman liked his speech and debate coach well enough (she was a youngish woman, after all; he liked to preen before all young and youngish women), but Georgina's mind was too quick for him. In Georgina's presence, the chairman wore a constant and uncharacteristic smirk on his face to indicate that he was keeping up with her sarcastic wit when actually he hadn't a clue.

At the front door Peggy said, "I'm getting a band together, Georgina. Do you play something?"

"Sorry, preschool rhythm class was as far along as they could bring me. Who's in the group?"

"You'd never guess."

"Faculty?"

Peggy nodded.

"Our division?"

She nodded again.

"How many?"

"Myself and four others."

Georgina put forth a number of wrong names. When Peggy told her, she said she was shocked. "You mean you're actually taking those four into the music wing on a Sunday afternoon? I'd be scared to death."

Peggy laughed. "Of what?"

"Well, of Victor, for starters."

"Victor's a pussycat."

"And Connor . . ." Georgina narrowed her squint, examining Peggy. "He's the most unlikely man in town for you to lose your head over."

"Who said I'm losing my head?"

Instead of answering this, Georgina moved on. "And Leland Edwards, he'll bore you to death."

"You haven't heard him play the piano."

"Have you?"

Peggy told her then about the gathering in Neil's basement. She told her, too, that she was invited to the Edwards house for the evening.

"God help you, Peggy. Lolly Edwards is trying to line you up with her son."

"Don't be funny."

"No, Peggy, it's what she does every year. She auditions new faculty women for Leland."

"Well, good. We can double-date."

For once, an expression crossed Georgina's face. Horror.

If Leland Edwards was known for anything beyond his slavish obedience to his mother, it was for his talent at the keyboard. He was the only youngster ever to perform at twelve consecutive recitals of Miss Carpentier's piano students. These recitals, held each year in the gymnasium of Paul Bunyan Elementary on the first Sunday in May, were occasions of such cultural importance in Rookery that they attracted people who weren't even related to the musicians. Clergymen brought their congregations, the sewing circle brought their husbands, and the overseer and his wife from the Poor Farm drove into town with a carload of codgers smelling of tobacco and urine.

The recital of 1952 marked Leland's final appearance. He was eighteen years old. He sat head and shoulders taller than the rest of the performers waiting their turn in the front rows of folding chairs. Next to him sat his mother, Lolly Edwards, a doting widow. She kept turning to her son to make sure he wasn't taking the crease out of his pants by crossing his legs, and now and then she reached up to pat his unruly cowlick into place.

At precisely two o'clock, Miss Carpentier, a pale, bony woman whose age was unknown and whose legs were acutely bowed, welcomed the audience, handed out cough drops to those in need, and introduced her pupils.

First on the program were the seven- and eight-year-olds playing pieces of nine or ten measures and striking eleven or twelve wrong keys. It seemed to Leland, a keyboard perfectionist, that he was witnessing a lot of sloppy fingerwork this year, and he wondered if Miss Carpentier was growing careless with age, or if talent was generally less plentiful since television had come to town. He recalled, with chagrin, his own first performance, at seven, when three-quarters of the way through "Anchors Aweigh" his fingers forgot what he'd memorized and he fled from the stage in shame. But he had not, as he recalled, struck even one wrong note up to that point, a fact that remained, to this day, a consolation.

Next came the intermediate students, who ranged in age from nine to fifteen and in height from four feet to five and a half. The range of talent was vast as well. Leland could tell by their applause that the audience had no idea who was good and who wasn't. He knew that Rookery judged performance artists not by their art but by their demeanor. If a youngster approached the piano with a sure step and acknowledged the clapping with a smile and a bow, there was no telling what a great artist he might become. On the other hand, it took but a glance at Carl Henderson to convince these untrained ears that he was pursuing music down a dead-end road. Carl trudged over to the piano as if the floor were a miry field, and he played with his red face hidden behind one of his shoulders. His fingers trembled on the keys.

Why didn't Mr. and Mrs. Henderson relent and free poor Carl from the piano? they asked one another during intermission. Couldn't his parents see his shame? Didn't they understand how wretched was his playing? Mingling with the audience at the refreshment table, Leland heard these comments and held his tongue. He was too shy to point out that Carl Henderson, though a victim of stage fright, actually loved the piano, and that his playing, far from wretched, was improving every year, right before their ears. They didn't know, as Leland did, that Carl hoped to major in piano or organ in college and go on to become the music director of some big Lutheran church somewhere.

As an only child and chronically lonely, Leland had hoped Carl might be his friend. Throughout Leland's boyhood, friends had been in short supply. There had been a neighbor girl when he was little, and a couple of boys in grade school and junior high, but after his father's sudden death, Leland had become more or less reclusive, taking pleasure in solitary things like fishing and coin collecting, and he became very serious about his music, practicing long hours in preparation for jivy jam sessions that existed only in his head. At one point he'd asked Carl, three years his junior, to work up a duet with him for this recital, say a Gershwin medley, but Carl's taste ran to the sort of moody compositions that Miss Carpentier loved so dearly and Leland couldn't stand. Carl wasn't the least bit interested in the jazzy showtunes Leland liked to play.

After the punch and small cookies of intermission, Miss Carpentier presented her prize pupils, five in number. Shirley Pribbelow was first. Shirley, like Carl, was still completely under her teacher's power, which meant she was still playing the convoluted melodies Leland loathed, written by Debussy and other sleep-inducing Frenchmen. There was languor in Shirley's stride as she approached the piano, her playing was faint and dreamy, and the movements of her wrist and head were studied, hypnotic. The audience, who at the beginning of her piece had been shifting gingerly in their seats and loosening their elastic and buttons and exploring their teeth for morsels of cookie, fell gradually into a trance so deep that the applause Shirley got when she finished was as faint and scattered as the notes she had played.

Then it was time for the Skoog sisters. These three small, high-tailed blondes could be counted on to play the audience awake with lively melodies arranged for six hands on two pianos. Brisk bundles of nerves, Judy, Trudy, and Cecilia Skoog went rushing at the pianos with their hair flying, and they bounced on the benches as they pounded out pieces with clowns and stampedes and shooting stars in their titles. Every year they played their encore number, "Qui Vive," with such gusto that listeners were known to leap to their feet and whistle and cheer—such gusto this year that Cecilia, the youngest Skoog sister, midway through the crescendo, broke her index finger.

Perhaps it was the commotion of three girls wailing, one in pain, two in sympathy, as their father and mother and aunts and uncles rushed them out of the gym and across the street to Mercy Hospital that destroyed the audience's concentration and left them restless during Leland's performance. Or perhaps it was his own fault, for his rendition of "Slaughter on Tenth Avenue," though technically perfect, seemed to lack heart or soul or whatever it was that had made him such a hit in years past—indeed had brought his mother to the piano more than once during this past week of practice to clap her hands with delight because the loud parts were so thunderous and the soft parts so tender and moving. But this afternoon all the parts were level and uninteresting. What a shame, thought his mother, something's got into the boy, maybe the flu bug; she must take his temperature.

But it wasn't the flu, it was reverie. Leland was dreaming while he played, imagining himself a member of a small jazz combo or dance band consisting of drums, a bass fiddle, a trumpet or two, his piano, of course, and perhaps a trombone. The players were men he would meet next year in college, or perhaps later when he became a teacher of English. The group already had a name—the Icejam Quartet or Quintet or Sextet, depending on their number. This vision had been occurring to him more and more often the closer he came to the end of his school days, and now, this being his farewell appearance, these fellow musicians joined him on the piece he was playing and made it much livelier in his head than it sounded in the gymnasium of Paul Bunyan Elementary.

Not that it mattered much to the audience after all, for he stood up and took his bows with such aplomb and received Miss Carpentier's kiss and his mother's kiss with such a handsome smile that everyone knew they must have heard something fine.

Leland had caught only a few fading minutes of his mother's voice before they outdistanced the signal of KRKU, so he switched off the car radio and turned his attention to Victor Dash, who was saying, "When Honey Oberholtzer brought in that artichoke and set it on the table in front of us, I didn't know what the hell it was."

"I knew what it was," Connor said, chuckling. "I painted a still life with an artichoke one time."

"I thought it was a goddamn thistle plant." Victor's laugh was shrill. Connor continued to chuckle.

Puzzled and a little hurt to think the Oberholtzers might have entertained without inviting him and his mother, Leland asked, "When was this?"

"Back before Christmas," Connor replied.

"Oh, the newcomers' party," said Leland, relieved. He'd heard all about the newcomers' party from Honey Oberholtzer—how Victor Dash had eaten part of a houseplant, how Connor had seemed so tense and silent before getting a couple of drinks under his belt, and how outrageously Connor's wife had behaved. Apparently, she'd sat there glowering for most of the evening, saying next to nothing, and then, when the party was breaking up, had called her husband a shit. "Come on, you shit," she'd said when Connor lingered on his way out the door to tell his host and hostess a joke. Everyone bravely pretended not to have heard, Honey Oberholtzer reported. Everyone, that is, except Connor, who turned crimson.

"Oberholtzer's wife brought in a very creamy dish of something," said Victor, "and said to dip our leaves in it."

"And then she brought in a very weird person," said Connor, "and said it was her son."

They laughed, all three, Leland perhaps not quite so uproariously as the other two. Leland's lightness of heart was caused less by his companions' account of the party than by their compatibility. It boded well for the music they would make. He just hoped they didn't go too far with their fun. The Oberholtzers were particular friends of his.

"Honey Oberholtzer is a particular friend of Mother's," he told them, expecting this to stop them short of disrespect.

"Then she brought in something else green and leafy," said Victor, "and I tore off a leaf. . . ." Victor's laughter overcame him.

"And you dipped it!" cried Connor.

"And I ate it!" roared Victor, whose eyes were tearing up so that he could scarcely see to drive.

"And she said . . ." Connor, too, was overcome, choking on his laughter.

"And she said . . ." Victor, snorting and gasping for air, had to brake and pull over on the shoulder and stop.

Connor was finally able to get it out. "She said, 'That's my jade plant!' "

Both men quaked breathlessly, their silent laughter punctuated by Connor's wheezing and Victor's pounding the steering wheel with his fist. Leland forced himself to chuckle.

Recovered, they drove on.

"That boy of theirs." Connor shook his head.

"A throwback," said Victor. "How did you know he was a boy? Hair down to his shoulders."

"By his name. She introduced him."

"Gary," Leland offered.

Victor began laughing again. "My wife thought he was a girl. She thought Mrs. Oberholtzer must have said, 'Mary,' not 'Gary,' so that's what she called him."

"Their youngest son," explained Leland.

"Did you hear what my wife said to him, Connor? Annie shook his hand and said, 'Hello, Mary,' and that was about the time she saw his chin whiskers." Victor roared as before. "She never saw hair that long on a guy before, and neither did I."

"Gary's been something of a problem to them," said Leland, not much amused.

Nor was Connor altogether amused. Aberrations in young people made him uneasy, now that his own daughter was manifesting signs of a troubled nature.

"He's counterculture," Leland explained.

"What the hell's that?" demanded Victor.

"Just what it says. On the order of hippies."

"Jesus—hippies! That whole ban-the-bomb crowd ought to be taken out and shot."

Leland fell silent, aware that the only way to quell Victor's more repellent opinions was to allow him the last word, and so they drove several miles in silence, snow falling in gauzy squalls, wind whistling around the windows, Leland passing the bottle left, right, left, right. He was aware of Victor's little sips, as compared to Connor's thirsty intake.

At length he asked Connor, "How did you like Honey Ober-holtzer? Isn't she a marvelous hostess?"

It took Connor a few moments to answer because his rate of drinking was already shutting down sections of his brain. "Marvelous," he agreed, as soon as he was able.

"And your wife?" asked Leland. "She enjoyed the party?"

A long pause. A bald lie. "Marcy thought it was marvelous."

"That wife of yours is a mighty good-looking woman," Victor prompted, hoping Connor would say more. It would be nice to present Annie with some new little clue to help her understand Mrs. Connor.

"Sweet-looking," Leland agreed. "That's what Mother says."

Connor, growing a bit dizzy, said nothing. He blinked at the road ahead, telling himself, not for the first time, that he ought to work up a stock reply to inquiries about his wife, something simple and final that would put the matter to rest. Addicted to certain medicines? Would that satisfy them? Or should he report the diagnosis of her doctor in Minneapolis—chronic depression? Or perhaps his own diagnosis after fourteen years of marriage: Marcy was simply the unhappiest person he'd ever known.

"Your wife too," Leland hastened to add. "Annie's the name?"

Victor confirmed it. "Annie."

"Mother saw her downtown with your children. She seems like such a good little mother, Mother says."

Victor confirmed this as well. "Annie's tops."

Connor, closing his eyes against his dizziness, fell immediately asleep. The other two rode on in silence. Here and there they passed a clearing containing a house or small farmstead; otherwise the countryside consisted of hilly forests of aspen and pine, and lowland swamps surrounded by bare tamaracks. Snow continued to fall, and so did the temperature, apparently, for the steam forming on the windshield required more frequent wiping.

Connor didn't wake up until the car was skidding to a stop on the snow-covered ice of Liberty Lake. Paralyzed by drink, he had to be told to open his door. He opened it. He had to be told to get out. He tumbled out and sprawled on the ice. He raised himself to a sitting position, grew dizzy again, and carefully lowered himself flat. He crossed his ankles, crossed his hands on his chest, closed his eyes against the snowflakes tickling his lashes, and said, "Go ahead and fish, don't wait for me."

While Leland bent over him, encouraging him to get up, Victor walked away, stretching his legs and surveying the vast white sheet of the lake. He saw that the nearest fishermen and vehicles were clustered a half mile or more to the north. He looked west, where the far shore was out of sight, twenty-two miles away, according to Leland. Facing all this emptiness gave Victor the willies. He called, "How do we know where the sandbar is?"

"We're on top of it," said Leland, lifting one of Connor's limp arms.

"How do you know?"

"Because I've been coming up here for years." Actually, since he was seven. From that year forward, Leland's father took him fishing at every opportunity. Summers, they tried many different lakes, fishing from shore, from bridges, from canoes, from launches. Winters, they concentrated on this lake, this very sandbar, because it never failed to produce walleyes for them. One summer when Leland was fourteen and away at camp, his father went fishing alone, in a canoe, and was killed by lightning. Fishing, ever after, was Leland's link with his father.

Victor returned to the car and drew Leland's ice auger out of the trunk.

"Hey, Victor, I think he's passed out."

"He'll be fine."

Victor removed the blade guard from the auger and began drilling a hole in the ice, pressing down on the handle with all his weight while turning the crank with his right hand. By the time he'd gone down eight inches, he was winded and his right arm was cramping. He turned the auger over to Leland, who ground down another ten or twelve inches and struck water.

Leland had brought along three fishing sticks. He unwound the line from one of them, clipped on a bobber, baited the hook, and sent it down into the water while Victor started another hole.

They caught two small walleyes before the second hole was drilled. With two lines they caught four more before the third hole was drilled. With three lines they caught seven more, and then the fish stopped biting.

Leland, who between fish had been urging Connor up off the ice, was now alarmed to see that the whites of his half-open eyes had turned a yellowish gray, and spit was freezing on his beard.

"Victor, his eyes are funny."

No response from Victor, who was kneeling at one of the holes, concentrating on a nibble. They needed five more fish for their three-man limit.

"Victor, he's unconscious. He'll freeze to death."

"He'll be fine."

Victor jerked the line, but felt no fish. He brought up the hook and found the minnow gone. He cursed, perturbed that Leland should have caught eleven of the thirteen fish thus far. Leland had the touch, knew when to set the hook and how to raise the fish gently through the hole. Victor had lost six or eight on the way up.

"Listen, Victor, this is serious. Help me get him into the car."

Victor ran to another hole where the bobber had disappeared. He lost this one too.

Leland, watching, reproved him. "You can't fish with your mittens on. You can't feel when to set the hook."

"What am I supposed to do, freeze my fingers off?"

The bobber went down in the third hole, and Leland hurried over and teased the fish for a minute by twitching the line. "I think we're into a school of bigger ones," he exclaimed, bringing up a walleye somewhat larger than the others. This fish had swallowed the hook, so he went to the trunk and opened his tackle box—his father's tackle box—in which he carried a probe.

"Hey, how about this!" shouted Victor, who was back at the first hole and holding a dripping, twisting walleye in the air. It was larger than Leland's. "Look at this beautiful goddamn fish, Leland. What do you think, four pounds?"

"Two and a half."

"Four pounds if it's an ounce," Victor exclaimed, hefting the fish like a yo-yo until it twisted itself off the hook and fell headfirst down the hole. Victor dropped to his knees and thrust his arm shoulder-deep into the icy water; then he was instantly back on his feet, cursing, fishless, dancing about, throwing off his mitten and kneading his coat sleeve, which was quickly stiffening with ice.

"Take off your coat," Leland advised, "before it soaks through to your shirt."

"My hand stings!" He rushed over to Leland and showed him his hand.

"Of course it stings. Take off your coat and get in the car. Start the engine and warm up."

"My *wrist* stings."

"What do you expect, with your arm down a fish hole?"

"My *arm* stings," said Victor, getting in behind the wheel.

The exhaust pipe rattled and chugged and spat smoke at Leland, who stood at the trunk working the hook loose from his fish's gullet. He dropped the fish into a pail, then went around to the passenger side and stood over Connor. "Help me get him inside," he shouted through the window.

"There's a bite," Victor shouted back, pointing to a hole.

It took longer to hook this one, Leland teasing the fish with little flicks and tremors of the line. It was well over two pounds. He unhooked it and threw it into the pail. He went around gathering up the others they had caught and left scattered on the snow, the later ones beginning to stiffen, the earlier ones frozen solid. Pausing, he looked north toward the cluster of fishermen and found that they had vanished. The snow, which had been falling lightly and intermittently all the while, was coming down thickly now, obscuring all landmarks, even the near shoreline.

He stood at Victor's window. "We'd better leave."

Victor was undecided. "How many we got?"

"Fifteen."

"Three more won't take long."

"We've got to get him home."

"Hate to quit so close to our limit." Victor could see all three holes from his window. The bobbers floated motionless.

"It's snowing pretty hard, Victor. Pretty soon our trail to shore will be covered up."

"Yeah, I guess." He got out.

First they gathered up the fishing sticks, then Connor. It was difficult lifting him into the car and impossible to keep him in a sitting position. Mumbling and coughing weakly, he fell across the seat. Mucus streamed from his nose.

"We'll lay him in back," said Victor.

"No, he needs to be up here close to the heater."

"What? Dripping snot on my upholstery?"

"Listen, this is serious. He's got to be warm."

Victor relented. They slid Connor to the center and sat on either side of him, supporting him with their shoulders, so that he rode in a more or less upright position, his chin on his chest. The sounds he uttered seemed not to be words, but foamy noises from deep in his chest. The car moved across the ice.

"We shouldn't have let him lie there, Victor."

"The fish kept biting."

"But even so."

"Christ, I never saw fishing this good."

"He sounds like he's got pneumonia."

"He'll be fine."

Despite the snowfall, they reached land without getting stuck and followed a winding lane through the trees and out onto the highway. They sped south in dying daylight.

"Victor, it's really cold over here by the door."

"Yeah, by this one too."

They met no traffic coming north. Leland grew dizzy watching the snowflakes shoot into the headlights. Now and then he felt a shudder run through Connor's body.

"Victor, what will we tell his wife?"

"Why tell her anything?"

"I mean if we have to carry him in."

This struck Victor as funny. He laughed softly, recalling the times he'd carried home drunken pipeliners. He never expected to carry home a drunken professor.

"Because I don't think he'll be able to walk, Victor."

"Tell her the truth. He can't hold his liquor."

"You tell her."

"Not me, I hardly know her."

"Well, neither do I."

Victor stopped chuckling as he pictured the forbidding Mrs. Connor opening the door on her unconscious husband.

Leland exclaimed, "I think he's going to throw up!"

"He'll be fine," said Victor.

"No, he is!"

Connor began to be sick into his lap.

"Jesus Christ, my upholstery!" shouted Victor, flooring the accelerator—an unwise tactic because the powdery snow on the highway caused the car to swerve. Held to forty-five miles an hour, he grumbled and fumed. Leland was relieved when they finally drew within range of KRKU and a diverting news program. A woman from Milwaukee, Golda Meir, had been named premier of Israel. A man from Rookery, Harold Hunsinger, had been elected president of the Minnesota Appliance Dealers Association. The Colts were favored by eleven points over the Jets in tomorrow's Super Bowl III. Connor was not voluminously sick. It was a recurring, dribbling form of sickness mostly absorbed in the folds of his coat.

At the heart of Rookery, Victor turned east and followed U.S. 2 to the outskirts of the city. "Is this where you live?" he asked, creeping along, peering into the darkness.

Leland answered for Connor. "There's no picket fence in front of his place."

"How about here?" he asked, stopping farther on.

"I don't think so," said Leland. "I think his house is closer to the road."

The third place they recognized even before the headlights picked up Connor's name on the mailbox. They saw his white station wagon drawn up close to the front door, an electrical cord connecting the engine heater to the light socket over the stoop. Through a large, square window they saw the gray light of a TV screen.

Switching off his headlights, Victor turned in at the driveway and stopped behind the station wagon. Leland opened his door and got out, urging Connor to follow. Connor appeared not to hear. Leland shook him, but to no avail.

"Come on, Victor, give me a hand."

"Not me, I'm not getting into a hornet's nest."

"Well, I can't carry him alone, for pity's sake. He weighs more than I do."

Victor was silent for a few moments, conceiving a method of avoiding Mrs. Connor. "All right, we lay him out under that window."

"Are you crazy? He's got the chills."

"They say she's a hellcat."

"Is that any reason he should freeze to death?"

"We don't leave him here to die, for God's sake. We let her know he's out here, but we don't hang around."

"Come on," said Leland, pulling Connor across the seat. Victor came around and helped. Connor was rubber. He moaned with displeasure as they half carried, half dragged him across the snow, Victor steering them away from the door and over to the dim patch of light under the window. Laying him down on his back, they heard him sigh as though happily satisfied.

Victor said softly, "Now what about fish?"

"Fish? What about them?"

"I'd be mad as hell if I was Connor and my friends didn't leave me my share."

Leland didn't argue. It seemed strange to Leland that the trunk light came on when so little else about the car was in working order. They stood over the pail, selecting the five largest walleyes, which by this time were hard as firewood.

Leland picked out a sixth one. "Let's give him his limit, as long as we're at it."

Victor bumped it out of his hand. "Are you kidding? That'd leave us one short."

They carried the five fish over to the window, and Victor lined them up neatly on Connor's chest and stomach. "So his wife doesn't miss them," he explained, standing back and admiring the sight.

"Okay, so now what?"

"So now we get in the car and honk."

"That's childish."

"We don't leave till we make sure she looks out and sees him."

"But how does she get him inside?"

"She's got a kid to help her, hasn't she?"

"The daughter's only twelve or so."

"That's her problem."

They got into the car. Victor turned it so the headlights fell across the recumbent figure covered with fish. He honked. There was no movement in the window.

"Maybe they're gone."

Another honk. A shadow fell across the window. A face appeared.

"Is that her?"

"It's the daughter."

Victor hit the high beam, and the girl, seeing her father, jumped back from the window.

Soon a second face appeared. "That's her, isn't it?"

"Victor, I can't believe we're doing this."

"Yep, that's her. Let's get out of here." Victor backed up, turned, drove out of the yard.

"How will we ever face the woman?"

"Who says we have to?"

"Department doings. Dinner parties. Potlucks."

"Maybe the wives won't come."

"Wives always come. It's the wives that plan them."

"Life was simpler on the pipeline." Victor shook his head sadly. "Wives never entered into things."

Marcy Connor, groggy from sleep, pulled her coat on over her nightgown, tugged on her boots, and followed her daughter out the front door. There was no light over the stoop (the bulb had been replaced by the cord from the car), and she was startled in the blackness by the touch of snowflakes on her cheeks. Shivering and waving her hand as though at a swarm of gnats, she trudged across the drifted yard to her husband.

"Daddy, get up, get up!" Laura pleaded stridently, brushing the five fish off her father's chest. "Come inside, you're freezing."

"Pneumonia again," said her mother evenly.

"Daddy, stand up!" Coaxing and tugging, the girl succeeded in raising him to a sitting position.

"Here, get behind him," said her mother.

By gripping him under his arms and lifting, they succeeded only in tipping him sideways, but Connor seemed to get the idea. He raised himself to his hands and knees with his head pointed toward the door. He crawled a short distance before he began treading on his coattails and fell forward, facedown, in the snow.

"Daddy, Daddy," Laura wept. "Get up, Daddy, you'll freeze out here."

"Listen to him breathe—if that's not a death rattle."

"Mother, don't *say* that!"

They raised him again to a crawling position, but he didn't crawl. He lifted his eyes and stared at the white station wagon looming faintly in the darkness, fully aware now of his whereabouts, of his daughter's voice, of his wife's. He was aware, too, of the blockage in his breathing, which meant he'd soon discover how the Rookery hospital compared to all the others he'd been in. He could expect four or five days, possibly six, of nurses and vaporizers, and then many more days of weakness in the classroom, weakness at his easel. Recuperation took longer each time.

"Daddy, you have to get in where it's warm."

He brought his right foot forward and tried to stand. He did stand, finally, and with his weeping daughter supporting him on his right and his silent wife on his left, he staggered halfway to the stoop. But walking through snowdrifts required more effort than he had breath for, and he went down again to his knees.

A truck rumbled past on the highway, lighting up the yard with its headlights, and Marcy pictured their tableau as it must appear to the driver—two solicitous figures bent over the wounded animal that was her husband. The truck fanned out a swirl of snow that came blowing across the yard and into their faces. Then darkness again. Stillness. The sound of his labored breathing. The sound of Laura's weeping.

"Daddy, you'll freeze out here!"

Connor began to inch forward again.

"We'll go straight to the hospital," said Marcy. "I'll get my keys."

She went inside, and as she put on a sweater and slacks, she spoke to Connor. "There has to be more to our lives than this torture over and over again. I can't believe Laura and I were brought into this world to be nursemaids to a drunk." Such was Marcy Connor's bitterness that she spoke to her husband only in his absence.

She carried her daughter's jacket outside, and there discovered Connor on his feet once again and Laura guiding him to the car. She unplugged the engine heater and got in behind the wheel. The engine groaned reluctantly, but started. Connor fell in on the passenger side. Laura lifted his legs in after him, then got into the backseat and put on her jacket. Shivering, she asked, "Do we know where the hospital is?"

"I've seen it."

They drove without speaking into the center of Rookery and beyond, to the campus neighborhood. There they caught sight of Mercy Hospital across the river. Distracted by the beauty of these residential streets—snow-molded yards glowing under antique streetlights—Marcy made a couple of wrong turns before she found Bridge Street. She crossed the Badbattle and followed the signs to the emergency room.

Two nurses and an orderly hoisted Connor onto a gurney, stripped him of his layers of heavy clothes, and wrapped him in blankets. A young doctor, after listening long at his chest and up and down his back, turned to Marcy and said, "Pneumonia."

Marcy said, "Of course."

He told her that his temperature was rising at an alarming rate. She responded with a curt nod of her head.

Connor was wheeled to an elevator, riding along the bright fluorescent hallway with his eyes closed, his breath coming out shallow and noisy. He was raised to the second floor and rolled into a room containing two elderly men who lifted their heads off their pillows and watched the nurses transfer him to the third bed and place an oxygen mask over his face.

When the nurses left, Marcy and Laura approached the bed and stood over him. Exhausted but fully conscious now, Connor looked at them with a forlorn expression that his wife had learned to despise and his daughter found endearing. To each of them it seemed to say he was helpless without her. Marcy turned away. Laura sighed, "Oh, Daddy."

One of the old men smiled at Marcy, revealing only one upper tooth, and asked, "What's he got?"

"Pneumonia."

"I'm in for piles."

"I'm in for my heart," said the other proudly, an outdoor man with a face as bleached and bluish as an old weathered board.

"Mother," said her daughter with alarm, and Marcy turned to find Connor shuddering violently. She pressed the button for the nurse.

"Lookit that boy shake, would you," said the weathered man. "You sure he ain't got malaria? I had a brother with malaria in the war shook like that. Got bit by a bug of some kind in Panama."

The nurse brought more blankets. The shaking subsided. Marcy led Laura out of the room and argued with her in the hallway, insisting they go home and get a good night's sleep. Laura had no alternative but to follow her out to the car.

Riding home in a dark, resentful mood, Laura said, "You think more of sleep than you do of Daddy."

Marcy drove dreamily through the fluffy snowfall, knowing her daughter was right. Sleep had become her greatest pleasure. She guarded her hours in bed like precious stones. She hadn't always been in need of so much sleep. Early in her marriage, when Laura was a baby, she'd gotten by on six hours or so. Now she needed ten. Some nights twelve.

"Admit it—you do. You think more of sleep than you do of Daddy or me or anybody."

Not you, she wanted to say, but didn't, fearing the effect on Laura of admitting that she no longer loved her husband. There was so much you couldn't say to a teenager. Daughters this age bruised so easily. There was so much you couldn't say to practically the whole world, for that matter, when you were boxed in like this, ashamed of your predicament, held hostage by your wedding vow.

Locking his fishing gear in the garage, Leland heard his mother calling through the haze of snow, "Honestly, you're just like your father—blizzard or no blizzard, there's no controlling you on Saturdays."

Despite her admonitory tone, Leland purred with satisfaction, glad to have proved once again, as she'd trained him to prove all his life, that he'd been created in the image of his sainted father. He snapped the padlock shut and crossed the yard toward the door she was holding open.

"Baseball, football, hunting, fishing," she reminded him as he drew nearer, "your father never spent a Saturday at home."

Fishing, of the four, was Leland's only interest. He was bored by team sports and afraid of guns. Bowling intrigued him, but his father hadn't been a bowler, so he didn't take it up. Some Saturdays, however, he did spend an hour or two at Lilac Lanes, watching. His pastime at home, like his father's, was the piano. Musically he went far beyond his father. He played hour after hour. He loved Scarlatti and Haydn, and he loved to experiment with tunes from the Hit Parade of his youth. Today's rendition of "These Foolish Things" on Neil's piano was the result of perhaps ten years of practice.

"I'd never have gone into radio if I'd had your father's companionship even one Saturday out of the month."

"Oh, Mother, of course you'd have gone into radio." He climbed the steps to the back entryway and saw that she was dressed for company—her favorite caftan, the one with the broad horizontal stripes, tan and red. She was a tall, heavy woman, broad of body, beefy of face. For some months now her beautician had been carrying out an experiment Leland didn't care for, allowing her chestnut-dyed hair to grow into a shaggy sort of ponytail which was now long enough to hang forward over her shoulder.

"That's where you're wrong, kiddo," she told him. "It was unbearable Saturday boredom that drove me to it."

Leland mumbled, "I see," acquiescing to this fiction, and wondering if his mother was truly unaware of her almost pathological need to inform the world of every little opinion that crossed her mind. And most of them were very little indeed. Which cleansing powders damaged porcelain. Who deserved an Academy Award. Whether white or dark raisins were best for fruitcake.

In the entryway leading to the kitchen, he hung up his coat and removed his boots, wondering, too, if she realized what an ideal medium radio was for anyone who hated to have her opinions contested. That original few minutes of "Lolly Speaking" on weekends had evolved into a daily show (ten o'clock weekdays, two o'clock Saturdays), and she often took phone calls on the air, but always with her finger on the switch that cut callers off when she'd heard enough.

"I've kept your hot-dish warm." She led him into the dark oak kitchen, where the appliances were avocado green, and a cork bulletin board covered one entire wall.

"We caught fifteen," he said, setting his bucket of fish on the drain board. He removed his down vest and his outer flannel shirt, revealing a similar shirt beneath it, while his mother heaped chicken casserole on a plate, and added a slice of buttered bread and a pickle. She carried it to the table, telling him, "Hurry and eat and then clean up. We're having a few people in."

"Honey and Mortimer?" he asked, turning from the drawer he was searching through.

She nodded her large head, causing her shaggy ponytail to dance on her shoulder. "And Peggy Benoit."

"Peggy Benoit?" Leland was surprised.

"She phoned for you, and I thought why not ask the poor thing over. It's so sad seeing a girl at loose ends on a Saturday night."

"What did she want?"

"Something about playing in a combo. There's more hot-dish, and you can have Jell-O."

Leland drew his father's fillet knife from the drawer.

"You haven't time to clean fish, Leland. They're coming at seven-thirty for dessert."

He obediently returned the knife to the drawer and sat down to his meal.

"Jell-O?" she asked.

"No, thanks."

She carried the bucket of fish across the kitchen and shut it in the entryway. "She said you played the piano for her."

Leland recognized the trace of anxious hope in his mother's voice. It signaled her determination to find him a suitable mate.

This was a change from his youth, when she defied the few young women who manifested the least interest in him. He'd first aroused this defiance when he was sixteen and reported to his mother that he'd walked Sally McNaughton home from the Homecoming bonfire. But it wasn't exactly defiance then; it was more like panic. Leland got the message. To lose her son two years after losing her husband was unthinkable. For a decade or more the message remained the same—no romantic attachment allowed. His compliance became so habitual that her change of policy took him off guard. For the past few years she'd been checking out new women on the faculty with increasing interest—Leland was now thirty-five—and had found more than one who might have qualified as her daughter-in-law. However, none of these women seemed to consider Leland a catch. This astonished his mother. He had tenure. He had clean habits. He was intelligent, responsible, and healthy. Wasn't it obvious to these women that someday he'd own this very substantial house? Why, when she enticed young women home for an evening and Leland played a piece on the piano for them, did they look unbearably bored? Well, this evening at last she was bringing in a woman with musical sensibilities.

"When did you play for her, Leland?"

"This afternoon, but not just for her. I played on Neil's piano."

"Neil has a piano?"

"It's pretty well shot."

"What did you play?"

" 'These Foolish Things.' They wanted 'Your Feet's Too Big,' but I couldn't remember how it started."

"Dum dum dee dum," his mother said helpfully. She turned to her bulletin board and pinned up a fresh index card, adding, "Dee dum, dee dum."

He said, "No, I think that's 'Josephine.' "

She drew a pen from a deep pocket of her caftan and wrote *Monday* on the card, and then *Steadman.* Before her Monday morning show, she would try to reach State Representative Harry Steadman and find out what was holding up the appropriation for college salaries. Judging by the number of heated calls to KRKU this afternoon, it was a hot subject.

"Did you listen in this afternoon?"

"No, I missed it."

She chuckled. "It was mostly about whether you deserve a raise."

"Do I?"

She laughed. "I guess not. It was four to one against."

Four out of five callers, fearing higher taxes, had deplored higher pay for professors—a stance she opposed. She did agree, however, with those who came out against the Faculty Alliance. She couldn't imagine her late husband belonging to a labor union. Nor Leland. Unions were for teamsters and telephone operators.

"I had one of those calls again. Very obscene."

"Did it go out over the air?"

"No, it was the same voice, so I was ready with the switch."

She turned back to her bulletin board and hummed a few bars of "Josephine" while Leland began to eat.

"Neil got out his clarinet."

"Oh, Neil plays?" she asked distantly, her mind on Monday's show. She would warn Representative Steadman about the Alliance. Heavens, she'd say, there was even talk of a strike.

"I don't know how well. We were interrupted by one of the men living upstairs. We woke him up from a nap."

His mother scanned her clippings, rearranged a few, threw a few away. "I had more calls today than any show since I gave away the Oberholtzers' puppies. Why didn't you listen?"

No reply.

She turned to look at her son. He had put down his fork and was staring out the window at the snow falling through the amber glow around the yard light.

"Leland, I asked you a question."

His words were directed toward the snowfall, his tone was somber. "Mother, I think I did something bad."

She anxiously creased her brow. It wasn't like Leland to bother her with questions of morality.

"Victor Dash and I," he added.

"Oh, that awful man." She sat down opposite him. "What is it, Leland?"

He watched her throw her shaggy ponytail back from her right shoulder and bring it forward over her left. "We left Connor lying outside in his yard."

"The artist?" She laughed a little. "Lying in the snow?"

He nodded. "With his fish."

"Leland, for shame!"

"I know. We shouldn't have."

"Too drunk to walk, I suppose. They say how he drinks."

"We honked so his wife would see him and take him in."

"But lying in the snow, Leland. Why didn't you help the poor man inside?"

"Because Mrs. Connor . . . you hear how strange she is."

She laughed again. "You leave a drunk out in the snow because you're afraid of his wife?"

Leland nodded sheepishly, and her expression changed from mirth to tenderness—dear Leland, her perennial little boy.

She said, "You'll have to call her, you know."

"Well, I was wondering . . ."

"We can't spend the night not knowing if he's frozen to death, can we?"

"I was wondering if you'd call."

"Leland," she laughed. "I wasn't the one left him lying there."

"But it might be better, you know, woman to woman." He was hunched over his plate of cooling hot-dish, his head hanging. He added, in a tone of abject helplessness, "I mean you've already spoken with her, this noon, and I've never actually spoken to her. . . ."

She sat for a moment, feigning reluctance, then went eagerly to the phone on the wall beside the bulletin board. She loved being strong for Leland. She loved making new acquaintances. She loved the telephone. Consulting a list of numbers on an index card, she dialed the one she'd written down earlier in the day. Turning to her son, she said, as he knew she would, "You won't always have me around to do your dirty work."

His appetite returned. He ate.

After many rings she said, "No answer."

He put down his fork. "What do you suppose that means?"

"You're sure there was somebody home?"

"We saw them in the window, his wife and his daughter."

"They must be still trying to get him inside. You'll have to go over there, Leland."

He grimaced. "I was wondering if you—"

"Not on your life. I've got company coming."

As though on cue, the front doorbell rang. Their eyes went to the clock on the stove.

"That would be Peggy Benoit," she said.

"It's only seven."

"I asked her to come early." She set off heavily through the dining room, calling back to him, "I want to set up a show with her, about her choir."

This was only half the truth. Her other motive was to observe her son in the young woman's company. She wanted to determine, undistracted by the Oberholtzers, whether there was anything like a romance to hope for.

She pulled open the heavy front door and enveloped Peggy on the threshold, drawing her to her bosom, planting a kiss on her cheek, and then standing back and sighing, "How lovely, how lovely," by which she meant that Peggy was truly gorgeous, coming in out of the night with snowflakes glinting in her black hair and her makeup applied so expertly and that wonderful smile playing on her beautiful lips. Here, God willing, was the ideal partner for Leland.

"Why would a lovely girl like you be free to accept a last minute invitation from the likes of me?" she wanted to know. "Why aren't men waiting in line to take you out on a Saturday night?"

"Out where?" asked Peggy sarcastically, and saw immediately that cryptic remarks such as this would be lost on Lolly Edwards. She was, after all, one of the foremost promoters of Rookery and its limited way of life.

"I'm not taking your coat, Peggy dear, because I have an enormous favor to ask of you. It seems my son has done something rather foolish." She emitted a booming laugh. "Would you mind terribly if we went straight into the kitchen and confronted him about it?"

Peggy followed the laughing woman through her living room, taking in the layers of rugs, the excessive number of overstuffed pieces upholstered in floral designs, the fresco of ducks and deer over the fireplace where a small fire sputtered and smoked. In the dining room, silver and china glinted behind glass. In the kitchen sat Leland, chewing and smiling self-consciously. He was still in his fishing clothes, still smelling, in fact, a little like fish. His uneasy expression seemed to ask Peggy to explain what in the world she was doing in his house.

"Did your mother tell you I called, Leland? We've got the room and the instruments. I can't get over what I heard you do on the piano, and with Connor on the bass, and if Victor is really the drummer he claims to be . . ." Here she turned to Leland's mother to explain that Victor Dash was mostly hot air.

"Oh, the worst sort of windbag," Lolly Edwards agreed happily.

"And then there's Neil on the clarinet—I don't think he's very good, but maybe if he practices . . . and I could take the sax on certain numbers, though I'm not very good either, but maybe I could make up for it by singing now and then. Is four o'clock tomorrow okay?" She sensed something less than eagerness in Leland. "We can't let this go, Leland. It's going to be great fun."

"You're right, we can't," he agreed halfheartedly. He felt an attack of cold feet coming on. With his dream of a musical group at last within reach, he was suddenly afraid of playing for others. Even when he was completely satisfied with his rendition of a piece (which was seldom), he was reluctant to go public with it.

"Leland, what's the matter? You're not backing out."

He looked sorrowfully at Peggy, wishing he could recover the assurance of his schoolboy recitals. He wanted to back out, yet he'd never learned how to disappoint a forceful woman. "Of course not," he said.

His mother, getting down to business, said, "Poor Leland has to make a quick trip to the Connors' house, and I wonder, Peggy dear, if you'd do us the great favor of going along with him. He'll need your moral support. He asked me to go, and I'd love to, but the Oberholtzers will be at my door any minute."

Mystified, Peggy said, "Sure."

"Leland, you can explain on the way, unless you think it too shameful." His mother laughed again.

Leland, embarrassed, left his meal and went to the entryway for his boots and his coat.

His mother couldn't resist explaining. "It's the craziest thing, Peggy. Leland went fishing with Mr. Connor the artist and Mr. Dash, and it seems Mr. Connor imbibed overmuch, and his two friends—you'd think they were little boys—left him lying outside his house in the snow."

Alarmed, Peggy asked why.

"Because they're both afraid of Mrs. Connor."

"No!"

Sorry to see Peggy's pretty smile replaced by a serious look, she added, "Isn't that hilarious?"

Leland came in from the entry and sat down to lace up his boots.

"How long has he been lying there?"

Lolly Edwards explained lightheartedly that in all likelihood the poor man had already been taken indoors, but since Mrs. Connor couldn't be reached by phone, they'd have to drive over and make sure.

"That's terrible," said Peggy. "What makes you think he's been taken in?"

"We honked," said Leland.

"Hurry up," cried Peggy, flying through the dining room. "You can lace your boots in my car."

Laura Connor heard the car. She opened the front door and peered out into the dark, past the station wagon. She made out two figures approaching the house. One of them said, "Hi, is your father home?" and the other said, "We just wanted to make sure he's okay." Laura recognized the voices. One was Dr. Benoit's. She'd led the singing at the Christmas party. The other one belonged to Dr. Edwards, who'd come this noon to pick up her father.

Peggy, followed by Leland, stepped around the car and up onto the dark stoop. Light from a lamp in the front room fell sideways across the girl's face, and they saw that she was crying.

Peggy asked, "Are your parents home?"

"My mother's in bed."

"My name is Peggy. I saw you at the Christmas party."

"I remember. You sang." Laura wiped her cheeks with the heel of her hand.

"Have you met Leland Edwards?"

"This noon."

Leland presented the girl with a calling card and shook her hand. "We just wanted to make sure he was okay."

Laura let them in and shut the door. They stood in a small sitting room, its walls and woodwork painted a smoky gray. The room beyond it, the dining room, was the same color. The furniture was unharmonious, unattractive.

The girl's eyes remained on Peggy. "I liked the way you got everybody to sing 'The Twelve Days of Christmas.' "

"Then why didn't you sing?"

"What? Me sing?" The girl was astonished to think this woman had noticed—and remembered—how she'd sat silently at her mother's side throughout the party. The only time she'd spoken was when her father made his periodic visits to the table and she asked him the names of his colleagues.

"You looked so unhappy," said Peggy.

"Did I? Well, I wasn't. I loved every minute of it." This was true. It was her mother who'd been unhappy, as usual. Laura herself had sat there eavesdropping and memorizing names and faces. She'd picked up words like "governance" and "collegiality" from a pipe-smoking, grandfatherly type named Dr. Oberholtzer. She'd heard Mrs. Oberholtzer refer to someone as a "perfectly atrocious hostess." She'd heard Victor Dash use obscenities, most of them describing an individual named Zastrow, who was apparently not present. Her father had pointed out a novelist named Novotny and offered to introduce her, but she'd been too shy. Creative artists were too godlike to talk to. Except her father, of course. Her father, though godlike, was approachable.

"Well, give your dad our best," said Leland Edwards. "Did you find the fish we left?"

"No."

"Goodness, the fish." Leland went out the door and dashed across the yard to the square of light under the window.

Left alone with Peggy, Laura lost her composure. "My dad's in the hospital," she cried.

"What is it? What happened?"

"Could you take me there?"

Peggy put an arm around her and asked again, more softly, "Why is he in the hospital?"

"Pneumonia," the girl moaned, covering her face with her hands.

"I could take you, but aren't visiting hours about over?"

"Please, I need to go." Laura picked her jacket off a chair and darted over to a dark doorway. "Mother, I'm going to the hospital with some people."

Peggy heard Mrs. Connor ask, "Who's out there?"

"Dr. Benoit the singer. She's going to take me."

She heard Mrs. Connor objecting, but Laura ignored her. She came away from the doorway zipping up her jacket and smiling tearfully at Peggy. She switched off the overhead light and followed Peggy outdoors.

Leland, suddenly in darkness, called, "I've got four of them. There was a bigger one I can't find."

Peggy led the girl to her Thunderbird, parked on the shoulder of the highway, and guided her into the backseat. "Come on, Leland, we're leaving."

He came to the car, the frozen fish piled in the angle of his arm.

"Get in, we're taking Laura to the hospital."

He stood at the open passenger door, perplexed.

"Leave them on the stoop, Leland. Connor's in the hospital."

He hurried to the house, tumbled the fish onto the stoop, and returned.

They sped off.

"What's his trouble?" Leland asked.

"Pneumonia," said Peggy. She sounded upset.

"My dad's got weak lungs," Laura explained from the backseat. She went on to say they'd moved to Rookery in hopes that the country air would be better for him. They'd been living the last

few years in Minneapolis, downwind from a factory with smoke-
stacks. He'd been teaching there, at Cass College. When Laura was
ten he'd almost died of pneumonia.

"It's nearly eight," said Peggy. "You'll just have time to run
in and out."

Laura didn't respond. She was remembering the hospital in
Minneapolis where children under twelve weren't allowed in.
With her father near death, Laura had had to wait hours in the
car while her mother sat at his bedside. She remembered being
wild with grief, afraid she'd never again see him alive. She'd
vowed never to be separated from him in any future illness.
Tonight she'd obediently gone home with her mother in order
to avoid a scene outside his room, but once home, she knew
she'd made the wrong choice. How stupid of her to leave her father in order to appease her mother. She'd phoned the nurses'
station several times. The last time, the nurse told her not to call
anymore.

"What grade are you in, Laura?"

"Ninth."

"Ninth? Somehow I thought you were younger than that."

"I am. They put me ahead a year when I moved here. I was in
this school in Minneapolis where they pushed us pretty hard."

Peggy made more inquiries, and Laura replied with only half
her mind, wondering all the while how her mother could walk
away from her father in his time of need. She'd peppered her
mother with questions all the way home. How long had he been in
the hospital that other time? Was his breathing worse this time?
Was his temperature higher? How could she stand to leave him
there delirious like that? This last question she'd asked over and
over until her mother snapped, "I've had all I can take, I've reached
my limit, I'm worn out!" How could you possibly reach your limit
with somebody you loved?

"Do you miss it, Laura?"

"Miss what?"

"That school in Minneapolis. Being pushed."

"School's always pretty boring no matter where."

"Exactly why is she going to the hospital?" Leland asked. "I
mean, how is she going to get home?"

"We're taking her home."

He bent his wristwatch to the light from the dashboard. "Mother will be wondering."

"Leland, it was your mother who sent us out."

"True," he said.

"I won't need a ride home. I'm staying all night."

This silenced the two in the front—Laura caught them exchanging raised eyebrows. She turned her attention out her side window. Snow piling up along sidewalks. Cozy lamps burning in houses. The street in front of the Paramount splendidly flooded with light from the green and pink neon. *True Grit.* John Wayne and Glen Campbell. How could you ever possibly wear out, if it was somebody you loved?

At the hospital she asked Peggy to drive around to the emergency room. She recalled that just inside that door was a waiting room she could slip into. There she would wait for a chance to sneak upstairs.

Peggy had misgivings. "Laura, I don't think they'll let you stay all night."

"I'm just going to sit by his bed—what's wrong with that?"

"But you can't sit there till morning. You have to sleep."

"There's a couch in the next room. Sort of a lounge."

Peggy pulled up and stopped under the red emergency sign. Neither she nor Leland made an effort to bend their seats forward, and Laura feared for a moment that they intended to keep her trapped there, forcing her to return home.

"Thanks for the ride," she told them.

It was Leland who finally let her out. "Tell your father I'll come and see him tomorrow."

She was about to dart away when Dr. Benoit said, "Give her your phone number, Leland, in case she changes her mind."

"It's on my card."

Peggy reached across him toward the open door. "Here, give it to me."

Laura dug his calling card out of the back pocket of her jeans and handed it to her.

"Leland, have you got a pen?"

"A pencil."

With his silver mechanical pencil, she jotted a number on the card and handed it back to the girl. "Here, this is my phone, in case you need anything later on tonight."

Laura thanked her and dashed away.

Leland pulled his door shut. He waited impatiently for Peggy to put the car in gear.

She asked, "Do you suppose we should go in and check on him? I mean, I hate to leave her, if he's in serious condition."

He looked out at the door the girl had gone through. "I'm not saying it's not serious," he said, "but if it *was* serious, wouldn't his wife be with him?"

"You'd think so." Peggy sat with her hand on the gearshift, undecided. "But just to make sure, maybe we should talk to a nurse."

"We can call the nurses' station from home."

She considered this, then shifted and drove away. They crossed the bridge to the college neighborhood. Nearing the Edwards house, she asked, "How come you carry calling cards, Leland?"

"So people know what to call me."

"Why not just tell them your name?"

"Because I can't very well introduce myself as 'Leland Edwards, Ph.D.' "

"Oh, I get it." Peggy laughed. "*Doctor* Edwards."

Leland, puzzled by her amusement, chuckled along with her, to be polite.

Honey Oberholtzer reacted with a sharp intake of breath and a look of horror when told about Connor lying drunk in the snow. She was a small, gray-haired woman with the beaky alertness of a wren. She was dressed tonight in a black knit dress with silver beads down her front, silver bracelets on both wrists, and silver buckles on her bright blue shoes. Seated near the fire which Leland was trying to stir to life with a poker, she turned to her husband and said, "Goodness gracious, Mortimer, it sounds like you hired a real washout."

Sunk low in the softest chair in the room, the chairman of the Division of Languages and Fine Arts groaned pleasantly and said, "He came with the highest credentials, Honey, the very highest credentials." Wreathed in pipe smoke, clad thickly in tweed, and smiling rather vacantly, C. Mortimer Oberholtzer looked impervious to all disorder and distress. Peggy wondered if he'd even caught what Leland had just said about Connor. The chairman's mental powers, according to Neil Novotny, diminished as the day wore on. "An intellectual giant mornings," Neil had informed her, "and by night a blithering idiot."

"Leland, go to the phone right away," demanded Lolly Edwards, entering the room with a tray of cups and saucers. "Call Victor Dash and tell him his friend's in the hospital. I'm sure he'll want to know."

"Yes, Mother." Leland replaced the fire screen and hurried away to the phone in the kitchen.

Peggy was amazed to witness firsthand this woman's control over her son. It had been at his mother's behest, and with a great deal of embarrassment, that he told the Oberholtzers the story of his afternoon, and she obviously wasn't done with him yet. Peggy was beginning to understand Neil Novotny's disdain—though she didn't share it—for Leland's slavish obedience. Cousin Neil, she knew, had grown up with parents who pulled his strings like this. Peggy, for her part, felt wonder rather than disdain. She'd never before known anyone in his thirties bound this tightly to a parent.

"And call the hospital, would you?" Peggy asked him, curious to know whether she might have the same power over him, but he was already out of earshot.

"A drunkard, my heavens, this is the most astounding news. And to think we nearly commissioned him to do one of his double portraits of Tracy and Casey. Isn't it lucky we didn't go ahead with that idea, Mortimer?"

"Lucky for my pocketbook, I'd say." The chairman snuffled and snickered noisily, indicating to Peggy that he was being funny.

Peggy acknowledged this with the same chummy smile and nod of the head with which she'd been humoring the man all year at division meetings. Seated as she was, on a couch facing him, she'd caught him sneaking peeks up her skirt, so she'd drawn a needlepoint pillow onto her lap and sat patting it absently as she tried to look interested in what his wife was saying.

"Tracy is our son Byron's wife," Mrs. Oberholtzer explained, "and Casey is their sweet little boy. We were thinking of making the portrait our Christmas gift to Byron and Tracy next year, but, my goodness gracious, you can't have a painting in your house that every time you look at it you imagine the artist stewed to the gills."

"I'm not sure he does mothers and sons anyway," Peggy told her. "I think it's just mothers and daughters."

"But in this case he'd do a mother and son," she replied confidently. "For his chairman, I mean."

Peggy made a mental note to repeat this to Connor. She could imagine him chuckling and shaking his hairy head. She loved to make Connor chuckle.

"I'd be careful with an artist of his stripe," warned Lolly Edwards, noisily distributing china and silver. "I'd hate to pay good money for anything like the one he did of Harry Steadman's daughter and granddaughter."

"I don't believe I've seen it," said Honey Oberholtzer.

Lolly Edwards straightened up from the coffee table and looked at her guest in amazement. "You haven't seen it? They had it over their mantel at Christmas."

"We missed the Steadmans' party this year, I'm afraid. I forget just why. Mortimer, do you remember why?"

"Yes, we probably weren't invited." He snickered as before, this time winking at Peggy.

"Oh, my stars, don't be funny. Of course we were invited. We're always invited."

"It's not a thing of beauty, let me tell you," Lolly Edwards continued. "He made their skin so rough-looking."

"Well, of course the Steadman women have always had complexion problems. It's as though they never learned how to take care of their faces."

"But all the same, you don't want your dermatitis hanging there for all your descendants to see."

"I'll tell you the sad thing about it." Honey Oberholtzer turned to her husband. "The sad thing is that now we'll have to think of something else to get Byron and Tracy for Christmas."

"Something that doesn't cost me an arm and a leg, I hope."

"Well, you have eleven months," Peggy interjected, stifling a yawn.

In the kitchen, Leland had reached Victor by phone. In the background were the painful screams and shouts and thudding noises of the three Dash children at play.

"Connor's in the hospital, Victor."

"So I heard. I'm not surprised. Any man who can't hold his liquor any better than that—"

"Who told you?"

"Annie."

"How did Annie find out?"

"When I told her how plastered he was, lying there in his own puke, she called up his wife."

"When?"

"Just now."

"We did a bad thing, Victor, letting him lie there on the ice all afternoon."

"Hey, Leland, as long as I got you on the line, tell your old lady to lay off the Alliance, would you? Annie heard her on the radio talking against the Alliance."

His *old lady*? Victor's disrespect astonished him. And so did the strange little twinge of delight it caused at the back of his neck. He replied, "Unions are for nonprofessionals, Victor."

"All the more reason we need one, then. This faculty is the biggest bunch of stumblebums I've ever seen in my life."

Leland was again delighted, and a bit riled. "Listen, Victor, you're not going to get to first base with the Alliance if you talk that way about your colleagues."

There was a long pause. "Just tell your old lady to keep her nose out of other people's business."

Again the strange little thrill crept over him. It was like the secret mirth he felt whenever Victor unsettled a faculty meeting with some vulgarism. Last week, after the faculty rejected his proposal to send President Gengler a vote of no confidence, Victor had stood up and shouted, "We are not doing ourselves justice, ladies and gentlemen. By not speaking up when our president disappears for weeks at a time, we are only shitting in our own hats!" Whereupon the recording secretary, Dr. Florence Finnegan of the Nursing and Public Health Division, stopped writing the minutes, and most of the others lowered their heads in embarrassed silence while a few, protesting his language, got up and left the room. But there was a raw kind of power in Victor's crudeness, which Leland, for all his fine manners and discretion, responded to. Though he voted nay, Leland had secretly hoped that Victor's initiative had been carried through. The president was not, even on those rare days when he showed up on campus, an inspiring educator.

"But it's everybody's business," said Leland reasonably. "We're on the public payroll."

At this, Victor grumbled something unintelligible, and Leland changed the subject back to Connor, asking if Annie had learned anything about his condition.

"Yeah, his wife didn't seem to know much, so Annie called the hospital. The nurse said he's doing okay, considering."

"Considering what?"

"Considering it's pneumonia."

"How bad?"

"She's seen worse."

"We'd better go see him tomorrow."

"Yeah, Annie'll make him some fudge."

Peggy, having left the Oberholtzers with the problem of next year's Christmas gifts to their children, came into the kitchen and asked, "Is that Victor?"

Leland nodded.

"Ask him if he got my message."

"Say, Victor, Peggy Benoit was wondering if you got her message."

"Hey, you bet," he shouted, "I'll be there. We'll do some Ellington, okay?"

"If you've got sheet music."

"I don't need sheet music."

"Well, I do."

"And how about we do 'Your Feet's Too Big'?"

"We can try."

"I'll bring some fudge."

"Okay, four o'clock in the music wing."

"Hey, Leland." There was a pause, then a lower, more serious tone. "I suppose you'll be one of the naysayers when it comes to voting on the Alliance?"

"I will," Leland admitted.

"Then you'll be shitting in your own hat." Victor hung up.

So did Leland, chuckling despite feeling wounded.

"We'd better call the hospital," said Peggy.

Leland looked up the number, dialed it, and handed Peggy the phone. There was a long wait while a nurse was summoned who could answer her questions. Yes, Connor's condition was satisfactory; he was wakeful, but not unduly restless; yes, his daughter was in the next room, sleeping on the couch; it was against hospital policy, but the nurse had provided her with a pillow and blankets. "Are you Mrs. Connor?" she asked.

"No, a friend."

"We tried calling Mrs. Connor to come and get the girl, but she won't."

"Just let the poor thing sleep."

"It's against policy, a child staying overnight. Children aren't immune to as much as adults are."

"I'll come myself and talk to her in a little while," Peggy offered.

" 'Preciate it," said the nurse.

It was nearly an hour before Peggy could politely leave. First there was coffee and pie and the chairman's lengthy explanation of how money was channeled from the Minnesota taxpayer into the fund for faculty salaries. Peggy was surprised to learn that despite the many letters the faculty had been urged to send off to their representatives, it was not ultimately the state legislature that determined next year's pay. It was a group of six people known as the State College Board who parceled out the legislative appropriations.

"But I thought the legislators specified how the money is to be spent," said Peggy. "Isn't that why we've been sending all this mail to this fellow Steadman?"

"Legislators can only recommend," said the chairman wisely. "The board decides."

"You mean six people can overrule the entire Senate and House of Representatives?"

"Can, and do." The chairman nodded serenely. "Four years ago most of our salary appropriation went to fix the boiler room. Remember, Leland?"

Leland remembered. "Badly needed. Used to be parts of Mc-Call Hall that never warmed up from November till April."

"My office," said the chairman.

"And classroom 204."

"I could see my breath some days, right there in my office."

"I could see my breath in 204."

As soon as Peggy said, "But that's illegal!" she saw the serene look disappear from her chairman's face. Having spent his entire career at Rookery State, C. Mortimer Oberholtzer had an unswerving respect for things as they were, and couldn't imagine things as they might be. Leland, too, looked a bit shocked by her protesting, "It's unconstitutional—it puts the College Board above the people we elect."

Honey Oberholtzer smiled tolerantly, calling to mind her own rebellious younger days. She recalled wearing slacks to a dedication tea when the new wing of McCall Hall was opened. She recalled expressing a political view opposed by the other women in her bridge club. And it wasn't too many years ago she'd told President Gengler that the words to the school song were a bit juvenile. All this was before she learned from her dear Mortimer to see the wisdom of the old ways, to concentrate on homemaking and leave the larger issues to those who understood them.

"And the gender lanes on the salary schedule," Peggy went on, her dark eyes flashing. "I couldn't believe it when I saw that the women's basic salary is two hundred dollars lower than the men's. Who's responsible for that?"

Dr. Oberholtzer said, "Now, now, girl" in a low voice, the same calming tone he used on his dog when it growled. "It's only the last four or five years we've had a salary schedule of any kind. Before that it was every man for himself, bargaining for a raise."

"And every woman?" asked Peggy. "Didn't women bargain?"

"Some tried. Maggie Anderson in home economics used to get on her high horse every year at contract time. But old Dean Smith refused to talk to women about salary. Said they had no concept of money."

"Dean Smith must have been a Neanderthal."

"No, an agronomist."

Lolly Edwards, entering the discussion on Peggy's side, said that old Dean Smith was a fool in more ways than one, and she hoped for better things from Dean Zastrow.

Peggy turned to her hostess. "Don't you agree it's wrong to have a salary lane for women lower than the lane for men?"

"My dear, it's the height of folly. At the radio station I demand the same rate of pay as the disc jockeys and the farm reporter."

"And you get it?"

"Of course I get it. The station would be defunct without me. Every time I go on the air, everybody over the age of twenty-five tunes in."

"And if they didn't meet your demands, what would you do?"

Lolly Edwards tried unsuccessfully to imagine the station manager denying her anything. She shook her head and said, "Impossible." She owned a major share of KRKU.

"But just suppose. Would you go on strike?"

"Oh." The large woman laughed and laughed. "Oh no, dear heart, I'd quit before I'd go on strike."

"I'd go on strike," Peggy declared.

It was Leland who seemed most astonished by this remark. Dr. and Mrs. Oberholtzer laughed along with their hostess, laughed quite uproariously in fact, as though Peggy's declaration was the funniest one-liner they'd ever heard, while Leland raised his eyebrows and studied her closely and warily, as though personally threatened by her audacity.

"You'd have to belong to the Alliance to strike," he delicately pointed out.

Her temper flared. "Oh, I'll belong to the Alliance all right. I'm voting to bring the Alliance on campus, and I'll be the first to enroll."

"I don't foresee any need, girl," said the chairman. "I foresee the legislature being good to us this year."

"And the College Board?" she asked.

"I foresee them being good to us too."

"Mortimer sees goodness in everybody," his wife testified. "That's what makes him such a superb chairman."

"And do you foresee them doing away with the two lanes on the salary schedule?" Peggy asked.

"Oh, well . . . I wonder really . . . long-standing tradition . . ."

He put his pipe in his mouth and sucked in his answer with his smoke.

Lolly Edwards, sensing Dr. Oberholtzer's discomfort, brought the discussion to an end by announcing Leland's party piece, something by Edward McDowell, who by coincidence was Peggy's least favorite composer. Leland stepped across the room, flexing his fingers, and sat down before a music book standing open and ready. Upon hearing the opening chords, Peggy knew she was in for one of the composer's more interminable works. Although the piano, a Baldwin baby grand, was in perfect tune, it seemed to contain only a small portion of the sound and spirit Leland had drawn out of the abused instrument in Neil's basement. His playing seemed strangely dead, causing even his mother's eyes to glaze. His heart wasn't in it, Peggy could tell.

This was because the piece had been chosen not by Leland, but by his mother. Lolly Edwards, leaving nothing to chance, had selected McDowell for this audience, assuming that Peggy and the Oberholtzers would be more thoroughly impressed by something she herself didn't understand or care for. Whatever sounded opaque and tuneless to her must be deep and satisfying, she thought, to those in the know.

When at last the final A-flat died away, his four listeners clapped solemnly and Honey Oberholtzer declared him a genius. "Oh, no, not a genius," said his mother, "but the dear boy works hard at it." C. Mortimer Oberholtzer said nothing encouraging for fear of having to sit through more of the same, but when Peggy asked, "Will you play something jazzy?" the chairman perked up and asked Leland if he knew "Twelfth Street Rag."

He did. He pounded it out with his elbows flying and his head wagging down close to the keys. On his face was an expression Peggy had never seen before—a smile and a crinkled, scowling brow. True concentration and joy. Leland Edwards caught up in wild abandon—who'd have thought it possible?

He played it once through and stopped. He quickly straightened up and was shy again, stiffly facing away from his audience.

"My, wasn't that peppy," said Honey Oberholtzer, getting up to leave.

The chairman, looking naughtily at Peggy, said, "Nothing like a little whorehouse music to wake us up, eh, girl?"

"Come, Mortimer, we told Boots we'd be home by nine."

Mrs. Edwards saw the Oberholtzers out, then pleaded with Peggy to stay longer, but Peggy in turn pleaded for her coat, explaining that she had to check on the girl they'd left at the hospital.

"Oh, my son will go with you, he's terribly ashamed."

Peggy glanced at Leland, who looked pained but not ashamed—pained, no doubt, at the thought of going out into the cold night. "Let me go alone," she said. "In case she needs someone to confide in."

Now Mother looked pained. Son looked relieved.

"By the way," said Peggy, "is Boots the name of the Oberholtzers' son? The one who's been giving them trouble?" She'd heard about this incorrigible boy. Somehow she couldn't picture a Hell's Angel sitting at home at nine on a Saturday night, watching the clock as he waited for Mother and Father's return.

"Heavens no, Boots is their dog," said Lolly.

A nurse showed Peggy down a bright yellow corridor to a small lounge containing a couch and two chairs, and there they found Laura Connor lying asleep under a light blanket. A lamp burned dimly in a corner. A magazine was folded open on the floor.

"How is her father?" Peggy whispered before entering.

"High fever," said the nurse brusquely, a woman of sixty years or more who seemed jaded or worn out by her work.

"Alarmingly high?"

The nurse shrugged. "I've seen worse. Will you take the girl home?"

"If she'll go."

"She'd better." The nurse turned and walked away, her shoes squeaking on the polished tile.

Peggy went in and lightly touched Laura's shoulder, but to no effect. Her sleep was profound. She spoke her name, but the girl slept on, lying on her side with her stringy blond hair swirled over her face. She sat down facing her and for several minutes watched the blanket rising and falling with the girl's shallow breathing. Warm in her coat, she grew sleepy herself, and might have drifted off in her chair if the nurse's squeaking footsteps, returning, hadn't roused her.

"Laura," she said again, and the girl opened her eyes. She gazed groggily at Peggy without raising her head.

"It's me, Peggy Benoit."

The girl's first words were, "She's not my mother, you know."

"Who's not your mother?"

"My mother."

Peggy didn't respond to this, believing it was dream-talk, the girl needing more time to come fully awake. The nurse stood in the doorway, a fist on a hip, and Peggy nodded her head vigorously, indicating that she understood her impatience and would soon be gone. The nurse was evidently satisfied, because she left the doorway and didn't come back.

Slowly, Laura sat up, drawing her hair out of her face. "She makes me call her my mother, but she's not really my mother. My real mother died when I was two, and my dad married Marcy just a couple of years ago." Her voice was dim, faraway, a little slurred from sleep. "I just wanted you to know that."

They regarded each other in silence for a time, the girl drawing herself up very straight on the couch, her shoulders thrown back, her hands lying limp on her lap. Peggy, waiting to hear more, wore an expression she'd learned to use in her office when counseling troubled students, a look eliciting secrets that needed telling.

"My real mother died of a heart attack. We were living in Minneapolis. That's where I was born. Her name was Naomi. She came from a family of artists. My dad met her in college."

Peggy said, "So you and your father were alone for a long time."

Laura smiled. "Years and years." Her smile disappeared. "He met Marcy in a bar."

Again silence. Peggy sensed that the girl wanted to be questioned. "Is Marcy good to you?"

"Neutral."

Peggy was struck by how ready she was with the word. Indeed

by the word itself. It seemed, along with her self-assurance, beyond the girl's years.

"How old are you, Laura?"

"Thirteen . . . I mean she's not bad to me, and she's not good to me. She's more or less nothing to me."

Peggy hesitated before prying further. "Is she good to your father?"

"Bad." A smile came and went. She raised a hand to her hair, straightening it. "I mean she's the same to him as she is to me, neutral. But being neutral with your husband is different from being neutral with your stepdaughter, wouldn't you say? Being neutral to your husband is being bad to him, if you ask me."

"Is your father good to Marcy?"

"Oh, he's so wonderful to her." This was delivered with unction, and it evidently concluded her message, for she then yawned and stretched, raising her long arms over her head.

"Let's go home," said Peggy.

The girl nodded and put on her shoes. "I'm starving," she said.

Peggy followed her into the dark room next door. By the light from the hallway she saw that it contained three beds. Connor was propped up on pillows, an IV in his arm, a mask over his bearded face. His eyes were closed and his breathing was quick and shallow. Laura kissed him on the forehead and whispered to Peggy, "His fever is going down. He looks more relaxed, he's not so flushed."

It was much too dark, Peggy knew, to judge his expression or color, but the girl might have been right at least about the fever. She wanted to verify it by placing her own lips on his forehead. This urge was sudden and very strong, but she resisted it as improper. Then, as Laura was slipping into her jacket, Peggy changed her mind. She kissed him.

Connor in his delirium was watching himself being lowered into a dry concrete minnow tank. Though he'd been pronounced dead and duly embalmed, he was aware of an angry conversation between two men who stood over the tank and disagreed about the correct level of water to be piped in. One of the men was the minnow dealer. He was scoffing and blowing cigarette smoke in the face of the other man, who seemed to be Dean Zastrow. A doctor wearing a white jacket entered into the argument and recommended that the tank be filled to the brim. Connor, hearing this, considered himself lucky to be dead, because if he were alive, it would be such a struggle to breathe underwater. He woke up drenched in sweat, and not altogether relieved.

Across town, Victor and Annie Dash were watching television. A girl of sixteen was dying of leukemia while her father was having an affair with a partner in his real estate office. The girl's mother, played by an actress who looked to Victor like an aging Rita Hayworth, was trying to hold their marriage together at least until the girl was dead. They watched from the couch, Annie nestled into Victor's arms and weeping profusely, Victor sipping from a can of beer and wondering how long you could put off cleaning fish before they went bad.

"Are you sure that isn't Rita Hayworth?" he asked for the third or fourth time.

Annie said she was sure because Rita Hayworth was a brunette, never a blonde.

"Yeah, I guess you're right," Victor agreed. "And didn't she have bigger knockers than this dame?"

At the next commercial break Victor went into the kitchen and picked the largest of the walleyes out of the sink where they had been left to thaw. He hefted it, recalling Leland Edwards's insulting estimate of two pounds. He carried it upstairs, trailing an elastic string of slime, and stood on the bathroom scale with it. He bent over and squinted at the dial. Victor and the fish weighed 181. He laid the fish on the vanity, pushing aside several bottles of Annie's perfume and the children's cough medicine, and he read the scale again, expecting it to register at least four and a half pounds less than before. It said 179. He cursed and returned to the kitchen, trying to convince himself that a fish could lose as much as two pounds by freezing and thawing. He spread newspapers on the kitchen counter and scaled the fish with the edge of a spoon, scales flying in every direction, and when he was finished with that, he began sawing away at its flesh with a bread knife too dull for the job.

Across town, Leland Edwards, too, was standing at his kitchen counter cleaning fish, reflecting as he did so that something quite extraordinary had transpired today. Thinking back beyond the stupid way he and Victor had handled the drunken artist, he realized that his attempt to create a bond of brotherhood among his colleagues might very well prove successful. He had sensed something very much like friendship for a few minutes around the piano in Neil's basement, and later in the car before Connor passed out.

He was extremely gratified. For the last several winters he'd been enticing his colleagues fishing, partly for his own sake (it was a lonely sixty miles to Liberty Lake, even for an introvert like himself) and partly at the bidding of Chairman Oberholtzer, who liked to see his division cohesive off campus as well as on. *It's a great morale builder, Leland, cementing division friendships the way you do. I'd rate you right up there next to Honey when it comes to building off-campus morale.* Leland was a sucker for praise like this from the man he looked up to as a kind of substitute father, and year after year he kept trying to play the role of elder brother to the new members.

But without much success, sad to say. The friendships Leland had striven to cement over the years had never actually set. There were two professors who now and then did continue to go fishing with him, but they were not of his division. Aaron Cardero in Accounting and Brooks Dumont in Manual Training. That's why today's gathering was such a breakthrough. He wished now that he'd told Mortimer and Honey about tomorrow's jam session in McCall Hall. They'd be so pleased.

How interesting, thought Leland as he sliced deftly along the backbone of a walleye with his razor-sharp boning knife, that a woman should have been present in the midst of this budding male companionship. He wondered if Peggy sensed their friendship forming around her. Then it occurred to him that it might have been Peggy who caused it. Was Peggy responsible for Connor's heightened good humor, and for the way Victor softened and joked about "Your Feet's Too Big"? Without Peggy present, would Neil even have invited them in?

Next day, Connor was surprised to have visitors. He'd assumed that his existence in Rookery had gone virtually unnoticed. Indeed, he'd worked to that end, avoiding social entanglements and faculty friendships in order to gain time for his art. Yet whenever he woke from sleep during the long afternoon, he found well-wishers standing beside his bed. First to arrive were Honey and C. Mortimer Oberholtzer, dressed in matching olive jackets with furry collars.

"Sorry you're under the weather, my boy," said the chairman. "Awkward, being out of commission so early in the semester. I can cancel a couple of your classes, but if you're out longer than that, we'll have to get somebody to fill in. Who would you like to do that, any ideas?"

"No," said Connor, lifting his oxygen mask away from his mouth. "Not at the moment." He spoke with great effort, each word needing to be shaped separately around a meager puff of air from his overworked lungs.

"Well, if it comes to that, and you haven't anyone else in mind, Honey here would be glad to take over, wouldn't you, Honey? She's had a few art classes in her day."

Mrs. Oberholtzer said she would, though her expression indicated otherwise. Standing at some distance from the bed, she looked upon the sick man with obvious revulsion.

Connor nodded his agreement, wearily settling his mask into place, and not caring in the least who took his classes. All he cared about was recovering. He had important work to do. He needed to paint mothers and daughters and he needed to guide his own daughter through her teens. He'd come back from the brink of death to do these things. This morning, between two and three o'clock, he'd begun to slip into the pit and fought his way out.

"That's fine, then, that's settled," said his chairman. "That's wonderful, that's superb."

He'd never been so frightened in his life. His breathing had become completely blocked and he'd felt his spirit being extinguished. He must have struggled and made noises, because one of the old men across the room woke up and rang for the nurse and a doctor was summoned. An injection saved him, but not immediately. After the needle went in, it took what seemed forever before he was able to inhale fresh oxygen, and it was during this interruption in his mortal life that he'd vowed to stop drinking and take care of himself. He lay there wakeful until morning, exhausted but unable to sleep, measuring the depth of each new breath against the last, and telling himself over and over that he needed to change his ways.

"Your medical coverage is first-rate, no worry there," his chairman assured him. "The college gives you medical coverage second to none. There's more to a contract than salary, my boy. I hope you realize that."

Again Connor nodded his assent, understanding this to be Oberholtzer's plea for a vote against the Alliance. His chairman would doubtless be happy to know that he didn't give a damn about the Alliance. Unions, contracts, fringe benefits—they were trifles compared to one's health, one's work, one's daughter. He might have explained this to Oberholtzer, had he breath for talk that small.

"You're in tremendously good hands here, my boy. Fantastic care they give here at Mercy. Your color shows it. His color looks first-rate, wouldn't you say, Honey?"

At this point Connor dropped off to sleep. A few moments later, feeling a hand on his shoulder, he awoke briefly to find his chairman bidding him good-bye and Mrs. Oberholtzer stepping forward to hand him the gift they'd brought—a small box of candy. She did this gingerly, as though the touch of his hand might be harmful. Connor, groggy with fatigue, tried to remember if the Oberholtzers had daughters. Well, it didn't matter—no painter could make Honey Oberholtzer's pinched face interesting. As they backed away, wishing him well and waving, he heard one of the old men across the room urgently describing for them the ordeal of hemorrhoids.

The rest of his visitors appeared and disappeared as though in a

dream. He opened his eyes and looked into the faces of Victor
Dash and a smiling little woman, apparently his wife. He opened
them again, and was startled to see looking down at him two elderly members of the banking family of Steadmans, for whom
he had done a mother-daughter portrait. Not that he recognized
the Steadmans. They had to tell him who they were. Not that he
cared.

Next time he awoke, he looked up into a woman's face of remarkable freshness and beauty, and he wondered if this woman
had a daughter, for this was a face that begged to be painted. The
eyes and lips were the most attractive features, but interesting too
were the forehead and cheekbones. Her hair was jet black. She was
wearing dark green. Wise of her, he thought, for green was certainly her color. This analysis was going through Connor's mind
during the several moments it took him to realize she was Peggy
Benoit. She smiled down at him, warmly and apprehensively. Leland Edwards came into view behind her. Leland was wearing a
black overcoat and a red necktie. Both of them spoke to Connor,
but he didn't catch the words because he was drifting off again,
picturing his daughter and Peggy Benoit sitting for their portrait
together.

They left the hospital in her red Thunderbird, Peggy scowling
fiercely into the late afternoon sun, and Leland sitting at her side,
uncertain whether to speak and try to relieve the tension, or remain silent until they picked up Neil. Peggy had been transformed
in the hospital. She'd gone in happy and come out all nerves.

Chatter, Leland had learned from his mother, sometimes altered a woman's mood for the better, so he opened the briefcase on
his lap and spoke about the sheet music it contained, displaying for
her the composers and performers pictured on the covers. Hoagy
Carmichael. Count Basie. Frankie Carle. She didn't even glance at
them.

They stopped in front of Neil's house, and Leland went to the
door. He was back in a minute with the message that Neil would
walk. Almost finished with a chapter, he'd be along within the
hour.

"Within the *hour*!" cried Peggy. She sprang out of the car and went to the door herself. Leland watched her enter without knocking and open the inner door to the stairway. In two minutes the outer door opened again and she emerged, followed by Neil carrying his clarinet case and pulling on a parka several sizes too big for him.

She drove to the campus in silence and parked in front of McCall Hall. They waited in the car for Victor because he, too, was untenured and keyless, and only Leland could unlock the door. Peggy turned to Neil in the backseat and told him about Connor's pneumonia.

"Serious?" asked Neil.

"Serious as hell," replied Peggy, looking anguished. "The nurse said he almost died in the night."

"There's a sign on his door limiting visitors to five minutes," Leland said.

Neil was amazed. "How could that be? He was fine yesterday."

Peggy turned to Leland with raised, insinuating eyebrows. "Leland?" she said.

So Leland reluctantly described their fishing trip, minimizing the part liquor played in Connor's collapse and leaving out altogether the shameful manner in which he was delivered home to his family. "Turns out his lungs were weak to start with—his daughter told us that—and he just couldn't stand all those hours out on the lake."

Neil shivered and pulled his enormous parka tight around himself. "Idiotic, fishing in winter."

"He's going to recover," said Peggy insistently, as though to reassure herself. "They figure he'll be at least a week in the hospital, but he's going to recover."

Neil looked disgusted. "So what do we do for a bass fiddle?"

"We hope Victor can keep a beat," said Leland.

Soon Victor pulled up behind them and got out of his car with two of his children, manifesting a side of himself his colleagues had never seen—Victor as family man. On their way up the walk to McCall Hall, Victor answered endless questions from his five-year-old and helped his four-year-old blow his nose. Both children had fudge marks on their faces.

Leland was disappointed. He recalled the wild noises of the Dash children over the phone last night, and he lost hope of achieving harmony in the music room. Following them inside, he stayed well behind, fearing they might wipe their hands on his suit.

But the children were no trouble at all. Both of them (a boy and a girl, as it turned out once their coats and caps were removed) lay down on the violet carpet and watched the musicians arrange themselves around the grand piano at the center of the room. The sound of the instruments seemed to enchant them. At the first broken blat out of Peggy's saxophone, at the initial toot of Neil's clarinet, at Leland's first scale up and down the piano, at the first thump of their father's kick drum, both children gaped with a kind of loving intensity, as though the dissonance of musicians warming up spoke directly to their hearts.

Snatches of "Ain't Misbehavin'," "Body and Soul," and "Cheek to Cheek" rose and fell and rose again over the racket Victor was making with his sticks and cymbals. This went on for perhaps five minutes before the noise died away and a kind of embarrassed silence filled the room. Peggy was surprised to see the three men looking expectantly at her—acknowledging her as their leader, she realized. Their expressions amused her, like those of three little boys asking permission to go ahead with some vaguely illicit fun, and she laughed her short, stuttering laugh, lifted at last out of the sadness she'd felt at Connor's bedside.

Neil asked, "What's so funny?"

She shook her head and resisted telling them how sheepish they looked. She asked Leland to play "These Foolish Things," in a simpler rendition than he'd played the day before, not so much inventiveness and elaboration. Victor should lay down a slowish beat, and she and Neil would come in as they went along.

Leland and Victor walked through the melody once, twice, three times, Victor a little hurried and heavy-footed at first, then going to brushes and finding the leisurely pace Peggy prescribed. Then she nodded at Neil, evidently before he was ready, for he joined in out of control, his clarinet unsure of itself, its voice like a pubescent boy's, changing register without warning, blaring where it should have been soft, momentarily disappearing when he meant it to sing. He dropped out in shame and waited for Peggy to lead the way back in.

She came in, then, with her understated sax and moved smoothly and steadily along with the keyboard and drums, not trying anything very surprising, her improvising very tame, only a hop and a skip here and there. She felt enormously relieved, almost euphoric to think it was working, they were staying together, they were a team. They were out for a walk in the country on a fine summer day. Look at the green fields, look at the cows grazing in clover at the top of the hill, look at the birds swooping above them, look at the puffy white clouds.

Neil's clarinet came in then, a little more gracefully this time, falling into step beside her, better modulated than before, not forced to make sounds it couldn't produce, yet not entirely easy on the ear. It was clear to Peggy (even without having heard Connor on the bass) that Neil would be the least talented of the quintet, would need the most practice if they were ever to close ranks around a pleasing, harmonious sound. But that was of no concern today. Today was just for fun.

Chorus after chorus, they continued with "These Foolish Things," no one wishing to let it go. "Sing," Leland told Peggy, letting the piano part lapse while he dug the music out of his briefcase, but she shook her head and went on playing the sax. Later she would sing a few numbers when their instrumentation fell into disarray, as it was bound to do, but for now she couldn't give up the warm, sisterly affection she was feeling for the quintet, each chorus binding her closer to her four companions: the shy and serious pianist, his head bent low over the keys again, brow to brow with the Steinway; the emaciated novelist, her cousin-in-law, tooting earnestly along with an expectant, approval-seeking look on his face; Victor the wild man, tamed and absorbed by his drums, turning now to wink at his children after a phrase of clever stick work; and Connor—even in his absence, she could hear the deep underpinning he would provide with his bass. Connor, she knew, would be their foundation.

PART 2

I'll Get By

Connor made his debut on "Stormy Weather." No sax, Peggy singing throughout. Victor shushing along softly with his brushes. Neil's clarinet weaving in and out, mostly out. Nothing from the piano except Leland lightly sketching in the melody at the beginning. Connor virtually her only accompanist because this was his first time and they wanted him to feel welcome. They were also curious to hear what he could do. At a table in the corner of the band room sat his daughter, her pencil poised over her homework, her eyes moving back and forth between Peggy, who sang with her eyes closed, and her father, who was laboring arduously at his bass and sweating profusely.

Peggy's voice built up to a height, then trailed off in what the four men assumed was a concluding fade-out, but then she hastily reverted to the opening and led them through it again. It was at this point that Connor's legs began to tremble. He knew he'd have to ask for a stool before the evening was over. He'd been back in the classroom for several days, and doing all right, but his strength flagged quickly at the end of the day. Besides the sweating and trembling, he was feeling light-headed. He probably should have put off his debut until the following Sunday. The group had added these Wednesday evenings to their week because their Sunday af-

ternoons had been spilling over into the supper hour, and Victor
and Leland were expected home to eat. Indeed, he *would* have
waited until Sunday if Marcy weren't such a strain on his nerves. It
was an intolerable life the three of them were living in that tiny
house beside the highway. He'd brought Laura along with him
tonight to give her a respite from her mother.

"Stormy Weather," this second time through, grew slower and
bluer, strictly a duet now, Peggy's voice and Connor's bass growling along together. She sang frowning, as though worried or in
pain. No strolling through fresh green meadows this time. No
chirping birds, no puffy summer clouds. This was a trudging, sor-
rowful progress through the night, with far-off thunder heading
this way, Connor slogging along at her side, slumped over his bass
as though about to embrace it or collapse upon it, his head down,
his eyes on the violet carpet, glancing sideways now and again at
his daughter, who seemed to be studying Peggy's every gesture.

When it ended, no one spoke. Nobody's eyes sought out other
eyes. Usually upon finishing a piece they had a dozen things to say
about it, except Victor, who had two dozen, but their rendition of
this one had been too tragic and wonderful to talk about. It required only meditation. Victor, examining his drumsticks, felt immensely pleased with himself for achieving finally what Peggy had
been asking of him—understatement. Now if Novotny could only
learn to control the squeaks in his goddamn clarinet, this would be
a swell combo. More than a combo, actually. This group of five
friends with a common cause took him back to the tight, professional comradeship he'd enjoyed as a member of the Brotherhood
of Pipeliners. He'd never expected to recover anything close to that
fellow-feeling among college professors.

Leland Edwards, taking out his handkerchief and lightly dusting the high and low ends of the keyboard, felt supremely satisfied
now that the quintet, with Connor in place, was finally complete.
Being an equal among these five elated him. Never, not even in
boyhood, had Leland been part of a circle of close friends. Now all
that remained for his dream to come completely true was to work
up a repertoire and find an audience. He supposed they ought to
start small, work out the kinks and overcome his shyness in places
like Martin's Rathskeller in the basement of the Van Buren Hotel,

but he couldn't help picturing grander venues. Onstage at the annual Elks dance, for instance. Or up on the makeshift bandstand in the college gymnasium for the spring formal. He also imagined playing on his mother's radio show.

For Neil, like Leland, this five-sided friendship filled the void an only child inevitably carries around with him while scarcely knowing it exists. Neil hadn't realized he was lonely until Peggy began trying to reform him in much the same way his parents used to. Her good-natured nagging, which had become part of these musical sessions, reminded him of his upbringing in that tight-knit three-member household in Dayton, with of course this difference: whereas his parents' concerns were tidiness, table manners, and making lots of money (things he had very little interest in), Peggy's object was to make a better teacher out of him—doubtless a worthier goal. Eventually, his novel would bring him the respect of readers, Peggy reasoned, but until it did, why not try to win the respect of his students? He thrived on Peggy's attention. The more she kept at him, the more he loved her. She never dropped in at his apartment anymore, so these practice sessions became the highlights of his week. He left sentences half finished, characters half formed, in order not to be late. He wished, for her sake, that he were really good on the clarinet.

Well, he hadn't been half bad on this version of "Stormy Weather." Perhaps less noise and more feeling was the direction he should be going with his music. Peggy hadn't been accusing him of overplaying the way she'd been accusing Victor, but if he was never going to play any better than he did now (and if he never got around to practicing, how could he hope to play better?), maybe he ought to settle for a minor role. The question was, could you go along forever merely laying out a few pretty edges around the main piece, and still keep your self-respect? You could if Peggy did the singing—anything for Peggy. And if Victor would tone down the deafening rat-a-tat of his everlasting drums.

Connor hadn't heard any drums, nor had he heard Neil's clarinet or Leland's keyboard. He'd only heard Peggy, and he was still hearing her. Putting his ear to his strings, tightening them and quietly strumming them, he went back over "Stormy Weather" in his head, noting where next time he would better anticipate her subtle changes of tempo. Her voice was a wonder, always on pitch, reaching the low notes and high notes with ease, always sounding somehow younger than her age, which was pretty young. He guessed she was around thirty, a dozen or so years younger than himself. Earlier this evening, waiting in the hallway for Peggy to show up with her key to the rehearsal room, Victor had declared his preference for female voices that were huskier or throatier than hers. "Thin" was Victor's word for Peggy's. Well, there was no arguing with Victor, but Connor couldn't have disagreed more. Purity, not thinness, was Peggy's quality. So fresh was her singing that even an old standard like "Stormy Weather" became something you'd never heard before.

The silence finally was broken by Neil, appealing to Peggy. "Let's do 'Misty.' "

"Hell with 'Misty,' " said Victor, punctuating his remark with a crash of his cymbal. "Let's do 'Your Feet's Too Big.' "

Leland asked if they shouldn't repeat "Stormy Weather" because it was the best thing they'd ever done. He explained to Connor that the best, before this, had been "These Foolish Things," which the four of them had been jamming on ever since that day three weeks ago when they first came together in Neil's basement.

"No, we'll come back to it later," Peggy declared. She recommended a change of tempo. " 'Goody, Goody,' " she said, glancing at Connor, who nodded to indicate he could play it.

And so they set off on a kind of furious and ragged footrace, out of sync, out of harmony, one or another of them falling behind Victor's raucous beat and then skipping and running and stumbling to catch up—but having great fun with it, Peggy blatting rudely on her sax, Neil producing wild falsetto squeals, Leland pounding out chords like Fats Waller, and Connor's string work all but buried under the noise because he was trying to save himself; it was too early in the evening to work himself up to the point of collapse. Strumming along weakly, he wondered how these four musicians had settled so quickly into their roles, how they had arrived at this system of deferring to Peggy. He wondered, too, how Peggy, with her musical sensitivity, could tolerate all their shortcomings. Was it torture for her to be surrounded by the mess they were making of "Goody, Goody"?

No, it was a joy. To Peggy, who came from a large family, her friendship with Victor, Neil, and Leland had come to feel like the loose but everlasting union between brothers and sisters, and tonight there was the added dimension of her adoration for Connor. She studied him as she blew on her sax. She could tell he was wearing out. She'd find him a stool and suggest a pause in their playing.

She swung her instrument around and studied Connor's daughter, who was now working out an algebra problem while keeping time with her foot. The girl was mature for thirteen, tall and lanky. Her face was thin and pale, her dark blue eyes commanding. Her haircut was too long to be given so little care, and her clothes were wrong. In about three years she would be beautiful, and quite likely wouldn't know it.

"Goody, Goody," despite the desperate efforts of all five of them to hold it together, came apart and collapsed like an old wooden shed, notes splintering and dying out in a rumble of laughter and heavy breathing. Leland moaned with delight and Victor laughed silently, wiping his eyes on his sleeve. Peggy cast her highly charged smile on Connor, who responded in kind. Even Neil, never much of a laugher, was shaking with mirth. Laura Connor, however, looked on with a face of stone, sensing the current running between Peggy and her father.

"The band'll be right back, folks," said Peggy, and she left the room while the others filled their paper cups from the thermos of coffee Leland had brought. Connor watched his companions move about to stretch their legs, then return to their instruments. He marveled at how congenially—without the help of drink—they fell into conversation with one another.

Peggy returned carrying a high stool. "What will you live on if you lose this job?" she asked Neil. "Will you go home to Ohio and live off Grandpa Jake all your life? How long do you think either of your parents will let you write in peace?" She paced back and forth across the room with her head down and her hands clasped behind her back. Connor counted the shades of color in her black hair (there were five) as she passed under the fluorescent lights. Neil, whose threat of dismissal seemed to be an obsession with her, was polishing his clarinet with his shirttail.

Leland was absently swiveling on his piano stool. Victor fussed with his drums.

"You know what they'll have you doing?" she asked. "They'll have you going around selling apples in all those high schools. They'll have you playing on people's sympathy as Grandpa Jake's idiot son." This enterprise of the Novotnys, known as Grandpa Jake's Fruit Basket, had long been the cause of derision in Peggy's family. Its customers were mostly high school students whose clubs or bands or athletic teams sold gift boxes of oranges and apples door to door in order to finance their field trips or proms or new uniforms.

During his college years, Neil had worked part-time in this lucrative business, and he hated every minute of it. The job entailed appearing before assemblies of students and their advisers and sometimes their parents, competing for their patronage. It had been humiliating to be part of his father's act, to stand at his side in a crowded high school gymnasium or band room or auditorium as his father, in broken English, pretended to be a naive, uneducated old-world peddler extolling his line of apples and oranges. Having arrived at these schools in a beat-up old car, with a three-day growth of whiskers, his father let it be known that he was a struggling immigrant trying to make his way against the slick competition in the fund-raising game, and he peppered his pitch with the cute things his grandchildren said. All of this was fraudulent. Neil's father had been born in the city of Dayton, educated at Ohio State University, and he traded his Cadillac for a new model every second year. He had no grandchildren, Neil being his only child.

" 'Dismissal with cause,' " Victor hissed over his drums, quoting the *Faculty Handbook*. "The only cause they've been able to pin on Neil so far is his small student load. Well, we've got that fixed, haven't we, Neil? You've got students hanging from the rafters. If they come after you now, without cause, the Alliance will fight the stupid clowns all the way to the Supreme Court."

The stupid clowns, of course, were Victor's enemies on Administration Row, primarily the dean. He rubbed his hands vigorously, anticipating a scrap. The Faculty Alliance of America was now installed as the faculty's official bargaining agent, having been chosen by a close vote (59–53) to replace the staid old Congress of

College Professors. Perhaps more surprising than that, and clearly dismaying to the administration, was the fact that Victor himself, a first-year instructor, had been elected president of the local chapter. President Gengler and Dean Zastrow let it be known that they would have preferred someone more deeply interested in academics than Victor, someone less fiercely committed to unions and less dogged as a bargainer, someone who wouldn't accuse people, in public, of shitting in their hats.

In his inaugural address to the membership, Victor had announced that his first order of business was to lobby, or strike if necessary, for higher pay; and his second order of business (at Peggy's urging) was to do away with the two-tier salary schedule, male and female. A third order of business (not made public) was to save his office mate's job.

"You've got what, eighty students in your classes?"

"Ninety-nine," answered Neil with pride. Neil was the only one of the five who hadn't gone home to freshen up before practice. He still had on his classroom outfit. His white shirt, old and carelessly laundered, was actually more yellow than white, and its collar and cuffs were badly frayed. His blue corduroy pants were stained with the things he had been drinking and eating for the past month or so.

"Ninety-nine! Jesus, just let Zastrow try coming after you with an enrollment like that."

"Yeah, just let him try." Neil smiled, happy to think that his Alliance membership (annual dues: $35) might actually pay off. Having condescended to join simply as a favor to Victor, he was amazed and pleased by the bracing solidarity it afforded him.

Leland Edwards spoke up then, in aid of Neil, offering him his old lesson-plan books from his days as a teacher of Freshman English. Leland's interest in Neil's rehabilitation went beyond his fear of losing a member of the quintet, even beyond his big-brother regard for the youngest member of the division and his need to please Chairman Oberholtzer. Not being creative himself, Leland loved being a patron to people who were. Unlike Connor, who came to Rookery with a reputation, Neil had been hired with little to recommend him except his grade point average in graduate school, and Leland, like Chairman Oberholtzer, had been happily surprised to discover they'd acquired a novelist in the bargain. True, they also acquired a fairly inept teacher, but Leland, while holding himself to high academic standards, felt that allowances must be made for the substandard ways of artists. That Peggy's advice might now prevail and Neil resolve to raise his standards would indeed be a stroke of good fortune.

"Make sure you divide the class hour into various activities," he advised. "You can't lecture the whole fifty-five minutes."

That's when Connor decided to join in, offering Neil a kind of pep talk about the teaching profession as one of the best ways for an artist to support his art. At the first word out of his mouth, the others fell respectfully silent. Connor's size (six-two) and age (forty-three) seemed to give his words power, and so did his weakened physical condition, his voice being somehow more authoritative for its raspy faintness. He was more heavily bearded than before his hospitalization, his brow more deeply lined. Slumped on his stool, his shirt wet, he spoke with his arms draped over the instrument into which, on "Goody, Goody," he'd poured too much of his energy.

"Stick with teaching, Neil. I tried other things. I wheeled cement for a contractor and I tended bar. It's no good working jobs entirely unrelated to your art, like selling fruit. Jobs like that wear you out. What good is your writing impulse if you're too tired to put it to use? Sorry, but selling oranges and apples?" He shook his head despairingly.

Neil, basking in all this attention, gave Peggy a shy smile she recalled from his boyhood.

"I tell you what I've done," Connor continued. "I've made it my goal the past few years to eliminate the distance between my job and my art. Teaching is the right line of work for doing that. Now, it's true that my students, if I let them, would sap me of all my juice, but I'm not letting them. I paint right there in my classroom. I'm paying less attention to my students' painting these days than I'm paying to my own. Introduce your novel into your class. Talk about it. Read it to them. Show them the problems you're having. That's how I do it."

"But English is different," Leland put in, worried that Connor might disturb the new leaf Neil intended to turn over. "In Freshman English we're teaching skills, remember."

"Writing skills, painting skills," said Connor, "I don't see a lot of difference."

"But what I'm saying is that you're teaching studio courses, so your own painting might very well make up a large part of your syllabus." Leland, unaccustomed to making declarations, except to youngsters on matters of literary taste and grammar, spoke haltingly, casting about for the phrasing he wanted. "But in Freshman English, Neil is teaching all sorts of skills of communication. Everything from how to use the library, to how to write a research paper, to how to read Milton. Therefore, I don't see the value, quite . . ." Actually, he didn't see the value, period, but he added the word "quite" as a kindness to a convalescent, and as a compromise to what he hoped was a budding friendship. ". . . the value, quite, of building his course around his novel."

Victor thumped a drum for attention. "Listen, Edwards, what a man teaches is his own business and nobody else's. Correct me if I'm wrong, you've been in this game longer than I have, but aren't we talking here about academic freedom?" He then brought his sticks down on his snare and worked the kick drum with his foot. Rattle rattle thump. Rattle thump.

"Leland might have a point," Connor admitted after the noise died down. "In English, Neil probably has a lot of basic material to plow through before he gets to the creative stuff."

They all turned to Neil then, who was making a breathy noise like a sigh. His head was bent to the clarinet lying across his lap.

"Cheer up," said Peggy, fearing he was downcast. She recalled how he'd never, as a boy, taken advice or criticism easily. "All we're saying is put on a suit and tie and give your classes ten minutes of thought before you walk in the door." When he didn't raise his eyes, she gave his arm a little shake. "What's bothering you?"

He looked up then, smiling wryly. "I forgot to teach the library unit."

Victor laughed and brought his sticks crashing down on his cymbal.

"Oh dear," said Leland, sounding injured. "How did your students ever manage their research paper?"

Neil looked away, not to hide embarrassment, Peggy saw, but
to hide the grin he couldn't suppress. "I forgot to assign the research paper."

"Oh my God!" Leland's wound sounded mortal.

Drumroll on the snare, cymbal crash, thump-a-bump on the
kick drum.

Spring semester seemed the ideal time for Neil to interest himself in his subject matter. This was the literature semester, the term
when the fresh air of masterful writing was allowed to mix with
the dusty research and rhetoric that the freshmen of Rookery State
College had been choking on since September. Fiction and poetry—these had been the staples of Neil's reading diet since he was
seven, and now he was free to communicate his enthusiasms to his
students. But despite his best promises to Peggy and to himself, despite his mushrooming enrollment, despite his necktie, his lecture
notes, and his haircut, he enjoyed no instant success.

For one thing, his students were suspicious. Here was a man
who had never before been prompt, never been known to lead a
coherent discussion or follow a lesson plan. For two and a half
years, they'd heard, it had been the style of this distracted, shaggy-
haired novelist to go directly from his manuscript to class and wing
it. A waste of tuition, they'd been told, and they signed up for his
three sections of Freshman English only if their schedules made al-
ternatives impossible—until this semester, when he promised an A
to everyone who enrolled. Now he had over thirty students per
section in a room with only twenty-eight desks.

B-18, before the enrollment boom, had been a janitorial supply
room in the basement of McCall Hall. A long, narrow room without windows or ventilation, it still smelled of the insecticide, floor
wax, and toilet disinfectant that had been stored there for decades.
The walls had been freshly painted a mustard shade of yellow, the
baseboards and door trim a lurid shade of green. At the front of the
room stood a coat tree, a lectern, and a portable blackboard on

three spindly legs. The shortage of desks presented no problem during the semester's first couple of weeks, when half the class naturally absented themselves, but since Neil began demanding regular attendance as a prerequisite for the A, there were invariably four or five students sitting on the floor.

On first meeting these classes, in early January, he'd been surprised by the scarcity of females. Three-fourths of his freshmen were young men, the great majority of whom, it didn't take him long to learn, were attending college for reasons other than mental stimulation. Many had come to Rookery on athletic scholarships. In his twelve o'clock class alone, he had four linemen and a running back. One of the linemen, a three-hundred-pound giant named Dickie Donaldson, intimidated Neil by glowering at him during lectures and making disapproving noises in his throat. The halfback, a little fellow named Swecker, bragged that he'd never read a book. Seven scar-faced hockey players attended his one and two o'clock classes—but not very often, the Blue Herons being far too accomplished for the Minnesota State College League and thus excused by the dean to make four-day road trips to Maine and Michigan and Colorado, seeking out teams of their caliber. On those few occasions when a goalie named Perkins showed up in class (an agreeable, smiling lad), he displayed new gaps where teeth had been. Also enrolled at two o'clock was the freshman basketball sensation from Staggerford, Phil Pflepson—enrolled, that is, but hardly ever in attendance. Absenteeism ran as high as fifty percent until Neil announced his new attendance policy.

But it was not athletic glory alone that these young men of Neil's were aiming at. This was the Vietnam era. Draft boards back home picked like buzzards through the mail from the registrar's office, smelling out their monthly contingent of D and F students to send to war. Dozens of borderline scholars, athletic or not, had crowded into Neil's classroom seeking academic deferment from the draft, their grades being such that they desperately needed his A to save them from suspension or expulsion.

It was these underachievers who were most alarmed by Neil's suddenly businesslike approach to teaching. As part of his new earnestness, mightn't he rescind his promise of the A? What a devastating betrayal, your harmless pushover of a professor suddenly developing standards and sending you off to death or dismemberment in the jungle.

Actually, they had nothing to fear on this score, for Neil was a man of his word. Pestered for assurance, he repeated over and over that he never made idle promises, and by February their anxieties appeared finally to be relieved. At least they began falling asleep more easily during his lectures.

One of his lectures, however, delivered on the last Wednesday in February, caused a revolt.

On this day (which he would later think of as the second-worst day of his life, soon to be followed by the first-worst), his freshmen were scheduled to hear one in a series of students reporting on their favorite poets. Today's designated student was Jodi Bukowski, a small, pale girl with earnest blue eyes all but hidden under long blond bangs. Miss Bukowski had written her name along with her poet's name, Velma Belvedere, on the sheet of paper Neil had taped to the classroom wall. That Neil had never heard of Velma Belvedere did not surprise or dismay him. Neil liked to think he was not above learning things from his students. Spring quarter a year ago, hadn't his freshmen introduced him to Robert Bly and Richard Brautigan? He assumed, therefore, that Ms. Belvedere was another young voice whose star had risen since he went underground with his novel. For the past three years he'd been reading dead writers of turgid prose almost exclusively, hoping thereby to lend weighty importance to his own narrative style.

Neil began his twelve o'clock class on this fateful Wednesday by reading aloud from his class roster, determined to learn every name in the room. (In the past, even in classes of six or eight, he'd known his students only as faceless delegations sent into his life to disrupt his fiction.) After roll call, he tried out a funny remark (Peggy said he should lighten up), but no one laughed, so he shuffled his papers, turned to the freestanding blackboard, and drew a stub of chalk from his pocket. He wrote as far as the W in SEVEN WEAKNESSES IN POOR POEMS when the blackboard collapsed.

In terms of student response, this was the most successful thing he'd ever done. It was minutes before the riotous laughter subsided, and even then, lecturing without visual aid, he was conscious of a continuing wave of suppressed giggles.

He forged ahead nevertheless, describing the damage done to poetry by clichés, platitudes, and the lack of concrete nouns. He read examples of stilted and old-fashioned language. He came down particularly hard on sentimentality, which he kept referring to as mush. Glancing up from his notes after half an hour, he saw that his lecture had succeeded in draining all mirth from the room. About half the class seemed to be following him, while the other half, including all four of the football linemen, were gazing like zombies at nothing.

"And now, Jodi Bukowski," he said, "I hope I've left you enough time for your report." He was counting on this girl to bring the zombies back to life, particularly the young men, for Miss Bukowski was attractive in a pallid, overserious way, and today she was dressed prettily for her appearance at the front of the room.

But Miss Bukowski did not rise from her desk. He was about to repeat her name when he saw, to his astonishment, that she was weeping. Splotches of red had sprung into her pale, wet cheeks, and she was shuddering with sorrow and searching her handbag for a hankie.

"What is it?" he asked urgently, hoping it was simply stage fright, although it appeared to be genuine grief.

She had no voice to answer him. She sobbed aloud, causing the eyes of the zombies to flicker to life. She wiped her tears with her knuckles until a friend handed her a tissue.

"If you'd like to leave the room . . ." said Neil.

She swallowed. Her voice quavered. "What you said about bad poetry . . ." She swallowed again, and moaned, "All of it applies to Velma Belvedere." She held up a little pastel book, which Neil recognized as the sort of inspirational and overpriced hardback displayed in greeting-card stores.

"I have not read Velma Belvedere," he said apologetically. "I had no idea."

"Her poems are wonderful, but you're saying they're mush."

Neil bristled. "I wasn't referring to Velma Belvedere. I have not read Velma Belvedere."

"She's wonderful. She speaks to the heart. I keep going back to her poems. She helps me through troubled times. That's a line in one of her poems: 'I'll help thee through thy troubled times.' I forget the next line. It ends with 'pantomimes.'" Jodi Bukowski's voice was growing stronger and steadier, although she still looked grief-stricken. Strands of her blond hair were stuck to her wet cheeks, which were coloring now with anger as well as sorrow. "My mother gave me one of her books when I was twelve, and she's been my favorite poet ever since, and you'll never, never, *never* change my mind."

"Yeah, Mr. Novotny!" said a masculine voice from the back of the room. "Who says you can go around telling people who their favorite poet should be?" The voice belonged to the mammoth and menacing Dickie Donaldson. This was his first coherent utterance of the semester.

"Yeah," added a friend of Donaldson's. This was the friend's initial statement as well.

Another friend agreed, calling out, "Yeah."

"Yeah," muttered about twenty-five others, their hostility as spontaneous and widespread as their laughter had been.

"I'm not telling people what to like, Mr. Donaldson. I'm only saying what's good and what's bad."

"Yeah?" Donaldson inquired. "What's so bad about Jodi's poet?"

" 'Thee' and 'thy,' for one thing. I'm judging by the line she quoted."

Here, a sigh of hopelessness from Jodi. A general murmuring of disgust from the others. A restless shifting of bodies in their desks. Neil sensed an uprising. The girl across the aisle from Jodi, a heavyset girl wearing a man's pinstripe vest and small rimless glasses, spoke up. "I happen to know how much Velma Belvedere means to Jodi, Mr. Novotny, and it's rotten of you to talk that way about her. I mean *dirty* rotten."

Others took up the cause. Neil was called a spoilsport, a Nazi, a snob, and a jerk. He was shocked by the intensity of their anger. Jodi Bukowski, weeping anew and clutching her pastel book of poems to her breast, made her way through the welter of tightly packed desks and left the room, and although the period was far from over, many others gathered up their books and followed her, drifting out into the dusky basement corridor.

"Hey, wait a minute, come back," called Neil, recovering his power of speech and realizing too late that this was a teaching opportunity. Forming now in his mind were additional remarks he could make about favorite poems as opposed to good poems. He would apologize for destroying Jodi Bukowski's illusions, while at the same time holding to his convictions. He would send his class away with a new awareness of literary standards.

But he had no class.

"Come back," he called again, addressing a procession of backs on their way out. Those few remaining in the room were on their feet and visiting among themselves as they prepared to leave.

"How can you be so uncivil?" he asked heatedly of the girl in the man's pinstripe vest.

Her reply was a shrug and a haughty smile of loathing, which he found extremely irritating. Struggling to control his temper, he stated evenly, "You realize, of course, that you're missing the rest of today's lesson?"

"So what?" she said. "We've already got our A for the semester."

While Neil's class was self-destructing in the basement, Victor Dash was upstairs in the office they shared, asking questions by phone of State Senator Harry Steadman in St. Paul.

"Who knows what's what down there at the capital? Who's running the show? Who's in charge of this goddamn state?"

Victor was devoting a great deal of time to the Faculty Alliance of America these days, stealing most of it from his students by cutting his classes short and reducing his office hours. The legislature had designated an unexpectedly large pool of money for college salaries, but there was a rumor going around that it might be drained off into campus construction.

"I go to the dean and ask are we getting a raise or aren't we, and he says talk to the president. Well, you know as well as I do that nobody talks to the president of this place, he's always in hiding somewhere, so I call the State College chancellor, and he tells me it's up to the State College Board. So what I want to know is, where the goddamn hell does the State College Board get its authority to override you lawmakers?"

"The board has certain discretionary privileges, Mr. Dash." From his office at the capitol, Harry Steadman was speaking in the overhappy voice he habitually used on disgruntled constituents, tones Rookery was used to hearing from him on Lolly Edwards's radio show. He was a good-natured man in his midfifties, the third Steadman in three generations to represent Rookery in the legislature. "They're entitled, as they see fit, to move around the funds we appropriate because they're appointed by the governor."

"I thought we sent you thugs to St. Paul to make laws, not kowtow to the governor."

Being referred to as a thug knocked the wind out of Harry Steadman. He needed a moment to recover, and when he did, it was in softer, breathless tones. "I assure you the governor only appoints people to the board who are specialists in higher education."

"Well, I'm a specialist in higher paychecks, and if the board doesn't come across with the money you guys earmarked for us, there won't *be* any higher education, at least not at Rookery State College, because we're going out on strike."

"Now, Mr. Dash—"

"On the peanuts I'm paid I can't even afford to buy my kids a bicycle."

"Now don't be hasty, Mr. Dash. There's a good bit of risk in striking. Lost wages and hard feelings all around. Think what it would do to your standing in the community. Striking is for miners and factory workers and their kind."

Victor exploded. "Their kind! What do you mean, 'their kind'?"

"I mean don't lose sight of your professional dignity up there on that beautiful campus of yours. It would be disillusioning to a lot of people in Rookery to see professors go out on strike. People have a lot of respect for—"

"Listen, I'll tell you how much respect they have for us on this beautiful goddamn campus. There's not a hardware store in this city will trust me to buy a bike on monthly installments."

"Can you imagine doctors striking, Mr. Dash? Lawyers or

priests or ministers carrying picket signs? I'm just saying keep your dignity, Mr. Dash, and you won't be sorry."

"Keep my dignity and my kids will never learn to ride a goddamn bicycle. Good-bye."

Dr. Warren W. Waldorf, chancellor of the Minnesota State College System, a man grown elderly and distinguished in this position, had been charged by the board nearly thirty years earlier with keeping its four campuses in smooth running order. In his prime he'd been a ubiquitous and charming public speaker, traveling the length and breadth of the state to confer his blessing on countless commencement exercises, retirement dinners, and alumni luncheons, but by the time Victor Dash began making revolutionary noises in the North, he'd lost his zeal for long ceremonies and long rides in his car. He hadn't visited the Rookery campus in several years. He felt somewhat guilty about this, but Rookery State seemed to be operating pretty well under its own power. If he were lucky, he'd be retired and living with Mrs. Waldorf in their condo in Florida well before any of his campuses were overrun with the faculty unrest and student militancy creeping into the Midwest from the East and West coasts. Although he'd been predicting difficult years ahead in higher education, he hadn't foreseen anything quite so outrageous as a faculty strike.

Nor anything so disrespectful as the words he was now hearing from Victor Dash: "They aren't lawmakers, they're chickens. They're letting the College Board piss all over them. If that money for salaries doesn't end up in our pockets, we'll be out on strike within the week." This was Victor's second call to the chancellor in a span of fifteen minutes.

Concealing his unease, Dr. Waldorf chuckled over the phone as though he thought the threat preposterous. "A strike, Mr. Dash? You can't be serious."

"What I want to know is this, Dr. Waldorf. Will the board negotiate?" This was Victor's concession to protocol. Any respectable union must offer to bargain.

The chancellor sounded even more amused than before. "Negotiate, Mr. Dash? With whom, pray tell?"

"With the Alliance."

"Alliance? What alliance?"

He knew goddamn well what alliance—Victor was sure of it. After pausing a moment to squeeze his eyes shut and blow out his cheeks—often useful in bringing his temper under control—he was able to continue in more tranquil tones. "The F.A.A., Dr. Waldorf. The Faculty Alliance of America. It's become our bargaining organization. You were notified."

"Oh *that* alliance," came the syrupy reply. "I'm so awfully sorry, Mr. Dash, but the board does not recognize the Faculty Alliance of America as a negotiating entity. Perhaps you're acquainted with the Congress of College Professors. That's your proper avenue for pursuing matters of faculty welfare."

"Hey, the C.C.P.'s gone belly-up in Rookery, Dr. Waldorf. We voted that bunch of old fogies out of existence almost a month ago. I'm sure you were notified."

"Oh?"

Convinced that the chancellor was playing dumb, Victor followed suit, asking the impossible. "Now if you'd kindly find a time slot for me and my steering committee to come down to St. Paul and meet with the board." He would be granted no appointment, of course. The board and the C.C.P. had been chums for generations. The Alliance was anathema. Furthermore, a meeting, even if it came to pass, would be fruitless, because the board, never having been seriously challenged by the timid likes of a college faculty, would see no need to compromise.

But Victor was under orders to offer to negotiate. A failed bargaining session, or at least a failed *attempt* to bargain, must precede a strike—a principle pointed out to him by Jack Short, executive director of the F.A.A., Midwest Section, in one of his pep talks from his office in Milwaukee. Picketing got tiresome, particularly in winter, Jack Short had told him yesterday. "Along about the second week, a striker gets to wishing there was an alternative to striking, and if he thinks there's been no serious attempt to bargain, he's liable to throw down his picket sign and say the hell with it."

Dr. Waldorf, responding to Victor's request, emitted a long, jolly laugh. He'd be happy to arrange a meeting, he said. The board would be in session this very afternoon, and they'd be more than pleased to see Victor and his steering committee between three o'clock and three-fifteen.

Victor was momentarily puzzled. Why was the chancellor acceding to his wishes, and with such an abundance of happiness in his tone? Then he glanced at his watch. One-fifteen. It was a four-hour drive to St. Paul. Still, he kept the lid on his temper. "What would you say to five-thirty?" he asked.

"Oh, no, quite impossible. A packed agenda, I'm afraid, right through into the evening."

"You're risking a strike, then, Dr. Waldorf."

"Well, we'll just see, won't we, Mr. Dash?"

It was the chuckle that came trailing after this remark that touched Victor off. He stood up from his desk and shouted, "You don't believe me!"

"Now please listen, Mr. Dash." The chancellor did not depart from his calm delivery. Indeed, his tone became warmer, more fatherly, more condescending. "You are only one campus of four, remember."

"You don't say."

"And you are the smallest of the four."

"So what?"

"And you are the farthest away from St. Paul. I daresay your impact will not be felt with quite the fear and trembling that you imagine."

"Who says we're the only campus going on strike?"

"I urge you to come to your senses. Who else went over to the Alliance? Surely you don't expect the Congress of College Professors to lead your three sister campuses out on strike."

"The C.C.P. couldn't lead a horse to water in a flood, but you're going to see faculties walking off their jobs all over this god-damn state. I'm talking about wildcatting, union or no union. We've been on the phone with the other three campuses. There's a hell of a lot of your professors ready to come over to the Alliance once Rookery leads the way."

"Good-bye, Mr. Dash," said the chancellor curtly, his patience suddenly gone.

"Hang on now. Do I have this right? Three o'clock this after-noon is the last possible time the board will meet with us?"

"You have it exactly right."

"And you understand it's a four-hour drive."

"You could fly."

"Fly what? There's only one flight south out of Rookery, and it already left. Besides, who can afford plane fare?"

"Well, I can only offer my regrets, Mr. Dash. After three o'clock the board takes up its full agenda."

"After three o'clock," Victor roared, "the board shits in its hat."

The office door opened and Victor turned to see Neil coming in. "The dean's been looking for you," Victor told him.

"What for?"

"Damned if I know. He stopped by when I was on the phone." He was holding the receiver to his ear and waiting to be connected with Alliance headquarters in Milwaukee. "If it's about those memos he's been sending you, tell him to stuff 'em."

Neil smiled weakly.

"I've just been on the phone with the chancellor. The board won't negotiate."

"No surprise, is it?"

"I'm alerting headquarters."

The effusive voice of Jack Short came over the wire. After an exchange of greetings and news, Victor confessed to a few misgivings:

"Now listen, Jack, we're a small faculty compared to the other three, and we're way the hell up here in the boondocks, so how do we know the others will follow our lead? I mean, hell, our strike might not even make the Twin City papers unless you start churn-ing out news releases, and how can you do that sitting clear over there in Wisconsin? You need to be up here wading into the loon shit with the rest of us. We can't do it *all*, for God's sake."

"Victor, Victor, the Alliance is behind you many hundred per-cent," Jack Short assured him from his office in downtown Mil-waukee. He did his best to sound hopeful, but as executive director of the F.A.A., Midwest Section, he wasn't betting on the Rookery chapter to succeed. He'd visited Rookery State on the day the faculty voted to align themselves with the Alliance—a surprising victory—and seen a faculty mostly grown long in the tooth. You could never get that many old men to carry a strike vote. Only someone as reckless and zealous as Victor Dash would propose such a thing.

"You promised us literature and bumper stickers, Jack. You said you'd start getting out news releases."

"Of course, of course, all in due time. Your College Board hasn't decided to screw you yet. We can't very well go on alert before we've been screwed, can we?"

"They're deciding this afternoon."

"Yeah? So where are you calling from, Victor?"

"My office."

"Your office in Rookery?"

"How many offices have I got?"

"Well, I should think you'd be in St. Paul trying to negotiate. Remember what I told you, your people will have to know you tried to bargain."

"Listen, I was told about the board meeting exactly five minutes ago, and I was given exactly an hour and forty-five minutes to drive two hundred miles."

"Hmmmm. And you're sure they'll vote to freeze your pay?"

"Spend it on capital outlay, that's the rumor. New buildings, scientific instrumentation, all that sort of stuff. Meanwhile, I can't afford a bicycle for my kids."

"What's your administration's attitude? Can they see your side of things?"

"Are you kidding? The dean's got sawdust for brains, and the president's a nonentity. They won't even let the Alliance meet on campus."

"Oh, wow!" said Jack Short, genuinely affected. He'd never run into this sort of discrimination before. "Where will you hold your strike vote, then?"

"I got a church reserved."

"Ha, good for you." He really had to hand it to this upstart. Perhaps the Alliance ought to take him on staff. They could always use an energetic malcontent foolhardly enough to take on the big boys.

"Victor, I'm not making you an offer or anything, but have you ever considered another line of work?"

"Other than teaching? Hell yes, I spent seven years laying pipe, and I'd still be doing it if they'd let me, but I signed off after rehab. I was in this gasoline explosion west of Sioux Falls that tore a hole in my head, and after they got my skull pieced back together, they kissed me good-bye. Not that I blame them. I cost them fifty thousand dollars, what with doctors and hospitals and retraining, so I can see their point. I mean, you can't put a man back on the job if his head's liable to fall apart every time you give it a good tap. Why do you ask?"

"I just wondered, say if we had an opening for a strike organizer someday, if you'd be interested."

"Christ, just try me."

The revolt of Neil's freshmen was followed that same afternoon by the first episode in what he and Peggy would come to refer to as the "Case of the Barmaid Who Couldn't Stand Death."

The barmaid was Helen Culpepper. She was older than the average freshman by perhaps fifteen years, although the extreme thinness of her body and the oversized dark glasses she never took off made it difficult to determine her age. She was one of those discontented wives Neil had lately been reading about in Ann Landers who were trying everything these days, even college, in order to find happiness. Upon the recommendation of her therapist, she had also taken up macramé to keep her hands busy. Each day, she carried a grocery bag full of rope to campus and spent the class period working on plant hangers.

Helen Culpepper was no stranger to Neil. He had first met her two and a half years earlier, when he was new in Rookery and would occasionally drop in at Culpepper's Supper Club for a drink and a steak. This was a bar and restaurant painted Kelly green and situated on the muddy river flats under the Division Street bridge. Because it was patronized mostly by laborers from the paper mill and the railroad yards, Neil was spared the company of academics, whom he found frightfully boring, and was free to meditate on his novel. Sometimes, in fact, he pulled a page of fiction out of his pocket and scribbled revisions while sitting at the bar nursing a beer, and it was one such page that first attracted the devotion of Helen Culpepper, wife of the proprietor and part-time bartender. She considered it terribly exciting to be serving drinks to a novelist.

In those early days, Neil had no idea that her husband, Sammy Culpepper, was a drunken brute in the habit of slapping his wife around and seeing other women. After a few exchanges of small talk over the bar, however, he did begin to sense that she was a nervous wreck and about to unload something like misery on him, so he stopped going there. In fact, he stopped going out for meals altogether, preferring to sustain himself with snacks at home, where he could eat while typing.

Thus, when she'd turned up in his one o'clock section this semester, Neil was wary, fearing she might open up the distressing conversation he'd fled from two years earlier, and he pretended not to remember her. "Am I changed that much in two years?" she asked after class the first day, having followed him to his office, found him alone there, and made herself comfortable in Victor Dash's desk chair. "I had my hair done and I've lost a few pounds, but I didn't think I'd changed so much you wouldn't know me."

"I guess it's your dark glasses," he said uneasily. Her highstrung nervous system was still giving off signals of misery.

"My therapist has me knotting," she told him, displaying her bag of rope.

The term was new to him, and he misunderstood. "Naughty?" he questioned.

Her screech of laughter was deafening in the small office. "Oh, you're terrible," she laughed. "You give me such a charge."

He smiled weakly. (Peggy had recommended that he smile more often on campus, that he look happy in his work.)

"Knotting," she repeated. "Like this." She pulled snakes of heavy purple cord out of her paper bag. It was a plant-hanger-in-progress, she explained. It had small ceramic birds and tiny pieces of driftwood worked into it. "What do you think?"

He thought it stupendously ugly. He said, "So that's knotting."

She had to stand up to display its full length. She wore a black dress and black stockings. The thinness of her legs, arms, and neck was alarming. Her dark glasses were very large, and so were her black furry earrings. She said, "Some call it macramé."

"Ah, yes."

"There's nothing naughty about it, Dr. Novotny," she said playfully. She sat down again and stuffed the rope back into her bag. "I hope you didn't mind I spent the class period working on it. My therapist says it's good for me. I suppose you heard about my divorce."

"Actually no, I hadn't heard." He had trouble maintaining his smile. He felt his face returning to its natural state—a fretful, inward expression. (*You look like somebody monitoring his own faulty heartbeat*, Peggy had told him.)

"It was hell. We ended up in court over custody of Alison."

"Your daughter?"

"She's a genius, Dr. Novotny, and she's sweet and sensitive."

"Who got custody?" (*Show an interest in your students outside of class*, Peggy advised.)

"I did. She's only ten but you'd think she was forty, she's so wise. Her sensitivity she gets from me, but I don't know where her brains come from."

"Not from you?" he asked charitably.

"I'm average. Alison's a genius."

"Not from your ex-husband?"

She screeched with laughter again. "Sammy's an imbecile. Sammy comes from a family of imbeciles. Do you like Sara Teasdale, Dr. Novotny?"

"Mister Novotny, not Doctor."

"What do you think of Sara Teasdale? I used to adore Sara Teasdale, but then I found out Sammy's mother likes Sara Teasdale, and now I can't stand Sara Teasdale."

Here the interview ended, because the campus clock struck two, summoning Neil to his third consecutive hour in the basement.

Each day thereafter, she followed him to his office in order to pose questions. What could be done about Alison's stodgy fourth grade teacher at River Grove Elementary? How late did Sammy have to be with his child support before she could take him to court? Where would she and Alison eat Easter dinner?—holidays were so lonesome. (Easter was sixty days away.) Should she complete her degree and become a teacher, or drop out and take a job at the paper mill? Didn't Dr. Novotny agree that she was too sensitive for working at the mill? Would she be better off, and would Dr. Novotny like her better, if she became less sensitive? Was Dr. Novotny married?

By sitting still for all this, by using Helen Culpepper as a test of the listening skills he was trying to develop, Neil quickly became the object of her dependence. She turned up in his office before class as well as after. On days when class didn't meet, she called him on the phone. In a few weeks he knew more about Helen Culpepper without trying than he knew about Cousin Peggy after months of inquiries.

It was the next period after the Jodi Bukowski debacle that Helen Culpepper's death phobia came to light. Without attempting to write on the flimsy blackboard, he began his lecture on literary standards by reading two poems about the death of children. One was "Ode to Stephen Dowling Botts," from *Huckleberry Finn*, a fine example of emotion run laughably amok, and the other was Ben Jonson's moving little elegy for his son. These poems, which an hour earlier had gone unremarked, caused a hitch in Helen Culpepper's knotting.

"How come you're so hung up on death, Dr. Novotny?"

"I'm not hung up on death, Mrs. Culpepper. I'm simply illustrating two approaches to the same subject."

"Yesterday it was 'Crossing the Bar' and the day before that it was 'Gather ye rosebuds while ye may.' It's a fixation and it's not healthy. My therapist says it's not good for me, all the death in this class. Call me Helen."

"Death is unavoidable in the study of poetry, Mrs. Culpepper."

"I don't believe it is. I know a lot of happy poems. Sara Teasdale wrote a lot of happy poems."

"I'm with Helen," said a young man Neil knew by name—Chuck Lucking—because he'd frequently spoken up, displaying a fairly astute mind. "We've already studied eight poems about death."

"Death is unavoidable, Mr. Lucking. In poetry as well as in life."

"So why dwell on it?" the young man asked.

"I told my therapist I was thinking of dropping your class." Obviously she meant this to be devastating news. "My therapist said she was glad. She said your poetry was giving me a lot of stress."

"It's not *my* poetry, Mrs. Culpepper. It's—"

"Call me Helen."

A young Indian woman seated near Helen Culpepper raised her textbook in the air and asked, "Who chose this book anyway? I think it stinks."

There was a rumble of agreement, and a gradual rising of voices, a groundswell of complaint against the textbook, against poetry, against death. Helen Culpepper, seated at the front of the room with her feet buried in rope, turned in her desk and trained her black glasses on her classmates, smiling and nodding happily at one and all—their reward for coming to her aid.

Minutes passed before Neil was able to quell the muttering, which he accomplished by calling for a student report and postponing the rest of his lecture. (*Be flexible,* Peggy advised.)

Today's reporter was the outspoken young Indian woman, whose name was Theresa Skip. Her poet was Wordsworth, not one of Neil's favorites but a writer with far better credentials than Velma Belvedere. Theresa Skip took Neil's place at the front of the room as Neil stepped to the back. She wore a pair of wire-rimmed glasses, and her black hair hung in two braids over her ears. He admired her self-assurance as she sped through a brief biography of the poet and then slowed down to recite a few quatrains chosen from his brighter-colored poems. Flowers in nooks. Children at play. Waves on the sea. She concluded with "I Wandered Lonely as a Cloud" in its entirety.

This left Helen Culpepper smiling blissfully. "Now that's more like it," she said, turning again to face the class as Theresa Skip returned to her seat. " 'A host of golden daffodils,' isn't that perfectly beautiful? Dr. Novotny needs to learn more poetry like that. Next time why don't we each bring a happy poem to class and help him get over his fixation on death."

The class studied Neil for what they expected to be a negative reaction. To their amazement, he condoned the plan, foreseeing here another teaching opportunity. (*Seize the moment,* Peggy had said. *Stay on your toes and look for openings*.) He was confident that most of them would bring inferior poems to class, and he would show them exactly why they were innocuous, wrongheaded, or sappy.

The period ended with no more unrest, his students filing peaceably out of the room and Neil following. (In the past he'd always been the first one out.) He climbed the stairs dreamily, imagining how swiftly his reputation would change. He imagined himself boasting to the quintet at practice tonight, describing how efficiently he'd turned his students' discontent to his advantage. He went to his office to tell Victor that he was, at last, coming into his own as a teacher.

Victor was still on the phone, so he climbed to the second floor, looking for Peggy, but she wasn't in her office. He climbed farther, to report his classroom triumph to Dr. Oberholtzer, but found a line of students waiting at his door. He idled about the building, looking out windows and trying to imagine further perils to lay in the path of his fictional heroine Lydia Harker, now that she had eluded Zastrow the repulsive courthouse clerk. He pictured his novel in print. He pictured Dean Zastrow begging him to remain on the faculty.

Next period, his lecture on poetry was interrupted by Dean Zastrow's rap on the door. "Let me speak to your freshmen, Novotny. We've got to get at least five of them transferred to other sections. I sent you a memo on this."

"Can't we talk about it later?" asked Neil, blocking the doorway. "You're interfering with my lesson."

"What?" The dean's shock was apparent in his face, all color draining instantly away. "What?" he repeated, examining Neil's eyes for signs of lunacy.

"The classroom is my turf," Neil proclaimed, bravely quoting a favorite line of Victor's, and he pulled the door gently shut. Today, for some amazing reason, he didn't find the dean intimidating. His resolve to be a good teacher was filling him with courage as well as pride. Returning to his lectern, he could not suppress a little smirk of glee. His freshmen, who had overheard the exchange, caught his spirit and chuckled happily, their eyes trained on the door. Of the three, this was Neil's most agreeable, malleable class.

Standing in the dark hallway, the dean spent a few seconds considering his next move—should he press on, or dump this case of insubordination in the lap of Chairman Oberholtzer? His anger dictated that he press on. He flung open the door and stormed into the classroom, growling, "Now listen here, Novotny, there are certain things just as important as academic freedom, and one of them is seeing that this campus operates in an orderly manner." Inflated with rage, he seemed about to pop all three buttons of his tight suit coat. He turned to the students and said, "There are too many of you in here."

Besides being Neil's most congenial students, these were his most athletically inclined, as well as the most intensely interested in the A he offered. (They were also the most wide-awake, which had puzzled Neil until he recalled from his own lie-abed youth that midafternoon was morning to a nineteen-year-old.) In addition to the hockey players (all present today, their schedule having brought them home for two consecutive games), there were three wrestlers (two middleweights and a mastodon), and four junior-varsity basketball players (three guards and a beanpole). Packed into this tiny classroom, they created a remarkable impression of strength and robust health. Gaping at the dean, they fairly gleamed with vigor.

"Five of you will have to go to other sections. I'm asking for volunteers."

No one volunteered. They met his scowl with a steady stare. So he beamed them a sudden, unnatural smile, hoping to win them over by goodwill and reason. Tapping the wart at the side of his nose, he continued, "Let's look alive, everybody. Tomorrow is the day class lists are finalized for the semester, the day when everybody has to be enrolled where they belong. There's another section this hour that can take all five of you. Come along now, chop chop."

They sat in perfect, unblinking stillness, as though studying a rare specimen in a zoo.

The dean's smile turned sinister. "Your instructor was sent

two memos on this." He turned to Neil as though daring him to deny it. "I sincerely hope your instructor has not been guilty of insubordination."

"I got the memos," said Neil, who'd not only received them, but done his best to carry out their demands. The first memo, a longhand scribble, had ordered him to reduce each of his classes to twenty-eight students, in order to bring certain other sections up to quota. The second memo, typed, with copies routed to Chairman Oberholtzer and President Gengler, had demanded the names of his students transferring out. Instead of following Victor Dash's advice *(Write "Kiss my ass" on the goddamn things and send them back)*, Neil had read both memos to his classes and asked for volunteers. He had not done so halfheartedly. He had no desire to deplete the rolls in other classes, and this crowded room was claustrophobic. Furthermore, he was having trouble learning all these names, especially with several students scattered around on the floor and scarcely visible. But of course his appeal had had no effect.

"You," said the dean, pointing to a girl sitting prettily in the front row with her admirable legs crossed. This was Sandy Hupstad, a basketball cheerleader. She smiled at him, crinkling her nose.

"And you, you, and you," he said, indicating the rest of the front row. "How many is that?" he asked Neil.

"Let's see, I believe one and three is four," Neil told him.

"All right, then, you," he said, pointing to another. "Come with me, you five," he ordered, and he marched out the door. In the corridor he halted, waiting to lead them upstairs.

The silence in the room was tense. No one drew an audible breath or moved a well-toned muscle. All eyes were on the doorway. Neil, embarrassed for the man standing stock-still in the shadowy hallway, while at the same time feeling triumphant, bowed his head at the lectern and shuffled through his papers. Ten seconds passed. Twenty.

It was Sandy Hupstad who finally ended the standoff. Flashing her crinkle-nose smile at Neil, she glided across the room on her silent white sneakers and pulled the door quietly shut.

At the click of the latch, Dean Zastrow climbed angrily and swiftly to the main floor and stood snorting and fuming in his outer office, while his imperturbable secretary, Mrs. Kibbee, continued typing without pause. His message, when he finally got it out, was that she must call Chairman Oberholtzer in for a conference immediately.

"Not now," she corrected, without looking up from her typewriter. "You have a meeting in room two hundred."

"I do?"

"Signage Committee."

Mrs. Kibbee, who was thought by many to possess the only sensible mind on Administration Row, was an efficient woman of few words who had served in this position through four deans and held a low opinion of this one. She was married to a farmer named Clement Kibbee and drove a heavy old pickup to work. On her desk were photos of her three grown-up children and a prize-winning pig.

The dean studied his watch. "What time does it start?"

"Twenty minutes ago."

"All right, tell Oberholtzer I'll see him later. Tell him it's about Novotny. And while you're at it, put a note in Novotny's file."

Mrs. Kibbee picked up a pencil and wrote the date on a notepad.

"Insubordination," Zastrow dictated. "He defied his dean. First he said his dean couldn't come into his classroom, and once his dean got in, he refused to release the students his dean asked for. Got it?"

She nodded, scribbling a word or two.

"Barring the door to his dean, Mrs. Kibbee—can you imagine?" Muttering furiously, he left the office.

Mrs. Kibbee tore the page from the notepad, pulled open the personnel drawer of her filing cabinet, and tucked the note into Neil's folder. It said, *Gave Z lip.*

The five members of the Signage Committee, including Peggy Benoit and Leland Edwards, were waiting for the dean in McCall 200, a messy journalism workroom seldom in use because the college newspaper came out only four times a year. They were sitting around the layout table eating doughnuts and happily discussing the state legislature and the money approved for faculty salaries, an appropriation of unprecedented generosity. Hearing the dean's quick step in the hallway, they fell silent. They greeted him with nods and mumbles and passed the bakery box and a paper napkin around to his place at the table. One doughnut left, Leland noticed—raised and sugared, not the dean's favorite kind.

"Strange time for doughnuts, right after lunch," said the dean, sitting down and biting into it. He turned to smile at Peggy, who was sitting on his right with a music score open before her. Being the only woman on the committee, she was naturally in charge of refreshments. "Not that I'm blaming," he added, aware of his power to frighten. "I'm only commenting."

Peggy, not frightened in the least, said pleasantly that the doughnuts had been ordered before the dean changed the time of the meeting from morning to afternoon.

"Of course," he conceded. "Couldn't be helped. Things come up. Hated to do it because morning is best, when the mind is fresh. Committees traditionally accomplish far less in the afternoon." He set what remained of his doughnut on the napkin before him and brushed his sugary fingers over the box. "But let's see if we can go against tradition today and get some business taken care of."

"We've only fifteen minutes left," said Peggy. "Some of us have a class coming up." Then she did something that would have shocked the rest of the committee had they not seen her get away with this sort of thing time after time. She nudged the dean with her elbow and said, "Not blaming, only commenting."

He actually laughed, though only momentarily. There were smiles and murmurs of amusement from some of the others, though not from Leland Edwards, who was discouraged by Zastrow's partiality toward the people he had hired since taking over as dean. Any older member of the faculty, predating the Zastrow era, wouldn't think of giving him an elbow to the ribs; probably not even the esteemed C. Mortimer Oberholtzer would have dared. Yet Peggy got away with such indignities. So, until recently, had Victor Dash. Leland had overheard Victor one day tell the dean that he was shitting in his own hat, and the dean laughed. But of course that was before the Alliance, before Victor was chosen its leader. Now the dean despised Victor.

Zastrow turned serious and lowered his voice, confiding that he had been running behind all day. "Personnel trouble at the moment. The worst kind. Insubordination. I won't say who, but he's not a beginner. Ought to know better."

"My division?" asked Peggy Benoit, guessing the truth.

The dean nodded.

"English?" She knew the dean loved posing riddles.

Another nod.

"His third year?"

A smiling nod. "Tut tut, Dr. Benoit, you're getting too warm for comfort." The dean's mouth was a long slit when he smiled. He tapped the wart on his nose. "Let's get down to business, shall we? Minutes of the last meeting, please, Mr. Dumont."

Brooks Dumont, a husky young man from Manual Training who was wearing a shop apron over his shirt and tie, looked to the committee chairman, Leland Edwards, for the go-ahead, then opened his notebook.

Leland watched an expression of childish bliss spread across the dean's face as he prepared to be read to. Of all committees, Signage was Zastrow's favorite. Its mission was to post new signs campuswide, identifying buildings and directing pedestrians and motor traffic. Nothing pleased the dean quite so much as routing masses of people through channels. He loved discussing at social gatherings, for example, the most direct way of walking from McCall Hall to the power plant, from the student center to the hockey arena.

Today's minutes, in their entirety, were these: "Dr. Quinn moved that we invite a member of the custodial staff to join our committee. Motion seconded by Dr. Cardero. Vote three to three, no majority, motion defeated."

"That's all we did last time?" asked the dean, crestfallen.

Peggy nodded sadly. So did Leland.

"It took us a long time to discuss the question, sir," said Brooks Dumont.

Quinn, of History, moved to accept the minutes as read.

Cardero, of Accounting and Office Procedures, seconded.

There were no objections, the motion carried.

Dean Zastrow asked, "Why didn't I break the tie?"

"You said you couldn't decide, sir." Brooks Dumont addressed all his elders and superiors as sir—a habit brought home from Vietnam.

"Then why did we vote? Why didn't we table it?"

"The question was called, sir."

"Who called it?"

"Dr. Benoit, sir."

The dean directed an unhappy chuckle at Peggy. "Far too impatient, you young people. This is deliberate work we're about here. Signs are permanent. We can't be making quick decisions we'll be sorry for later."

"It wasn't about signs," she snapped. "It was whether to ask a janitor to join us." Peggy had not yet digested the dean's reference to insubordination. She was full of anxiety for Neil, full of resentment that an oaf like Zastrow should be invested with the power to hire and fire.

Leland, sensing her emotion, nimbly diverted their attention to the problem of the college motto. The manufacturer, he said, was waiting to add a motto to the Rookery State College sign to be erected at the corner of Sawyer and Eleventh, the point where most visitors entered the campus. The sign was to be made of varnished butternut and edged with wrought iron. The problem was that the college had no motto.

Accountant Cardero asked to hear again the suggestions submitted by the faculty.

Historian Quinn asked to be spared such inanities. He said they were offensively stupid, and why did Rookery State need a motto anyway?

Shopman Dumont, his notebook open to the motto page, waited for a signal from Leland, who said, "What's our pleasure?" to the other members.

"By all means run through them," said the dean.

"Oh, by all means," echoed Peggy, perhaps sarcastically, Leland couldn't be sure.

Leland next looked to Reginald Fix, the scientist, for an opinion. Fix, a mousy little man with a mouse-colored beard, nodded, complying with the dean's wishes. Since this group began meeting in September, Fix had uttered no words except (on voice votes) "aye" and "nay" and (on motions to adjourn) "I second." Was he chronically obsequious, afraid of offending the administration, or was he, like Quinn, just plain bored by any topic outside his field? Leland, his colleague for twelve years, hadn't a clue to what went on in Fix's head. His field was organic chemistry, his specialty was compost.

Brooks Dumont, at a nod from Leland, read the mottos. As in past readings, as recommended by the dean, he paused for a moment of meditation after each item. "Academics in the Northland," he read. Pause. "Higher Education for You and Yours."

Leland, who knew the list by heart, had to agree with Quinn that nothing worth carving in butternut had yet been suggested. He cringed at the next one, "Princeton of the Northwoods," because it was so far from the truth. There were two dozen more, all of them submitted in a contest. The winning slogan would win for its creator a lifetime pass to Blue Heron athletic events, home and away.

"Excellence Since 1929."

Pause. A groan from Quinn.

"Scholarship and Hockey."

Giggles from Peggy. She, like Leland, recognized this one as Neil's.

While Dumont droned on, Leland's thoughts wandered back to his main worry of the hour—faculty pay. Leland did not share his colleagues' optimism. Few of his colleagues seemed to believe what his mother had assured him of—that the money for salaries from the legislature was in danger of being channeled elsewhere by the State College Board. His mother had learned from President and Mrs. Gengler that the board would vote today on this matter, and that all six members were already committed to reallocating the funds into dormitory construction and classroom equipment, even though these areas, too, had been provided for—but apparently not sufficiently.

The board was of the opinion, according to the Genglers, that in this year of surging enrollment, campus facilities were pressed beyond their limits. The Genglers had seemed confident that the professors on all four campuses statewide, if they waited patiently (which of course they would do if they were truly committed to higher education), would be amply rewarded in the next biennium.

Leland's mother had been skeptical. "Do you buy that?" she'd asked Leland. "Your father always said, 'Better a postman than a professor if it's income you're after,' though goodness knows he managed to leave us comfortably fixed, but of course money went farther in those days."

Leland would gladly wait two years for his increase in pay. Not only did he trust the College Board to do right, he was committed to the long-term welfare of Rookery State. Furthermore, the prospect of striking appalled him. Classes canceled, students idle, professors picketing—how messy and loathsome.

And yet a strike seemed a strong possibility. The local Alliance, under Victor's direction, was putting out a stream of inflammatory memos. The local steering committee, commonly referred to as Victor's Viceroys, had their ears constantly to telephones, listening to strike talk from labor unions all over the nation, listening to instructions from Alliance headquarters in Milwaukee. Aaron Cardero was one of them. Just yesterday the Viceroys had instituted something called the Telephone Tree, a system by which each professor passed along strike-related news and rumor to a colleague, and the colleague in turn was expected to pass it further along his branch. Leland's antistrike attitude was apparently well known, for he turned out to be an endmost twig, given no number to call.

As Brooks Dumont went on with his recitation, Leland saw Peggy suppressing further giggles, her head bent to her musical score. He rather liked the blue woolly shirt she was wearing, with the coral turtleneck underneath. It was an awfully casual outfit for a professor, and surely too informal to be wearing a string of pearls with, and yet on Peggy the pearls looked just right. Women of striking looks, he concluded, could get away with things like that.

His eyes moved over to Quinn, whose frown mark was growing deeper with each motto. It pleased Leland to suppose that Historian Quinn would vote against the strike. Negativity had become Quinn's guiding philosophy. Last month, in an uncharacteristic moment of what looked like enthusiasm, Quinn had agreed (along with Accountant Cardero) to serve on the Alliance steering committee. Later he'd quit, saying he couldn't stand Victor Dash. It seemed that Quinn couldn't stand much of anything these days. He claimed to despise change as much as the status quo. At faculty meetings he voted no on every issue. Any issue not up for a vote—the harsh winter weather, the stark ugliness of new campus architecture—he dismissed with a sneer. It was rumored that his sour outlook was related to some secret and serious illness, and that poor Mrs. Quinn had been terribly frightened lately by his references to suicide.

Leland's eyes moved over to Dr. Aaron Cardero, who moonlighted as a financial planner to practically everyone of means in Rookery. Leland's mother, with her few shares of inherited stock in Minnesota Mining and Manufacturing and her investment in KRKU radio, was one of his clients. It wasn't hard to predict how Cardero would vote. Contrary to Leland's theory that a financial theoretician should see the long-term wisdom of not striking, Cardero was proving to be an adventurer. As a lover of committee meetings, he hadn't been able to resist Victor's invitation to become an officer of the Alliance.

On Cardero's left sat Reginald Fix, the cipher, who at the moment had his eyes fixed on his lap, where he was trimming his nails with a manicure scissors and catching the clippings in a tiny pillbox. (Experimenting with various compost ingredients, he'd lately been soliciting nail clippings campuswide.) Leland guessed that anyone with Fix's long years of tenure and his short attention span on every topic but fertilizer would not vote to complicate his life. Surely he could be counted on to vote no.

Next to Fix sat Brooks Dumont, whose no-vote was as good as tallied. You could see it in his deferential treatment of the dean and all other administrators.

Dean Zastrow, of course, was not a member of the Alliance and would not cast a vote. The dean, in Alliance terms, was management. Opportunist that he was, and hoping to bring glory upon himself in the eyes of the College Board, Dean Zastrow instead of President Gengler was setting himself up as the voice of Administration Row. He was management's counterpart to Victor Dash, scoffing at the threat of any work stoppage. His secretary, Mrs. Kibbee, had been seen at the mimeograph machine preparing a memo enumerating the personal risks that went with striking—dangers which, to Leland, seemed drastic enough to bring any half-hearted striker to his senses. Loss of paycheck, for one. Loss of health insurance, for another. For the untenured, the possible loss of their jobs. For one and all, a diminished standing in the community, stemming from unprofessional behavior. And worst of all, in Leland's opinion, an undying rift between strikers and those who crossed the picket line.

Leland wondered if he would have the courage to cross such a line and risk the undying hatred of his colleagues. Would he have the courage *not* to cross and risk the anger of the administration and the disappointment of his mother? This problem had been keeping him awake nights.

Shopman Dumont droned on, and Leland's eyes circled back to Peggy again. Her willingness to strike was a great disappointment to Leland. It was the double salary schedule, male and female, that had put her in Victor's camp. She seemed obsessed by the notion that women be paid what men were paid. She'd been busy alerting the other women on the staff to this injustice. Well, it *was* unjust, but wasn't she overreacting? Wasn't the two-hundred-dollar difference something the Alliance could easily negotiate out of existence without resorting to a strike? How appalling to imagine a woman so graceful and smart and well-meaning carrying a picket sign.

"Learning for Life," said Dumont.

And there was much more than disappointment in Leland's heart where Peggy was concerned. Peggy was on his mind more than his mother was—a distinction no other woman had ever achieved. He'd never in his life had music dreams, but lately he'd been dreaming about Peggy on the sax. In one such dream, two weeks ago, she was making up the melody as she played it, and Leland actually remembered it when he awoke. He'd switched on his bedside lamp, drawn five lines on the endpapers of the book he'd been reading (his father's first edition of Hemingway's short stories), and jotted down the notes. In the morning, before leaving for class, he'd tried them out on the piano, and was charmed—a melody vaguely reminiscent of something of Scarlatti's he'd played as a boy. He played it half a dozen times, and then, in an unprecedented flash of inspiration, he extended it by several more bars straight out of his imagination.

He'd been working with it ever since, perfecting it and looking forward to playing it for Peggy and Connor and Neil. For Victor, too, of course, but the others especially, because Peggy was its inspiration, and Connor and Neil, being the creative geniuses they were, would doubtless appreciate it more than Victor. He played it at home every evening, trying out various tempos. It was turning out to sound like something Hoagy Carmichael might have done, but with a jazzier spirit. He thought of calling it "The Old Lamplighter Takes the A Train," but decided not to be derivative. He'd ask Peggy to name it.

"The College with a Heart." Pause. "Live and Learn."

Every time he played the piece, he felt Peggy tugging at him in a way he'd never been tugged before. Neither erotic nor motherly, it was more of an intellectual tug, a desire to achieve a meeting of minds. It grew out of his strong feeling of indebtedness to her for being the heart of the quintet. When he considered all she brought to it—her singing, her saxophone, her showing the four men how to blend the noises they made into something close to music—he realized how impossible it would have been to get the group going on his own. He lacked the authority to tell Victor not to drum so loud, to urge Neil to practice more, to encourage Connor to be more assertive on the bass. Leland wasn't good at telling people what to do. And even if he knew what to tell them, which quite often he didn't, he was too busy at the piano to hear truly what the group sounded like. Peggy had the ear for that, knew the instant their music began to fall off, knew right away what the problem was and how to talk about it. Well, why wouldn't she, with her doctorate in music?

Brooks Dumont changed his tone slightly, trying to instill some life into the meaningless phrase, "Healthy Minds on a Healthy Campus."

He rather liked it whenever his mother had Peggy in for an evening and she'd sing to his accompaniment. The only problem was that these duets made his mother a little silly. They fueled her expectations. The other night they'd worked out a rendition of "I

Only Have Eyes for You" that was really superb, Peggy's voice being perfectly attuned to that sort of love song, and after she left, his mother said it was clear that a romance was germinating. He'd forced himself to laugh at that.

At some point in every practice session, Peggy praised him. She seldom had anything negative to tell him, and when she did, it always came down to the same flaw. He couldn't fully relax and let go. He couldn't follow the leader when the leader—say, Peggy on the sax or Neil on the clarinet—really began to fly. "You've got to be ready to change your style, Leland, you've got to jazz it up when the rest of us get wild and zany, or if you can't do that, then you've got to drop off a little, give us a few background chords and let it go at that. Why do you have to play everything like a solo?"

Well, of course the answer was that he'd been playing nothing but solos since he was seven.

"Education for the Future." The words dropped like lead from the lips of Shopman Dumont, and he said it was the final motto.

Peggy rolled her eyes in relief, the historian sighed, and the accountant urged that the vote be taken.

Leland passed around slips of paper.

The dean jotted down his choice and showed it to Peggy, hoping she would concur.

She copied it, which would have pleased him immensely if she hadn't laughed while doing so.

Victor Dash skipped his late afternoon Business English class and went instead to the student center to meet with his Viceroys. The cafeteria was chilly and almost empty. A foursome of late-lunching students sat at a table tearing apart a deep-fried chicken, and off in a corner booth he found half of his steering committee, the two female members, sharing a plate of carrot sticks.

"Where the hell are the others?" he asked, dropping into Kimberly Kraft's side of the booth because she was skinny. Alex Bolus took up most of the seat on the other side. Kimberly Kraft, professor of Educational Tests and Measurements, was proving very useful to Victor, given her orderly mind. As secretary-treasurer of the

Alliance, she kept him on course, reminding him of duties and deadlines. He thought her quite attractive today, dressed in her blue suit, though not so attractive as his wife Annie, who had a more substantial body and prettier hair. Besides being a color he'd never cared for, Kimberly's ash-blond hair was too thin and airy, floating out from the sides of her head in wisps. His wife's thick dark hair was beginning to gray. Nothing prettier, in Victor's opinion, than a brunette turning a little gray.

"Aaron Cardero's in a committee meeting," Kimberly told him, unfolding with some distaste a page of handwriting too sloppy to be her own. "He sent his notes with me."

"He's not hopeful," added Alex Bolus, a beefy professor of Physical Education, and women's athletic director. As usual, and in defiance of the dean's dress code, Alex Bolus was wearing gray sweatpants over her ample hips and a gray sweatshirt over her muscular upper torso. A referee's whistle and a stopwatch were suspended from leather cords around her neck. Year-round, indoors and out, her face appeared windburned. Like Kimberly, she was a hard worker, though perhaps slightly less committed to the Alliance. Neither woman would ever see fifty again, which was why Victor had enlisted them, their reputations long-standing and sterling.

"Where's Quinn?" he asked.

"Larry quit, remember?"

He'd forgotten. Larry Quinn, the sardonic senior member of the four-person history department, and probably the wisest head Victor enlisted, had quickly lost interest in the Alliance—and in life too, perhaps, given the way he slouched around campus looking despondent.

"Christ, we can't have people quitting on us."

"Have a carrot," said Alex Bolus, as though to cheer him.

"Not on an empty stomach," he snapped. "I haven't had lunch." This woman, a health freak for all her size, was forever foisting vegetables on him.

"Mankato says no," Kimberly Kraft reported, showing him Aaron Cardero's scribbles. "They say maybe next biennium."

Victor gave the table a resounding slap. "Goddammit!"

"It says here they need new classrooms bad, and they're willing to put off their raises to get them."

"Doesn't surprise me," he growled, turning away in disgust. "I never had faith in Mankato."

"And Winona says no."

He turned and glared incredulously at his seatmate. "You're kidding."

Kimberly shook her fluffy hair regretfully.

He raged, "Winona promised they'd go out if we did."

Kimberly squinted at the paper. "Says here there's just not enough interest. They're in the middle of some big upheaval in Winona—hiring a new president and a new dean."

"Tell them they can have ours."

"You can see their point," said Alex Bolus. "It's no time to cause trouble if you're bringing in a fresh crop of administrators."

"No better time," Victor fumed. "Strike when management's on the ropes. What about Moorhead?"

Kimberly ran her crimson fingernail along a line of Aaron Cardero's illegible writing.

Victor couldn't read it. "What the hell's it say?"

"Moorhead."

"Yeah, but then what?"

"I don't know, it looks like 'mayor.' Or is it 'mulch'?"

They turned the paper toward Alex, who interrupted her noisy mastication of carrots to say, "Looks like 'mucus' to me."

"Christ, you'd think a college prof could write English. Why isn't he here? What committee's so goddamn important he's got to miss this meeting?"

"Signage," said Kimberly.

Victor's anger was causing his face to turn colors—red at the temples, bone-white around the eyes, pink along the ridges of his ears. "Since when does Signage take precedence over the Alliance?"

"Since the dean fell in love with the Signage Committee," Alex explained. "He shows up for all their meetings and keeps track of attendance."

"What does Cardero care? He's got tenure."

"Oh, Victor." Alex drew this out in a sigh, as though addressing a slow-learning child. "Tenure only guarantees your job. It doesn't prevent your job from becoming torture." Waving a carrot in one hand and fingering her stopwatch with the other, she went on to tell a story of a former Blue Heron hockey coach with a losing record who, despite tenure, was hounded off the faculty by a former athletic director. The athletic director, it came out later, had recruited students to dump garbage on the coach's front porch for as many as fifty consecutive nights. It was the coach's wife who finally broke down, and they moved away for her mental health.

"And the athletic director?" asked Victor, obviously moved by the story. "What became of that son of a bitch?"

"He retired to California."

"Arizona," Kimberly corrected. "We had a banquet for him."

"Christ, and people wonder why colleges need labor unions."

Kimberly, neatly folding Cardero's report, offered the example of a colleague of hers when she taught in a high school years ago, a home economics teacher driven to the point of a nervous breakdown by a superintendent who took an intense dislike to her. He did not trust, or pretended not to trust, her management of the department budget. He alerted all the merchants in town—the town was Owl Brook—to her supposed dishonesty and ordered them to phone him the moment she left the store with a purchase, never mind if it was paid for with a school voucher or her own money. He made a list of all these purchases, both school items and personal items, and confronted her with it every Friday morning. This wore her down. She became physically ill on Thursday nights and often had to take sick leave on Fridays, whereupon he would call her house and read the list over the phone. The Friday he read "sanitary napkins" over the phone, she went completely 'round the bend. Had to take sick leave for the rest of the year.

"Christ," whispered Victor, truly aghast.

"What a scumball," said Alex Bolus.

"And listen to this—he'd been married to her."

"Oh, sure," seethed Alex, as though the evil of all husbands was well known.

"Why didn't the rest of you come to her aid?" Victor asked.

"What could we do?"

"Go over his head."

"Who's over a superintendent?"

"Well, somebody must have *hired* the son of a bitch."

"The school board, but the school board were those very same merchants. He had them all in his pocket. They admired the tight hold he kept on the school budget."

He shook his head. "And people wonder why we got unions."

The third of Victor's Viceroys, Aaron Cardero, made his way between the tables of the cafeteria, greeting the four students sucking on chicken bones. He pressed himself into Alex's side of the booth, smiled happily at Victor and Kimberly, and said, "Sorry, Signage ran a little over." Accountant Cardero was energized by committees. He loved everything about them—the minutes, the motions, the endless and convoluted discussions. "What have I missed?" he asked Kimberly Kraft, of whom he was especially fond because of her fussily bureaucratic mind.

"Penmanship in grade school," answered Victor, unfolding the sheet of paper. "What the hell does this say about Moorhead?"

Cardero glanced at the word Victor pointed to. "It says 'Maybe.'"

"Maybe!" Victor couldn't believe it. "Yesterday Moorhead gave us their word."

Cardero seemed untroubled. "Today they said maybe."

Victor then reviewed for them his day of phone calls—the College Board about to do them in, the tepid support from Milwaukee, the diminished chances of success if the other three campuses didn't follow their lead. One by one he looked narrowly at his advisers and asked, "Do we call a strike vote anyhow?"

"Are you saying we should back down?" asked Cardero in disbelief.

"I'm asking your opinion. Do we call a strike vote?"

"Well, of course," said Cardero, relishing the countless meetings entailed in a strike.

"Alex?"

The heavy woman looked uncertain. "You mean if the board actually does us in . . ."

Victor glanced at his watch. "We're being done in at this very moment."

Alex shuddered and looked to her companion across the table.

"What's to lose, except our chains?" said Kimberly rather

grandly, by which she meant the second-class treatment accorded to women. It had taken a newcomer, Peggy Benoit, to alert her to the unfairness of the two-tiered salary schedule. Peggy herself ought to be on the steering committee, thought Kimberly, but she claimed to be too new in the system and too busy teaching music to be an effective member. Kimberly understood that. Your first year in the classroom was a killer. She often conferred with Peggy anyhow. She drew strength from her. She respected Victor for his energy and union savvy, and she was an old friend of Alex's, having taught with her for over twenty years and roomed with her for part of that time, and of course Aaron was a dependable workhorse, but it was young Peggy Benoit she counted on for direction.

"Alex?" Victor said again.

"Well, I don't see the harm in at least *voting*." If not actually striking, she seemed to mean.

"All right, how's Sunday afternoon?"

"Why Sunday?" asked Alex.

"Nobody's in class."

"How novel," said Kimberly excitedly.

"Two o'clock at Mount of Olives Lutheran. I've got it reserved. If it carries, we give the board forty-eight hours to back down while we get our picket schedule made out, our signs ready, news releases out, and then"—he squealed gleefully, smacking the table with both hands—"we walk off our goddamn jobs!"

His ardor was infectious. Kimberly gave him a peck on the cheek. Aaron Cardero shook his hand warmly while blowing a searing blast on Alex's referee's whistle.

Victor gave Aaron and Kimberly a ride home in his drafty convertible, the three of them packed into its front and only seat. As they passed through the intersection of Sawyer and Eleventh, Aaron said, "We voted on a college motto—it'll go right there, carved in butternut." He pointed to the little snow-crusted hillock in front of McCall Hall.

"I'm afraid to ask," said Kimberly.

"Scholarship and Hockey?" asked Victor, chuckling and pulling at his mustache. He'd put Neil up to submitting that one.

"No, that came in second." Cardero, too, was chuckling.

"Well, tell us," said Kimberly.

"Paul Bunyan's Alma Mater."

Meanwhile, returning from a voice lesson to her office, Peggy was summoned to the phone by the second-floor secretary, a curvy young woman named Deelane Villars, who apparently found it amusing that the beautiful, young newcomer to the music department should be addressed as Dr. Benoit, for she giggled each time she said it.

"She told me not to bother you if you're busy, Dr. Benoit, but it's Lolly Edwards, and I know you just love her radio show."

"I do when I'm on it," Peggy replied. She followed Deelane Villars to her desk, which, because of the office shortage, was located in the language lab, a small room of earphones and travel posters at the head of the stairs. Half a dozen students sat at tables wearing headsets and murmuring to themselves in foreign tongues. The posters displayed airplanes with propellers and women in swimsuits long out of style. Next to Deelane's desk stood an enormous coffee urn giving off the metallic smell of hot wiring.

"Hi, Lolly," said Peggy, stretching the phone cord out into the hallway so as not to disturb the language students.

"Peggy dear, would you mind terribly stopping over tonight after your jam session so we can go over Saturday's show? I realize it's only Wednesday, but I'm swamped the next couple of days and I would dearly love to get this taken care of. It will take us ten minutes at the most."

"Fine, I'll stop in." In order to catch her so often and so precisely by phone, Lolly Edwards had obviously researched her schedule. Either that or she'd put Leland on her tail.

"What I'll need is the names of the choir members you're bringing with you, and their hometowns, and which are the well-spoken ones I can ask questions of. Would you mind terribly? Ten minutes at the most, unless you have time for coffee and a cozy chat in front of the fire."

"I'd better not stay. I've got an early class tomorrow."

It was a fine line Peggy walked with Lolly Edwards. The voice of KRKU was courting her with offers of airtime, every

minute of which Peggy eagerly accepted for the good of the college music program. By appearing twice on "Lolly Speaking"
thus far, Peggy had attracted an audience of unprecedented size
to her winter choral concert. Even President and Mrs. Gengler
had come out to listen—their first public appearance in months.
From the wings, Peggy had watched the president come stooping
down the aisle of the auditorium looking furtive and sickly in
his black suit and his collar too big for his neck. Between numbers, turning to acknowledge the applause, she noticed Mrs.
Gengler giving the president little pats on the arm and whispers
of encouragement—lending him the strength, evidently, to remain in his seat until intermission, after which their places were
empty.

A fair number of faculty couples had turned out as well, including the Oberholtzers, both of them kissing Peggy's cheek at
the postconcert reception and expressing their delight in the size of
the audience, the quality of the music, and the comeliness of
Peggy's gown. Honey Oberholtzer said she was enchanted by its
color—dark green with a scattering of tiny sequins. Her husband, it
was obvious, was intrigued by the dip in its neckline.

Lolly Edwards pleaded, "Because if you *do* have time, Peggy
dear, I'd love to go through some wallpaper samples with you."

"I guess not, Lolly. I'm pretty busy this week." The trick was
to stifle every one of the woman's matchmaking efforts except the
radio show.

"Of course you're busy, you little dynamo. I don't see how
you do everything you do. Leland and I are thinking of redoing his
room, which you maybe haven't seen. Have we ever shown you
Leland's room?"

Peggy rolled her eyes at Georgina Gold, who was hurrying toward her in search of coffee, her empty mug in hand. "No, Lolly, I
haven't seen Leland's room," she said for Georgina's benefit.

This remark brought Georgina to a halt. She leaned far back,
pointing her large nose at the ceiling, and groaned.

"What was that noise?" asked Lolly Edwards.

"Just one of our nutty students going by," said Peggy.

Finding the coffee urn drained dry, the two women put on
their coats, descended the narrow back stairway of McCall Hall,

and made their way against a stiff wind to the student center. Sunlight was flashing on and off between swift-moving clouds. There were hard patches of old snow lying in cloudlike shapes on the dead gray grass.

"When does it get warm?" Peggy asked.

"Any month now," Georgina replied.

"It was sixty in Boston yesterday."

"Count your blessings, it was nine in Winnipeg."

They drank coffee with their coats on because the student center, a new, barnlike structure, was designed to be chilly, its walls of single-pane glass facing the prevailing winds of winter.

"Tell me honestly, Peggy, are you getting serious about Leland?"

"Don't be funny."

"But I mean, his bedroom, Peggy! Lots of us have been given the ground-floor tour, but you'll be the first one upstairs."

"I'd like to change the subject, Georgina. I'd like to know if you've heard what's going on in St. Paul."

"Ron's been down to the basement—he installed their water heater—but nobody's been up where the bedrooms are."

"Georgina!"

Georgina dipped her head, smiling her crimped, humorless little smile. "Sorry."

"Victor says we might be picketing by next week."

Georgina smirked disapprovingly. "Victor Dash," she said with distaste.

"Will you picket with me, Georgina?"

"Are you kidding? Ron would die."

"Listen, we're making two hundred dollars less on every step of the schedule because we're women. It's going to take a strike to get us up where we belong."

"Where we belong! We belong two hundred dollars *above* the men."

"Exactly, but we can pull even with them at least. I can't see you not striking, Georgina. You're not the type to sit back."

Looking out the window at the wind bending the jack pines, Georgina adjusted her engagement ring on her finger. She said, "Let's get back to you and Leland."

Peggy ignored this. "Victor says it's going to happen fast. The

College Board is probably going to freeze our salaries and put all the money into typewriters and toilets."

Georgina looked uncomfortable.

"The Alliance isn't asking for the moon, Georgina. We just want the raise the legislature intended us to have, along with a single salary schedule." Peggy felt herself heating up. "Isn't it time Rookery State joined the civilized world?"

A look of pain crossed her friend's face. She spoke with her eyes on the trees outside. "You're free to go in for that sort of thing, Peggy. You're not engaged to be married."

"For God's sake."

"Ron belongs to the Chamber of Commerce."

"So what, I had a husband straight out of the chamber of horrors—it didn't stop me from living my life."

Georgina shifted her serious gaze indoors to Peggy, who thought she saw a trace of fear mixed with the pain.

"Look, Peggy, most people in Rookery despise college teachers, don't you realize that?"

"They do?"

"They think we're snobs. They think we're lazy because we don't work a forty-hour week."

"Well, we don't. You and I don't, anyway. We work sixty."

"They see us off campus at odd times of the day and they think we're loafing. Ron sees Neil Novotny walking to work at noon and it irks him."

Peggy resisted the urge to say *Ron's a jerk,* and asked instead, "Is that any reason we should go on living like peons—because Neil Novotny writes in the morning and teaches in the afternoon?"

Georgina shook her head vigorously, shook the serious expression off her face and replaced it with an unconvincing smile of goodwill. "I can't picket with you, but I'll vote to strike if it means that much to you."

"Promise?"

"As long as it's by secret ballot. Ron would blow his cork if he thought—"

"Ron's a jerk!" The words were out before she knew it. She reached across the table for her friend's hand, but Georgina withdrew it, her face again registering pain. She sat back, deflated, her eyes riveted once more on the swaying trees.

"God, I'm sorry, Georgina." She tried to expand on this, but words wouldn't come. "Georgina, I'm sorry," she repeated uselessly as her friend got to her feet and left the table.

Peggy watched her walk out the door, watched her walk stiffly along the wall of windows, her coattails whipping in the wind.

The mysterious and handsome new music teacher came to Peggy's high school the year she was a sophomore, and under his direction the music program, never strong, took a turn for the worse. Membership in his choir soon dropped from thirty-two students to nineteen, and about half of them had no talent. His band, at their spring concert, got lost in the middle of "The Skater's Waltz" and had to leave it unfinished and go on to something harder, an arrangement for brass of a Rossini over-ture. This they stumbled through to the end, but shouldn't have, because the disharmony was so hard on the ears that a committee of parents was formed to seek the director's dismissal.

The principal, sent by the committee to confront the music teacher, advised him to resign his position, effective in June.

He said, after a long, thoughtful pause, "I have no intention of re-signing."

"Resign this year," countered the principal, "or I'll fire you next year."

"I'll not resign," he said.

His name was Tillemans. He was a heavy-shouldered, dark-haired man who lived alone in a small apartment and seemed to have no friends. Students called him Tillie the Turtle, a reference to his deliber-ate movements and manner of speaking. Ask him a question or say good morning, and he needed time to formulate a reply. Climbing the school stairways or moving along the narrow passageway leading to the music room, he caused traffic jams. He was about thirty-five years old, not as old as he acted, and the tip of his right forefinger was missing— shot off, it was said, in Korea. While most of his students paid him very little respect, Peggy thought him a genius.

Peggy loved music. Beginning in the seventh grade, she'd sung in the choir, played the saxophone in the band, and now, as a sophomore, she went to Mr. Tillemans for piano lessons. It was clear to Peggy that his shortcomings as a teacher lay in the area of classroom management and had nothing to do with his musical talent. One on one, she found him patient and wise.

She also witnessed, in November and December, the wonders he could work with older, more serious musicians. Having put out a call for adult voices and instrumentalists, with a view to performing Han-del's Messiah *at Christmas, he was gratified by the great number of singers who turned out, along with a few string players and a trumpeter.*

Peggy's brother and sister, Kenny and Connie, were among them. Both Kenny and Connie had moved away from home, Connie to take a job on the other side of Boston, and Kenny to attend law school. Peggy missed them acutely, and it was in order to be near them that she first went to watch them rehearse. Loving the music and intrigued by Mr. Tillemans's methods of putting the choir together, she went back to all the subsequent rehearsals and attended the single public performance, which she thought exquisite beyond any concert she'd ever heard.

She was particularly impressed by three of the soloists: a baritone with a beard, who'd come to rehearsals straight from his job as a meat cutter in a packing plant; a radiologist who, despite missing three of the six rehearsals, sang tenor like James Melton; and a soprano named Diane Kunkel, who moved Peggy practically to tears every time she opened her mouth. When Diane Kunkel sang "I know that my redeemer liveth," Peggy was overtaken by the closest thing she'd ever had to a religious impulse, a feeling that her soul was leaving her body and floating to heights of pure satisfaction. That's when Peggy knew what she must do with her life. She must sing.

The following year, Mr. Tillemans did it again, rose above the discouraging chaos of his high school classes and put together a choir and orchestra of even greater beauty than last time. This year it was Haydn's Creation. *Again Diane Kunkel was the star, but she didn't monopolize Peggy's admiration quite so much as before, because Peggy herself was now in the choir, the only high school student who tried out, and she was enchanted by the graceful way Mr. Tillemans drew melodies in the air with his baton. Her own voice in particular he seemed able to pull effortlessly and magically out of her chest. That's when she made up her mind to do more with her life than simply sing. She must direct other singers.*

It was about this time that Peggy began to sense Mr. Tillemans's fondness for her. He liked to talk with her in the privacy of the practice room during her piano lessons. He told her she was destined for a musical career, perhaps not in piano, for her keyboard accomplishments were quite ordinary, but most certainly in voice because of her timbre and perfect pitch and enunciation and sense of pacing.

"How about band?" she asked breezily, half expecting him to say something scornful about her saxophone playing, which she'd never taken very seriously.

"Yes, band too," he said, "because band is enjoyable for you, more enjoyable than piano, but your voice is your treasure, Peggy." Here he pulled his chair up close to the piano bench and studied her face very intently in an odd way he had, as though her expression were telling him more than she meant it to. She was made uncomfortable by the silence that ensued. Coming back to himself finally, he sat back in his chair, drew in a deep breath, and spoke very ponderously, like someone drugged or brain damaged. "It will be a very great tragedy . . . if you don't become a professional singer or teacher of singing." Then he sat forward again and laid his hand on her arm, brushing his fingertips lightly across her breast as he did so. "Peggy, you owe the world . . . the gift of your voice."

She laughed self-consciously, while resolving to become worthy of his praise.

When in the spring his teaching contract wasn't renewed, Peggy was both sad and relieved. She still felt privileged to be taking lessons from a genius, but less and less of her lesson was devoted to her playing and more and more of it to conversations which, given his long pauses and penetrating gaze, she found hard to sustain. Filling one such pause one day, she asked, "What have you composed lately, Mr. Tillemans?" During rehearsal for Creation, he'd asked the choir to run through a brief hymn of his own, something about the Christ child, which everyone had thought very beautiful. They suggested it be sung in performance, as a lead-in to the oratorio, but he scoffed at the idea, claiming that not only was it unfinished, it would be presumptuous to ally himself with anyone so gifted as the incomparable Haydn.

"Oh, I have not composed for three or four years," he told Peggy.

"What about that little hymn at Christmas?"

"Oh, that old thing . . . very old . . . no, nothing new for three or four years."

"Why?"

"Because when I try to work on something, all I do is doodle."

"Doodling's a start," she told him.

Two lessons later, he placed on the piano a sheet of music with the notation done in his own hand, in pencil, with many erasures. It was called "Bagatelle Number Six."

"Something new?" she asked.

"I wrote it because of what you said."

"What did I say?"

"Doodling was a start, you said."

"Oh." She'd forgotten. "Well, I'm glad I said it, then."

"It isn't finished, but I would like to play it for you."

She started to rise from the bench, but he insisted she remain there, and he sat down beside her. He hunched over the keys for a time, as though he were praying or working up courage, and then he began playing very deliberately, holding the chords much longer than Peggy would have, playing it so slowly, in fact, that it wasn't until the second time through that the melody came clear to her. It sounded like a lullaby, slow and then slower and all of it quite beautiful—though it was hard for her to concentrate on the music rather than the movements of his mutilated finger. The piece ended in midphrase, and he held the last chord until long after its sound had died away. Then he lifted his hands and looked at her.

"Beautiful," she said. "Just beautiful."

"I know it," he said. "I can't believe I wrote it." He said the conclusion was just now coming together in his head, and he asked if she would make the notations while he worked it out on the keyboard.

"Oh, yes," she said, eager to be his accessory.

"It saves time if I don't have to interrupt myself to write." He went to his desk and found new sheets of staff paper and returned to sit beside her, on her left so her right arm would be free for writing.

It was slow work. When the half hour drew to a close, they had covered only four measures. She thought it sounded odd, mostly music for the left hand, and therefore darker and more disturbing than what had gone before. At one point he dropped his idle right hand, not onto his own lap, but onto her left forearm, and this aroused her to feelings far greater than admiration. It set off the alarms of love. She kept glancing at him, unsure if he realized where his hand was. He seemed too engrossed in composing to notice. At the bell, she hurried off to her English class, feeling feverish.

The next week they went at it again. This time, late in the session, she was startled to feel his hand on her shoulder.

"I'm afraid this is turning very somber," he said. "What do you think?"

She thought of pointing out that perhaps the piece needed more of his right hand, but she was breathless and didn't trust her voice. Nor was she sure what she ought to be feeling. His hand was very warm and comforting, but when he moved it slightly toward her neck, she flinched. Again the bell rang, as though his advances were carefully timed to be interrupted. For the rest of that week she thought of little else but her body and how its various parts would feel if touched by the hand of the composer.

At the next session, her last before summer vacation, Mr. Tillemans's hand was very low on her back when the bell rang. She didn't get up to go. She'd confided in her best friend about the composer's wandering hand, and this friend, a boy-crazy girl named Anita, had shrieked excitedly and said kissing was next. Peggy sincerely hoped so. She wasn't yet permitted to date boys, not till next year, and had never kissed one. She was certain that no boy her age could ever measure up to this sensitive man home from the war with a shortened finger and mysterious, penetrating eyes. She lost sleep yearning for the kiss of this genius and imagining intimacies beyond that.

But there was no kiss, only the hand on her lower spine. "I guess this is as far as we can go," said Mr. Tillemans, his eyes on the unfinished score. Withdrawing his hand, he rose from the bench. She rose too, and studied his face for a sign of longing or love, but she saw nothing of the sort. When he offered to shake her hand, she ran from the room and wept in the lavatory.

The rest of the week she skipped choir and band, and avoided running into him in the hallways. When she got her report card and found her grade lowered from A to B for these absences, she felt no resentment or anger. What she felt was sad for a while, then wistful, and finally privileged to have known Mr. Tillemans and to have been some small help to him as a composer, and to have learned so much by his example as a director, and perhaps—who knows?—to have been a bit of a comfort to him as a lonely, friendless man. She would go looking elsewhere for the kiss of a genius.

Across campus, in his studio-classroom on the second floor of the industrial arts building, Connor laid his palette aside and studied the two faces smiling at him from the canvas. He was getting nowhere. Belinda Ashby's smile was cloyingly sweet. Some girls of seven had personalities (his daughter Laura had been a clown at that age), but this one's face was angelically bland. He guessed he'd have to quit trying to make it interesting. He couldn't paint what wasn't there.

This double portrait had been commissioned by J. W. Ashby, president of Rookery Power and Light, as a gift to his wife on their tenth anniversary. Mrs. Ashby, a handsome woman much younger than her husband, loved her daughter's image on the canvas, but was dissatisfied with her own. Yesterday, at the end of their third and final sitting (after three sittings, Connor worked from photos), Mrs. Ashby had given the canvas the briefest of glances and Connor the stiffest of good-byes. He assumed she didn't like the way he'd thrust her head forward and worked the tightness of apprehension into her neck muscles and brow. On her lips was the smile she had requested and painfully held throughout all three sittings, but the eyes belied the smile. He had given her face so much power that it dominated the seven-year-old at her shoulder. Her expression said to the viewer, *Here you see my beloved little daughter—admire her, but keep your distance.* Hanging in a gallery, the intensity of the mother's expression might very likely stop even the casual viewer and instruct him in the anxieties of parenthood, but as J. W. Ashby's gift to his wife, it was certain to be a failure. Well, he had to paint what he saw.

He turned politely away from the canvas and yawned. This was the point in Connor's afternoon when he either judged himself fit for more work or gave up and quit. On a good day he could paint longer before putting down his palette and hurrying over to the music department for an hour or so of practice on his bass, but today, because of the noise from downstairs and because of his failure to bring the sweet-faced doll to life, he decided to call it quits. A machine of some kind, probably a band saw, had been screaming in the woodworking shop for an hour or more, compounding the edginess he normally felt when a day's work brought him no closer to achieving his vision. What were they sawing down there—entire oak trees lengthwise? What ran in Belinda Ashby's veins—Kool-Aid?

He made quick work of cleaning his brushes, for he was eager to make music. The quintet had come into being at the most propitious time for Connor, reawakening his boyhood interest in popular songs and filling the space in his life formerly occupied by alcohol. Three or four afternoons a week he spent an hour in one of the tiny practice rooms in the music wing of McCall Hall. This hour of private playing, formerly his hour of private drinking, was a holy time for him, the kind of relaxing reprieve he required between painting portraits and going home to Marcy, both of which tightened him up.

Marcy, though physically present, seemed to have packed up her soul and fled. While Connor was in the hospital, she'd gone out and bought a single bed and had it installed in the dining room, the only space large enough for it in the tiny house. She'd done this, she said, because Connor would need their bedroom all to himself while he recuperated. Although he hadn't understood why this should be so, he hadn't argued. Breathing, at that point, required all his attention. But now, although he was far along on the road to recovery, Marcy did not return to their marriage bed. Instead, she went back to the store for a dresser and ordered a cardboard armoire from a catalog; then she completed the separation by hanging a curtain across the doorway to what was now her bedroom, though she still referred to it as the dining room.

She spoke to Connor only when necessary, and then usually from behind the curtain, for she seldom came out when he was home. He made a point of going in and standing at her bedside every evening, and there he would talk to her remorsefully about his years as a drinker, taking the blame for their damaged relationship. He'd offer to help her find counseling or whatever she needed in order to rise out of her depression. She seldom responded with anything but silence. The other day she'd ordered him never again to say the word "depression" in her presence. She said it depressed her.

He'd hoped that his sobriety might arouse her interest, but if she noticed this monumental change in him, she did not rejoice or say encouraging things or act relieved in any way. She seemed to have decided to sever her links with everyone but Laura, whose access to her mother's thinking, though limited, was not completely cut off, and to live out the rest of her life in bed.

Connor carefully laid his brushes out to dry on his worktable, then he carried his palette into the office he shared with the other art professors and slipped it into the freezing compartment of their small refrigerator, in order to preserve the glistening gobs of color. Until January, the shelf designated as his in the lower half had contained mostly soft-drink bottles with rubber stoppers filled with gin and vermouth, but now he used it only to keep his orange juice cold. Since he had the office to himself for the moment, he sang softly the opening bars of "Stormy Weather" as he hung up his paint-spotted smock and zipped himself into his coat, a bulky sheepskin garment of wooden toggles and large front pockets containing pencils and a couple of small sketching tablets.

He went down the steps and outside into the bracing wind. Crossing the campus in the direction of McCall Hall, he stopped between the library and the power plant and looked out over the river valley. Taking in the shades of gray and blue in the river ice and the snowy shadows on the far bank, he thought back to the first years of his marriage. He wished he could have them back. They were the only time he could recall, boy or man, when his home life was unclouded by smoldering tempers or black moods—his parents' as well as Marcy's. And quite often, of course, the blackest moods had been his own.

The cold wind made him shiver. He went into the student center for a hot drink, and there he saw Peggy Benoit sitting alone at a table and staring out a window. Her posture suggested inertia, which struck him as curious. She was known for her nonstop energy. He'd never before seen her woolgathering.

He carried his cup of hot water to her table, and she brightened at the sight of him. He wasn't surprised. Ever since that Saturday afternoon in Neil's basement—the afternoon of his last taste of alcohol and very nearly his last day alive—he'd been aware of this woman's fondness for him.

"Mind if I join you?"

Her smile was her answer. It speeded up his heartbeat and made the nape of his neck tingle. The smile today contained a hint of melancholy, which he thought made her particularly beautiful.

Sitting down, he unbuttoned his coat and reached into his shirt pocket for a tea bag. His shirt was faded blue denim, with a streak of fresh blue paint between the top two buttons where his ragged smock had left him unprotected.

"Sky blue," she said, lightly touching the paint with her little finger and smudging it on a paper napkin.

"Eye blue," he corrected her. "The eyes of Mrs. J. W. Ashby and her daughter Belinda."

"How's it coming?" Several days ago, popping in on her way to a committee meeting, she'd seen the canvas in its early stages.

"It's half good," he said, unwrapping the tea bag and lowering it into the water. He smiled and added, "The half they won't like."

"Commissions must be hard."

"Hard to come by. Around here."

"I mean having to please yourself and your sitter both."

He nodded. "And in this case the sitter's husband, who's paying for it."

"Do you ever not get paid?"

"Never so far."

They fell silent and studied each other for a moment. Under her smile he saw gravity, worry. Then the smile faded and he saw more. Sadness. Yearning.

"What's the matter, Peggy?" His voice was little more than a whisper, all but lost in his beard.

She blushed a little, sorted through the three or four things troubling her at the moment, and picked out the least serious. "Connor, is it true that we're hated?"

He looked puzzled. "Hated? Who's hated?"

"The faculty, by the rest of Rookery."

He chuckled behind his beard. "I'm no expert on the local worthies, but I should think 'hated' might be overstating it."

"Georgina Gold claims they detest us."

"Does she say why?"

"Because we don't punch a time clock."

He looked skeptical. "Hardly seems a very good reason, does it?"

"And we're snobs, she says."

He mulled this over and decided Georgina Gold was wrong. "This is the second faculty I've been on. The one in the city—Cass College—has far more snobs. Of course, it's also a better faculty."

Peggy nodded regretfully. "By and large we're not an inspiring bunch, are we?"

He chuckled.

"Why did you leave Cass?"

He smiled and shrugged, unwilling to go into it.

"I mean, you left a very good campus of your own free will."

His beard rearranged itself over a broader smile. "How do you know?"

"Because no college likes to lose an artist like you."

He made a scoffing noise in his nose. No need to go into all the things he'd hoped to leave behind in Minneapolis, including his attachment to the Lock and Dam Saloon on University Avenue. Cass College had been good to him, had provided him with an adequate salary, a solitary studio, and a light load of fairly gifted students. His colleagues and a regent or two had implored him to stay. However, he saw this move into the Northwoods as a chance, perhaps his last, to save his health and his marriage and set his daughter on a fresh course through adolescence. His daughter, despite her intelligence, had a talent for attracting sinister companions.

"I adore your paintings, Connor."

"Which ones?" he asked, aware that many of his patrons had been disappointed when he turned from landscapes.

"All of them." She said this firmly, and watched him color and squirm. Was this false modesty, or didn't the man really know how good he was? "What's the matter," she asked, "can't you take praise?"

"Please," he said. He removed his tea bag and sipped.

"You're the opposite of Neil—do you realize that? Neil can't take criticism and you can't take praise."

"I worry about Neil," he said.

"I know. His students don't have much respect for him."

"I don't mean his teaching, I mean his writing. He's too private about it. Too intense."

"More private than you."

"With me it's okay, I'm older. My training's behind me. But this is Neil's first novel, am I right?"

She nodded.

"So who's reading it? Who's advising him?"

She shrugged. "He says he learns by reading."

"Well, of course, but reading will only take him so far. I mean, I learned a lot from looking at paintings, but to get started I had to be taught technique. Nobody's teaching him technique."

"Tell him that."

"I can do better than tell him. I can put him in touch with somebody who'll read his book and judge it."

"Oh, do, Connor." Her eyes got big and serious. "Oh, please do."

"A fellow I know at Cass. He owes me any number of favors. He knows good writing from bad."

"Wonderful. Will you bring it up tonight?"

"Maybe *you* should."

"No, he thinks of you as the master."

"Oh, I doubt that. I don't think he cares much for my work."

"He doesn't. He's told me. But he has this enormous respect for *how* you work. Remember last week, your little pep talk about mixing art with teaching? Well, you had such an impact, he's even been trying to be a good teacher."

"We came at him from four directions, as I recall."

He recalled, too, that there seemed to be a good bit of sexual energy in Peggy's impact on Neil. It had been more obvious on Neil's side than Peggy's, as though she might be oblivious to the enchantment she was working on her cousin-in-law. But you never could tell. Maybe her blithe way with him was a disguise, and she knew exactly what she was doing. Hell, for all Connor knew, she might be sleeping with him.

Peggy looked at her watch and stood up from the table. They carried their cups to the counter, where she replenished her coffee, he his tea, then carried them outside.

"And you?" he asked, raising his voice above the wind. "What brought you here?"

"The only job I was offered. A fluke year for music majors. I'm told a lot more positions are opening up for next fall."

"Will you move?"

She shrugged. "If you'd asked me a couple of months ago, I would've said yes, definitely. Now I don't know. I've started some things here that might take a while."

"The quintet."

She laughed, and this puzzled him. "Building up the choir—it was really pretty ragged. Also building up the women's salary schedule."

They entered McCall Hall through the rear door, at the bottom of the narrow back stairway.

"Will you vote to strike?" she asked, and in the same breath answered for him. "Of course you will. Don't say no."

He looked amused. "It won't come to a vote."

Big eyes again, not amused. "Connor, haven't you heard? The board is almost certain to withhold our salary appropriation."

"It's all just a game," he said, climbing the stairs at her side.

"No it's not. Victor's already having the ballots printed."

He wasn't convinced. "College faculties never strike. They make threats and hope for a compromise."

"The board isn't about to compromise."

"Boards don't have to. Faculties always back down."

"Not this one. We need your vote."

He shook his head. "I never go to meetings."

"But *this* meeting, Connor. This once."

"Meetings take the edge off my painting. This week alone, if I let myself, I could be sitting with three committees."

"This week I have six."

"Good God." He looked horrified. *Was* horrified. "Six!"

When they reached the second floor, he said, "I wonder, would you have any records I could practice with? Some old standards like the ones we play? Ella or Sarah or somebody?"

"Come on, there's a stack of records in the music library." She led him along the hallway and into the language lab. "I've been meaning to see what they are, but I haven't had time."

The shapely Deelane Villars, at Peggy's request, drew a key

from her desk, wiggled her way to the back of the room, and unlocked the closet known as the music library.

"Thank you," said Peggy and Connor together, and Deelane blushed and giggled.

There were stacks of records in dusty jackets, also many tattered volumes of Czerny and Thomson and other exercise books for the piano, as well as cantata scores from earlier regimes—Handel, Haydn, Vaughn Williams. Most of the records were 78s, including a number of singles from the big-band era. They found several vocal numbers, but not a voice Connor was looking for.

"Joni James?" Peggy offered.

"No. She overdoes it."

"Rosemary Clooney?"

"No, it's got to be somebody doing what you do with a song."

"What do I do?"

He paused in his search, a record in each hand, and considered how he might describe her voice. "You just sing it."

She laughed. "Well, that's what every singer does."

He looked irritated by this, and a little hurt. "Don't play dumb, Peggy. You've got the perfect voice for the pieces we do, and we're all trying to be good enough for you."

She made no reply. His earnest tone, the seriousness in his eyes, confirmed how intensely important the quintet was to him. She was moved by his gravity—indeed, it excited her—and yet she felt daunted by it. How could anything so crucial be any fun?

"What time is it?" she asked.

"Four."

"I've got time to be Ella myself. Come on."

While she hurried down the hallway putting her ear to the doors of the five practice rooms and finding the last one unoccupied, Connor went into the band room and came out with his bass.

Deelane Villars, continually fascinated by Peggy, was so excited to see the two of them enter the room at the end of the corridor that she immediately phoned her friend in the bursar's office, a gossipy young woman named Nicole, and reported what looked like a budding romance. "They're in there together right now, as I speak, and what do you want to bet they're kissing and stuff? Students do it all the time in these rooms."

"Is he the one with the beard?" Nicole wanted to know.

"That's him. The big guy, over in art."

"The one with the mystery wife?"

"Next thing to a mental case, they say."

"So you think they're fooling around?"

"Well, I can't see through doors, Nicole, but what would you make of it if you saw them go in that tiny, tiny room together? I mean he's this shaggy, handsome man, and she's got these real kissy lips and I think she's got a crush on him."

Deelane, an authority on crushes in the workplace, was never wrong. On the narrow back stairway, Peggy had trembled at Connor's nearness, his furry voice so close to her ear, his casual touch, elbow to arm, as they climbed, and now crowded into an eight-by-ten room with an old upright piano and a bass fiddle, she was suddenly warm—actually perspiring—with anticipation. Exactly what she expected she couldn't have said, perhaps something as simple as a word of brotherly reassurance, some sort of salve to heal the abrasion she'd suffered with Georgina Gold. She removed her coat and laid it together with his on top of the piano.

Bending over his instrument, his ear to the strings as he tuned them, he revealed a slight balding spot at the crown of his head. Gazing at this bit of scalp, she imagined herself kissing it. Insane, she thought, and turned abruptly away. She stepped around the piano, putting it between them, and hummed a few experimental notes as she looked out the small, grimy window. The sun was lowering itself into a stand of pines, but the diminishing light seemed not to darken the campus so much as to leech it of all color—the stark blankness of a February afternoon in the North.

Then she began to sing. She sang several bars of "I'll Get By" before Connor came in with his bass, and when he did, her voice quavered with emotion. He assumed this was stage emotion, manufactured and rehearsed, and he thought it very convincing, her tone so much fuller than usual, her low tones heavier and deeper. Playing very softly, allowing her to be quietly breathy, he wondered why she didn't sing this way with the group.

It wasn't stage emotion, that was why. Singing without the rest of the quintet, she was feeling so close to Connor, so helplessly entangled in his strings, and at the same time so lonely and sad, that she was moved nearly to tears. Singing with her back to his slow, thumping rhythm, she felt as if he were tenderly strumming her spine.

The second time through, in order to keep from weeping with desire, she teased him into a slightly faster tempo, but it felt wrong. "I'll Get By" was not written as a lament, but today the words struck her as lamentable. As long as I have Connor, she was thinking as she sang, while assuming she never would.

So the third time through, she gave in to her mood and made a dirge of it, sang low and slow and a little on the sour side. Connor filled in her long wordless pauses by somberly climbing and descending the scale and wishing she would turn and face him so he could indicate by a nod of his head how fantastic she was. He'd never before been instrumental in anything so heavy with emotion. Indeed, he'd scarcely ever heard its like on record.

Her pauses grew longer and longer as she neared the end, and then seeing her suddenly straighten her shoulders and lift her head, he improvised a cadenza leading up to what he expected would be a strong finale delivered with renewed energy in her voice. But her silence continued. He plucked his strings softly and more softly, until he was barely touching them, and then, assuming that she was caught up in some private reverie (which she was), he stopped playing altogether and sat down on the piano bench to wait respectfully for her to turn and face him.

She did so, eventually, with tears running down her face. Color had risen in her cheeks, and the whites of her large eyes were pink and damaged-looking. Her sorrow was accentuated by the smile she was trying to show him.

"What is it?" he asked, alarmed, but not so alarmed that he wasn't picturing the colors he might mix in order to capture her flushed complexion.

She dug into her coat for a hankie and blew her nose. "You caught me on a bad day."

He shifted himself on the bench, indicating there was room for her, but she didn't sit. She turned back to the window and said, "When you found me in the cafeteria, I had just insulted Georgina, and she left me sitting there remembering the day my husband left me."

"Your husband? You had a husband?" Because there was such a young and innocent aspect to her beauty, he'd been thinking of her in a daughterly, virginal way. He was astonished.

"It was a day a lot like this one. Clouds and sunshine and a nasty wind off Boston Harbor. I was researching Rameau."

"Wait a minute, I didn't know you had a husband."

"For eight months. A photographer for the *Globe*. His name was Gene." Her words became steam on the window glass as she spoke, clouding her view. "I came home from the library and found our turntable and speakers missing from the living room and most of his clothes gone from the closet. At first I couldn't believe he'd cleared out. *I'd* been the one threatening to leave."

There was a long pause, and then she told Connor, as though he'd asked, "Because he wasn't nice to me."

She said no more for a while. She wiped her breath from the windowpane and watched a pair of students leave the library and lean into the wind, heading for their dormitory. She saw Leland Edwards, holding his hat on his head, cross Eleventh Street on his way home.

When she took up the story again, it was to say she didn't believe at first that he'd left for good. Weeks passed before she stopped listening for the car at the curb and his heavy step on the stairs, and it was longer than that before the shock of it was entirely dissipated and she realized how relieved she was to be free of him. Up to that point, she'd spent her idle moments going over his character traits, looking for those she'd have difficulty living without. There were some. Not many, but some.

A knock on the door. Connor, without rising from the bench, leaned over and opened it. Deelane Villars handed him a slip of paper. "Phone call for Dr. Benoit," she said, giggling. "I'm leaving now, so I thought I should tell her."

"Thank you," said Connor.

Deelane leaned in for a better look at Peggy, who did not turn from the window. "See you in the morning, Dr. Benoit."

"Thanks, Deelane."

"Bye-bye," she chirped, pulling the door shut.

Peggy came around the piano and picked up her coat. She stood facing Connor on the bench as she read the slip of paper.

"I've got a student coming in." Smiling down at him, she applied a hankie to her reddened eyes.

"I can go and tell him to come back another time," Connor offered.

"Thanks, but no," she said.

Connor made a move to rise from the bench, but she stood so close in front of him that their knees were practically touching.

"Thanks for the song," he said. "It was . . ." No adequate word came to mind for its beauty.

"Sure," she said, continuing to smile sadly down at him.

Before embracing her around the hips, he sat there for a moment, prudently making sure her closeness was an invitation and not necessitated by the smallness of the room. It had been months since his wife had allowed him to touch her, and so the feel of this woman's flesh through her wool skirt caused a roaring in his ears that intensified when she dropped her coat, lowered herself to her knees, pressed herself between his legs, and kissed him.

When Connor arrived home for supper, his daughter asked him what was wrong, he looked so distracted. He told her it was nothing.

"No, it's something," Laura insisted. She had just applied fresh lipstick and was wearing one of her mother's aprons. She enjoyed playing housewife, a role her mother had relinquished. She was chewing a large wad of gum.

Slowly, as though in a trance, Connor removed his coat and laid it across the back of the couch.

"Daddy! When will you learn to hang up your clothes?"

"I'm going out again," he told her.

"That's no excuse."

He forced Peggy from his mind and stepped over to the curtain dividing the dining room from the rest of the house. He said, "Hi, Marcy" in a tone Laura hated. It was higher and happier than his normal voice, entirely out of place in these depressing gray rooms.

Marcy spoke from behind the curtain. "Did you get my medicine?"

"I did." He returned to the couch and took a bottle of capsules from his coat. It was a mild tranquilizer prescribed by her doctor in the city, a poor diagnostician, in Connor's opinion. She needed stimulation, not sedation. "Here it is," he said, drawing aside the curtain and stepping over to the bed.

She lay, facing away from him, in a tangle of bedclothes—a red Hudson Bay blanket, a yellow afghan, and a patchwork quilt. The sheets and pillowcases were not fresh. "Put it on the table," she mumbled.

"It's your last refill, Marcy."

"Well . . ." she said, indicating she had more to say, but not quite yet. It required great effort for her to speak to this man standing over her bed, this selfish, improvident husband who had removed her from the city to this squalid little house in the wilderness. She drew in a long breath and let it out slowly. Her voice came out cracked and flat. "I can write for a new prescription."

"You can," he replied, "but you ought to see somebody in Rookery. I can ask my doctor who he'd recommend for problems like yours." Connor had already proposed this a number of times, but he wanted her assent before going ahead.

"Problems like mine?" There was the slightest hint of a laugh in her voice as she spoke to the wall. "Nobody has problems like mine."

"I know it seems that way, Marcy. But they do."

"No, not for long. If they have problems like mine, they get over them."

"And you can too."

"By dying."

"Marcy."

"By their own hand."

He stood there in silent anguish, not wanting the conversation to end on this low note, yet lacking the words to elevate it.

Laura called from the kitchen: "Daddy, would you come and set the table?"

He bent over and laid his hand gently on his wife's cheek. "Come out and eat with us."

She said nothing.

The phone rang in the kitchen. Laura answered it. "Daddy, it's for you."

"Please come eat with us," he repeated.

His wife pulled the sheet up over her cheek. "Your hand is cold."

"Daddy."

He went to the kitchen, where Laura was standing over a double boiler on the stove.

"Have you ever had tuna before?" she asked, looking amused.

"Yesterday, as I recall."

"Oh, really? Then you must like it." Laughing, she tipped her head back and shook her long blond hair away from her eyes.

He picked up the phone. He didn't recognize the woman's voice declaring stridently, "This is the Telephone Tree!"

"What did you say?"

"The Alliance Telephone Tree."

"Who is this?"

"Alex Bolus. We met last fall, I'm in phys ed."

"Oh, yes."

"Big news from St. Paul, Connor. The board just took all our money and poured it into cement, so we've set our strike vote for Sunday at Mount of Olives Lutheran—two o'clock. Got your numbers handy there?"

"What numbers?"

"We gave you three numbers."

"When? What for?"

"The Telephone Tree. There's twelve numbers on your branch."

"Look, I have no idea what you're talking about."

"You call three people and they each call three more. We gave out the numbers at the last Alliance meeting."

"Well, that explains it. I don't go to meetings."

"Besides that, we sent out the whole list through campus mail."

"I must have lost it." He didn't admit to Miss Bolus that he seldom checked his campus mailbox.

"Anyhow, here's your three numbers. Got a pencil?"

Connor stepped over to the kitchen table, where Laura had been doing her homework. He wrote the numbers and names on a sheet of her scratch paper. One of the numbers was that of a colleague named Sims in the art department. Another belonged to an academic counselor named Mackensie. The third was Neil Novotny's number.

He thwarted Miss Bolus's attempt to dictate all twelve numbers. "These three can call you if they don't have the numbers you gave them."

"Okay, just make sure you give them the whole message. All our salary money's going down a rat hole, and we're voting to strike Sunday at two. Mount of Olives Lutheran."

"Why in a church?"

"Because—I'm quoting Victor now—because our dean's a slimy bastard."

"So we're praying for him, or what?"

Alex Bolus laughed. "He won't let the Alliance meet on campus."

Connor said good-bye and hung up. He cleared away his daughter's schoolwork and set the table. Then he stood transfixed for nearly a minute, his mind drawn back again to the practice room of the music wing, the woman kneeling before him, the feel of her narrow waist between his thighs, the warmth of her mouth on his.

"Daddy! Tell me what it is. Your eyes are funny."

He said wearily that it was probably Belinda Ashby's fault. "She's seven, and her portrait's giving me a lot of trouble."

Laura turned back to the stove and resumed her strenuous stirring of the thick concoction in the double boiler. "After this, don't try to hide things from me."

He promised he wouldn't.

"What are those numbers?"

"People I'm supposed to call." He told her about the strike vote.

"Can't it wait? The tuna's ready."

"It can wait." He went to the doorway and called to Marcy, then he and Laura sat down and waited to see if she would join them. They heard the squeak of bedsprings, the jingle of hangers—she was rising from bed. In a minute or so she emerged from behind the curtain wearing her shapeless brown robe over her pajamas. Her graying hair was uncombed. Connor hadn't yet grown accustomed to the roundness of her face. She'd put on twenty pounds this winter.

They greeted her, Connor in his falsely hopeful tone, Laura half swallowing the word "Mom" and looking away.

Marcy sat down at her place. Nibbling a lettuce leaf and bits of macaroni, she watched her daughter's attention turn inward. It was one of the reasons she hated coming to the table—Laura greeting her coldly and then swiftly retreating inside herself. It was a great sorrow of Marcy's that their mother-daughter bond was all but severed, but she was much too tired to do anything about it.

They ate in silence. She saw that her husband, too, was distracted. His painting often caused him to look unfocused like this, which was fine with her because it kept his mouth shut and left her in peace. The worst thing was when she joined them for supper and he said cheery things like what a nice day it had been, or how much brighter her eyes were looking. As a drunk, he'd been hard enough to take. Playing Pollyanna, he was insufferable. She lowered her eyes to her plate of too much food.

"Marcy, I'm going to see my doctor about your tiredness."

So it was tiredness now. Well, that was more accurate than depression. She wiped her mouth with the back of her hand and pushed her plate away. She was extremely tired.

"I've been waiting for you to give me the go-ahead, Marcy. I don't think we can wait any longer."

She gathered her robe tight to her throat and faced him with an expression she hoped he'd interpret as hate.

"I mean if we're going to have any kind of life, the three of us . . ."

She rose from the table and dragged herself back to bed.

Neil's writing had slowed nearly to a standstill. While Lydia moved stealthily downstream, running from Zastrow, the libidinous courthouse clerk, Neil was scarcely able to put one word in front of another. It had taken him a week to get his heroine up over the top of the wooded knoll where she discovered herself at the edge of a small town. Her skirt is torn and her hair hangs in strings over her eyes. She has lost a shoe and her foot is bloody. She follows the dusty street downhill to the center of town, ignoring the curious stares of the townspeople. She finds a wharf, peopled with riverboat travelers and a man with a dray wagon full of wooden crates and bags of grain. Lydia prays that the boat they're waiting for is headed downstream. If it's going upstream, Zastrow's direction, she won't dare board it. "Oh Lord, dear Lord, spare me from this fiend who is determined to have his way with me."

The ringing telephone drew Neil out of his work. He pushed his chair back from the Ping-Pong table and went into the bedroom, where a pan he'd forgotten on the hot plate was giving off the searing aroma of scorching soup. It looked and smelled like tomato. He hadn't read the label when he opened the can.

"Neil speaking."

"Neil, it's Connor. Did you know you're on my branch of the Telephone Tree?"

"Sure, you don't share an office with Victor Dash without knowing things like that."

"Well, I've got it straight from the trunk—the board took away our increase in salary, and we're voting Sunday on whether to strike."

"No surprise."

"Tell me whose side I should be on. I haven't been paying attention."

"I'm voting to strike."

"Why?"

"Because you can't share an office with Victor—"

"Yeah, I see that, but is a strike really necessary? Are you an avid member of the Alliance, or what?"

"I'm not an avid member of anything."

"I didn't think so. Is the quintet together on this?"

"I doubt if Leland is. He gets real quiet when Victor starts preaching."

Connor was silent for a few moments before asking, "Isn't it risky, giving up our paychecks for the duration of a strike? Who can afford that?"

"I hear the Alliance has a fund to pay us."

"They do? You mean our whole salary?"

"I don't know. We'll have to ask Victor."

"And then there's health insurance. That stops, doesn't it?"

"Maybe not. Maybe the Alliance takes care of that too."

Another pause. "Don't you sometimes wonder if the Alliance is all sound and fury and no logic?"

"I guess I haven't given it that much thought, Connor. I've been working on my novel."

"Ah, yes, of course. How's it going?"

Coming from an accomplished artist, this question went like a probe to the heart of Neil's self-doubt. He had all he could do to keep fear out of his voice. "I'm worried, Connor. I can't get up any speed. I can't turn it out the way I did at the beginning. I go plodding along, stopping and starting. Right now I'm trying to get my main girl to board a riverboat, but I can't get the riverboat to come down the river. Do you ever have times like that?"

"Sure. Today was one of them."

"But I mean more than a day. I mean all last week, all this week. I mean ever since I started getting serious about teaching."

"It can happen. It's temporary."

Neil's voice took on a whiny undertone. "Connor, you said I should do it."

"Do what?"

"Teach and write."

There was a long pause before Connor replied icily, "Sorry, Neil, I'm not responsible for your writer's block."

"But you said I could do both." He realized how childish he must sound, but he didn't care.

"That isn't what I said." Connor sounded perturbed. "I said teaching can often fit very nicely into an artist's routine. I didn't mean every artist in the entire world. I imagine there are cases—"

"What made you think I'd even *want* to be a good teacher? It's thankless work, Connor. It takes everything you've got, and what does it give back? I worked hard to build up my enrollment, and I stayed up till two o'clock this morning working on my poetry lecture, and what do I get for it? I get the dean interrupting my class to give me hell, I get a neurotic student saying I'm driving her crazy with poems about death, and I get three dozen students in revolt because one of them loves a poet who turns out to be a sobsister. Jesus, Connor—"

Neil grew suddenly short of breath. Fear was drying up his mouth, fear that his desire to be a novelist, no matter how intense, might not be enough to produce a publishable book. What if he didn't have the talent? The patience? The publisher? Until this moment, he'd never seriously imagined failing.

There was a drawn-out "Aaaah" on the wire, as if Connor were having his throat examined, but his words, when they came, were quick and sharp. "We all know how you built up your enrollment, Neil. You put out the word that you were handing out A's."

If this was indignation, it fit Neil's desperate mood. He packed all the defiance he could into a single syllable. "So?"

"So I'm just saying it couldn't have been *too* much work filling your sections."

"Well, that's beside the point, isn't it? Isn't the point that I'm being treated like scum?" He felt himself sinking into a warmly satisfying pool of self-pity. "Doesn't how I'm treated mean anything to anybody?"

Connor said softly, "Relax, Neil."

"How long am I expected to go on trying to make silk purses out of sows' ears if the administration and the student body treat me like scum?"

There was no reply to this.

"Connor?" he said, chagrined now, afraid he'd gone too far.

After a few moments he said it again. "Connor?"

"Neil, you need a break from your book."

"I do?"

"You live with it day and night. Sometimes an artist needs time away. How long have you been working on it?"

"Since I moved to Rookery."

"With how much time off?"

"Christmas, both years. I went home for four or five days."

"How about summers?"

"Stayed and worked on it. Minnesota's cooler than Ohio summers."

"And this is your first novel."

"Right."

"It's time for somebody to read it, Neil."

"I've read parts to Peggy. I don't think she likes it."

"I mean a mentor. Somebody to take it off your hands and give it a thorough reading and tell you what he thinks."

"I don't know anybody like that."

"I do. His name is Emerson Tate."

Silence on the line.

"He's at Cass College. He writes literary criticism."

"No thanks, I'm not writing for eggheads." Handing Lydia over to a professional critic seemed as cruel as turning her over to Zastrow. In both cases, she'd return to him violated.

"Tate's a practical sort of guy. He's on the editorial board of a small press in St. Paul. I did some charity work for his board one time—illustrated a little book they put out for unwed mothers. I could ask him to return the favor and read your novel."

"What press is that?"

"T. Woodman."

"Never heard of it."

"Neil, for God's sake!" Connor sounded as if he might hang up in disgust, but the connection remained open.

"Well, what I mean, Connor, you can't have just anybody pick up your novel and pass judgment on it." T. Woodman Press. No doubt some stuffy little print shop putting out books only a scholar could love. *The History of the Hyphen Since 1066.*

"Connor?"

"You got your three numbers to call?"

"Yeah, somewhere around here."

"See you tonight, then."

"Say, Connor." He hated to lose the artist on the line. "Thanks."

"Don't mention it."

"It's just that you have to know a guy's credentials before you turn your work over to him."

"Emerson Tate's got the credentials, trust me on that."

"Okay, put me in touch," said Neil, but Connor had already hung up.

He stepped over to his hot plate and burned his fingers on the handle of the pan. Cursing, he opened another can of soup. Bean, said the label. He poured it over the crusted remains of tomato. He wadded a slice of bread into a ball and put it in his mouth; then he opened a beer and carried it back to Lydia Harker. There she stands on the worn, sun-heated planks of the wharf, concealing her bloody foot under her long skirt and anxiously waiting for a boat to carry her away to safety.

On his way home, Victor had stopped at a garage to have his idling adjusted, and then he went shopping for groceries, so the news didn't reach him until he sat down to supper with his family. As soon as Annie said Aaron Cardero had called, he shot out of his chair and dialed the phone on the kitchen wall. At the first words over the wire, he emitted a broken howl, like Tarzan's.

"What's the matter with Daddy?" asked his seven-year-old, a dour little boy whose habit it was to cringe in his father's presence.

"Nothing's the matter, Donnie," said his mother. "Daddy's just heard some wonderful news."

Five-year-old Vicky shared her brother's misgivings, gaping with apprehension at her father, who hung up the phone and turned to his family with a renewed and louder cry of triumph.

The youngest of the three children, a four-year-old boy, turned red in the face and cried tears of happiness. This was the Dashes' overwrought child, Marky by name, who strove nervously to conform to his father's moods.

"Goddammit, Annie, you're looking at the George Washington of campus work stoppage. Can you believe I'm leading that bunch of bookworms out on strike? The College Board doesn't believe it either. They think we're nothing but sheep." He wheeled on Donnie, who hunkered down in his chair. "The College Board is about to get the surprise of their lives, so don't think they aren't." Then to his wife: "Aren't they, Annie? Aren't they going to just piss their pants?"

The Telephone Tree (Kimberly Kraft's branch) conveyed the news to the Edwardses as Lolly was serving Leland a bowl of chicken soup. She stretched the telephone cord across the kitchen so her son wouldn't have to rise from his chair.

"I'm not surprised," he told Kimberly. "What surprises and disappoints me is the number of old hands going over to Victor's side, including yourself."

"We don't think of it as Victor's side," she replied. "It's the side of justice for women and enlightenment for all."

Oh, my. Kimberly was given to this sort of grandiose language. He responded in like terms. "You've been the heart and soul of the education department for as long as I can remember, Kimberly. Why would you ever want to throw aside your reputation for the sake of two hundred dollars a year?"

Kimberly was adamant, though not unkind. She said she was throwing nothing aside but her bondage, and she hoped Leland would come to understand that. The last thing in the world she wanted was for Leland to lose his respect for her.

"No, it's your position I can't respect, not yourself, for pity's sake." He was rather amazed to be speaking out like this, amazed to realize this issue was causing something like defiance to boil up in his rib cage. He was about to add that after the strike vote failed to carry, Kimberly must not be ashamed of her mistake; she must hold her head high and go on as before, sending superb young teachers out into the world. This statement was forming in his mind when his mother snatched away the phone.

"Kimberly dear, I'm sketching in my show for the next few weeks. How would you like ten minutes at the end of the month to promote your Future Teachers of America?"

Kimberly said that would be lovely, and they set the date. Kimberly was in charge of the day each year when the education department cast its net, hosting Future Teachers clubs from the surrounding high schools, plying them with lectures, jelly dough-nuts, and lots of promotional materials from the admissions office.

"Now, Kimberly dear, what's all this foolishness about a silly old strike?" The "dear" attached to Kimberly's name designated her as one of the women Lolly had tried to match with Leland. Actu-ally, she'd been the first. Though nearly fifteen years his senior, she'd seemed just Leland's type—earnestly dedicated to the college, conservative in her habits, rather good-looking in a prim, sexless way.

At tedious length Kimberly explained to Lolly why a strike vote was necessary.

"Well, I just wanted to caution you, Kimberly dear. On TV the other night they showed the telephone operators striking in Berrington, and it looked so horribly crude and unladylike, women on the picket line, that I had to laugh at the poor things. How can ladies go back to being ladies after going public with their greed?"

"Ladies!" said Kimberly with surprising force. "Who said we're ladies? What we are is slaves."

Lolly assured her that professors had come a long way out of slavery. Years ago, when her husband was young, there'd been no salary schedule at all. Everyone negotiated individually. The brassy bargainers were better paid than the timid; friends of the division chairmen were the best paid of all.

Kimberly countered by saying professors were pawns of the board, and women were lesser pawns than men. She said a strike would rectify all that.

"Oh, my stars," sighed Lolly, hanging up and joining her son at the table. "I'm afraid I'm beginning to see her side of it."

"Not me," said Leland staunchly, hoping to conceal his sudden panic at the prospect of losing his mother to the side of labor. He had no memory of ever occupying any position, on any question, but his mother's. Except her position on girlfriends, of course. "Next thing we know"—he laughed nervously—"you'll be out on the picket line yourself."

"Now, now," she cooed in the voice she had used to put him at ease as a baby, laying him down for his nap. She saw the alarm in his frown, in the set of his underbite.

"But seeing her side of it? I mean, really, Mother."

"Now, now, Leland, can't you take a little kidding? What I may do, though, is have a remote broadcast from the picket line one day. My listeners enjoy it so when I leave the studio and go out in the field. Remember all the nice calls I got after my remote from the mink farmers' picnic?"

"Yes." His frown mark grew less deep. He had taken some of those felicitous calls himself—evidence that his mother was universally loved.

"And that time from the mayor's funeral?"

He nodded. The tension went out of his jaw, and he smiled.

"How do you like the soup?"

"Fine. Very tasty."

"Made from a package, would you believe it?"

They heard the outer door open on the enclosed back porch, heard a bark and a growl and a man's voice urging a dog to behave.

"Mortimer and Boots," said Lolly, blushing with pleasure.

Leland rose to open the door, but his mother instructed him to finish his soup before it cooled. He sat.

C. Mortimer Oberholtzer came in looking distracted and worked up, doubtless over the strike. She invited him to the table for soup.

"No, thanks, Lolly. It's Gary's birthday and we're going to the Van Buren for dinner, so I'll abstain just now. However, I wouldn't turn down a glass of something to drink." He hoped it would be strong spirits of some kind and not the dry white wine Lolly and Leland customarily drank with their meals.

"Chicken soup," she cooed. "Surely you'll have a small taste."

"Just a taste, then, Lolly." He unleashed his enormous collie, Boots, who went directly over to Leland and slobbered saliva on his lap; then he stole off into other rooms, sniffing in corners. "Have you heard the awful news?" he asked, removing his checkered Tyrolean hat and sitting down opposite Leland.

"We have," said Leland, reaching across to shake his chairman's hand.

"A minute ago, from Kimberly," said Lolly, "and we're not surprised, are we, Leland? Herbert Gengler saw it coming."

Leland said, "It'll be nice to have our offices and classrooms updated." He paused a moment, and then added, "Don't you think?" in case his chairman held a different opinion. What was eating his chairman tonight? He seemed untypically twitchy.

"What's awful about it?" Lolly wanted to know, bearing another bowl to the table. "Surely you can see the board's side of it, Mortimer. There are just oodles of things need doing on campus. Have you noticed the rusty arbor vitae in front of McCall Hall? And the parking lot is all mud whenever it thaws."

"I don't mean the news from the board is awful, I mean the news from the Alliance. I'm beginning to believe we might actually have a strike on our hands." Looking distraught, the chairman unbuttoned his jacket and pulled at the collar of his black turtleneck.

"Mother says she might go on the picket line," Leland joked, hoping to relieve his anxiety.

"Lolly, you wouldn't!" said the chairman, believing it. His old friend Lolly had an unpredictable streak.

She disabused him of this absurd prospect, laughing and painfully pinching her son's earlobe, admonishing him not to make trouble.

Over soup and whiskey, Oberholtzer laid out the untenable position a strike would put him in. Where was a chairman's place if the faculty went to war with the administration? No-man's-land, that's where. He had no intention of joining the strikers and thereby losing the respect of the dean and the president and the whole college hierarchy in St. Paul, to say nothing of his own self-respect as a full professor with a doctorate in Eighteenth Century English Prose. And yet by crossing the picket line he'd be divided from his division.

"Irreparable harm to the division, Leland. Can't you see it? Our Languages and Fine Arts family coming apart in factions? Do you realize that some of our best people are likely to follow Victor off the job? Dr. Benoit, for one? Lolly, you've had Dr. Benoit on the radio. You've had her in your house. Such a gem she is. Such a presence. Can you believe she's going over to Victor's side? I don't mind saying I'm hurt by that." He tapped his scrawny chest. "Hurt right here, in the heart."

"I know," said Leland. "It hurts me too." It made tonight's practice session problematical. He foresaw Victor full of strike talk, and Peggy speaking on Victor's behalf. What if Connor and Neil took their side, leaving him the lone reactionary? What would become of their music? Their friendship? He pictured himself playing solos again in his living room. That's what hurt.

"Aren't you two getting ahead of yourselves?" asked Lolly. "Save your worry till after the vote."

Her son brightened, telling his chairman, "Mother's right, you know. I really don't believe Victor can carry it off. Just too many old hands on the faculty for the Alliance to win."

"But look at Aaron Cardero," said the chairman sadly. "Look at Larry Quinn. Look at Kimberly Kraft and Alex Bolus. Who'd have guessed *they'd* go over?"

Leland lowered his head and shook it slowly, his napkin to his mouth, his appetite gone. "Oh my."

Oberholtzer took a big swallow of whiskey, closed his eyes till his throat stopped burning, then continued, leaning forward over his soup. "We need a spokesman for our side, Leland. Someone to stand up at the meeting on Sunday and remind everybody we're professors and not teamsters. Would you do that for us?"

He gaped at his chairman.

"You're our man, Leland. You've got to stand up and speak for dignity and right reason."

The momentary pleasure Leland felt in being so designated was replaced—crushed—by the weight of it. He shook his head mournfully. "That's not my strong suit, Mortimer, advocating things."

"Nonsense. Don't forget the year you got the English teachers to agree on Lane and Peters."

Leland smiled faintly at the memory. By proposing that anthology of essays, he had actually, for once in his life, swayed the thinking of the textbook committee. Too bad he'd overestimated the freshman mind. They found the essays unreadably dense and dry, and Lane and Peters was thrown out the very next year.

"Why not you, Mortimer?"

"Well, as I told Honey, I'm in charge of people, I'm partly an administrator. You belong to the rank and file, Leland."

"But we need somebody with more seniority than I've got."

"No, that's exactly what we *don't* need. We can't risk a break between young and old. A model for the younger professors to follow is what we need, and that's you. Sterling reputation. Ten years on the staff—"

"Twelve."

"Twelve years on the staff, yet young enough to sway the newcomers. They'll look to you for guidance."

Again Oberholtzer drank deeply. Lolly held the whiskey bottle out to him, but he waved it away. She poured a bit of it into her empty wineglass and said to her son, "Your father would be so proud."

Oberholtzer drained his drink and smiled at her, waiting for Leland's consent.

Looking into his soup, Leland pictured himself addressing the faculty, impassioned and eloquent. Somehow the setting—Mount of Olives Lutheran—made it easier to imagine, his message enhanced by the holy surroundings, his listeners neatly arranged in pews, afternoon light falling in through the blue-tinted windows. Though Episcopalian himself, he'd always felt comfortable at weddings and funerals in Mount of Olives. Would he stand at the altar rail, or climb into the pulpit?

"Well?" the chairman asked.

"He'll do it," said Lolly decisively.

He raised his eyes to his mother and asked, in genuine curiosity, "I will?"

The chairman stood up, buttoned his jacket, and called Boots away from the table leg he'd been gnawing in the dining room. Lolly saw them out through the back porch, sending her love home to Honey and to Gary on his birthday. Leland would deliver the faculty vote to the side of right reason, she said. No worry there.

Leland, meanwhile, to relieve his anxiety, slipped out of the kitchen and went to the piano, where he pounded out a loud and weighty version of the piece that Peggy had taught him in a dream.

Kimberly Kraft, whose branch she was on, had tried several times to reach Peggy with the news, but to no avail.

Peggy hadn't gone home after class, but carried her supper—a Coke and an egg salad sandwich—from the student center to the band room, and was sitting cross-legged on the violet carpet listening to the records she and Connor had discovered in the closet off the language lab. They were the wartime songs of her early girlhood, and she knew most of the lyrics by heart. "I Don't Want to Walk Without You." "Don't Get Around Much Anymore." "This Is the Army, Mr. Jones." She sat with a notebook in her lap, into which she jotted down titles suitable for the quintet, and she noted as well certain lyrics that had slipped her mind in the twenty or twenty-five years since she'd heard them last. "I'm Beginning to See the Light." "Sunday, Monday or Always." "The White Cliffs of Dover."

The records were dusty and scratched, some of the music lost under the hissing needle, which now and then jumped a nicked groove, but she played all of them, engulfed in nostalgia. She pictured the radio over which she and her older brothers and sisters had listened to the Hit Parade every Saturday night, a large table-model Philco of polished walnut with a rounded top and a grill-work face. It stood within easy reach of her father's easy chair, so that he could dictate, most evenings, what the family listened to. Dull, esoteric stuff mostly. "The Bell Telephone Hour." "H. V. Kaltenborn." The children considered themselves lucky on Saturday nights, when their parents went out to play bridge and they were left with free rein of the dial. Sue, the oldest, was nuts about Frank Sinatra; Bill wanted to play the trumpet like Harry James; Kenny's taste ran more to novelties such as "Pistol Packing Mama" and "Mairsy Dotes." Lucy, for some reason, perhaps because she loved horses, made everyone listen to "National Barn Dance," and wept tears of ecstasy whenever she heard "Deep in the Heart of Texas." Connie, closest to Peggy in age, was the only one in the family with no interest in music. Give Connie "The FBI in Peace and War," and the rest of the week you could do what you wanted with the radio.

When one by one they all went off to college and careers, Peggy, the youngest, suffered intense bouts of loneliness. They all seemed so willing to shut her out of their lives. They hardly ever came home or answered her letters. Her mother and father were no consolation; they were strict and chilly with Peggy, having overextended themselves on the other five children and exhausted their supply of parental nurture and love. Her sense of abandonment was terrifying, and now, nearly thirty, she wasn't able to put it completely behind her. Every so often it came rushing back at her with no loss of intensity—as now, since the moment Connor had left her in the practice room upstairs.

But it helped to remind herself how her family, after coming apart, had more or less pieced itself back together. Sue, the oldest, after spending ten years in England, first as a student and then as an artist in stained glass, returned to the States with her English husband and set up a fairly successful mail-order business on the coast of Maine. Their line was pottery. Sue was the one Peggy now felt closest to. They talked on the phone nearly every Sunday evening.

She'd come to know Connie all over again, though perhaps without achieving the closeness they'd enjoyed as girls. Connie, unmarried, was now conducting workshops in customer relations for an insurance firm in Connecticut.

Lucy, the lover of horses, was currently the least involved with the family. Lucy was a high school science teacher in Laramie, Wyoming. She and her husband, a rancher, had two babies Peggy had never seen.

Their father was dead. He'd died of cancer when Peggy was an undergraduate at Boston University. Her mother lived in an apartment in Salem, near Kenny's house.

Bill and Kenny both married women to whom family connections were important, and, living as they did near Boston, they formed a kind of hub for the others. Until she married Gene Benoit, Peggy was often a guest at Bill's house or Kenny's house.

The family had disliked Gene Benoit from the start. Indeed, they despised him. This surprised and angered Peggy. She'd introduced him at a Sunday brunch at Kenny's, and afterward she couldn't get anybody to say a word in his favor. She'd expected them to be impressed by Gene's credentials as a photographer, also by his wide-ranging knowledge of world affairs. As a stringer for the *Boston Globe*, he'd spent time in every troubled nation in Central and South America, and a downtown gallery regularly displayed his photos of suffering humanity. He wasn't the gregarious type, that was the trouble. He said very little at the brunch, and what he did say gave Kenny and Connie the impression (they said later) that he was a know-it-all.

This reticence of Gene's she'd thought a virtue, expecting it to remind her brothers and sisters of their father, whose silences had always been such an intriguing mystery. Sue and Bill, however, told her that her boyfriend seemed to be sitting back smirking the whole time, and judging them all. She'd imagined her brothers drawing him out on the subject of the Red Sox (Gene had begun his career as a sports photographer), and she'd imagined her mother being interested in the fact that she and Gene's mother, as girls, had attended the same academy. But none of this came to pass. He got off on the wrong foot with her mother by turning away from her as she spoke to him, looking about for an ashtray, finding instead an unfinished plate of food, and putting out his cigarette in the yolk of someone's fried egg.

Nor was Gene Benoit any more pleased to make *their* acquaintance. He and Peggy left the brunch after an hour and a half, and the only favorable reaction she got out of him concerned Kenny's gun collection and the silver service Kenny's wife had brought to their marriage. He pressed Peggy to tell him how her brother first got interested in guns (Kenny had hunted deer as a boy), whether he ever took them out of the cabinet and shot them anymore (occasionally, at a rifle range), and what the collection was worth (she had no idea). In order to get him past the silver service, which he spoke of with the same urgency, she told him, without really knowing, that it was worth three thousand dollars.

Six months later, her brothers and sisters rose up in alarm when she said she planned to marry him. Kenny told her Gene Benoit was arrogant. Sue said he was egotistical. Bill said he had the manners of a derelict. They predicted he'd never give her the life or the love she deserved. Her brothers' wives in particular said they couldn't imagine entertaining that boor down through the years, not if he was going to stub out his smokes in other people's eggs. By marrying Gene Benoit, said Connie, Peggy was certain someday to be the first divorcée ever to disgrace the family tree.

Peggy's mother kept her counsel. Peggy knew her mother well enough to understand her misgivings, but took her silence as a kind of grudging approval. It wasn't approval at all, as it turned out. Her mother saved her opinion until after the wedding—three minutes after, to be exact. It was a single word, whispered desperately into the bride's ear on the steps of the courthouse. The word was "Why?"

It was a fair question.

Gene Benoit came along just when Peggy was feeling the rather desperate need for a husband. The single life was getting her down.

Whenever she looked ahead to life after graduate school, she felt twinges of the horrifying solitude that had been dogging her since she was twelve. To anyone with three sisters and two brothers, it was unnatural to have only silent thoughts day after day, with no one to express them to; unnatural to depend entirely on oneself for the countless little decisions and diversions of daily life. Then too, there was her money problem, and she wondered later how much of her desperation was due to that. Tuition had risen to well over a hundred dollars a credit, her rent kept going up, and music texts were far beyond her means. Gene Benoit had money.

Moreover, to give him his due, money and companionship weren't all he offered. Gene was an artist. Peggy wanted to be allied through life with a man who understood her devotion to music, and this man did. They attended classical concerts and exhibit openings, and he brought the same sensitivity to Peggy's music that he'd cultivated for his photography. They also read to one another, biographies mostly, sitting in the cozy apartment they'd decorated together. Were these the qualities of an arrogant egotist with the manners of a derelict?

And he could be quite funny in his mumbling, ironic way, and he could be helpful around the apartment when she was too deeply immersed in her studies to keep up with the housekeeping. And he could be lavish with gifts when he returned from a foreign assignment.

Could be. That was the problem—his unpredictability. Tender and kind one day, disagreeable the next. Over time, his better days dwindled, and the irksome ones increased. He became, on those bad days, someone she hadn't married, dark of mood, selfish. He would brood. He would insult her and make her cry. Whenever he came out of it and said he was sorry, which he often did, she wiped away her tears, gathered up her hope, and started over.

But with time, he stopped saying he was sorry, stopped coming out of it. He sometimes left the apartment and didn't come back for days. A couple of times, his photographs in the *Globe* told her where he was—Panama, for example—but usually she had no idea. He'd return exhausted, needing lots of sleep. "Gene, tell me where you went," she'd plead.

"Ends of the earth," he'd say.

The ends of the earth turned out to be about seven blocks away, where there lived a young woman he was having an affair with. Peggy learned this only much later, after he moved out of her life, taking with him her hi-fi, some of her jewelry, and various other valuables.

She sought legal assistance to recover these things, but her lawyer, who was also her brother Kenny, together with Gene's lawyer, determined that when you took their expensive wallpaper and furnishings into account, what he had taken was a little less than half of their joint assets. Despite his hasty getaway, his calculations had turned out to be pretty shrewd, they told her. Kenny said she ought to divorce Gene Benoit immediately and get on with her life.

Was that good advice? She couldn't think straight, due to her suffering. It was the same old panic, brought on by desertion, intensified in this case by her suspicions that she might have been partly responsible. Perhaps by concentrating so intensely on her graduate work, she had failed him as his wife. Her brother Bill said this was pure bullshit. Kenny agreed. Kenny's wife recommended a psychotherapist.

Her trouble was compounded at this point by her husband's change of heart. He'd broken up with the woman seven blocks away and wanted Peggy to take him back. He besieged her with phone calls and gifts of records and flowers, begging her to start over again and promising he'd be a changed man now that he was free of this other woman who, he said, worked a kind of evil spell on him. He did not, however, return the hi-fi or any of her jewelry. He couldn't stand giving them up, he said, because they were all he had left of her.

Peggy's therapist, a young woman with the unlikely name of Lois Latitude, immediately won Peggy's confidence by resembling her sister Sue, particularly when she smiled, which she did easily and often. It took only half a dozen sessions for this woman to help Peggy get her self-confidence back. She did this by convincing her that Gene Benoit's erratic and abusive behavior was in no way caused by her conduct as a wife. Caught up in an illicit love affair, he'd seen Peggy as interfering with his pursuit of happiness, and he'd been striving, by his misbehavior, to drive her out of his life. "If I may be so bold," said Lois Latitude, "your husband sounds like an absolute meathead."

Over his protests, then, she divorced him. She did not, however, give up his name. She feared this final act of separation, and the panic that might ensue. Sometimes she thought of their happy times together and missed him quite terribly. Her feelings for him never hardened into hate or bitterness, as she'd been told they might. What she felt was a mixture of pity and regret and anxiety, this last caused by his distraught condition when they met in Kenny's office to sign the divorce stipulations. Parting for the last time, he'd wept and promised to make her life as miserable as she'd made his.

She heard footsteps in the corridor outside the band room and assumed it was Cousin Neil. Now that she was seeing him twice a week in the band room, she'd stopped visiting his dismal basement, and he, in turn, had started arriving early at rehearsal in order to talk with her about private things such as family news, his plot-in-progress, fresh complaints from the classroom. He'd stopped giving voice to his feelings for her, thank God, evidently recognizing it as the unrequited crush it was.

The footsteps halted outside the door, and she heard a moment of throat-clearing and the jingle of hangers on the coatrack. This wouldn't be Neil. He'd never in his life hung up an article of clothing.

It was Leland. He came in frowning deeply, looking burdened, crossing and uncrossing his lanky arms. As usual, his attire was attractive—a maroon sweater-vest over a starched white shirt, sharp creases in his gray pants, shiny black loafers. "Hi," he said shyly.

"Gee, you look nice, Leland. I should have gone home and changed, but I've just been sitting here. . . ." She got up off the floor and tried brushing the wrinkles from her brown wool skirt. She felt worn-out and grimy, certain that her blouse must look wilted, her hair stiff and oily.

"I thought I'd come early and ask if you think we're good enough yet to be on the radio. Mother would like to have us on KRKU someday, either her Saturday show or her weekday show."

"Sure, we're good enough." For the likes of KRKU, she thought, but didn't say. "I'm dropping in at your house tonight—we'll set a date."

Ordinarily, Leland went straight to the piano and played scales, but tonight he held out a folding chair for her to sit on, and then sat down next to her, shoulder to shoulder, facing the band director's podium and the open doorway beyond it.

"You know better than I do what we sound like. It's hard for me to tell when I'm at the piano."

She turned to him with a smile and patted his arm, hoping to soften the lines of strain in his face. "We sound like the bunch of inspired amateurs we are, Leland, good on some pieces, sloppy on others."

"That's what I told her. I said we could probably put together enough respectable music for the weekday show if not the half hour on Saturday."

Noise in the corridor—students arriving at play rehearsal. One of them, a pretty young woman Peggy had seen leading cheers at basketball games, stopped in the doorway and said "Hi, Dr. Edwards."

Leland raised a hand. "Hello, Miss Hupstad."

She was joined by a young man, who greeted Peggy. "Hi, Dr. Benoit, I hear you got a band going."

"We're working on it." It took her a moment to put a name to this open, innocent face: Chuck Lucking, her advisee from Loomis, back for another try at college. She hadn't seen him since the day she helped him in the library with his late registration. "How's it going this time?" she asked.

"Pretty good. I'm doing props for the play."

"How about your classes?"

"A lot of reading."

"That's college," she told him.

"Yeah. History especially."

"How about English?"

"English?" He thought about it. "It's not what I expected, but it's okay."

"What did you expect?"

"Well, I heard you could get an A from Mr. Novotny even if you didn't go to class, but it's not true."

She laughed. "You mean he expects you to actually *be* there?"

"Every day."

"Wow, that hardly seems fair."

Departing, the cheerleader said, "Good luck with your band."

"Yeah, good luck with your band," said Chuck Lucking, trailing after her.

A minute later their drama coach, Professor Bernard Beckwith, appeared in the doorway and asked how the quintet was progressing. He was a round, pink man in his midforties.

"A collaboration is something we should be thinking about," he said. "I'd love to direct a cabaret-style Christmas show next year, and your ensemble is just the right size."

Peggy was skeptical. " 'White Christmas' and 'Jingle Bells'? I'm afraid we're not very strong in that area, Bernard."

Leland, at her side, cleared his throat in a manner that said he begged to differ. "But, Peggy, are we wise to rule it out altogether?"

Seeing the eagerness in Leland's eyes, she patted his arm again and relented. "No, you're right." And to Beckwith she added, "Maybe you should check with us in the fall. We might be able—"

"Say!" Beckwith interrupted, coming forward into the room and peering intently at Peggy. "I heard you cast your lot with the Alliance." He had the unsettling habit of closely examining the face of anyone he addressed as though studying a bust on exhibit. "I heard you've gone over to Victor's side."

"With all my heart," she replied.

Beckwith then regarded Leland with the same intensity. "But not you—I can't see *you* voting to strike."

"No," was the subdued reply. Leland hadn't meant to declare himself quite yet. It was Sunday's meeting at Mount of Olives Lutheran (not his mother's radio show) that had brought him so early to the band room. He needed Peggy's assurance that the quintet would survive his speaking for the opposition, but he hadn't yet summoned the courage to bring it up.

"Who's voting to strike?" asked Peggy. "You mean it's official?"

"Straight from the Telephone Tree," said Beckwith fussily. "The board has elected to freeze our salaries."

"Those idiots!" cried Peggy with satisfaction. "They don't know what they're letting themselves in for."

Both men were astonished by the gladness in her voice. Beckwith said, "We're taking a strike vote on Sunday."

"Two o'clock in the afternoon," added Leland with trepidation in his voice.

"What a break for the women of Rookery State. While you men are picketing for higher pay, we'll be picketing for *equal* pay."

Beckwith rolled his eyes at Leland, indicating how droll women could be. "Who in the world said anything about picketing?" Because his question was met with silence, he looked a little alarmed. "Well, you and I aren't picketing, are we, Leland?"

Again Leland spoke timidly. "No."

Beckwith said, "Good," and swept dramatically out of the room.

Left alone, Leland cringed, expecting Peggy to confront him. But she didn't. She clasped her hands high over her head and stretched, yawning, arching her back. When she spoke, it was to ask, "Is there a piano at the radio station?"

"No, Mother can do a remote, from right here in the band room."

"It would have to be a Saturday, then. We're all in class during her weekday show, aren't we? All except Neil?"

"Well, what I was thinking . . . if there really is a strike . . ." There—he'd said the word.

"Yes?"

"I mean, all that free time on our hands."

She surprised him by laughing. "No, Leland, if there's a strike, who'd want to cross the picket line?"

Well, of course *he* would, out of duty to everyone he owed his allegiance to, including his dead father. Strike or no strike, he intended to report to his office as on any normal working day. Tightening his jaw and working it nervously, he suggested, "Bernard Beckwith might."

This amused her. "Oh, I suppose. He's such a drip."

Leland's heart sank.

More footsteps in the corridor. This time, to their surprise, it was C. Mortimer Oberholtzer who put his head in at the door, smiled benevolently, and asked if either of them had seen his son Gary anywhere in the building.

"I haven't," said Leland, adding, "Sorry," because he could imagine the frustration of having to go looking for the son you were about to treat to a birthday dinner at the Van Buren Hotel.

"Nor I," said Peggy. She shuddered slightly at the thought of the sinister Gary Oberholtzer at large in the corridors of McCall Hall. She'd met him the night his parents entertained the newcomers (the same night Victor ate the leaves off a jade plant), and she'd seen him since, walking the streets of Rookery. She could tell that something sour and virulent was boiling up in his soul. The first couple of times she came across him downtown, she greeted him, but he directed his smoldering, defiant eyes away from her and said nothing. On subsequent sightings, mostly from her car, she noticed that the angry set to his mouth was permanent, and so was his habit, even on the coldest days, of wearing his brown leather jacket unzipped and hanging open. It was an old motorcycle jacket crisscrossed with the deep abrasions one acquired by skidding along pavements after losing control of one's motorcycle. Although the crook in his nose might have been a birth defect, she imagined that this, too, was caused by an accident. And although long hair on men was becoming fairly common, Gary Oberholtzer's hair, well beyond shoulder length, was a startling curiosity in Rookery. She thought his mouth hideous. It was so tight, so defiant. He seemed never to open it except to hang a cigarette from his lip.

Chairman Oberholtzer, straightening his red silk tie and fidgeting with the buttons of his overcoat, explained to Peggy that Gary turned twenty-one today, and now that it was time to go out to dinner, neither he nor Honey could recall if they'd actually finalized their plans with Gary. Smiling helplessly, the chairman added, "Shows you what communication is like at our house." He backed away from the doorway as Connor approached with his daughter.

Connor exchanged a few pleasantries with his chairman in the corridor, while Laura, carrying books, came in and greeted Peggy and Leland in a rather sullen monotone, "Hi, Dr. Benoit, hi, Dr. Edwards." She settled into a corner with her homework. She was wearing blue jeans and a black satin blouse. She had been working, ineptly, on her long blond hair, curling the ends. Her mascara and blush were overdone. Peggy wanted to take the girl home and start over.

"Do you play an instrument?" she asked her. "Would you like to join in on a piece or two?"

The girl said no.

"Would you like to learn? I'd be happy to give you some lessons."

The girl shook her head no, distracted by voices in the corridor—three or four of Beckwith's stage crew going by.

Oberholtzer departed, and Connor advanced upon Peggy with an expression of something like amusement on his face. Her heart fell. Had he thought over the kiss and decided it was frivolous?

"I suppose you've heard the news," he said, removing his jacket and dropping it over a chair. "Our salaries have been frozen."

"In the long run, we might be better off," Leland blurted immediately and bravely. "I mean when you consider the state our campus is in. I mean the physical plant."

"But two years?" said Connor. "This is for the biennium."

"Well . . ." Leland shrugged helplessly.

"We're voting Sunday on whether to strike." He went into the instrument room and carried out his string bass, unzipping its black nylon cover. "The meeting's at Mount of Olives Lutheran, wherever that is."

"Just across the river," Leland told him. "Turn right at the foot of the bridge."

"What do you think? Will it carry?"

Peggy answered for Leland, "Of course it will carry. The opposition isn't organized. Who's speaking for them anyway? Nobody, as far as I know." She stood up and crossed to the instrument room.

Leland, spokesman for the opposition, was about to declare himself when Neil swept through the door, carrying his clarinet case in one hand and a manila folder in the other. "Victor can't make it, he called me, he's all tied up with strike business. He wants Peggy to call him. Hey, where's Peggy? Her car's out there."

In Neil's face was an energetic freshness that the other two men had never seen there before. Surely it wasn't strike-related. Neil was too self-absorbed to care what happened on campus.

It was novel-related. Dropping his instrument carelessly on the floor, Neil sat down, opened his manila folder, and riffled through the manuscript pages it held. "Look, would you mind if I read you people some of this out loud? I mean we've got no drums tonight, so what do you say we knock off early with the music because I need to see what you think of this chapter. It won't take a half hour of your time." He turned to Connor. "You're right, Connor, I need feedback." He turned to Peggy emerging from the instrument room with her saxophone. "It's about how Lydia runs away from this dirty old man."

His proposal was met with what he considered an insulting lack of enthusiasm. He added, "Well, I mean, what are friends for, right?"

Connor and Leland turned to Peggy, awaiting her judgment.

"No, I don't think so, Neil."

He looked at her in disbelief. "Twenty minutes," he pleaded.

Peggy shook her head. She didn't want to spoil the evening with Neil's deadly prose. Tonight of all nights, she wanted to sing. She'd risen out of her somber reverie over her failed marriage and was high on the news from St. Paul, higher yet on the vibrations from the string bass, which Connor was absently plucking. She was ready to belt out a happy cry from the heart—"Too Marvelous for Words" or "Singin' in the Rain."

"Fifteen minutes?" pleaded Neil, losing hope.

She said, as gently as she could, "This isn't a writer's workshop, Neil. It's a musical quintet."

"Jesus!" He closed his folder, picked up his clarinet, and strode angrily from the room.

She bit her lip regretfully, watching him go.

Connor continued slowly strumming. Leland listened intently, then swiveled around on his stool and picked out a one-finger rendition of "Bye Bye Blackbird." Connor increased the tempo slightly. Leland added chords. Peggy joined in, filling in the lines she couldn't remember with scat singing. The wildness in her voice was startling. It spurred the two men to play louder and faster. Leland set up a syncopated, one-chord pounding with his left hand and kept it up, measure after measure, never mind what his right hand was doing with the melody. Connor followed him into this reckless rhythm, slapping his strings roughly and making gasping noises in response to the nonsense syllables Peggy was uttering. After about five minutes of these high jinks they calmed down, returning to the slower pace of the opening. Here Peggy picked up her sax and "Bye Bye Blackbird" grew very elemental, very deliberate, as though they were following sheet music for beginners. Finally, when it grew too staid to be interesting, Leland and Connor began ever so gradually to pick up the pace again. Peggy put down her sax and began moving her hips with the beat. She didn't sing, but stood there with her eyes closed, facing away from both men, transported by their playing.

Leland's eyes were fixed on his keyboard. His pounding in the lower register was starting up again, while his right hand kept approaching the melody and backing away from it. Connor set up a rumble in his strings. This blackbird was no bird. It was a night train in the distance, headed this way, picking up speed as it approached. Peggy was on the train. She was swaying slightly, her arms out for balance, her eyes still closed. Leland was the engineer, taking surprising turns with the melody, while Connor, the engine, kept chugging steadily along. Connor couldn't take his eyes off Peggy's movements, her rhythmic knee bend, her ankle turning in, turning out, her black hair falling forward, hiding her face whenever she dipped her head. He kept his gaze trained on her until Leland ran out of fresh ideas and brought the music to a halt.

Peggy opened her eyes and faced Connor with a self-conscious smile, aware that he'd been concentrating on her.

Leland opened a piece of sheet music and ran through a few measures of "Twilight Time."

Connor turned to look at his daughter and found her gone.

Neil was energized by the quintet's rebuff. He retreated directly from the band room to his typewriter, where he discovered that anger could be a strong propellent for his prose—strong enough to power a riverboat downstream and steer it over to the landing where Lydia Harker stands waiting.

Lydia, relieved beyond measure to be delivered from her menacing pursuer, sits on a bench at the rail and examines her foot. The abrasions don't look serious, so she quickly tucks it back under her skirt and looks around her, studying the other passengers.

She notices a man who resembles her brother Alphonse. He is standing at the forward rail, looking out over the bow. The likeness is so striking, from behind, that she flies to him and throws her arms around him from behind, crying, "Alphonse, Alphonse, I ran away in a fit of temper. I'm sorry, I'm lonesome, I'm scared, please take me home, oh please, please take me home."

The man, struggling to free his arms from her embrace, turns around and faces her. She wipes the tears from her eyes and sees, to her supreme embarrassment, that this is not her brother. He's a handsome stranger, a little older than Alphonse, a little paler. He has steady blue eyes and a small mustache. His smile is both quizzical and kindly. He says . . .

What would he say? Neil sat back and tried to imagine the man's words. They must indicate to Lydia, without threatening her, that he finds her highly desirable. He got up and paced around the room, mumbling possibilities.

Hi, good-looking. No, definitely not.

Fancy meeting the likes of you on this lonesome old riverboat. Better, but no.

Well, well, aren't you a sight for sore eyes. He was getting closer.

He continued to pace, turning perhaps a dozen such responses over in his mind before picking out what he considered the most apt. He sat down and typed *I don't mean to threaten you, young lady, but I find you highly desirable.* He studied it. It didn't have quite the charm or wit he'd been aiming at, but he let it stand. Dialogue always came hard for Neil.

Among the several things Chuck Lucking found attractive about Sandy Hupstad were her car (a twelve-year-old Hudson Hornet) and her grades, which were nearly as poor as his own. He liked dating a girl for a change who was struggling, like himself, to maintain a C average so as to avoid suspension. He couldn't believe his luck when this blond cheerleader from Fargo with the knockout legs and the cute way of crinkling her nose turned out to be fond of him.

It wasn't luck from Sandy's viewpoint. It was a case of common interests. The Hudson, for one. Chuck understood engines.

On below-zero mornings, all she had to do was phone him in his dormitory across the parking lot, and he'd go out and start the engine and scrape ice off the windshield, and by the time she was dressed and ready to drive to class (four blocks away), the car would be nearly warm enough to be comfortable. He also made repairs, or paid for those he couldn't fix. Sandy's parents, having sent her off to college with the Hudson, kept her on a budget too tight to keep it running.

He also shared her love of beer. Two or three nights a week, after basketball games or play practice, they liked to drive out to Rocky Point Lodge and certain other taverns where underage drinking was permitted. Because Sandy was quick to get snaky, Chuck always drove, and because she was always short of cash, he paid for the gas and the beer and their midnight hamburger at Claudia's Lunch on their way home. These evenings ate up most of his earnings as a part-time employee of Hunsinger Appliance, where his work consisted mostly of muscling refrigerators around on dollies under the direction of Ron Hunsinger, Georgina Gold's husband-to-be.

Tonight, again, they were leaving campus on their way to Rocky Point Lodge when they saw in the headlights two forlorn figures, a boy and a girl, standing at the foot of the Eleventh Street Bridge, thumbing a ride. They slowed to a crawl and examined them.

"Who *is* that long-haired creep?" asked Sandy.

"Which one?"

"The guy. I see him around all the time. And look at her—she looks about twelve."

"Jailbait," Chuck agreed. "Let's give them a ride."

"Really? But he's such a creep."

"Yeah, but they look froze."

He stopped the car. The boy opened the back door and tumbled in, shuddering with cold. The girl hopped in behind him and pulled the door shut.

Sandy peered into the dark backseat. "Hi, where you going?"

"Looking to get a beer someplace," said the boy through his chattering teeth, his eyes glinting and shifting like an animal's.

"Us too," said Chuck, driving carefully across the icy bridge. "You like Rocky Point?"

The boy's answer, hard to interpret, was the sniffling sound of a runny nose.

Chuck asked again. "Rocky Point suit you okay?"

"You name it, you're driving."

They traveled a few blocks without speaking, the boy continuously sniffling, the girl coughing delicately into her hand. Sandy continued to stare at them.

"My name's Sandy, and this is Chuck."

The boy said nothing. The girl spoke weakly. "I'm Laura."

Sandy knew by her voice how young she was, how mismatched they were.

"You from Rookery?" she asked them.

"My dad teaches at the college," said the girl. "So does Gary's." Before continuing, she looked apprehensively at her companion, as though to make sure she wasn't revealing too much. "My dad's in art, Gary's dad's in English." She turned back to Sandy. "Where you from?"

"Fargo." Sandy laid her hand fondly on the driver's shoulder. "Chuck here's from Loomis."

"Loomis?" Laura inquired.

"Podunk," Gary explained to her.

After another pause, Sandy asked, "What's your dad's name?"

"Connor."

"In art, you said?"

"Yes."

"I guess I don't know him. Do you, Chuck?"

"Yep." Chuck was hunched over the wheel, rubbing frost from the windshield.

Laura asked, "Do you know Dr. Benoit?"

"Yeah, I know her," said Sandy. "Great voice, they say."

"She's my adviser," said Chuck. "Nice lady."

"She's sort of a whore." The enormity of the lie caused Laura's voice to tremble, but she pressed on. "I mean, she tries to get men to have sex with her, did you know that?"

"You're kidding!" Sandy was truly astonished.

Even Gary Oberholtzer was amazed. "You're shitting us."

"She never tried it with me," joked Chuck, but none of the three paid him any attention.

"She keeps trying it with my dad, but he won't do it."

"Geez," said Sandy. "Wow." She turned and faced front. "Holy Toledo."

No more was said for a while, then Laura piped up proudly: "Gary's turning twenty-one today."

This was an eminence neither Sandy nor Chuck had achieved. Sandy said, "Wow, happy birthday," and Chuck said, "Hey, yeah, happy birthday."

No response but a long drawing up of mucus.

"So you can drink legal now," said Chuck.

"Been drinking all along," growled Gary.

"You ought to get yourself some wheels," Chuck advised. "You could freeze to death waiting for a ride in this town."

"Got wheels. A Harley."

"Where is it?"

"Banged up."

"Too expensive to fix?"

"What's the use of fixing it? I'm going to get drafted."

"Oh, that's the shits. When?"

"Draft board says my number's coming up this spring."

"Hell of a note."

Beyond the city limits, Chuck speeded up, and the roar of the engine made conversation impossible until they pulled into an icy clearing in the woods and parked near a large building made of log and stone. Hanging crookedly over the front stoop was a neon beer sign, which suffused the clearing with an eerie pink light. The stoop itself was crooked, and so was the door Chuck pulled open with some difficulty.

A black cat, trying to slink outside as they were going in, caused Gary to stumble, and this enraged him. He cursed, and kicked the animal savagely, sending it twirling off into the night. He continued cursing as he followed the others across the gritty floor to the bar. The room was dim and smoky. The bar was very short, and a pair of men in blaze-orange caps had to move over to make room for the four of them. The only other patrons were five young women sitting at a table, sharing a pitcher of beer. Sandy had seen them around campus, but knew only one of them by name, Charlotte Giddings, a senior nursing major.

The young man tending bar wore a canvas hunting jacket with a large button pinned to it, four months out of date—NIX NIXON '68. "Whatcha want?" he asked.

"Tap for us," said Chuck, indicating himself and Sandy.

"Same here," said Gary Oberholtzer.

"Same here," said Laura.

The young man looked her over. "Not till you're about ten years older."

"Go hump yourself," Gary told him.

The young man, choosing to ignore him, drew three foamy beers. Laura said a Coke would be fine.

Sandy looked Laura up and down, and was appalled to think that this innocent girl-child was attaching herself to someone as full of anger as Gary Oberholtzer. She nudged Chuck away from the bar, and he followed her over to the table of college girls. She squeezed a chair for herself between two of them, making sure that Gary, if he joined them, wouldn't sit beside her. Chuck, too, pulled up a chair.

Laura, meantime, could hardly contain the excitement that had possessed her since meeting Gary at the water fountain outside the band room. Surely she was the only sophomore in Rookery High School asked out for a beer by a twenty-one-year-old. If only someone from the school newspaper could see her and get it on the Couples page. She'd stepped out for a drink of water while the quintet was playing something boring and found him standing beside the fountain smoking a cigarette. She was pleased by the way he looked her up and down. Her legs especially seemed to interest him. Her legs were long, and her jeans were tight because she was outgrowing them, but hardly any of the boys in high school ever gave her a second look.

"You in college?" he'd asked, and she explained about her father and the quintet. She bent over to drink, half expecting him to turn on the stream of water for her, but he didn't. What he did do, however, was offer her a drag of his beat-up cigarette. She took a tentative puff, half expecting it to be grass, but it wasn't. It was a dry old Camel.

"What's your name?"

"Laura." She took a second, deeper drag and made sure he noticed her inhaling. She blew out the smoke very slowly. "What's yours?"

"Gary."

"Are you in college?" she asked, sensing he wasn't. College students could be pretty sloppy-looking, but not this sloppy. His fingernails were chipped and dirty, and he wore his soiled sweatshirt inside out. His hair lay in thick, greasy folds across the shoulders of his scarred leather jacket. However, it wasn't primarily his clothes or his hair that marked him as an alien on campus; it was the sneer on his face when she said the word "college." Laura could see how much he hated the place. She found this refreshing, because her father was forever extolling higher education. Her father (she knew) was brainwashing her, lest she do something stupid after high school, like become a waitress. True, she'd threatened to do this, but there was actually nothing to it. She'd never pass up the chance to go to college, but she liked to keep her father in a state of anxiety. That way, she made sure he stayed interested in her.

When they finished the cigarette, handing it back and forth, Gary ground it into the varnished wooden floor with his boot and said, "Let's go out for a walk."

"Are you out of your mind?" It was about ten below zero.

"Well, then let's have another cigarette."

"No, I've got homework to do."

They spent an awkward few moments trying to effect a graceful leave-taking, moving away from each other without quite knowing how to suggest another meeting, Laura calculating that by hanging around with a guy like this she'd give her father something substantial to worry about, besides giving herself something to brag about to her dreary friends at Rookery High.

Gary, for his part, had sexual intercourse in mind. He'd had it in mind for about ten years, without once successfully acting on the impulse. Here at last was a girl young enough not to be afraid of.

It was Laura who finally figured out what to say. "Good-bye," she chirped, carrying herself stiffly back toward the band room, feeling his eyes on her seat.

"Hey, let's go get a beer," he said.

And now, sipping her Coke at the bar, she was gazing around at the interior of Rocky Point Lodge, which had obviously declined from its better days as a resort. For warmth in winter, Sheetrock covered most of the windows, and a dirty green tarpaulin was draped across the enormous hearth. The wall opposite the bar was crowded with dusty old cabin furniture brought in for storage when the Rocky Point Cabins were sold off and hauled away (as one of the men standing near Laura was explaining to his companion), and the table occupied by the students stood beside a row of seven old refrigerators that had their doors tied shut with rope. So people wouldn't crawl inside and suffocate, said the man. It was the law.

"This is my kind of place," said Laura, believing for a moment that she meant it.

"It's a dump," said Gary, wiping mucus and foam from his upper lip in a swipe of his sleeve.

"It reminds me of the place near our apartment in the city where my dad used to drink. When I was little, he used to take me there and feed me potato chips while he had a couple of quick ones."

"Cool," said Gary.

If only her father could see her now, out with this surly creature nearly eight years her senior. He'd be alarmed and understand immediately how vulnerable a daughter was, how desperately she needed a father's undivided attention. It had been horrible in the band room, seeing her father and Dr. Benoit conveying with their eyes things she hated to think about.

"Your dad's my dad's boss," she said.

"My old man's stupid. He's in love with books."

"Oh yeah? Well, that's real interesting. My dad's in love with paint."

"My old man don't give a shit for me, or nobody." Gary's eyes flashed with a surge of hate so steely and strong that Laura trembled with fright.

"My dad isn't like that." Her voice quavered. "My dad loves me."

"Just books is all he gives a shit for. Just books and the humping dog."

"Doesn't he like your mother?"

This question seemed to catch Gary by surprise. He squinted, as though the answer might be on the shelf of bottles behind the bar.

"You ought to see how bad it is at my house," she said after a long silence, sensing he was too self-involved to ask about her parents. "My mom never gets up."

This seemed to bring him out of himself. He looked impressed. "Never gets up?"

"You know, out of bed."

Gary's laugh was brief and humorless. "You mean he's humping her all the time?"

Laura turned scarlet and looked away. "I mean she's depressed."

Gary laughed again. He bit off a sliver of thumbnail. He put his nose close to her hair and asked, "But they hump, don't they?"

She couldn't look at him.

"I mean, you ever actually *see* them hump?"

"No!" she shot back.

"You?" he asked.

"Me?"

"Yeah."

"Me what?"

"You know—hump?"

She looked at him fearfully, then moved over as far as she could, putting space between them. This was about as much excitement as she could handle for one night. She wanted to leave.

"Well?" he said, waiting for her answer.

She turned her back on him and studied the college students at the table. They were all laughing and talking at once. She wondered if Sandy would make room for her if she pulled up a chair.

He repeated his question about humping, and she shivered, for his voice was again very close to her ear. In the safety of McCall Hall, at the water fountain, she'd found his surliness attractive, but here in these strange surroundings it was surliness raised to a dangerous power. She kept seeing the cat twisting in the air as he booted it off the stoop.

"*Do* you?" he asked more insistently.

Two of the young women rose from their places at the table, one of them drawing a key ring out of her handbag. If they were leaving, she would ask them for a ride back to campus. They stood for a time, finishing their conversations. She felt his hand on her arm. At length, the young woman with the key ring moved toward the door and the other followed. Laura made a move to join them, but he held her by the wrist.

"Hey, let go," she told him, still unable to face him, tears of fright springing to her eyes because of the menacing power of his wiry grip.

She pushed herself away from the bar, and luckily he was light enough to be pulled with her; he didn't have the bulk to resist. In spite of his tough appearance, he was actually (she realized) pretty scrawny. She was halfway to the door when he let go and turned back to the bar and hunched over his beer. He had seen what Laura had failed to notice: Chuck Lucking rising from his chair and taking a step in their direction, ready to defend her.

"Can I get a ride with you?" she asked, following the two young women out the door.

They halted on the crooked stoop and regarded her in the pink neon glow. "Depends where you're going," said the one with the keys.

"Rookery State."

"Come on—oh, look at the kitty."

The black cat came slinking up onto the step.

"The poor thing's cold, let it in."

They held the door open, but the cat backed away. One of them picked it up and set it inside.

Gary, turning from his beer, regarded the cat. The cat raised its hackles and darted behind the bar.

Chuck Lucking sat down again at the table, next to Sandy.

Gary ordered another beer.

———

Returned safely to campus, Laura found no one in the band room. The door stood open and the lights were on, but her father's string bass had been put away. She stepped back into the hallway to look at the coatrack. His coat hung there beside Dr. Benoit's. Dr. Edwards's coat was gone.

"Daddy," she called.

Silence along the corridor.

She went in and sat down at her homework. She read a paragraph of history, forgetting each sentence the moment she finished it. She tried a short story by Katherine Mansfield which was even less absorbing—some old lady sitting on a park bench listening to a band concert. Five minutes went by before she heard a door open and close and her father's footsteps approaching along the corridor.

"Ready?" he said, putting his head in at the door. He looked very grim.

She gathered up her books and followed him out. On the stairs he asked, "Where were you?"

"In the library," she lied. "Where were you?"

"Looking for you."

She sensed that this, too, was a lie. She asked, "Where's Dr. Benoit?"

"In her office."

Laura imagined the woman in her tiny office down the hall getting back into her clothes.

"What's she doing in her office?"

"Schoolwork, I suppose. Laura, why did you tell her Marcy's not your mother?"

"I never said that." She remembered saying it, but couldn't remember why, except she enjoyed testing people's gullibility, and Dr. Benoit seemed the type who'd believe anything.

"When I was in the hospital, you told her your real mother died when you were two. Why?"

"I never did."

In her office, meanwhile, Peggy, naked to the waist, paused with her ear to the door, listening to their voices fading down the stairwell. Then she continued dressing.

PART 3

Mood Indigo

Connor, numb with sorrow, dropped off his daughter at the Paramount. He switched on the radio as he drove away, tuning into a special Sunday afternoon edition of "Lolly Speaking."

"Hi, Lolly, love your program. Say, about those college teachers threatening to strike—haven't they got their nerve? I always used to come to their defense when my husband called them goldbricks—our daughter Sarah got her degree there—but I'm done defending them. They're already such a tax burden to all of us, and it's like they want to rub our noses in it."

"Hi, Lolly, I missed your recipe Friday for crumble cake. Please give it out again, would you?"

At a stoplight, Connor took a deep breath and vigorously rubbed his face with both hands, trying to recover the energy his wife had drained out of him. He'd spent the morning trying to convince her not to kill herself. He and Laura had finally succeeded in urging her into her clothes, then into her coat, then into the car, and they'd taken her to the hospital. Getting her admitted was an awkward, drawn-out procedure, as though no one on the staff had ever been presented with a case of mental illness before. She was admitted over the phone, finally, by the doctor who had treated his pneumonia.

"Say, Lolly, this is Bill Chapman down at the Standard station. What the blazes are you doing on the air—it's Sunday afternoon? The Blues are playing their biggest game of the year in about twenty minutes."

The light turned green and Connor proceeded along River Drive in the direction of Mount of Olives Lutheran. He hadn't intended to take part in the Alliance meeting, hadn't planned to vote one way or the other, but now he was suddenly in need of uninterrupted health insurance.

"Lolly, when are you going to have Herbert Gengler on the radio? He *is* the president, for pity's sake. Isn't he going to step forward and stop these people from striking? I've called his office every day for a week, I've even called his house, and I'm told he's either out of town or under the weather. I'm beginning to wonder if Rookery State even *has* a president."

"Hi, Lolly, it's me again. It wasn't crumble cake, it was peach delight I missed—if you've got it handy there. And tell Bill Chapman at the Standard station there's a few things in life more important than hockey, and I think you ought to be able to come on the air with a special show like this anytime you please."

It was a sunless, frosty afternoon. Driving slowly along the Badbattle, he saw skaters with shovels clearing last night's snow from a circle of ice. His wife had been given a bed in the geriatric wing because there was no section devoted to psychiatry. A psychiatrist, he was told, visited Rookery on Tuesdays. He and Laura hung around feeling useless for a time, and then Laura said she wanted to see the movie at the Paramount.

"Lolly, this is Ron Hunsinger. I just want to tell your listeners, in case they don't know it, there's certain professors on that campus drawing down fourteen thousand dollars a year for teaching two classes a day. Now is that, or is that not—"

He switched off the radio and parked at the end of a long line of cars. He sat for a few minutes watching latecomers hurry into the church and wishing he could go to his studio instead, take up his brush and pallette, and try painting his way out of despair. He heaved himself out of the car and climbed the steps to the church because Marcy's double room cost fifty-five dollars a day and psychiatrists were known to charge up to thirty dollars an hour.

Inside, he was jolted by the high spirits of his colleagues, the shrillness of their voices. He was handed a pamphlet by a man standing in the aisle, one of his colleagues, no doubt, but he didn't know him. He looked around for a familiar face, then slipped into a pew at the back, beside Professor Shea. He gave his face a vigorous rub and asked, "What do you make of all this, sir?"

The old man looked amused. "Not my sort of thing, I'm afraid."

"You're not taking sides?"

"Not yet. I'm waiting to hear the oratory."

Mount of Olives was small and chilly. It gave Connor the impression of icy purity. Everything, including the plaster altar of intricate design, had been painted white. A few dim lamps burned along the walls. The only color in the place came from the weak rays of afternoon light falling through the pebbly, pale blue window glass. This light made Professor Shea and all those around him, despite their high energy, look sallow.

He saw Victor up front, waving Kimberly Kraft and Alex Bolus forward to sit with the other officers and functionaries of the Alliance. In an alcove on the far side, he saw Leland standing beside the baptismal font in animated conversation with a small circle of his advisers. Bernard Beckwith, the drama coach, was one of them. Chairman Oberholtzer was another.

So tense and vociferous was the faculty that they seemed to be giving off sparks of electricity. Connor had been a college teacher long enough to understand their excitement. Scholars had very few opportunities like this to stir up reactions in the outside world. A campus was a kind of asylum where professors diverted themselves year after year with academic questions Connor didn't concern himself with. Which student should be spared an F as too demeaning? Which colleague should be denied tenure as too ennobling? How big a budget for hockey sticks?

Neil Novotny plumped into the pew next to Connor. He was wearing his soiled parka and his weekend whiskers. He said, "Well, I mailed it off to your friend. The first seven chapters."

Connor nodded approvingly. He hadn't seen Neil since he stalked angrily out of the band room on Wednesday evening.

"Is he a fussy sort of editor?"

"Well, I'm sure he has his standards."

"What I'm asking, will he read a dirty manuscript?"

Connor shot him a quizzical look. "Pornographic, you mean?"

"No, I mean food stains, wrinkled pages, scratch-outs. The pages I sent him had some chocolate where you couldn't see the words, and I typed those places over, but he can't expect me to re-type every little smear and coffee stain, can he? That would impede my progress."

"I'm sure he'll understand."

Neil looked relieved. "I've got my heroine involved with a man she met on a riverboat."

"A breakthrough, obviously."

"Clipping right along. I really shouldn't have left it, but I promised Victor I'd vote." In contrast to his sloppy attire, Neil's eyes looked unusually fresh; his voice sounded cheery. "Victor's going to go nuts if he loses, but I tell him he's got it sewed up. Don't you think it's sewed up?"

A worried look crossed Connor's face, his bushy eyebrows coming together in a troubled squint. "I can't say."

Neil leaned forward to look around Connor. "How about you, Mr. Shea? Don't you think it's sewed up?"

"Sorry?" The elderly man hadn't been paying attention.

"The strike vote. I'm saying it will carry."

"I'll be surprised. You have to remember we're a faculty not wild about new ideas, most of us."

"Does that mean you're voting no?"

"I haven't decided."

"Vote in favor. Do it for Victor."

Mention of Victor, for some reason, caused the old man to laugh with glee.

Neil sat back and scanned the assembly.

"I'm voting against," said Connor.

Neil drew back, astonished. "You?" He looked betrayed. "But Connor—"

"Self-serving of me, I know, but I can't risk losing my health insurance."

"That's a consideration all right," said Professor Shea.

"Why? Are you guys sick?"

Neither man answered.

"But, Connor, you *can't* vote no."

Victor Dash, up front, called for order, but to little effect. He opened the low gate in the communion rail and stepped up into the sanctuary and repeated his plea. In vain. The faculty was giddy. Connor noticed that even the tired old veterans were debating and guffawing and calling to one another across the church. He saw Peggy sitting several pews ahead of him and over to his left. Her loveliness caused a hitch in his breathing. She was one of the few people serenely facing front, attentive to Victor's appeal for quiet.

"Shut up, goddammit!" came the order from the sanctuary, and the faculty was startled into silence.

"The meeting of the Rookery chapter of the Faculty Alliance of America is now called to order," said Victor, and he introduced a young man named Jack Short, from Alliance headquarters, Midwest Section, in Milwaukee.

Jack Short stepped up through the low gate and stood at Victor's side, acknowledging the spirited applause with a broad smile.

The proceedings were then interrupted by a lean, ministerial-looking man who came through a dark doorway on the left side of the altar to have a word with Victor, presumably about his blasphemy, or perhaps about his invasion of sacred territory, for Victor and Jack Short quickly descended from the sanctuary, closing the gate behind them. The lean man faded back through the doorway.

Jack Short was a wide little man with a voice like a foghorn. He wore a gray, double-breasted suit and a tomato-colored necktie. He began by cracking a joke about the backwoodsy aspect of Rookery. The joke fell flat, Rookery's remote location being no laughing matter to most of this audience.

He turned serious then. He said he'd driven seven hundred miles to address them on the subject of exploring new territory. He called them pathfinders. No college professors in his jurisdiction had ever before gone out on strike. High schools, yes. High school teachers were doing it all over the place, he said, but college faculties were generally too fragmented, too divisive, too independent, to agree on anything.

Here the churchful of professors, for a reason Connor didn't understand, broke into wild applause. The clapping and shouting energized Jack Short. He enriched his delivery with a stagy kind of mugging and posturing, assuring them that they'd been betrayed by the highest level of state government, and they must serve notice that such treatment would not be tolerated. Not only did they owe it to themselves to strike, he roared, they owed it to all workers employed by heartless bureaucrats everywhere.

More applause.

"In conclusion," he said in a quieter voice, and with the smirk of a man with something up his sleeve, "it is fitting that this giant step in labor relations—and I mean *giant* step . . ." Here he paused and closed his eyes blissfully, as though overcome by his own eloquence. ". . . should take place at Paul Bunyan's alma mater."

The effect was immediate and sophomoric—shrieking, moaning, clapping, foot-stomping. Up front, Aaron Cardero leaped to his feet, faced the congregation, and whistled with two fingers in his mouth. Peggy covered her face. Professor Shea wiped tears of mirth from his eyes.

Connor was mystified. "Why is everybody going nuts?" he asked.

Shea said, "You haven't heard about the college motto?"

"No."

The old man explained. He said the Signage Committee was responsible.

"Including Peggy," Neil put in bitterly, still resentful that she hadn't let him read to the quintet.

"Paul Bunyan's alma mater," groaned Connor in disbelief.

When order was finally restored, Victor introduced an attorney who'd accompanied Jack Short on his drive from Milwaukee. His name was Laraby. He was large, white-haired, and the more rumpled-looking of the two men, as though the car might have been too small for him. His message, though delivered in a weary voice, was interesting. He said the Alliance was about to institute a pair of lawsuits on the faculty's behalf. First, the six individual members of the College Board would be sued for overstepping their constitutional powers in withholding the money appropriated for salaries. "This, together with the strike, will hit the board like a one-two punch," he said without emotion. "The board will be much more inclined to cave in to your strike, knowing that any fair-minded judge will eventually rule against them anyhow."

"What's the point in striking, then?" came a voice from the baptismal alcove. It was C. Mortimer Oberholtzer, standing straight and tall in elbow patches and French cuffs and twirling his smokeless pipe nervously in his fingers as he spoke. "My considered opinion is that we should take the high road. Let the courts lift this burden from us. Our place is the classroom, our mission is educating the young. I firmly believe that unless we—"

"Lawsuits take forever," the attorney interjected. "Next summer is the soonest you can expect a ruling from a judge. Meanwhile, your salary money is being used up, and how do you recover it?"

Oberholtzer answered glibly, "Why, that's simple—the court simply orders the board to hand it over."

"By next summer the board no longer *has* the money. It could take years for them to make it up to you in dribs and drabs."

The chairman wasn't convinced. "I think we can presume that the court will order the board to borrow it and pay it back to us in a lump sum."

"That's presuming too much." The rumpled attorney, having heard enough from Oberholtzer, moved on to his next point. "Our second lawsuit will be against your dean."

"Yippee!" cried someone at the back. Cardero, up front, leaped to his feet and repeated his two-fingered whistle.

"Your dean has violated your civil rights by not allowing the Alliance to meet on campus."

There was scattered applause, Neil's the most vigorous. "That stupid bozo," he said in Connor's ear.

"In plain language, it's discrimination," the attorney added. "We go to court with both of these suits next week."

He sat down to renewed applause, but not from everyone. Connor sensed that this talk of litigation had caused about half the gathering to lose their enthusiasm, and he wondered if the tide might be turning against Victor. He was tempted to help turn it by standing up and mentioning loss of insurance, loss of paychecks.

But he didn't have to. Leland did it for him. Leland, next on the agenda, spoke with amazing authority. Loss of paychecks. Loss of insurance. Loss of public respect.

"What if this year's seniors can't finish their course work?" Leland asked. "What if they can't graduate on schedule? Those who are able to transfer to another college will leave us, and those who can't transfer will have their lives set back half a year, maybe a full year. What happens to our reputation then?" Leland held notecards in his hand but didn't seem to need them. Looking his audience in the eye, he pleaded earnestly, "Is this any way to be the beacon of learning in the Northwoods—teaching only when it doesn't interfere with our internal skirmishes and squabbles? Ever since the founding of Rookery State College, ever since we were a Normal School with nothing but an office and a classroom on the second floor of Rookery High School, our noble work of educating the youth of northern Minnesota has never once been interrupted, and a temporary salary freeze is not reason enough to interrupt it now."

Connor could scarcely believe this was the self-effacing man who hung his head over his keyboard at the end of a piece of music. Here was eloquence and presence. Who coached him? His chairman? His mother?

Leland concluded with a warning about the dissension inherent in a strike. His final phrase, "friend against friend," rang ominously in the little church as he retreated to the baptismal alcove. There was a ripple of subdued applause, followed by a thoughtful silence.

Then Victor, after conferring briefly with his Viceroys, got to his feet and vehemently summed up the issue, calling upon his colleagues to close ranks for the sake of their families and the Alliance and justice in the world. He spoke of the gender discrepancy in the present salary schedule. He displayed a newspaper ad for bicycles and pointed out the model he couldn't afford for his children. He displayed a ballot. Yes meant strike, no meant two more years of slave wages. A simple majority was assured, he said, because he'd already spoken to over fifty professors who intended to vote yes, but he wanted a hundred percent. Unanimity would send a message of strength to St. Paul. He paused for effect.

The room grew so still that Connor could hear the scrape of skate blades on the ice below the church.

Then Victor's voice rose excitedly. The strike would begin on Wednesday morning, he said, the first of March. That would give the faculty forty-eight hours to put their classes in cold storage and get organized for picketing. It would also give the administration forty-eight hours to back down. He said that he himself would search out President Gengler this very afternoon, report to him the outcome of the strike vote, and urge him to make a last minute appeal to the College Board. "It could well be," Victor said stridently, "that as Wednesday approaches, management will fold."

It was obvious to Connor that Victor's loud and overwrought delivery was an attempt to recover the brisk vitality that had permeated the church at the start, but it was lost. Referring to his colleagues as slaves probably didn't help his case. These people were not very defiant by nature, and many of those around Connor hung their heads in what looked like slavish defeat. Nor had he been wise to bring up the bicycle he couldn't afford. It was somehow too pathetic an example to inspire vigorous resentment. Victor sat down to another round of polite, restrained applause, which was followed by another few moments of prayerlike silence, and then the question was called.

Alex Bolus and Aaron Cardero made their way down the middle aisle, passing out ballots. Kimberly Kraft followed with a box of stubby pencils. The ministerial-looking man emerged from the shadows again, and stood at the communion rail as though to consecrate the voting.

Neil voted yes. He glanced left and spied Connor marking his ballot no. He spied Shea voting yes. Historian Quinn, on his right, also voted to strike. He couldn't quite see over the woman's shoulder in the pew ahead. Sensing that Connor's side would surely lose, Neil felt suddenly magnanimous.

"I suppose with a family and all, you have to worry about insurance."

Connor nodded, his troubled frown returning.

"But remember you're an artist, Connor. Nothing can stand in the way of our art."

Connor looked him over. "What pompous bullshit."

Neil drew back, wounded. "Well, I beg your pardon."

"Being locked out of my studio would sure as hell stand in the way of my art."

"Oh," Neil murmured. "I hadn't thought of that." Then, thinking of it, he asked, "Why would you be locked out?"

"As a rookie, I haven't been given a key to my building."

"But why would you need one?"

"I'm assuming there'll be a lockout."

Neil, looking puzzled, scratched his head and his throat and various itchy places under his parka.

The ballots were collected and laid on the communion rail. Two professors of opposing views were summoned to assist Kimberly Kraft in the tally. This was the work of five minutes. Kimberly handed her notebook to Victor, whose ears and forehead glowed as he scanned the results.

Connor, regretting his brusqueness, leaned toward Neil and asked, aspiring to levity, "What does it mean when Victor turns red?"

Neil shrugged. He was pouting.

"It means he's pleased," said Professor Shea. "I watch him change color at division meetings."

"We're striking, then."

"I'd say so."

Victor announced the results. Sixty-four in favor, fifty against.

While many clapped, others looked stunned and disbelieving, as though they'd been tricked.

Victor said they all must check their campus mailboxes every morning and afternoon for Alliance memos. He said they would all be contacted at least once a day on the Telephone Tree. He said his house at 311 Trillium would be strike headquarters. "Come on over, all of you, right now. It's open house. My good wife Annie's got the coffeepot on."

The professors rose from the pews, mingled in the aisles, moved toward the door.

"God bless you, goddammit, you did it!" Victor called after them, raising his hand in happy benediction.

———

Ron Hunsinger, waiting for Georgina, stood in the middle of the narrow sidewalk, partially blocking the stream of professors pouring out of the church. Having just made a house call to fix a faulty refrigerator, he wore a dark blue coverall with soiled knees, tattered cuffs, and his father's name—HAROLD—stitched in red on the breast pocket. Ron was a short man with a large, handsome head and quick, darting eyes.

"Pardon me," said a sarcastic woman who had to step into snow over her shoes to go around him.

"For what?" was Ron Hunsinger's defiant reply.

"Hey, Hunsinger," called a man halfway down the steps, "I heard you on the radio. I'm one of your feeders at the public trough."

Ron Hunsinger knew the man. Quinn. A history prof with a poor credit rating. He'd sold him a humidifier for his basement.

"Some days I teach two classes, as you said, and some days I teach three," declared Historian Quinn, making his way through the crowd to face him. "I also spend three to four hours a day preparing for those classes and correcting the papers they generate, and I spend at least four or five hours a week helping seniors with their independent research."

"Okay, okay," said Hunsinger, turning away from him.

"To say nothing of the time I spend on committee work."

"Okay, okay," he repeated, watching for his fiancée to come out.

"You see, it all amounts to well over a forty-hour week. Which means my own research is conducted on my own time, and that means the information along the history trail hasn't cost the county a penny."

"What history trail is that?" asked Hunsinger, who liked to pretend that innovations he'd failed to thwart didn't exist. He'd campaigned against the referendum to put up historical displays along old Highway 21 where it wound through the forest. It defied logic that such a useless idea should have come to fruition. Who cared where logging camps had stood eighty years ago? Who wanted to look at laminated black-and-white pictures of old-time people standing along the crooked streets of old-time settlements that died out when the virgin timber disappeared? Nobody stood to make any money on a history trail.

Quinn shakily buttoned his coat and straightened his cap. "We're underpaid, Mr. Hunsinger. All we're asking for is a living wage."

Hunsinger, the shorter of the two, trained his steady blue eyes up at the historian and said, "I'm not against a living wage. What I'm against is having it come out of my pocket."

Quinn went kicking off through the snow of the churchyard. Hunsinger called after him, but Quinn didn't turn around. He wanted to ask Quinn why the public should have to pay for the livelihood of professors. Why didn't professors sell their teaching the way he and his father sold refrigerators? Why didn't they raise tuition so people who wanted a college education paid the full price? It didn't make sense that people who didn't use them should pay for microscopes and library books and air conditioners in faculty offices. Nobody subsidized Hunsinger Appliance.

He saw Georgina step out of the church. When she waved at him, he timidly lifted his gloved hand and wiggled his fingers. He wished she'd learn to be less public with her affection, but of course nothing could be done: she was too deeply in love to exercise any sort of restraint. Good old Georgina. He proudly watched her descend the steps and move toward him through the crowd. She had promised to vote against striking. How could you not be fond of an intelligent woman who, by the force of your logic, came around to your way of thinking? And this was over and above his many other reasons for being fond of her. Good old Georgina was about the right size for a man of his height. She didn't paint her face and get herself up like Peggy Benoit and these other overdecorated women. She'd expanded his idea of entertainment; they'd seen *Oklahoma!* on the campus stage. Above all, she had a remarkable head for money and his father approved of her—which meant she'd fit nicely into the appliance business when she quit teaching, which she kept threatening to do because it bored her.

When she rushed up to him and took his hand and kissed him, he looked stone-faced, hiding his embarrassment.

Then along came Leland Edwards, a man he'd gone to school with, kindergarten through high school. Leland tried slipping furtively past him, but Hunsinger reached out and grabbed him.

"Edwards, tell your mother she's doing Rookery a world of good with her programs about the Alliance."

"Thank you, I'll tell her." Leland stood looking off into the middle distance while doing his best to ignore the hand wrinkling the lapel of his coat. It was a new coat of tan poplin, and today was the first time he'd worn it. Throughout their schooldays, Hunsinger had been a bully.

"It's good to hear the true feelings of people come out on programs like that. Almost everybody's against you guys striking."

"I'm against it too," said Leland, glancing sideways at Hunsinger, hoping this would qualify him for release.

Peggy Benoit came up to them. "Leland, I had to admire you up there, in spite of what you said."

"Thank you." Leland, prohibited from turning to face her, was warmed by her voice and relieved beyond measure. His plea for votes had obviously not antagonized her.

"Me too, I was impressed as hell," Georgina told him, reaching over and lifting her fiancé's hand off Leland's lapel. "You'd have earned an A-minus in my speech class."

"Thank you," Leland repeated, backing away. "I'll see you at four, then?" he asked Peggy.

"On the dot."

Ron outmatched Peggy's chilly smile with one of his own. Peggy had that eastern way of talking, as though she were above everybody.

Peggy saw how much more antagonism his smile contained than hers. Where hers conveyed indifference (she hoped), his was full of hatred. Did he know she'd called him a jerk? Had Georgina told him?

"See you tomorrow," said Georgina blithely.

Watching them walk away, Peggy shivered with trepidation. Here was a couple as dangerously mismatched as she and Gene Benoit had been. Mystery of mysteries, Georgina truly loved this clod. You could see it in her expression and body language. At the church door she'd looked momentarily delighted when her eyes fell on him, and now, stepping out into the street, she took his arm and leaned into him while Hunsinger held himself rigid, an ungiving man, incapable of returning her loving gesture with a hug or a pat on the arm or even a slight bending in her direction.

Kimberly Kraft came down the steps calling, "Peggy, we're all going to Victor's house. It's headquarters." Kimberly's eyes shone with joy. "Isn't it terrific, Peggy? I've never been so excited. The moment the ballots were counted, I knew there was no turning back. It's like a roller coaster starting down and there's no getting out."

Peggy tried to imagine Kimberly Kraft, so prim and prudent, allowing herself a roller-coaster ride. She was dressed today in an elegant gray coat. The stand-up collar of her cream blouse showed above the fur trim.

Alex Bolus came lumbering down the steps. "Peggy, come on, everybody's going to Victor's."

"I'll drop you off," she said, "I've got quintet practice."

"Oh, skip your music for once. Victor wants your input especially."

Peggy's eyes were on the appliance truck, which was double-parked. It was an old van with dents. She watched Ron accompany Georgina to the passenger side and hold the door open for her. Studying him in profile, she saw that his short legs and big head gave him a babyish aspect. Even his straight back and his fine blond hair somehow contributed to this infantile effect, as well as the way he moved his head in quick little jerks. And of course his coveralls. Georgina might have been engaged to an oversized preschooler.

"Come on," Alex pleaded, wrenching her pink nylon jacket around in order to dig a large red handkerchief out of its pocket. "Victor mentioned you especially. He wants your input on the women's salary schedule."

"My input is simple. Equality."

The Dash house on Trillium Street was a white, shrubless, story-and-a-half colonial with childish paper cutouts pasted in all the downstairs windows. Lumps of ice in the yard were all that remained of ruined snow forts and snowmen. Leaning against a tree was a sled with a missing slat, and leaning against another tree, near the street, was a little boy with gaps in his mouth where baby teeth had been. He'd been watching hordes of people stream into his house, and now he saw yet another car, a red one, come to a stop in the street and two women get out, a big one and a little one.

"Oh, come on in, at least for a while," begged the big one. "Victor's wife is serving snacks."

"I can't," said the driver. "The quintet's at four o'clock."

"Quartet, you mean. Victor won't be there."

"I know, but the others will."

"Tell them to come too," the other woman urged in a high-pitched, laughing voice. "Tell them it's a victory party and we need music."

"Impossible," said the driver. "Leland, you see."

The women apparently understood, for they quit begging, and the driver added, "We're nothing without Leland on the piano."

"Is he really that good?" asked the big one.

"Our heart and soul."

The car sped off and the two women spied the boy before he was quite hidden behind the tree.

"Oh, look, a little *boy*," trilled the smaller woman, as though she'd spotted a monkey or a stork. She was wearing a gray coat and gray gloves. They both came at him, the one in the gray coat asking his name, the one in the pink jacket lifting off his stocking cap and saying she wished she had one just like it. The house was already full of people like this, saying dumb things to kids. He'd escaped them by sneaking away, but Marky and Vicky were still trapped inside. One of his father's friends, a jumpy man named Neil, had picked up Marky and accidentally dropped him. Another friend named Cardero, who'd been at the house a lot lately, bounced Vicky on his knee until she threw up.

"Aren't you cold out here?" asked the gray coat.

He was, but he shook his head no.

The pink jacket said, "You must be wondering why your daddy has brought home all these oddballs."

"I know why!" he blurted, then wished he hadn't, for both women laughed at his sudden excitement.

"Why?" they asked together.

He lowered his voice and told them confidentially, "So he can buy us a bike."

After several rings a woman's voice answered Victor's phone call. "Yes?"

"Hello, is this Mrs. Gengler?"

"Yes, it is."

"Can I talk to President Gengler?"

"I'll see if he's able to come to the phone. Who shall I say is calling, please?"

"Victor Dash."

"Who?"

"Dash." He spelled it for her. "I teach English."

"At the college?"

"Yes, at the college."

"And what do you wish to talk to the president about?"

For God's sake, it was like calling the King of France. "Alliance business," he told her.

"Just a moment, Dr. Dash."

"I said Victor, not Doctor."

Waiting, he turned to Cardero standing beside him in the kitchen. "Tell everybody to pipe down, Aaron, I can hardly hear." Then he turned to his wife, who was making a lot of noise with a spoon in a jar, replenishing a bowl of mayonnaise. "Be quiet a minute, would you, Annie? I'm getting the president on the line."

Annie put down the jar and spoon and gave her husband a loving pinch in the ribs on her way into the dining room. She was wearing a flowered apron with flounces over the shoulders. Cardero went ahead of her, pressing himself through the small rooms, urging quiet. The three dozen guests were mostly clustered around the table where the food and wine had been set out.

"Here's more mayo," called Annie, plopping down the bowl. She picked up the bread tray, sweeping the remaining rolls onto the tablecloth. She also picked up the nearly empty plate of sliced ham. "Just hold your horses, everybody, I'll be right back with more sandwich makings."

"You got any more herring, Mrs. Dash?"

"Sorry, we ran out."

"Hey, Annie, how about pickles? You got any pickles?"

"No pickles. Victor ate them all before you got here." Laughing, Annie disappeared into the kitchen.

"How about liquor?" came a call from the living room. "I don't see any hard liquor."

The noise level was rising, due to the inept way Kimberly Kraft was picking up four-year-old Marky Dash, causing him to shriek in fear, while his five-year-old sister Vicky, wearing vomit stains down her front, pounded a miniature xylophone with a carpenter's hammer.

"Quiet now, quiet now," pleaded Cardero. "Victor's trying to get Gengler on the phone." By planting the word "Gengler" here and there, he achieved near silence among the adults, the president's name casting something of a spell over the faculty, many of whom had never been introduced to the man. He was a phantom, glimpsed at fall workshop and spring commencement and practically nowhere else, always rumored to be gravely ill or traveling afar on fund-raising junkets. One constantly heard about some incredibly huge endowment Dr. Gengler was on the verge of attracting. Reports differed about its purpose: an electron microscope, a natural gas heating system, a new hockey arena.

A dozen professors packed themselves into the kitchen to hear Victor on the phone. They gobbled up the ham nearly as fast as Annie could slice it, and they ate the last of the rolls. She passed word into the living room, requesting that someone quiet her children. She also passed along a handful of saltwater taffy for this purpose, but it disappeared en route.

"Seems to me the Alliance could afford a phone extension for Victor," said Laraby, the lawyer from Milwaukee. He was hemmed in beside the refrigerator and had been knocked nearly off balance by someone looking for beer.

"Agreed," said Jack Short, with an empty wineglass in his hand. "For the duration of the strike at least. I'll see that he gets it."

"Shhh," said Aaron Cardero, pointing to Victor, who had resumed his conversation with a look of amazement on his face.

"Vacation, Mrs. Gengler?" He covered the mouthpiece and

spoke to his audience in the kitchen. "The Genglers are leaving for a week in Florida in the morning."

"Ask her, vacation from what?" somebody said.

"How about I come over for a few minutes right now, Mrs. Gengler?" After another moment of listening, he nodded happily, indicating assent.

"Can I go with you, Victor?" asked Kimberly Kraft. "I've always wanted to see the inside of that odd-looking house."

"Cats? Why do you ask, Mrs. Gengler?" Victor gave the voice on the wire a few moments to explain, then he called out to his wife, "Annie, we haven't got any cats, have we?" His children were known to adopt homeless dogs and cats, then lose them after a few days, the normal ruckus of Dash family life proving too chaotic for animals.

"A kitten," she said happily. "Donnie found it yesterday, eating garbage in the alley."

"Yes, Mrs. Gengler, we have one, but it's just a kitten." This time, as he listened, he turned to his followers and pointed to his other ear, making a spiral gesture indicating lunacy. "All right, Mrs. Gengler, I'll send one of my associates instead. I'll send Kimberly Kraft. . . . Yes, she's right here by my side, she'll be glad to serve as my spokesman. . . ." Then his eyes opened wide, in wonder. "But Mrs. Gengler, she's only been here twenty minutes and she hasn't even *seen* the cat."

He covered the mouthpiece and addressed his audience with a mixture of anger and mirth. "The president's allergic to cat dander. Have you ever heard such—"

"Now, Victor," Annie cautioned, smiling benignly, "don't say things you'll be sorry for." Annie was an expert at gauging the rise or fall of her husband's temper.

"But they're all here in my house, Mrs. Gengler, all my steering committee. You mean not one of us can come and see him? I don't even know where the cat *is*. I've never even *seen* the cat."

He listened further, his eyes narrowing, his cheeks turning ashen. Twice he stuttered with rage, and was interrupted. The third time he opened his mouth to speak, Annie snatched the phone away from him lest he tell the president's wife that she was shitting in her hat.

"Hi, Mrs. Gengler, this is Annie Dash. Just tell us what time would suit the president and I'm sure we can find someone. Yes, you have my word. Yes, I understand perfectly. Just a second, I'll see." Annie looked from face to face in the kitchen; she jumped a couple of times to see over their heads into the next room. "No, she's not here, Mrs. Gengler. Yes, we'll get ahold of her and send her right over." She bade the woman a cordial good-bye and hung up.

"Peggy Benoit," announced Annie. "She's asking for Peggy Benoit."

"Of course, Peggy," sighed Victor with relief.

"Perfect," said Kimberly Kraft and Alex Bolus together.

"Why didn't we think of Peggy in the first place?" asked Aaron Cardero.

There were noises of agreement from one and all. Who better than Peggy Benoit to appeal to the president's better nature, if he had one?

The quintet was a trio today, and so much the better, in Leland's opinion. Lacking Neil's off-key piping, "Mood Indigo" became as shadowy and touching as rain in the night. "Little White Lies," without Victor's frenzied drumming, went bubbling along like a clear little brook.

After they played each of these through in a straightforward manner—no scat, no riffs, very little ornamentation—Leland suggested they not go on to other songs, but devote the rest of the afternoon to these two pieces. Leland never grew weary of polishing his keyboard work. With Victor absent, they wouldn't be continually pressed to move on to the next piece before the last one was correctly disposed of. Whereas Victor enjoyed the novelty of trying out new rhythms, Leland found novelty of any kind disheartening. Where was the satisfaction if each song wasn't presented flawlessly for that appreciative audience he had been imagining since he started lessons with Miss Carpentier at the age of seven?

Peggy and Connor agreed to his request, but Connor less eagerly, it seemed. Connor looked distracted today. Was he deep in some artistic problem, Leland wondered, or simply deep in his music? His eyes had a hidden look, even when he directed them at Peggy and smiled. His movements, apart from fingering the strings of his bass, were wooden.

So they backed up and concentrated on "Mood Indigo," he and Connor teaming up on a few experimental openings while Peggy applied various vocal intonations to the words. She faced away from the men, singing to the west window and looking down on the hockey fans streaming out of the arena and creating a traffic jam on Eleventh Street. When she settled on the right voice to convey the song's torchy message, she turned to them and nodded, indicating she was ready when they were. Both men bent eagerly to their instruments, awaiting the downbeat, their eyes fixed on the pencil she held in the air, and it was during this moment of silence that footsteps sounded in the corridor. They turned to face the doorway, expecting Neil, all three of them concealing their regret.

There was no concealing their surprise when Kimberly Kraft walked in, followed by Annie Dash.

"Sorry to break up the fun," Kimberly said to Peggy, laughing her nervously musical laugh, "but you've been named ambassador to the president." She turned to Leland and Connor, explaining, "The Alliance wants her to go to the president's house right away and tell him the results of the strike vote. He's leaving for Florida in the morning."

Peggy, playing along with what she assumed was a joke, fluttered her eyelashes and spread a hand across her breast—mock humility. "Whyever me?"

"Because the president's wife asked for you especially, and because you don't have a cat. President Gengler won't talk to anybody who's been around cats."

"I've met you all before," said Annie, stepping forward and planting herself boldly and cheerfully at the center of the trio. She shook Leland's hand, then Connor's, then Peggy's. "Victor asked me to drive Kimberly over here because he couldn't leave those high-up mucky-mucks from Milwaukee. I met you all at the Christmas party."

"Yes, I remember," said Leland, who had risen politely to his feet.

"Of course," said Connor from his high stool. "How are you?"

Peggy said, "Annie, this is a party joke, isn't it?—let's send Peggy to the president's house with the bad news and see what happens."

Annie's laugh was a roar. "No joke," she said. "Cross my heart."

"Annie's a marvelous hostess," said Kimberly. "You should have seen the food."

"Ham," Annie said proudly. "The Alliance paid for it, otherwise it would have been bologna." Her deep, full-throated laugh was surprising in a woman so small. She was smaller even than Kimberly, Peggy observed, but without Kimberly's frailty. Here was a wiry little dynamo, a resolute woman of happy disposition— the perfect wife, in other words, for the likes of her hotheaded Victor. Like her husband, she filled any room she was in, but filled it with brightness and cheer, her lighthearted nature unsullied by any trace of Victor's petulance. Below her short coat hung the bottom half of her flouncy apron.

"You've never seen people eat like that crowd," she went on. "When I left, they were digging through the freezer looking for more ice cream. Victor used to bring friends home when he was working on the pipeline that ate a lot, but nothing compared to this crowd of professors. My God, they polished off a nine-pound ham in forty-five minutes." Again the loud, surprising laugh. There was something sensual and reckless in the way she gave herself up to it.

Kimberly said, "Grab your coat, Peggy, the Genglers said to come over right away."

"They did not."

"You or nobody," confirmed Annie Dash.

"But they don't even *know* me."

"It's Alliance policy," said Kimberly. "We can't strike without offering to negotiate with local management."

Leland spoke up, stating fussily, "Local management is Dean Zastrow."

"The dean doesn't count," said Annie excitedly. "The men from Milwaukee told Victor a dean doesn't amount to a hill of beans, not if there's a president."

Peggy looked from one woman to the other, beginning to believe them. "You mean I go now, this minute, without putting on lipstick?"

"We'll take you in Annie's car, so grab your coat," Kimberly said.

Connor began picking out "Sunny Side of the Street" on his bass.

Peggy put on her coat. "What do I say when I get there?"

"Simple. Tell him the vote count, sixty-five to fifty."

"Sixty-four," said Leland.

"And tell him he still has forty-eight hours to prevail on the College Board and get us our salary money."

Peggy, as though for support or advice, turned to her fellow musicians. Leland frowned sadly, shaking his head. Connor, still plucking away at the song, was smiling mysteriously.

"Will you wait for me?" she asked them.

Both of them nodded—where else would they rather be?

Leland sat down at the piano and followed Connor's lead into "Sunny Side of the Street," which had a magnetic effect on Peggy. She could hardly bear to leave it. It was only by telling herself, *For the good of the Alliance, equal pay for women, a bicycle for the Dash kids,* that she was able to follow the two women out of the room.

"I'm so glad it's you instead of Victor," said Kimberly in the corridor. "I mean, can't you just imagine what Victor would say to the president?"

Imagining it caused Annie Dash to fill the corridor with a great echoing laugh that overspread the strains of music floating after them.

Peggy drove alone to the Genglers, having turned down Annie's offer of a ride because the old Dash convertible didn't seem classy enough to represent the Alliance. Annie and Kimberly followed her as far as Claudia's Lunch, where they were to wait, over coffee, for Peggy's report. Nor had Peggy agreed, as requested, to go to the Dashes' house afterward and report directly to Victor and the potentates from Milwaukee. She needed to get back to her music.

The president's house on River Drive, with its flat roof,

rounded corners, and white pebbly walls, put Peggy in mind of a cake. Its few windows, reflecting now the rosy light of late afternoon, were bordered by art deco ornamentation. She got out of her car and followed a walkway of frosty stone to the front door. There was only one tree in the yard, a high old oak, and perched on its topmost branch was a crow squawking at another crow circling overhead.

Finding no knocker or bell button, Peggy pounded on the heavy oak door. It was opened almost immediately by Mrs. Gengler, a very tall, white-haired woman of stately demeanor bent forward slightly from the waist. She wore a woolly black shawl over an ankle-length dress of some dark material as heavy as tapestry. At her throat was a brooch of silver and pearl. On one hand she wore three rings, emerald, diamond, and ruby. She gave off the aroma of mint.

"I'm so glad you could come, Dr. Benoit."

"Glad to, Mrs. Gengler."

The rooms were large and underfurnished. Three of the walls in the room where the president waited to receive her were papered in huge violet flowers. The fourth wall was given over to a larger-than-life portrait of a pretty young woman in a yellow sun hat.

The president rose from his straight chair next to a bare table and said, "We're so glad you could come, Dr. Benoit." He was a bony, emaciated man. His face, white as paper, was dominated by an enormous nose supporting a heavy pair of horn-rimmed spectacles.

"I'm very glad to be here, Dr. Gengler." This wasn't entirely a falsehood. She was fascinated by the mysteriousness of the house and its two inhabitants. She had a feeling of anticipation, as though something astonishing was hidden here. She thought it odd that the mystery seemed to emanate, like the aroma of mint, not from the president, but from Mrs. Gengler. The president smelled of medicine.

Verifying Peggy's intuition, he said, "My wife has been wanting to have you in for a month or more, haven't you, Justine?"

Mrs. Gengler nodded solemnly and asked Peggy to make herself comfortable on the only other chair in the room, a spare, Shakerlike piece with a straight back and a hard seat. The president, his shirt collar open under his suit coat, sat down again, and Mrs. Gengler went over and stood behind him with her jeweled hand on his shoulder. His itchy affliction was apparently flaring up, for his neck was raw-looking and glossy with salve. Despite his emaciated look, he wore a self-satisfied expression on his face, like someone unhealthy by choice.

His wife said, by way of breaking the ice, "Neither of us comes from a music background, but we thought your choir concert rather good."

"Thank you," said Peggy.

"At least the half we saw. It is hard for Herbert to sit for very long, so we don't go to many things."

"Not many," her husband agreed, passing his fingertips delicately over his throat, checking for loosening scabs.

"I'm sorry," said Peggy, her hand going involuntarily to her own throat. She'd never seen a skin problem this severe.

"But we made the effort in order for me to have a look at you," said his wife.

Peggy grew uneasy, unsure how to reply to such a curious statement. This woman had a snappish way of speaking, accompanied by a shrewd narrowing of her right eye.

The president seemed altogether friendlier. He asked her softly, "Is it warmer today? It looks warmer out."

"Quite nice, actually. Cloudy, but not awfully cold."

"I take it you're not from these parts?"

"No, the Boston area."

"You don't talk like people from here."

"So I've been told."

"Something of an adjustment, then, Rookery."

"You people *do* have long winters."

He nodded thoughtfully. "Yes, long months of dry indoor air is hell on dermatitis." His hand went again to his throat. "A week in Florida will see us through to the fifth of March. Justine isn't from these parts either. She comes from Tennessee and had to get used to the unrelenting cold. I'm not sure she ever did, to tell you the truth." He looked up at his wife to confirm this.

"I never did," she agreed.

"No, she never did. That's why we're going to Florida."

"That will be nice for you."

"Yes, a week in Florida will see us through to the fifth. Or did I say that." Stiffly, he slipped his hand behind him, under his suit coat, and tried scratching a spot he apparently couldn't reach, for he signaled with his eyes, and his wife picked a long-handled, ivory back-scratcher off the table (Peggy had seen one like it in a museum; it was molded like a tiny human hand) and stuck it down inside his shirt collar.

Discreetly averting her eyes, Peggy got down to business. "Victor Dash asked me to come and tell you about the action the Alliance is taking."

Because this statement was met with silence, she wondered if she should back up and explain who Victor Dash was. Had the president even heard of the Alliance? Seeing his expression would have helped, but the scratching operation was still going on ("There, yes, ah, right there") and she didn't want to look. Her eyes wandered through a doorway into the next room, and there she saw an even larger painting of perhaps the same sun-hat woman. Both portraits were interesting for their color if not for their insight into character. The faces were sketchier than the women in Connor's work, the effect more decorative, the tone altogether happier. She wondered what Connor would say about them. She wondered who the woman was. She seemed not to be Mrs. Gengler in her younger years. She wasn't severe enough.

"How well do you know this Dash fellow?" asked the president.

She risked a look. The scratcher was back on the table, the hand of his wife back on his shoulder. "Pretty well. We play in the same musical group together."

"Odd duck, wouldn't you say?"

"Odd? Well, yes, I suppose you don't see many labor agitators on a campus like this."

"No." The president looked vaguely amused. "Ill-advised, bringing unrest like that onto a campus, barking up the wrong tree entirely. Man like that makes you wonder why Oberholtzer hired him."

"Actually, he's quite a good teacher."

Dr. and Mrs. Gengler frowned simultaneously, as though skeptical that good teaching should be a qualification.

"Students like him," she added.

Apparently a bad sign, judging by their deepening frowns.

"The Alliance called for a strike vote this afternoon."

Their faces turned blank, their eyes shifting slightly away from her.

"Because the State College Board is withholding our salary money for the next two years, and because women are paid less than men."

President Gengler raked his throat, drawing blood.

"And the vote was sixty-four to fifty, in favor. The strike is called for Wednesday, and we are hoping—"

"When I say odd, I mean the plate in his head. I'm told he has a steel plate in his head."

"A vulgar man, from what we hear," said Mrs. Gengler, dabbing at her husband's bloody neck with a hankie. "Saying the most outrageous things at division meetings. Obscenities. The Oberholtzers have said so."

"It's the plate, Justine. Makes you funny, having a plate in your head."

Peggy forged ahead. "So I guess what the Alliance would like me to say to you is that we're hoping you might use your influence on the board, Dr. Gengler. Two years without even a cost-of-living raise is going to create a lot of hardship."

The president nodded, as though he agreed. It was his wife who resisted. "The campus comes first, Dr. Benoit. How do you teach without classrooms?"

"Well, I realize there are needs on both sides of the question, but why wasn't the faculty at least consulted?"

"I can tell you why." Her forefinger was lifted in the air, its emerald ring glinting. "You had no one looking after you in St. Paul. Had you been content to remain with the Congress of College Professors, things would have gone differently for you. The C.C.P. always looked after their own."

Was this true? Was Rookery being punished for going over to the Alliance? "No," said Peggy. "The other three campuses still *have* the C.C.P. and they're in the same boat we are."

At this, the husband and wife exchanged a grave look, he craning his neck upward, she patting him gently on the shoulder. There was a long silence before the president went back to Victor's plate. "I've wondered if this Dash fellow incurred his injury in Vietnam."

Peggy was suddenly enraged. She was talking to a pair of ninnies. This poor encrusted fool of a president avert a strike? Fat chance.

"I guess that's it," she said, getting to her feet and buttoning her coat. "We just thought we should tell you in person, rather than have you learn about it through hearsay."

"Oh, we learned about it from Lolly Edwards," said Mrs. Gengler. "She called right away after the meeting. Now if you can spare just a moment more, Dr. Benoit." Stepping out from behind her husband's chair, she swept toward Peggy with her jeweled hand extended. "I have something in the other room I'd like to show you."

The other room, the one with the second portrait on the wall, gave out on a pleasant view of the Badbattle, and was as sparsely furnished as the first—a desk, a wastebasket, a dining table with two high-backed chairs, and a sideboard. No rugs on the tile floor, nothing on the walls except the painting Peggy couldn't resist asking about.

"Herbert's mother," was Mrs. Gengler's cold reply. "As a girl." From the drawer of the desk she drew out a large white envelope and handed it to Peggy. "This is why I asked you to come, Dr. Benoit. I was at a loss for words when I saw it, as you will doubtless be."

Peggy drew a photo from the envelope and stopped breathing. An eight-by-ten glossy of herself, smiling and nude.

She slipped it back into the envelope and hid her face behind it, squeezing her eyes shut.

"It came addressed to the president, with no written message. The postmark, you'll notice, is Boston. Please take it with you. It has sullied the drawer of my desk for a month or more. Have you any idea who might be sending these things out?"

Things, plural? Peggy peered over the top of the envelope, shaking her head in horror, and asked in a whisper, "Are there others?"

"None that have come to my attention. I have not shown it to Herbert, though it's addressed to him. I would have destroyed it

immediately, had the face not been one I recognized from somewhere and couldn't place. Later, when we attended your concert, it
came to me—I had seen your picture in the *Morning Call* last September, among the rest of the new faculty. You know nothing
about it?"

She shook her head in denial, though she did recall the morning she stepped out of the shower and found Gene Benoit's lens
trained on her. She laughed and chased him from the bathroom,
snapping her towel at his bare legs.

"You're smiling at the camera," said the president's wife
accusingly.

Peggy shook her head again, in disbelief. This was the perilous
side of Gene Benoit, the side her brothers and sisters had tried to
warn her about.

"Take it now. I'll not say anything."

"Thank you."

Mrs. Gengler led her through the other room, where they
paused for the president's farewell, and then to the front door,
where they parted with an exchange of anxious, embarrassed
glances, but no words.

The movie was a disappointment. Stepping out of the Paramount into the gray afternoon, Laura put on her earmuffs and mittens and set off for campus a mile or more away. She'd liked
Newman and Redford separately in other pictures, and the ads for
this one said they were dynamite together, but they weren't. Silly
was what they were. Besides, the Paramount had a bad smell, like
garlic.

She left the business district and walked along River Drive,
wondering if her mother was truly over the edge, or just pretending. Either way, it was imperative that she, Laura, start working on
her father to return to the city before all three of them rotted away
up here in the forest.

Her route to campus took her within two blocks of the hospital, and she considered dropping in for another look at her mother
in her new robe and her new personality, but she decided no, her

mother was too weird. The nurses had no more than settled her in her room when she started acting perky. In the pink-flowered wrapper Laura had given her Christmas before last, and which she'd never worn at home, she sat in the chair beside her bed and smiled and said gushy things to her roommate. Color, as though by force of will, had even begun to appear in her cheeks.

In the car on her way to the movie, Laura had asked her dad if her mother was trying to fool the nurses into thinking there was nothing wrong with her. Her dad said he didn't know, and he didn't seem interested in speculating. He just stared ahead at the street, steering with one hand and smoothing his beard with the other. There was a time not so long ago when she wasn't upset by the way he'd be silent and mysterious and make her guess what he was thinking, but now it irked her no end. In the past she could be certain his thinking was confined to safe areas, like painting or teaching or speculating how much time till his next martini. Now she feared his mind was on Dr. Benoit.

She walked past several large houses with their backs to the street and their fronts to the river. She came to Mount of Olives Lutheran—no cars, the voting apparently over. She hoped the strikers prevailed. Maybe if her dad lost his insurance he'd be more inclined to move.

Next door was a house that must have been the minister's because it was so drab-looking and built so close to the church. Laura's classmate Sara Langerud, the minister's daughter, had been mentioned on the Couples page of the school paper three times this year, and with three different boyfriends. Well, sure, give them what they wanted, and who couldn't get boyfriends by the dozen? Sara Langerud was an easy lay. Laura's triumph, when she achieved it, would be in getting herself a boyfriend by the other method— teasing and withholding. Preferably, he'd be a hippie or a Hell's Angel. Nothing got her father's attention like a sleazy boyfriend.

Gary Oberholtzer, for example. What was he up to this afternoon? Maybe she ought to saunter past his house on Sawyer Street on the chance he'd come out and talk to her. She had time. The quintet wouldn't break up until six or later. She'd looked up his address in the phone book.

She came to the bridge and was starting across when a car came up beside her and stopped. Down came the driver's window and Dr. Benoit put out her head.

"Hi, Laura, hop in, I'll give you a ride." Peggy lifted her gloves and a large white envelope off the passenger seat and set them on the dash as Laura, after a moment's hesitation, went around the car and got in.

That night in January, on her way to the hospital, Laura hadn't noticed how nice and velvety the interior was. It smelled a little like perfume. The driver looked a bit on the gray side today, especially around the eyes—not her normal colorful self. Her hands were jittery, shifting gears.

Laura asked, "Isn't the quintet playing?"

"I got called away. Where would you like me to drop you?"

She shrugged. "Wherever you park. I'll go to the library."

They glided across the bridge and climbed the slope toward campus.

The woman looked at her rather sternly. "Laura, why did you tell me your mother's not your mother?"

She shrugged. "Oh, you know, a girl likes to pretend once in a while. She's in the hospital, did my dad tell you?"

"Why? What is it?"

"Insanity."

The woman's eyes bored into her. "Really?"

Laura maintained a steady, matter-of-fact expression. "Crazy as a loon."

The car came to a stop in front of McCall, and the look Laura had been waiting for came into Dr. Benoit's face—sadness and pity. This woman was a pushover.

Laura brushed away an imaginary tear. She considered trying out further manipulations, but if she were going to lure Gary Oberholtzer out of his house, she'd better do it now, because it would soon be dark. She opened her door.

"I have to drive over to Claudia's Lunch," said the woman. "Why don't you come along? We can talk."

"Thanks, I'm not hungry."

"Not to eat. I've just been to see President Gengler, and I've got to report my findings."

"To Claudia?"

This made Peggy laugh, as Laura knew it would. The proprietor of Claudia's was a dumb, greasy woman so inarticulate she never even said thanks when you paid her. But Peggy's laugh wasn't the clear, ringing call of joy Laura usually heard at rehearsals. It was forced, and it didn't last very long.

"I had to tell the president that his faculty is about to go on strike. A couple of friends are in there waiting to hear how he took it."

"How did he take it?"

"Like a man." Again the brief laugh. "In other words, no reaction. It was like talking to a mummy."

"Thanks for the ride." Laura got out.

"Look, if you need to talk, have you still got my phone number?"

"Sure," she lied. She'd thrown away Dr. Edwards's card, with her number on it.

"Call anytime."

Laura slammed the door.

It was twilight by the time Gary Oberholtzer woke from a three-hour nap and saw Laura Connor standing across the street staring up at his window. He put on a torn flannel shirt over his T-shirt and went downstairs and out the door, ignoring his father's request to know where he was going and his mother's demand that he put on a jacket.

"Hey," he said angrily, slouching across the empty street.

"Oh, hi," Laura answered.

The streetlight above her was flickering to life. The shadows made her face sort of homely, he thought. He asked, "What the hell you doing?"

"Walking by."

He stepped up close to her, dragging his dyed blond hair out of his eyes. "Don't give me that. You weren't walking by. You were standing here trying to see in my house."

"I wasn't. I was walking by." She hoped her steady voice belied her fear, for there was something savage and scary in his eyes, a wildness that needed to be broken and tamed. "Geez, how would I even know where you live?"

"Everybody knows where the Oberholtzers live. My old man was born in this house."

"And besides, why would I care?"

He lifted his lip and squinted, trying to look angrier than normal. "I figure you're here to apologize for walking out on me the other night."

"Walking out on you? Why, was it a date or something?"

He tried to look hurt. "It was having a few beers together."

"A few beers. Huh! I don't even like beer."

Women with smart mouths made him mad, but he supposed men had to put up with stuff like that. His old man, God knows, put up with plenty of stupid crap from his mother.

"So you want to do something?" he asked.

"Do something?"

"Yeah, you know, like go out to Rocky Point again."

"Rocky Point?"

Jesus, what a stupid broad. "How come you say everything I say?"

"Everything you say?"

"See?" He laughed a nasty, triumphant laugh. "Like that."

She said, "Huh!" and turned and walked swiftly away. She hated to be sneered at. This was enough of Gary Oberholtzer for today.

"Or we could go to a place and smoke some weed." He tried to keep up with her without running, but she kept a step ahead of him. "We could talk."

"Where?" she asked over her shoulder. She was angling across the street toward the campus library.

"Under the bridge." He pointed down the street. "Come on."

She was arrested by the note of supplication in his voice. She stopped and regarded him, more fascinated now than afraid. Here, under a campus lamppost, she saw the insecurity in his shifty, worried eyes, saw childishness in his pouty mouth. He looked so innocent standing there pleading, his nose running and his teeth chattering, that she felt suddenly far superior to him in looks and brains and cleverness. Here was an ignorant man-child she could lead around like a dog.

"Come on," he repeated, shivering and wiping his nose on his sleeve.

"I wouldn't really mind a smoke," she said. She'd tried grass in the city, with friends.

He took her hand and they hurried down the sloping street in the dusk.

The trio, once more in session, did not produce the sublime music Leland expected. Both of his partners struggled and strayed. On "Little White Lies," Connor was continually off the beat and Peggy was flat.

Leland himself had never felt more like a virtuoso. His fingers drew lovely harmonies out of the old Steinway while scarcely touching the keys. He was able to connect phrase after phrase with the intricate little ripples he'd been trying for years to copy from his Teddy Wilson records. With each of these keyboard triumphs he was filled with the same thrilling confidence he'd felt earlier this afternoon, at Mount of Olives, when he came to the end of his speech and saw the impact on his listeners, how serious they'd become, how thoughtful. Leaving the front of the church and returning to his place in the baptismal alcove, his chest kept expanding until he feared he'd hyperventilate. When had he ever before felt this proud and accomplished?

Twenty-odd years ago, he guessed. He remembered the day he went fishing the Badbattle with his father—he was twelve or thirteen—and he hooked and played and netted a fierce twelve-pound northern pike all by himself. In a canoe, no less, without shipping a drop of water. "Nice work," his father had said. "You've got a nice touch, Leland, a good sense of balance." The man's words somehow made Leland a man, convinced him there was nothing grown-up he couldn't accomplish if he put his mind to it. After his father was killed by a lightning bolt, the words were still with him. In college whenever he found himself in a difficult course, or later, faced with a difficult student, or at home, when his mother was acting difficult, it would be the memory of his father reminding him of his sensitivity and balance that saved the day. This afternoon, speaking at Mount of Olives, he'd pretended he *was* his father. "Just the right touch," Mortimer Oberholtzer had told him afterward.

Now, in the band room, Connor and Peggy must have been aware of their shortcomings, for they seemed more than willing to follow him out of "Little White Lies" and into "Mood Indigo," but here there was no improvement. Connor kept gumming up the piece with his imprecise rhythms. Peggy, her voice foggy and faltering, drained all the vitality out of it. Worse yet, she kept going astray, as though she had a different song in mind. What possessed them? Connor flailing away at his bass, looked anxious or angry. She looked so grave. She'd returned from seeing President Gengler in what seemed to Leland like a high state of nerves. Without a word, she'd thrown a large white envelope down on a chair, slipped out of her coat, hung her saxophone strap around her neck, and blew a note like a factory whistle. She blew another note, half a tone higher and even harder on the ears. "I'm sorry about your wife," she said. "I just saw Laura."

Leland turned to Connor. "What's the matter with your wife?"

"Some nerve problem."

This reply was curt, precluding further discussion. An awkward silence filled the band room until Peggy's saxophone blurted again. "Well, aren't you guys going to ask me about my audience with the president?" she said.

"I'll bet he wasn't the least bit disturbed," said Leland. "Herbert's always very calm."

"Calm?" Her laugh struck him as disrespectful. "More like in a coma."

"Will he appeal to the board?" asked Connor.

"Hell no." She looked over the scores on her music stand. "Where were we?"

Leland played the opening bars of "Little White Lies."

"One, two, three," she said, and they began.

That was half an hour ago. So discouraging was the ruin they were now making of "Mood Indigo" that Leland did something false and unprecedented. He claimed to have to leave early for an appointment. He said Sunday evenings during Lent he and his mother were expected to take part in a discussion group at the Episcopal rectory.

Both Peggy and Connor appeared to believe him. He gathered up his music and left them in the band room waiting for Laura. In the hallway, putting on his coat, he heard them get going on "I'll Get By." He stood and listened. No sax. Just the words against the soft thud of the string bass. It was slow, much slower than he would have thought to play a song like that. More like a lullaby. Or a dirge. But actually quite good. Very good, in fact. The longer he stood and listened, the more affected he was. It was actually quite wonderful. It couldn't be luck that produced such an exquisite harmony of voice and strings; anything this polished had obviously been rehearsed. When had they rehearsed? And why without him? He descended the dark stairway, wishing he hadn't heard it, feeling intensely lonely and left out. What a devastating shock: the quintet, reduced to its heart and soul, wasn't a trio after all. It was a duet.

They spent nearly twenty minutes fussing over "I'll Get By," going so slow and deep with it that they forced it nearly to a standstill. Then they tried working it toward a brighter mood, but they soon backed off, each of them sensing the other incapable of brightness today. They ended it with a kiss perpetrated by Peggy.

Or, rather, half a kiss, because they heard the door open at the bottom of the back stairwell, which they had left unlocked for Laura. They sat down on folding chairs with a discreet distance between them and listened to the footsteps coming up, both of them savoring the kiss and weighing its meaning. It was the sort of kiss that signaled more to come. Connor, his heart racing, imagined himself free of the pledge of lifelong constancy he'd made to a mental case. Peggy wasn't the first other woman he'd been attracted to, but the first since he'd stopped drinking. Drink, in copious amounts, had been a marvelous aid to suppressing adulterous desire.

He turned in his chair and busied himself with his bass, licking a finger and thumb and running them up and down the strings.

"Is it a nervous breakdown?" she asked.

"I'm really at a loss how to describe it. Or handle it. I'm not any good with mental problems." He was facing away from her. "This morning I'm pretty sure she would have done herself in if . . ."

The footsteps weren't Laura's. They were too heavy, and there were voices. Bernard Beckwith and some of his cast members passed the band room with a glance and a wave. The clock on the wall, formerly equipped with a buzzer, sounded its characteristic click and hum at the top of the hour. It was six.

"If what?" she prompted.

He swallowed, uttered a nervous, throat-clearing grunt, then said, "If I hadn't been there to talk her out of it."

She sat looking at the back of his gray sweater, at the wavy, graying hair, carelessly cut and curling over his ears.

"She talked about suicide before, but not seriously, I didn't think. I mean, it was always casual. Some passing remark."

He turned and looked up, not at Peggy but at her reflection in the darkening window—a faint, three-quarter profile, an unfinished portrait in the nearly colorless manner of Whistler.

"She always used to seem too tired for suicide. I'd read somewhere that the reason more depressives don't kill themselves is that they're too depressed. Well, this morning she talked about it with a kind of energy I hadn't sensed before. Not crazy energy, not manic, but a current running underneath what she was saying. Something in her voice, something new, something heightened, that told me she was determined. . . ." He shrugged and looked at his hands.

"So you took her to the hospital."

He nodded.

"Are they equipped to handle mental illness?"

"On Tuesdays."

She was saddened by the smile he gave her—the smile of a severely damaged spirit. "In the meantime?" she asked.

"She's okay. On her best behavior, in fact. I suppose so the psychiatrist will pronounce her stable and send her home."

"You look worn-out, Connor."

His smile faded. "Worst day of my life."

"Mine too," she said. "Or nearly."

He looked at her closely then, and saw for the first time her pain. "What is it?" he asked.

She drew the white envelope onto her lap and gazed at it. "I don't mean it's anything like what you're going through, but . . . damn it . . . President Gengler got this in the mail." She peeked into the envelope. "It's a picture my husband took of me. . . ."

He looked into the envelope, then raised his eyebrows, not meaning to be humorous, but his expression struck her as comic. Before kissing this time, they paused to make sure no one was approaching in the silent hallway. This kiss was savagely consuming. It left her panting, Connor wheezing. Again they kissed, even more roughly, their hands moving in quick, exploratory touches.

Again the back door opened. This time they heard the light, quick footsteps of a girl. He handed her the envelope, saying facetiously, "Could I have a copy of this?" She cupped his face in her hands, pressed her forehead to his for a moment, then moved away before Laura appeared in the doorway.

"Hi, you two." The girl breezed into the room with unusual grace, unusual cheer. "What a drippy movie. Redford and Newman trying to look comfortable in old clothes."

Peggy saw Connor brighten, infected by his daughter's cheer. He seemed unaware of the smell of pot that followed her into the room. The girl helped him carry his string bass into the instrument room.

"It's home to tuna hot-dish," he said, putting on his coat.

As he left with his daughter, Peggy handed him the white envelope.

Entering his office at noon the next day, Neil found Helen Culpepper sitting at his desk, busily knotting. A girl of nine or ten occupied Victor's chair, swiveling around at high speed.

"Mr. Dash said it was okay if we came in and waited for you. I talked to my therapist over the weekend and she said it's obvious you're picking on me."

"Later, please, Mrs. Culpepper, I'm going to be late for class."

Neil shed his parka and stuffed it into a shelf of his bookcase. He was light-headed from lack of sleep.

"My therapist said she went through eight years of college including graduate school without reading more than three or four poems about death, and when I told her we were already up to nine in your class, she said it's obvious you're trying to work some kind of harm on me." Mrs. Culpepper smiled pleasantly as she spoke, her eyes on her handiwork. She was wearing a black sweater with a black scarf tied tightly at her throat. The girl, having stopped swiveling, was scowling suspiciously at Neil. "This is my daughter Alison, isn't she charming?"

"Hello, Alison." He scanned his bookcase for his literature text.

"She's the reason I'm stuck in Rookery, and she's with me today as a witness."

"Witness to what?" he said absently. He couldn't find his book. He tried to remember what he'd assigned. He'd intended to read it over the weekend, and hadn't.

"My therapist says she's sick and tired of people playing mind games with her clients," she placidly continued. "She says it's time professors like you were brought before the dean."

"You're paranoid, Mrs. Culpepper."

"Of course I'm paranoid, and with good reason."

"Look, would you mind? I need to get into my desk." He threw his hip into the arm of the chair and rolled it aside with her in it. He pulled open drawers, searching desperately and angrily for his textbook and his list of assignments. It had been a bad night, a bad morning. Around midnight, kept awake by the noise of his typewriter, his housemates the steelworker and the cement worker had stormed into the basement threatening bodily harm, so Neil had had to stop working just as Lydia Harker and the man she'd met on the boat were about to consummate their love in a riverfront hotel in St. Louis. He'd lain awake for hours, going over the scene in his head, and finally got up and tried writing in longhand, but the scene was somehow much less convincing in pencil than in pica. This morning, groggy, he read random pages of the manuscript and was shocked to find very little of it lively or authentic-seeming. He'd walked to campus feeling rheumy and defeated, wondering if he hadn't mailed some of the weakest pages to Connor's friend the editor. He pictured himself living back in Ohio, peddling fruit to high school students, his novel too insipid to publish.

"The judge ruled that Alison and I have to stay in Rookery until she's eighteen so Sammy-my-ex can have visiting rights. Isn't she darling today, Dr. Novotny?"

Neil glanced at the girl, who continued to hold him in her dark, watchful gaze. He thought she looked pathetic, her oversized black pinafore covering her like a sack, her hair done up in a curly style beyond her years.

"I'm spacing out my degree work so it will take me the whole nine years to finish. Is it any wonder I'm in therapy—nine more years in this backwater? College is my salvation. I mean, if it weren't for college, I think I'd go absolutely bonkers. But I worry that you're not going to be here for my whole nine years, Dr. Novotny. You'll become a famous novelist and leave for New York, and who will I feel close to on campus?"

He picked a tangle of her hairy twine off a stack of books on his desk and dropped it in her lap. "Have you seen my textbook, Mrs. Culpepper?"

"Here, take mine." She reached into the bag of rope at her feet and drew out her book. "You need somebody to organize you, Dr. Novotny. I'm a great organizer. Culpepper's Supper Club has gone all downhill since I left. Sammy-my-ex, he's okay as a front man, he can greet people at the door and see they get the wine they want, and he's got this never-ending line of chummy lingo, but he's worthless as a detail man. My lawyer tells me his record-keeping could get him arrested it's so sloppy. He reminds me a lot of you."

"My lingo's not that chummy." Neil looked at his watch. He was already five minutes late for class. Taking the book from her, he asked, "Do you have a pen or pencil I can use?"

"Here." She handed him a bright green ballpoint with CULPEPPER'S printed on it. "When he had me doing his books, there was never once a mix-up in the work schedule, never once a late payroll. I tell you, sometimes I'm so frustrated living in Rookery, I'd like to break the law and leave town."

"What did we read for today?"

"I couldn't read it. You assigned it with me in mind, it's obvious, and I wasn't done with the first page before I had to quit. Looking at that man's face in his coffin—my God, Dr. Novotny, you're some kind of perverted ghoul, you know that? I gave it to Alison to read." Remaining in her chair, she turned to her daughter, who was now standing at her shoulder and fiddling with her curls. "Tell him what you thought of it, Alison. Tell him what you said to me when you finished."

Comment was unnecessary. The ten-year-old's expression told him how intensely she despised the excerpt from *The Death of Ivan Ilyich*.

"Alison's in fifth grade and reading at high school level. She's outstanding in every subject but art. They're thinking of accelerating her next year, because she's so bored in class."

"Come out," said Neil in the doorway, poised to run to the stairs. "I have to lock up."

"That's all right, I want to finish this piece"—she held up what looked like a series of strung-together pot holders with lumps—"and Alison has homework to do. Go sit down, Alison, and get busy with your civics paper."

"Why isn't she in school today?"

"It's parents-conference day."

"Then go to it."

"I've been."

"Come out," growled Neil, coloring with fury.

"I'll be bringing her to class with me at one, and then at two I'll be leaving her with you while I see the registrar. We're planning my course of study today, and my financial aid package."

Neil heard his name called. He turned to see Peggy coming down the stairs from her office. He thought she looked unwell. "Can I use your phone for a private call?" she asked. "I'm supposed to call my brother at one o'clock Boston time, and it's already five after." She looked harried and bilious. "Why aren't you in class?"

"You're welcome to the phone, but . . ." He tipped his head, indicating his visitors.

Seeing who it was—his loony nemesis—she didn't even slow down. "I'll try somebody else," she said, hurrying on.

Victor Dash came down the hallway, loudly discussing the strike with one of his students, a tall young woman Neil recognized as president of the student senate. Two young men followed after them, leaning forward to catch his words.

"I figure two weeks and they'll fold," he was saying. "The more students you can get down to St. Paul, the sooner it'll be over. Make sure the rally's on a day when the governor's in his office and the legislature's in session. I'll call down there right now and find out when. You can get all the picket signs you need from Cardero."

"They're all yours," Neil said to Victor, referring to Mother and Daughter Culpepper.

Ignoring Neil as well as the Culpeppers, Victor went straight to his phone and spoke to the operator. The three students stood in the doorway, trapping Neil inside.

"I love rallies," Helen Culpepper told them. "If there's a rally, count me in."

"Have you got a car?" asked the young woman. "We need cars."

"I've just got a little old Studebaker, but Sammy-my-ex has a Lincoln. Let me know what day and I'll sweet-talk him out of it."

"Hey, wow, a Lincoln," said one of the young men.

"Hey, wow, cool," said the other.

Neil shouldered his way out, crossed to the stairway, passing a classroom where the instructor was saying, "Macrobiotics, class, macrobiotics," and descended to his freshmen in the basement.

"Don't worry, Peggy," said her brother on the phone. "I'll find that pervert and sue the eyeballs out of him. Nobody sends a naked picture of my sister through the mail and gets away with it. When did it turn up?"

"I'm not sure. Sometime after Christmas, I guess."

"So what took you so long? You should have called me right away."

"I just found out yesterday. The president's wife gave it to me."

"The nerve of that bastard! Send it to me immediately."

"Kenny, no. I haven't got any clothes on."

"It's evidence. We'll need it for evidence in court. Now let me tell you how it works."

She sat in Kimberly Kraft's office in the education wing, listening to her brother, the Boston attorney, speak lovingly and at length about litigation. "No, no," she put in when he paused for breath, but to no avail. Last night, in a phone call to Maine, Peggy had told her sister Sue about the photo, and Sue advised her to tell Kenny despite his tendency to overreact. True, he'd want to go public with a lawsuit against Gene Benoit, but Sue and Connie and Bill would rein him in. "We'll convince him that the mere *threat* of a lawsuit will be enough to squelch the dirtbag," said Sue. Discussing it long past midnight, the two sisters talked themselves into the conviction that this reprehensible act had been out of character for Gene Benoit, that he'd probably done it on some drunken or drug-induced impulse and wasn't likely to do it again. A good scare, and he'd slither back in his hole and dry up.

"Please, Kenny, listen to me. Gene Benoit doesn't have the guts to persist if he feels threatened. I'm sure a letter on your legal stationery will put a stop to it."

"Look, he ought to be behind bars. I never trusted the bastard from the first day I met him. What did you marry him for? You broke your mother's heart, you know."

"Kenny, look, I married him and it was a mistake, okay? It's over. Just find out where he's living and write him a letter and let it go at that."

"And if another picture turns up? What then?"

"Then we'll sue the eyeballs out of him."

"Promise?"

"No holds barred, Kenny. How's Kate?"

"Fine. Busy."

"Kids?"

"Kids are fine."

"How's Mother?"

"Fine. Sort of bitchy. Say, are you coming out here for Easter?"

"I don't know yet. We only get one day off, Good Friday."

"Come anyway. We're all going to be at Bill's."

"Maybe I will. Depends on my choir, whether I can spare the time."

"When's the concert?"

"The weekend after Easter. April second."

"Well, save a seat for your mother. We're thinking of sending her out to see you."

"Really?"

"Then on to see Patty in Wyoming. She needs a change of scene."

"That would be nice," said Peggy, less than excited.

"Well, don't go into raptures."

"I'm really not set up for company. Just a rollaway in my living room, overlooking an alley."

"Put her up at a hotel. We'll pick up the tab."

"In Rookery? The only hotel's full of derelicts."

"Well, you must have an airport hotel. They usually aren't bad."

"Are you kidding? The airport's a landing strip between a tree farm and a pigsty."

"Jesus!"

"Next year I'm going to get a better apartment. I'll have a guest room."

"Next year? You're going back there next year?"

"I can't very well leave after one year, can I? How would that look on my résumé?"

"Like you came to your senses."

Neil found Dean Zastrow and Chairman Oberholtzer waiting for him outside his basement classroom. The dean was plainly agitated, pacing about in the dim hallway, tapping his nose, and snapping his expandable watchband.

The chairman took his pipe from his mouth, smiled sadly, and said, "You're a bit on the tardy side, my boy."

"Sorry, I had a student in my office."

"A bunch of them got out," said the dean, as if Neil's classroom were a holding pen for livestock, "but we got them back in."

"Thanks." Neil entered the room, prepared to cover his unpreparedness by asking a student at random to summarize today's story for him. He'd never read *Ivan Ilyich*.

"Not so fast," said the dean, following him in. "We've got some logistics to take care of." Not risking defiance this time, the dean had decided to take a more civil approach. "How do you do, ladies and gentlemen, I am your dean and this is C. Mortimer Oberholtzer, chairman of the Division of Languages and Fine Arts." He beckoned the chairman into the room. "Now I will be asking five of you to move to different sections of Freshman English, but before I do so, I would like the chairman to explain the logic of it. Dr. Oberholtzer?"

"The logic of it is parity," said the chairman mysteriously. "We strive for parity in all classes where rhetoric and written expression are the major pedagogical elements."

The students looked to Neil for a translation. He gave them an eye-rolling look of despair, which he immediately regretted because it caused a few of them to giggle. He had no desire to foment another confrontation.

"Now, I realize that after this passage of time you have become accustomed to the pedagogical methods of Mr. Novotny," continued Mortimer, who subscribed to the theory that you promoted learning by demonstrating how learned you were. "To say nothing of his engaging traits of personality and character." Here he directed his fatherly smile in Neil's direction. "But sometimes for the amelioration of the commonweal we must sacrifice our individual wishes."

There was a moment of silence before Dickie Donaldson, the behemoth in the back row, spoke up. "Hey, would you say that in English?"

A look of pain crossed the chairman's face. It had been many years since he'd taught a class of unpolished freshmen, and longer ago than that, decades perhaps, since anyone had dared challenge his love of fustian. However, being a man of strong pedagogical instincts, he undertook to give Dickie Donaldson a lesson in etymology.

"Parity," he said. "Evenness. Equivalency. From the Latin *paritas*, meaning equal."

"In other words, they like to have twenty-eight students in each section of Freshman English," Neil added, in aid of his visitors.

"Amelioration," said the chairman, trying to engage the shifting eyes of Dickie Donaldson. "Betterment. Improvement. From the Latin—"

"Now, do I have five volunteers," asked the dean impatiently, "or shall I pick and choose?"

Two young women shot their hands in the air, eager to flee Neil's class, A or no A. They were Jodi Bukowski, whose favorite poet he had defamed, and Jodi's defender, the girl with the tiny round glasses. Another hand went lazily up, that of a young man who more than once had surprised Neil by making insightful remarks about literature, the only truly promising student in the room.

Dean Zastrow flashed these three his slit-mouth smile and said, "Two more, then."

No one else volunteered.

"Very well, then." The dean put one forefinger to the wart at the side of his nose. With the other, he pointed to his choices. "You and you."

One of his choices, a young woman with serious acne, got obediently to her feet and carried her jacket and books out into the hallway. The three volunteers followed her. The desks they vacated were quickly taken over by those who'd been standing or sitting on the floor.

"Well?" said the dean, waiting for the other designated student to respond.

Despite his determination to cooperate, Neil felt a little thrill of joy when he realized this other student was the immovable Dickie Donaldson.

"Not me," said Dickie.

The dean shot a murderous look at Neil, clearly holding him responsible.

There was no change in Chairman Oberholtzer's benign expression. "For the amelioration of the commonweal," he reminded Dickie.

"Pick on somebody else," was Dickie's response. "I ain't going nowhere."

"Insubordination," exclaimed the dean, his eyes still on Neil. "What's that boy's name?"

Neil courageously deserted and went over to the other side. "He doesn't have to leave, Dr. Zastrow. He can stay."

There was a moment of indecision on the dean's part; then he stalked out, taking Oberholtzer with him. They led the four students to classrooms aboveground.

Neil opened his book at random and buried his nose it, trying to conceal from his students the wonderful surge of triumph he was feeling. Selecting a name from memory, he said, "Jendro, would you please summarize for us what you read for today?"

No response.

Neil looked down the long room.

Came the voice of Dickie Donaldson. "Jendro just left."

The dean and the chairman made no demands of Neil's one o'clock students. By that time, the two men were sitting in the chairman's car at the Rookery airfield, waiting for the daily flight from the Twin Cities. When they saw the little craft come into view high over the forest, they got out of the car and stood at the chain-link fence, cringing in the cold wind and watching the plane wobble and waver down through the troublesome air currents. It was a boxy orange plane with one propeller and two passengers. Zastrow and Oberholtzer raised their hands in a kind of timid salute as it bumped along the airstrip with the aged face of Warren W. Waldorf glaring at them from the side window.

Dr. Waldorf, chancellor of the State College System, had been severely offended by the news from Rookery. Having focused his attention on his approaching retirement, he took it as a personal insult that the Faculty Alliance of America should have invaded Minnesota and stirred up trouble before he had quite brought his glorious term as chancellor to a close. How unthinkable that a faculty should threaten to shut down a campus midsemester for a reason as mundane as salary. He could only assume that the long northern winter had unhinged at least sixty-four professors. Victor Dash, it went without saying, had been deranged all along, for it was rumored that he had a steel plate in his head; but the rest of the faculty—what, if not lunacy, would cause them to throw down their chalk and their slide rules and follow this madman out on strike?

"Are your people insane?" was the first question he put to Zas-

trow and Oberholtzer as he stepped off the plane, looking distinguished in his camel-hair coat and paisley necktie. His incisors were
outlined in gold. "Out of their minds?" he added, defining insanity.
Though Oberholtzer was taller than the chancellor by an inch or
two, he felt somehow diminished by him. Both he and the dean
murmured a reply the chancellor didn't hear in the wind.

So he asked it again, sitting in the cramped front seat of the
chairman's Ford Falcon, raising his voice over the roar of its tired
old engine. "Are your people insane?" He was glaring at Oberholtzer, at the wheel.

"A work stoppage is certainly without precedent in my considerable experience," replied the chairman, blowing out pipe smoke
and shaking his head in shame. He felt embarrassed, transporting
the chancellor in his second-best car. Had he known earlier, he
would have asked Honey to postpone her shopping trip to Berrington, but by the time the chancellor's surprise visit was announced,
Honey had left in the Oldsmobile. Dean Zastrow had a fairly new
Buick, but it was up on a hoist at the muffler shop.

The dean, sitting in the backseat, thrust his face eagerly forward and assured the chancellor, "It wasn't the whole faculty that
voted to strike, Dr. Waldorf, it was only sixty-four of them."

"*Only* sixty-four!" The chancellor wrenched himself around in
his seat and scowled fiercely at the dean, who sank back and looked
away.

"Where's your president?" was the chancellor's next difficult
question.

Chairman Oberholtzer, friend and defender of President Gengler, changed the subject. "We've lined up the committee of nonstrikers you requested, Dr. Waldorf. A wonderfully superb
committee, if I may say so, the cream of Rookery State. You may
have met Professor Edwards before, his father was here in History
for many years."

Dean Zastrow, no friend of the president, answered the question. "Gengler's in Florida."

Competing, Oberholtzer continued, "And then there's Professor Gold, a very gifted young woman in speech."

The dean said, "He flew out today, not an hour and a half ago."

The chairman said, "And our drama man, Bernard Beckwith.

We're very proud of our theater program. He's presenting two one-acts by Ionesco this spring."

The dean said, "Doctor's orders, he claims. Says he needs moist air for his skin. Well, I wonder . . ." The dean fell silent at this point, lest the chancellor get it into his head that the president should be replaced, for although the curious fact that Gengler's reputation never seemed to suffer was a source of frustration to the dean, the president's habitual absence from campus was a major source of the dean's power.

The chairman said, "And then, let's see, oh yes, we've asked Mrs. Kibbee to join us. She's the chief administrative secretary. That way we're certain not to overlook the consequences of the strike on the support staff."

"What about students?" demanded the chancellor.

"Students?" asked Oberholtzer. "We didn't realize you wanted to consult with students."

The chancellor leaned close to him. "Tell me, who does a strike *really* affect?" Then he turned in his seat once again to address the dean. "I really believe students could break up a strike faster than anybody. Who are your most popular students, what are their names?"

The dean lowered his eyes, not wishing to admit he had no idea.

"Who's president of your student senate?"

The dean didn't know this either, and so brought out his handkerchief and took a long time attending to his nose. Oberholtzer could have answered these questions, but rather enjoyed letting his companion squirm.

"And townspeople. I want to talk to your taxpayers. People won't let us build up our campuses if we let salaries skyrocket out of sight."

"For townspeople we could go to the Elks," said Oberholtzer halfheartedly. It struck him as self-defeating to arouse the resentment of taxpayers.

"We're too late for lunch at the Elks," the dean pointed out.

"That's okay with me." Dr. Waldorf broke out in a sudden astonishing laugh. "I've eaten exactly one thousand Elks chickens over the years."

They traveled the rest of the way in silence, neither host willing to tamper with the chancellor's amazing change of mood.

The chancellor, for his part, was happily calling to mind the days when he used to be constantly on the move, speaking to Elks, dedicating buildings, giving pep talks to faculties. These memories placated him, buoyed him up, softened him, reminded him of the fun it had been to travel the state, patronizing the natives. He actually felt younger, remembering. Carried along in the little Falcon, past frozen swamps and dilapidated farmsteads, he felt his spirit rising, transcending the officebound bureaucrat he'd become. By the time they reached McCall Hall, he felt like the cajoling, speechifying trouper he used to be. He was ready to be friendly.

The three professors—Edwards, Gold, and Beckwith—were waiting for him in the dean's inner office. As they stepped forward to shake his hand, the chancellor noted that the woman and one of the men wore fairly expensive suits, while the other man, no doubt the drama coach, was dressed like a vagrant. The men asked him about his flight and the weather in St. Paul. The woman hung up his coat and poured him a cup of coffee.

"Edwards, is it?" The chancellor feigned a thoughtful expression, as though the name rang a bell. "I recall a professor of history here by that name," he lied. "A very great educator. A relation of yours, by any chance?"

Leland swelled with pride. "My father, sir."

"Very good." He turned to Georgina. "Dr. Gold, they tell me your field is speech. I gave a good number of speeches in my day, some on this very campus."

"So I've heard," said Georgina blankly. She'd heard they were numbingly boring.

"It's mostly tricks—you learn that."

"Tricks?" she asked.

"Public speaking is tricks. I learned them all at Toastmasters."

"Such as?" she inquired.

Such as humoring you poor deluded hicks as I'm doing now, he thought as he shifted his attention to Bernard Beckwith.

"Glad to meet you, Bedwin. Glad to hear you're doing plays for Unesco."

"Ionesco," Beckwith corrected him.

"A fund-raiser, is it? Mighty worthwhile cause, Unesco. Did a lot of good for poor people in Greece or some such place."

Beckwith turned his back and sat down, which irked the chancellor. The others, he noted with pleasure, politely waited until he himself was seated. He also appreciated Mrs. Kibbee's coming into the room with a box of doughnuts and giving him first choice.

"Frosted cake doughnuts, my favorite," he said, peering into the box. "How did you guess?"

"I didn't guess, I remembered," Mrs. Kibbee replied curtly.

"My my my." His chuckle of pleasure, which began in his throat, came out as a tight little whistle through his nose. "In that case, you go back a few years. I haven't been here since, let me see . . ."

"April of 'sixty-three, six years ago," she said, sitting down beside him and arranging her steno pad, her ashtray, and her pack of Chesterfields before her on the table.

Dean Zastrow and Chairman Oberholtzer dragged chairs in from the outer office. They squeezed into places between the others, for the round table was designed for a foursome, not for seven people with notebooks, briefcases, and snacks.

"You're fifty strong," the chancellor told them, getting straight down to fundamentals. "I spoke this morning with the governor's man in labor relations. It's his guess that with fifty people remaining on the job, plus maybe two dozen short-term substitutes, you should be able to break the strike within three or four days. Strikers need attention, you understand, and with things humming along smoothly in the classroom, everybody will forget about those communists outside with their picket signs."

"But I don't quite see, sir," said Leland, bowing his head deferentially, "how two dozen substitutes can quite do the job of the sixty-four people on strike."

"You're right, Edwards. Skeleton crew is what I'm talking about, just to keep the essential programs going."

"And how do we decide what's essential?" asked Georgina.

"You don't. It's already decided. An essential program is one where the student needs to be certified by some outside agency at the end of the semester. The nursing program. Student teaching. Like that."

Dean Zastrow said the nursing program would not be a problem; the nursing professors were nonstrikers. In education, however, Kimberly Kraft was a striker, and so were certain others who supervised the student teachers.

"That's where your substitutes come in," said the chancellor.

"You mean scabs," piped up Mrs. Kibbee, her eyes on her notes.

The chancellor chose to ignore this remark. "Now, it's important to get your side of things out where the public can see it. Who's the newsman on campus?"

The group shifted uncomfortably in their chairs, unwilling to admit that their public information officer was certain to be a striker.

"Mrs. Kibbee here can take care of publicity," said the dean.

The chancellor looked doubtful. "News releases, letters to editors, things of that kind. Be sure you make the most of the war."

"Ah, but really," said Chairman Oberholtzer sagely, "I don't see what Vietnam has to do with it." He waved his hand before his face, clearing his vision of pipe smoke.

There was a shrewd narrowing of the chancellor's eyes. "Of course, you're right, Oberhammer, it's pure deceit. But it's only temporary deceit. We must play on the mood of the moment. Make the public think that by disapproving of the strike, they're joining forces with a great patriotic movement."

"Ah," said Oberholtzer, not entirely won over. He leaned back behind his smoke screen to give it more thought.

The chancellor was still uneasy about Mrs. Kibbee's role. He didn't like to entrust delicate work to people who looked as if they hadn't gone beyond high school. Further, he sensed her proletarian sympathies. "Now, I think we have to be careful not to overwork the dean's good secretary. I suggest all of you, as a committee, join in to help her with the news releases."

She was visibly offended. "I can handle it," she snapped. She lit up a smoke, flicking her lighter dangerously close to his sleeve.

Oberholtzer agreed with the chancellor. Mrs. Kibbee, though a whiz on the mimeograph, did not write complete sentences. He leaned forward out of his smoke to say, "Leland, my boy, I appoint you our editor."

Mrs. Kibbee removed her smoking cigarette and made a hissing sound.

Oberholtzer consoled her. "Only so we don't duplicate our efforts, Mrs. Kibbee, we'll channel our written efforts through Leland."

"Before you mail out any letters, make sure every one of them portrays the strikers as irresponsible with money," the chancellor advised Mrs. Kibbee, attempting to return to her a little of what had been taken. "And the nonstrikers must be portrayed as keepers of the purse strings. Also, does Rookery have a radio station? I'd like to broadcast a statement."

"Indeed, KRKU is top-notch," blurted Oberholtzer with an enthusiasm that hardly seemed called for. He was thinking of Lolly's show and others he was fond of: "Up-to-Date Obituaries" at five-thirty, the stock market report at six-fifteen, Pastor Bob's recorded "Prayer at Sign-off."

Bernard Beckwith and Georgina exchanged a look of disdain, in agreement about the loutishness of KRKU.

Leland, catching sight of this look, was pained for his mother's sake. He was pained as well for Mrs. Kibbee's sake, and by the skirmish that followed. It began with Dean Zastrow suggesting, "Wouldn't it be well to remind the public that Rookery State College lies at the heart of the poorest county in the state of Minnesota?"

Mrs. Kibbee came back at him with surprising heat. "That's not true."

"Not true?" said the dean, angrily. "Well, it's in the new economic survey from St. Paul."

"You don't need a survey to know it," said Chancellor Waldorf. "Just drive down a road."

"Yes, you see it, don't you, coming in from the airport." The dean was glad of the chancellor's support. "Scrubby-looking places— you don't see how people can live in poverty like that."

"There's that farm with pigs, first place this side of the airport," said the chancellor, to show he was alert to his surroundings. "It's got holes in the foundation of the barn."

"And the next place—remember that one?" said the dean, not

to be outdone. "All that broken-down machinery standing in the yard?"

"The pig farm is mine," declared Mrs. Kibbee, her face ashen with fury. "That's where we live, I and my husband, but not in poverty, thank you very much. We raised our family there."

"Well, we were only saying . . ." said the dean, deciding definitely to do what he'd been intending—fire this overbearing woman without delay, and bring someone more docile into his office. There was that sexy young body up on the music floor, Deelane something or other.

"Yes, we were only saying . . ." said the chancellor.

"I know what you're saying. You're saying we live in poverty because there's two holes in the south side of our barn." Mrs. Kibbee touched the lapel of the chancellor's blue gabardine with the eraser end of her pencil. "Pigs are hard on buildings, Dr. Waldorf. They don't like going in and out of doors if they can make themselves a hole to go through." She pressed on the pencil and the committee watched a deep dent appear in his lapel. "One of our pigs won a ribbon at the state fair."

"Are there any questions?" asked the chancellor, trying to ignore her, which was difficult, her pencil drilling into him.

Leland looked anxiously at Georgina and Bernard, signaling that it was time to bring up the conundrum they'd been discussing before the meeting began.

Georgina took over. "I don't see how we can plan on all fifty nonstrikers teaching while the strike is going on. How do we know some of them, or even all of them, aren't going to honor the picket line? I don't even know if *I'm* going to teach."

"Just one more thing, and then I'll shut up," said Mrs. Kibbee. She still had the chancellor pinned. "That farm was my husband's family farm. There's been Kibbees supporting themselves on it since nineteen eight, and there's not one of them wouldn't of punched you in the mouth if you called them poverty-stricken."

She withdrew her pencil and wrote down Georgina's question. *GG: Who teaches? Who doesn't?*

The chancellor drew himself up in his chair, cleared his throat, straightened his tie, and said, "I'll see what I can do along those lines, Dr. Gold. I would like to have a list of all those you think are definitely against striking, as well as those who seem to be on the fence. I'll do a little evangelizing." He might as well make the rounds, he decided. He was stuck here till tomorrow's flight home.

Mrs. Kibbee wrote, *WWW: wants list of weak sisters to browbeat.*

He stood up from his chair, thanking the committee for their time. "Now if I could somehow be put in touch with your radio station."

"That's easy," said the chairman. "Leland, my boy, see to it, would you?"

And so the meeting broke up. Leland used Mrs. Kibbee's telephone to call his mother, while Georgina Gold and Bernard Beckwith hurried off to class. From the bursar's office down the hall, Mrs. Kibbee placed the first of several surreptitious phone calls, warning the faculty that the chancellor was coming around to put the squeeze on them.

The only other passenger on today's flight to Rookery was a sallow-faced man not quite so tall, so old, or so distinguished-looking as Dr. Waldorf. This man, Emerson Tate by name, had recognized the chancellor aloft and introduced himself, hoping to share with him a taxi to campus. No such luck. Upon landing, he'd watched Waldorf carried off by two men in a little brown car, and so he looked around for a taxi. Seeing none, he looked for shelter from the wind and saw that the shabby building he'd taken for a toolshed was actually the airline terminal. He stepped inside and was told that taxis served the airfield only when summoned by phone. He considered calling Connor, his former colleague at Cass College in Minneapolis, but the plan was to surprise him, so he called a cab.

Emerson Tate wore a threadbare black raincoat over his baggy corduroy suit. He had small blue eyes that were at the same time bleary yet shrewd, and a complexion made scaly and splotchy by his long-standing thirst for hard liquor. His necktie was the same shade of purplish red as the broken capillaries in his cheeks and nose. Not only was he head of the American Studies department at

Cass College, he was the distinguished author of five books of cultural criticism, the latest being *The Tracys, Spencer and Dick: The Influence of Comic Strips on Movies*, which was still in print and available from T. Woodman Press of St. Paul for nine dollars, or seven to anyone buying three copies or more.

"Take a day and go up there, Emerson," one of the Cass College regents had said to him a few weeks ago, after learning that an art museum in Illinois had purchased a Connor landscape for its American wing. "Snoop around a little, find out what he's got at Rookery State that he didn't have at Cass. Tell him we'll match it if he comes back."

"Losing the likes of Connor to a state institution makes us look second-rate," the academic vice-president had told him. "You're his friend, Emerson, go have a talk with him. Ask him what he needs to move back here and give Cass another chance."

Although retrieving his friend Connor from the northern wilderness was a cause close to his heart, Emerson Tate had delayed this trip because he'd been toiling desperately to save T. Woodman Press from bankruptcy. The Woodman family of bankers and brokers, having subsidized the press for two generations, was about to withdraw its support, and Dr. Tate, who sat on its board, had been devoting all his spare time lately to pleading with creditors and courting a couple of high-profile authors from the Twin Cities—a writer of mysteries and a writer of westerns—in hopes of enticing them into the Woodman stable. The survival of the press was crucial to him, since T. Woodman had published three of his five books thus far, and was under contract to publish his next.

Rescuing the press with a line of popular fiction had struck the other directors as a betrayal of their exalted academic mission. Like Tate, all of them were scholars, and like most scholars (but unlike Tate), they held everything written outside their disciplines in low esteem. A scholarly press publishing mysteries and westerns? How base. But so stubborn had Tate been in his appeal, and so desperate their straits, that his fellow board members grudgingly agreed to the experiment, at least with mysteries. Westerns they would consider at a later date.

Then, over the weekend, two things had come to Tate's attention that prompted him to reserve a seat on this morning's flight north. One, he heard on the radio that the Rookery faculty was about to walk off their jobs. This confirmed him in his suspicion that teaching at a state college must be the equivalent of working in a sweatshop. He could imagine Connor's disgust. Connor abhorred campus politics and went to great lengths to avoid all events and procedures that stood in the way of his painting. What better time than now, with a strike pending, to approach him about returning to his cozy surroundings at Cass?

His second spur to action had been the manuscript sent to him from Rookery, a piece of fiction by some amateur named Novotny. It was atrociously written—the language stilted, the proportions ungainly, the characters drawn as though from a soap opera—but running underneath all its infelicities was a pretty good story line. There was something undeniably affecting about an immigrant girl, lost and frightened, wandering the mysterious land that pioneer America must have seemed to her, with a lecher pursuing her downriver and chasing her into the arms of a handsome stranger on a riverboat, while her brother all the while went searching without quite catching up with her.

Tate was convinced that the historical romance was to be the next big fad in fiction. This story, published with a sufficiently lurid cover, might very well appeal to a wide readership. He would introduce himself to the author and feel him out about signing on with T. Woodman. Of course, the book would have to be completely rewritten, himself no doubt the ghostwriter, and the author's name would have to be something more glamorous than Novotny, preferably a woman's name. Lydia, too, was an inadequate name. Call the heroine Lynda or Lucinda or Lizbeth. He assumed that Novotny, typical of most young writers, would agree to these minor compromises for the sake of seeing his work in print.

After twenty minutes, a cab arrived and delivered him to campus. The driver was not aware of the faculty's threat to strike, had never heard of either Connor or Novotny, and had no idea which building housed the art department. He spoke of the college as though it were a compound of mysterious aliens. He said a friend's son had gone there and come out a different person than he went

in. "He went in planning to take up manual training—be teacher of
it, you know—and he came out brainwashed. Some goofy guy in
science got ahold of him and turned his head around, and now he's
off somewhere studying bugs for a living, don't ask me where."

Alighting at the corner of Sawyer and Eleventh, Emerson Tate
gave the driver a two-dollar tip (unprecedented generosity, judging
by the driver's reaction: "Holy buckets!") and carried his briefcase
up the slope to what looked like the main building—three stories
plus turrets and the word McCALL engraved in stone over the pil-
lared doorway.

Inside, he stopped two students and asked them what they
thought of Connor's painting. Neither student had heard of Connor. He stopped a man and a woman who looked like professors
and asked where he might find Professor Connor. The man said,
"Connor—is he the new man in social science?" and the woman
replied, "No, he's the new man in art, the one we saw drunk at the
game last fall, remember?" "Oh yeah, him," said the man. "He's
over in manual training. Go out the back door here, and then
straight downhill to the doors big enough to drive a truck through.
You can't miss it, it says Woodworking and Metal Shop out front."

But Tate lingered in McCall Hall, stopping a dozen or more
students to ask about Connor. Only two had heard of him, only
one recalled seeing his work. The artist was clearly out of his element here. He belonged back at Cass College, where he was something of a legend among the student body and his paintings hung in
every building. Moreover he belonged back in the Lock and Dam
Saloon on Riverside Avenue, sharing with Tate his love of gin.

The imparting of literary knowledge and taste, always an ardu-
ous procedure for Neil, came to a standstill near the end of his one
o'clock class when Helen Culpepper, seated front and center with
her black skirt hiked up suggestively over her knees, accused him
of racial bigotry.

"You're not the least bit nice to Theresa, Dr. Novotny. Are
you prejudiced against Indians?" This was delivered in her most irritating singsong voice, and was followed by a smirk and a know-

ing nod of her head. Across the aisle, in a desk her mother had usurped for her, sat the beady-eyed Alison, holding Neil, as before, in her steady, distrustful gaze.

"Mrs. Culpepper, that's unfair," he said softly, straining to hold himself in.

"It's so obvious, the way you treat her. This is the third time today you put her down. I've been keeping track."

"Put her down, Mrs. Culpepper?" This, he knew, was in reference to the three times he'd called on Theresa Skip, an irrepressible hand-raiser, and been given three incorrect answers to his questions.

She paused in her knotting. "You ask her things nobody could possibly know. Name other books by Neil Tolstoy? Come on, Dr. Novotny, who could possibly know a thing like that? Who'd even care, after reading today's disgusting assignment?"

"*You* didn't read it."

"Alison read it. She hated it."

"And the name is *Leo* Tolstoy, Mrs. Culpepper, not Neil Tolstoy." His voice was beginning to rise in pitch, and he was aware of a kind of volcanic rumbling below his rib cage—his insides churning with fury. He clamped his mouth shut, fearing that if he opened it once more, he'd spew fire.

"Go ahead, attack *me* while you're at it, I don't care. It's Theresa who deserves your apology." She sat half turned in her desk, playing interlocutor. "Theresa, would you accept Dr. Novotny's apology and give him one more chance?"

Neil, to his great satisfaction, saw Theresa Skip glance bemusedly at a friend across the aisle as if to say, *What's with this nut?* He saw a few others rolling their eyes or crimping their mouths in disgust, obviously fed up with the antics of Mrs. Culpepper. This calmed him down somewhat, made him feel no longer embattled and alone. The barmaid who couldn't stand death had finally gone too far, even for her classmates.

"Well," she sang, "we're waiting."

And because she spoke in such a girlish, teasing tone while adjusting her skirt to reveal another inch or two of thigh, it dawned on Neil that the everlasting insults and complaints of Helen Culpepper were meant to seduce him. Had he been quicker with psychological insights, he might have realized weeks ago that she had a crush on him—Peggy had even suggested as much—but no, he'd assumed her antagonistic behavior was driven by hate or jealousy or a severe inferiority complex, not by anything so simple and tender as love. How horrible, he thought, watching her turn back to face him and fold her hands primly on her desk, that for some perverse reason, perhaps a twisted upbringing, this woman equated a foul temperament with romantic attachment. He could just imagine the explosive scenes leading to her breakup with Sammy-her-ex. But maybe they were no more terrifying than the scenes leading to their marriage. She definitely had a screw loose.

"Come on, Dr. Novotny," she teased, looking demurely up from under her eyelashes. "Be a good boy and apologize."

For once, Neil was moved to do the appropriate thing. Keeping a lid on his temper, he looked at his watch, saw there were a mere five minutes of class remaining, and left the room.

He climbed the stairs to his office, proud to have maintained his equanimity despite his fatigue, which he'd done by shifting his thoughts to "Losing Lydia." As though in recompense for restraining his temper, he was granted a wonderfully lucid vision of a reunion scene between Lydia and her brother Alphonse, who'd found his sister at last, in the lobby of a St. Louis hotel.

Intending to jot down some details of the vision, he hurried up the last few stairs, crossed the corridor at a dead run, and threw open the door of his office, only to find a meeting in session— Victor's three Viceroys taking instructions from their master. "No, no, I'm not staying," he said, assuring Aaron Cardero he needn't give up his chair. He backed into the hallway, determined to find a quiet nook somewhere. What were her brother's first words upon finding Lydia? What did she say in response? What about the man she met on the riverboat—was he present? A moment ago all this had been clear to him, but the details were fast disappearing.

In the hallway, he saw his students climbing up from the basement and dispersing in three directions, Mother and Daughter Culpepper among them. He drew back into his office and shut the door. He would give them a minute to disappear. Victor was lecturing intensely, spitting out his words in short bursts, his eyes darting among his three listeners, his chair creaking under his constant tipping and turning. He didn't waste even a glance at Neil. Since becoming president of the Alliance, he'd had very little time for his office mate. Neil was sorry about this. He was indebted to Victor for going to bat for him against the dean. He wished, in return, that he could be more zealous about labor relations, but all his waking moments—even his dreams—were given over to his book.

"Hope for a week, but plan for a month," Victor declared. "My time on the pipeline taught me that much. If it isn't settled in a month, one side or the other will cave in from lack of heart. Let's hope to Christ it's the board that caves in." Victor looked disheveled, the strain of leadership evident in the way his clothes were coming apart—his collar unbuttoned, his tie askew, his shirttail half out of his pants.

Kimberly Kraft asked, "What about strike pay, Victor? What can we tell our departments?" Kimberly stood primly in front of Neil's bookcase, her eyes not on Victor but on the gauzy green bow at the throat of her creamy angora dress. She was trying to get the bow to stand out and not droop.

Victor screwed up his face to look regretful. "Thirty dollars a week," he said.

"Thirty dollars a week!" exclaimed Alex Bolus, heaving herself up out of the visitor's chair. "Thirty dollars a week won't do it, mister—you've got to do better than that."

Victor went to work on his mustache, smoothing it down, hand over hand. "Jack Short says thirty's the limit."

"But my rent's almost that much."

"So is mine," Victor snapped. "More than that much. And I've got a family to feed."

Alex stalked over to the window, plucking her sweatshirt away from her sweaty chest, and said, "Damn, damn, damn," to the snowflakes blowing past.

"Listen, nobody said striking's a picnic." Victor picked up his feet and spun his chair around in a complete circle. "When you strike, you give up things."

"In hopes of a better tomorrow," added Kimberly the romantic, as though they'd rehearsed it. From what Neil had heard of the

Kraft family fortune (a farm implement dealership somewhere), she could afford to be an idealist.

He peeked out into the hallway and saw the Culpeppers walking away. Another few seconds and the coast would be clear.

Victor swiveled back the way he had come, facing Aaron Cardero now, who sat with his elbows on Neil's desk, lazily fondling his ears. "Aaron, tell Alex what it feels like to go into a strike with five kids."

"You tell her," answered Cardero, smiling blissfully, "you're the one with strike experience."

"But you're the one with five kids."

"Well, feels great so far." He repeated "Feels great" in a softer, fonder tone as he continued tracing with his fingertips the whorls of his ears. Neil wondered if Cardero's serene behavior was pathological or a drug-induced condition. How could a family man in his right mind face an approaching strike with this level of cheer and goodwill?

The thought of families brought Connor's dilemma to mind. "What about health insurance?" Neil asked, picturing himself going over to the art studio and reassuring Connor about his wife's hospital bill. It would mend the little rift that had opened up between them at Mount of Olives yesterday.

Victor looked darkly at Neil. "Health insurance stops," he said.

"Damn, *damn*," Alex exclaimed at the window.

Kimberly said, "But surely our coverage won't lapse if we pay our own premiums."

"Well, that's the sticky part," admitted Victor. "I've got Jack Short looking for a carrier to cover us while we strike. Seems our regular insurance company's beholden somehow to the College Board, and they're dropping the whole faculty for the duration."

Kimberly lost some of her brightness. "You mean even if we pay our own premiums?"

"That's right. It's called leverage."

"No problem," Cardero happily pointed out. "Just don't get sick."

At this point, Alex Bolus deserted. "That does it!" She turned from the window and made for the door, charging stumpily past Neil and out into the hallway, her whistle and stopwatch swinging from their leather loops, a hiss of anger sounding through her nose.

"Alex," Kimberly called after her.

"Let her go, she needs to let off steam," said Victor, well acquainted with the process.

But Kimberly, well acquainted with Alex, said, "No, once she makes up her mind . . ." She went running daintily out into the hallway on high heels, calling, "Alexandra, Alexandra."

Victor fumed at Neil, "Jesus Christ, why did you have to bring up health insurance?"

Neil made a blame-accepting face, squinting and grimacing regretfully, and backed out of the office and shut the door. He looked at his watch. Eight minutes before his two o'clock class convened, not enough time to go to the library. He was desperate to make notes before any more of the reunion scene evaporated. He headed for the men's room, trying to recall the hotel lobby he'd seen in his imagination, and wondering how what's-his-name, Lydia's brother, happened to find her there. What the hell *was* his name? Neil's brain, lacking sleep, was working only in fits and starts.

Ten feet short of the men's room he heard his name called. A man in an overcoat came hurrying toward him lugging a heavy satchel, a dark-skinned man with heavy brows and sweat running down his cheeks. He gripped Neil's hand and didn't let go until he'd made him understand that he represented Kriss and Dale Publishers of Philadelphia and was eager to know how Neil liked Kriss and Dale's new textbook for Freshman English. Had he noticed the wonderfully cogent sections on linguistics, on rhetoric, on strategies for stylistic options? The book was sweeping the country, adopted by teachers of freshman writing from Oregon to Alabama.

"Freshman writing!" Neil shot back. "My freshmen can't even read, much less write."

The heavy-browed man laughed falsely at what he assumed was a joke. "Now, Mr. Novotny, tell me, what has your committee decided?"

"My committee?"

"Your freshman textbook committee. I've just spoken with Dr. Oberholtzer, and he tells me your decision is a bit overdue."

Neil covered his eyes and moaned, remembering with something close to despair that he'd been charged last September with overhauling the freshman syllabus, had been empowered by Oberholtzer to appoint his own committee and come up with recommendations to the division. So that's why he'd been getting so many unrequested textbooks in the mail. He'd sold most of them to an itinerant book buyer and couldn't remember what he did with the money. He had yet to form his committee.

The heavy-browed man began to look wary. "You *are* Mr. Novotny, are you not?"

"No," said Neil in a flash of inspiration. "My name is Johnson."

"But you were pointed out to me."

"Upstairs," said Neil, giddy and pleased at his own cleverness. "I just saw Novotny upstairs."

The man begged his pardon and lugged his fat, book-laden satchel up the stairway, sweat dripping off his chin.

"Neil, Neil, my boy." This was Dr. Oberholtzer emerging from Administration Row, accompanied by a tall, distinguished stranger. Neil shook a cold dry hand, looked into cold blue eyes, and tried to say warm things. "Chancellor Waldorf, well, well, very happy to meet you, sir."

"Neil's our novelist," the chairman explained, as though to justify his shabby attire. "We're incredibly proud of him. Works like the devil on his book, year-round, day and night, just simply incredible dedication, and his classes are full to overflowing—can't keep students away with a stick. Remember the name, Dr. Waldorf. Novotny. You'll be seeing it on book jackets before long."

The chancellor looked dubious. "A striker, are you, Novotny?"

"More of a fence-straddler, sir. Not committed either way."

"Then I suggest, come Wednesday, you get off the fence and keep teaching. You'll be amply rewarded next go-round for your patience this go-round. Trust me on this, Novotny." He said this heartily, with a flicker of something like cunning in his cold eyes.

Neil, to be rid of him, said unctuously how fully he trusted him.

Waldorf warmed up then, smiling and clapping him on the shoulder. "Two years down the road and I wouldn't be surprised to see you making twenty percent more than you're making today."

"Thank you, sir," said Neil in a servile tone. He knew the chancellor had no business forecasting the next biennium, but he also knew he was near retirement. Some other poor ass would be on the job then, taking the heat.

Oberholtzer pointed his wet pipe stem at Neil and said, "Just a little reminder, my boy—your committee's decision on textbooks."

"Yes, sir. Any day now."

"Strike or no strike, we have to plan for next year."

"Of course."

"A couple of bookmen stopped by my office this morning. Have they found you?"

"No, sir."

"Seems they heard about the strike vote and hightailed it up from the Cities. They want to get our book orders wrapped up in case there's a work stoppage."

"I see."

"McGraw-Hill and Kriss and Dale. If either one of them is your committee's publisher of choice, you could save yourself a peck of paperwork by telling them today."

Neil was spared chagrin over his nonexistent committee by Helen Culpepper, who emerged from the women's room and came rushing up to them, dragging her daughter by the arm and declaring, "Dr. Novotny, I'm sending Alison to class with you and I'll pick her up when I'm done at the registrar's."

"Ah, Mrs. Culpepper," he said warmly. He introduced her to the chairman and the chancellor, expecting her to entangle them in nonsense while he escaped to the men's room. Alphonse was Lydia's brother's name—it came back to him. But now he couldn't remember her lover's name.

Mrs. Culpepper spouted nonsense all right, but not the sort he could escape from: "Hi, guys, I have to tell you Dr. Novotny's prejudiced against Indians."

He fought down a rising surge of temper. "Now, now, Mrs. Culpepper, these are my bosses, don't go joshing them."

She flashed him a wicked grin, then turned to the chancellor with a helpless expression. "And he's giving everybody an A for the semester just for showing up."

It was Chairman Oberholtzer, not Neil, who looked embarrassed by this. Neil simply looked sick, smiling a tremulous smile and fixing his eyes on the middle distance. The chancellor appeared to be fascinated.

"And that's not the worst thing." She shot out her arm, gripped Neil by the chin, and gave his head a rough little wag. "The worst thing is, he makes us read about death all the time. Nine poems about death so far, and now an endless story about a man lying in his casket. My therapist about flipped when I told her. She says I'm way too sensitive for all that death, and I'll probably have to drop the course."

"Let's get back to the A he's giving everyone," said Chancellor Waldorf. "You're not serious about that, Mrs. Peppercorn."

Shrieking with delight, she leaned into the chancellor and hugged his arm to her breast, not realizing that he was habitually careless with names. She thought he was teasing her.

The book salesman Neil had sent upstairs reappeared on the steps, still lugging his heavy bag and looking very hot in his overcoat. Chairman Oberholtzer called to him, "Here's your man, Gleason. Come down and I'll introduce you."

Whereupon Dean Zastrow popped out of his office and hurried over to the group. He asked Oberholtzer to accompany him to Neil's next class.

"Certainly, Dean, certainly," the chairman said. "Glad to, glad to."

The dean then asked the chancellor if he would please come along with them. "Worst classroom on campus, Dr. Waldorf. I want you to see what we'll be needing in the way of remodeling."

The chancellor gave his assent, and Zastrow, having enlisted these two eminences, cast a triumphant look at Neil, as if to say, *Now I dare you to defy me.*

Meanwhile, Oberholtzer was introducing Neil to the perspiring bookman. "Professor Novotny of the textbook committee, Gleason. Neil, this is Gleason from Kriss and Dale."

Neil shook Gleason's hand for the second time. The bookman's facial movements suggested puzzlement evolving into anger.

"Well," said Neil, glancing at his watch, "I'm off to class."

"Just a second," said Chancellor Waldorf. "What's this about handing out A's?"

The bookman, dropping his heavy bag at his feet and shedding his overcoat, said, "Somebody's giving me the runaround."

"It's out-and-out fraud." Helen Culpepper giggled. She left the chancellor's side and twined her long fingers around Neil's upper arm. "I shouldn't talk, I'll be getting one of the A's myself, but Willie LeBlanc calls it intellectual fraud."

This was the spark that touched Neil off. He exploded, though wordlessly at first, opening his mouth wide and turning very pale and making a wet sound deep in his throat. When he was able to put words together, they were "Goddamn it to hell!" and they came out in such a piercing falsetto that it drove the bookman Gleason and Chancellor Waldorf into retreat; they disappeared around separate corners. Even Mother Culpepper looked a little fearful. Not her daughter, however, who stared at him with contempt.

"Who in the hell is Willie LeBlanc?" he raged. "Some drunk you met in your saloon? What right does he have to accuse me of intellectual fraud?"

"Willie sits behind me in class."

"Get off my back, Mrs. Culpepper, or I'll get a restraining order forbidding you to set foot on this campus as long as you and your beady-eyed daughter remain in this city."

She gave ground as he advanced on her, thrusting his chin forward, throwing his arms out left and right and shouting, "I hope to God you're simply stupid, Mrs. Culpepper, because if you're stupid, you probably have no idea what a pain in the ass you are, no idea how dangerous you are, no idea how you're ruining my career—but if you're *not* stupid, if you're tormenting me as part of some scheme you've hatched in your perverted little brain, then so help me God . . . I'm warning you, Mrs. Culpepper, so help me God . . ."

Here he turned away from her for lack of a fitting conclusion, and directed his fury at Zastrow and Oberholtzer, accusing them of ganging up on him and making it impossible to concentrate on either his novel or his students.

Seeing the disbelief in his chairman's face, he intensified his attack. "Yes, I'm talking to you, Dr. Oberholtzer, you with your smug little pipe and your smug little smile and your smug little wife raffling off her weedy little African violets at your smug little division meetings." Even as he spoke, he saw that his diatribe was causing more injury than his stuffy, well-meaning chairman deserved, yet the man looked so shocked and vulnerable he couldn't resist finishing him off: "You don't understand the first thing about an artist's sensibility, Dr. Oberholtzer!"

The chairman caved in, his shoulders slumping, his head hanging down. He reached out to the wall for support.

"You're finished on this campus," the dean said flatly to Neil, and he led Chairman Oberholtzer down Administration Row in the direction of Mrs. Kibbee, who had left her desk to see what the shouting was all about.

Neil, raging, stalked after them. "And you, Zastrow, you warty little tyrant, you've embarrassed me in front of my students and you've made a shambles of my reputation all over campus and it's because of you that I've come to hate teaching as a profession. Yes, hate, hate, hate!"

Mrs. Kibbee restrained him from following the two men into the inner office. "Watch it, big boy!" she said, forcefully turning him around and steering him back down the corridor. "Don't make it any worse than it already is. This washes you up here, but I might be able to find you another job—English teachers are scarce. Let me know if you want me to type up a résumé and get you some names and addresses."

He shook off her touch. "Mrs. Kibbee, I wouldn't be a professor again if it was the last job on earth. Tell the dean to find my replacement as soon as he can—I'm leaving!"

"Now, now, don't lose your head. We might be able to keep you on the job till your contract runs out in June. Go home and cool off."

But Neil repeated his intention to quit without delay. She left him then, bustling back to her desk and her ringing phone.

In the hallway, only one figure remained at the explosion site— Daughter Culpepper standing her ground in her oversized dress and her unbecoming hairdo and conveying with her eyes a degree of loathing so intense that he lost his will to bark at her, scare her off, warn her away from his classroom. He knew from his own childhood how difficult it was to outhate a ten-year-old.

He went into the men's room and commandeered a pencil from a student standing at a urinal. He then closed himself in a compartment and scribbled copiously on paper towels the details of the reunion. It was all there—St. Louis in the 1860s. The hotel lobby had dark green textured wallpaper. Moving around the edges of the scene were bellboys, clerks, drifters, and men and women in traveling clothes. The lover Lydia had recently acquired on the riverboat (his name was Randolph) stood aside while brother and sister embraced, and then stepped forward to be introduced. They went into the tearoom for a heartfelt talk. Randolph and Alphonse took an immediate liking to each other. The three of them decided to have a celebratory dinner together.

When he left the men's room, it was twenty minutes after two. No use going to class now; his students would have left—unless the chairman, the dean, and the chancellor were down there restraining them. Well, to hell with the chairman, the dean, and the chancellor. He was too high on his novel to worry about teaching. He'd go straight home and type what he'd scribbled. Except for a little dizziness from lack of sleep, he was feeling in top form—eloquent, wise, and creative.

He found Victor alone in the office, talking feverishly on the phone. He slipped into his parka and was about to hurry away when a frail-looking man, a stranger in a well-worn black raincoat, appeared in the doorway.

"Mr. Novotny?"

"Yes?"

"I've come to talk books with you." He wore a corduroy suit and a stained necktie. There was a liveliness in his eyes that belied his age, which Neil guessed to be about fifty-five.

"I'm sorry, I'm mentally incompetent," Neil told him. "I'm not allowed to talk to strangers." This was out before he quite knew it, and he shrieked with wild delight, overjoyed by his own cleverness. Why hadn't he used this method, instead of a false name, on the other salesman? "Actually, I'm a certified maniac. I'm let out sometimes in the afternoon like this, when I've been good, that is, and my metabolism settles down." Again he laughed a maniac's brief laugh.

But Emerson Tate, a writer himself, was undeterred. He stepped into the office and set his black briefcase on Neil's chair. "Let's talk business for a minute," he said in a dim voice. "I'd like to make you a proposal."

Neil laughed once more. "No proposals. No business. There's a perfectly good committee for you to see about all that, not a loonybird among them. I'm going away now. I'm due back at the hospital at three." He circled around the man and backed out the door.

"Wait." The man was struggling to draw a sheaf of pages out from under the shaving kit, socks, and underwear in his briefcase. "You don't understand what I'm saying. I'm saying I think we could get together on this."

"Bye-bye," said Neil, fleeing down the hallway and out the front door.

Pausing on the steps amid dizzying flurries of snow, he zipped his parka, tied the hood tight under his chin, and patted his pocket, making sure his manuscript of paper towels was there. He was suddenly very tired. His explosion had drained him. But of course it was well worth it, and long overdue. He'd finally put all those exasperating jerks in their place, and probably spared himself the trouble of walking into a classroom ever again. He put his head down and strode home, leaning into the wind, happy to think that by blowing his cork, he'd unstopped his fiction.

When Neil was almost four years old—too young to know who his friends were—he received an invitation to Dottie Harris's birthday party. His mother was thrilled. For a long time his mother had been yearning to be noticed by Mrs. Harris, who lived with her husband the doctor and their well-dressed daughters in a two-and-a-half-story house with a limestone facade and a yard big as a park. Dr. Harris was an osteopath. Neil's father, a corporal in the army, was overseas.

The moment she opened the envelope, his mother began referring playfully to Dottie Harris as "your little girlfriend," and Neil had no reason not to believe her. He could only assume that's how you acquired girlfriends, by an announcement in the mail. Dottie had been his classmate in Miss Lesmeister's rhythm class for preschoolers. He had no special feeling for the girl. His only impression was that she made a lot of noise. She liked to defy Miss Lesmeister and play the triangle too loud to blend in with the things the rest of the children were hitting with sticks.

On the morning of the party, Neil and his mother went shopping for the gift. They spent a long time in the toy aisle of Kruger's Variety. When it became apparent that his mother was about to buy either a doll's dress with a matching jacket or a blanket and pillow made to fit a doll buggy, Neil had a tantrum. He wept and howled and collapsed on the floor, refusing to rise and stand without aid until his mother paid attention to his choice, a motorcycle with a sidecar and wheels that actually turned on their axles. "Not for girls," she declared so decisively that his second tantrum lacked conviction. They compromised and bought a kazoo.

At home, before wrapping it, his mother demonstrated how it was played, and then, warning him neither to dribble spit into the mouthpiece nor leave teeth marks on it, she allowed him to try it. He played what sounded to him like a sublime rendition of his favorite song, "Jingle Bells." How marvelous that this simple device, which was shaped like a cucumber, should transform his ordinary humming into music of unspeakable beauty. When he began "Jingle Bells" for the second time, his mother said it was a silly thing to play at this time of year (it was April) and she took it away to wrap it. He fell onto his back and howled and wept and kicked the floor with his heels until she promised to buy him a kazoo of his own the very next day.

So he had a bath and put on his white shirt, blue tennis sweater, and short pants with suspenders. His mother, too, changed her outfit, in case Mrs. Harris invited her to join the party. They walked the seven blocks to the stone-fronted house, for they had no car, this being wartime, and they were met at the door by a maid, who ushered Neil inside. His mother was not invited to follow. She was told that the children would be driven home after the party.

He was the last guest to arrive. In a large room at the back of the house, he was introduced to chaos. Holding his gift behind his back, he stood in the doorway with his stomach aching with anxiety and his ears ringing with the shouts of children he didn't know playing games he didn't understand. There were streamers, balloons, and red and yellow lanterns. He was an only child whose previous venture into society—rhythm class with his mother in constant attendance—had been orderly and safe and nothing like this. He had to go to the bathroom. A large boy wearing a dog mask came at him, growling. A girl with her mouth full of popcorn pointed out that his underwear was showing. Dottie Harris came rushing up to him and asked for her gift. She wore a dress of powder blue, over white petticoats, and a silver ribbon in her hair. "Hand it over," she demanded.

Neil withheld it. He couldn't give up his marvelous kazoo. Dottie threatened to tell her mother, but still he resisted. He could hardly wait until he was driven home and allowed to resume his lovely rendition of "Jingle Bells." Dottie summoned her mother with a scream. Her mother was a large woman with purple eyelids who knelt down before him and asked very kindly if he didn't want to be a little gentleman and give her daughter what he'd brought. The answer was no. Dottie screamed again and punched him in the stomach. Her mother gave her hand a weak slap. Dottie punched him again. Her mother asked Neil if he'd at least let them look at the gift in order that she might describe it to Dottie's father over the telephone and he could buy one just like it on his way home from the clinic.

No.

At this, his little girlfriend screamed most horribly and tears sprayed out of her as she punched her mother, punched Neil, and punched herself. Neil, despite the pain in his lower abdomen, was mesmerized. He obviously had a lot to learn about truly great tantrums. She finished her performance by falling to the floor and making an ugly face while holding her breath and rolling her eyes back in her head. So shocking was the sight of her all-white eyeballs that he lost control of his *bladder. Mrs. Harris, immediately aware of this accident, summoned her maid, who steered him out of the house and into a car and drove him home.*

Because of his embarrassing accident, and because she'd been snubbed by the Harrises' maid, his mother didn't reprimand him for bringing home the kazoo. She merely said he was silly. She told him he could keep it, and she would send another one to the Harrises' house someday. Neil was ecstatic. He changed his clothes and played "Jingle Bells" on the kazoo. His mother said if he insisted on playing the same silly piece over and over, he must go outside and do it. On the doorstep, therefore, warm in the afternoon sun, he played "Jingle Bells" five or six dozen times, all the while reviewing in his mind his little girlfriend's tantrum and planning how he might upgrade his own hysterics in the future.

Emerson Tate climbed to the second floor of the industrial arts building and found Connor alone in his studio-classroom. He was standing with his back to the door, spreading out eight or ten charcoal sketches on a large table.

"I say, isn't it about time for a drink?"

Connor, laughing, wheeled around to face his old friend, taking the man's hand eagerly, shaking it, dropping it, then snatching it up again for a second handshake and refusing to let it go. Tate knew he'd be welcome, but hadn't expected to be clung to like this, hadn't foreseen the emotion in Connor's eyes as he purred, "Em, Em, welcome to the provinces, Em." They were older eyes than the ones he'd said good-bye to last fall, heavy and careworn eyes, but with genuine delight showing through.

"What in God's name are you doing in Rookery, Em?"

"That's what we've been asking about you, and I'm here to ask it again today." Tate hoisted his black leather briefcase onto the table and patted it fondly. "You recognize old Rosinante surely."

Connor's heart fell. Into this briefcase years ago had been sewn a special pocket into which a pint of liquor snugly fit. Painter and writer, they had occupied neighboring offices at Cass College and emptied countless bottles together. Tate, unlike Connor, was a discreet alcoholic, requiring an infusion of spirits so small that many of his colleagues at Cass still hadn't caught on, and yet so steady that he sipped from his concealed bottle day and night, maintaining a level of harmless, good-natured inebriation most people thought of as his natural self. Harmless except for the toll it was obviously taking on his health, thought Connor, dropping his friend's hand and watching him shakily unbutton his coat and smile devilishly at him out of a beaky face that looked remarkably unwell, the complexion pinched and seamed, the eyes watery. Good-natured, Connor remembered, except when the booze ran out.

"Connor, why didn't you tell me Novotny was a madman?"

"Neil Novotny? Mad? A little odd, a little careless maybe. Not mad."

"No, I mean really. On leave from the mental hospital."

Connor looked vastly amused. "He told you that?"

"Well, isn't he?"

Connor shook his head. "Sane as certain other writers I know."

"Then why does he wear rags? He looks like a hobo."

"That's his style—no style."

"Well, he gave me the brush-off, but I'm not giving up."

"You like his book?"

"It's got possibilities, if I can find time to rewrite it." Tate circled the table of sketches, glancing from one to another and sneering.

"What do you think of my students' work?"

"I hadn't heard you were teaching ten-year-olds."

Connor moaned. "Hey, go easy, Em." Cynicism was what he expected from Tate. What he hadn't expected was to be injured by it.

"Well, just look at them." But Tate was no longer looking at them. He'd caught sight of the Ashbys on the easel, mother and daughter. "What the hell is *this*?" He approached the easel warily, as though the overprotective mother might reach out and claw him. "Connor, what *is* this?"

"My best since I left the city." Never, in Tate's company, could he get away with false modesty.

"Why, it's your all-time masterpiece." This from a critic not generous with praise.

They stood side by side for a time, their eyes on the canvas, Tate pulling at his chin and making appreciative humming noises, Connor turning his head slightly to the side and looking at it out of the corner of his eye, trying to see it freshly, as his friend was seeing it.

"It's so absolutely right, Connor. This woman's deep commitment to this girl, and the girl doesn't have a clue, does she? 'One-way Love'—if you're looking for a title. God, it's wonderful. So damn sad it's almost funny."

"I'll tell you what's sad. I might not get paid for it."

"You're kidding."

"It was to have been a gift from her husband. He's some kind of public-utilities tycoon. He was up here this morning looking it over—said it was wrong."

"Wrong? What's wrong?"

"Her expression. It's not sweet."

"Well, for God's sake, it isn't *about* sweet. It's about anxiety."

"That's what I told him. I said his wife sat here looking anxious the whole time, but he said no, she never looks like that. He expects me to fix it. He's coming in day after tomorrow for another look."

"Bank the advance and sell it to somebody else."

"What advance?"

He gave Connor a reproving look. "You didn't get half in advance?"

"I never do."

"For God's sake, Connor, how many times have I told you: half in advance, half upon completion? Why can't you get that simple principle through your head?"

"I never had this happen before."

Tate stepped over to the table and opened his briefcase. "Take the tycoon to court."

"Sure. Pay a lawyer half of what I collect."

Tate thought for a moment. "Forget the tycoon and sell it to somebody else."

"Who?"

"Your public in the Twin Cities, for God's sake—who do you think?"

"My public wants landscapes."

"This'll make them forget landscapes. Get faces like this in galleries and I promise you, they're going to be hotter than Picassos. But you can't be hiding up here in the woods and hope to maintain a career. You need to be accessible. How's the family?"

Connor furrowed his brow and rubbed his eyes.

"What's the matter? Marcy?"

He nodded.

Tate gave him a knowing grimace. "I figured."

"She's in the hospital."

"Good. Keep her there."

"It's mental this time."

"When *wasn't* it mental?"

"I don't see an end to it, Em. I see it like this for the rest of our lives."

"Yes, well, that's why you're such a great painter."

Connor made a scoffing noise.

Pulling Neil's manuscript out of his briefcase, Tate said, "The madman's book." Next, he drew out a pint of vodka, handling it ceremoniously, like a sacred vessel. He uncapped it, smelled it with his eyes closed, then stood it on the table next to the manuscript and rubbed his hands together. "Do you keep glasses here, Connor, or do we toast your masterpiece straight from the jar?"

Connor didn't reply immediately. He was gazing again at his canvas, intrigued to see what his friend the critic saw. The girl's expression of pure vacancy was precisely what gave the mother's face, by contrast, such power. No wonder the finishing touches had been eluding him all this time. It was already complete.

"Connor?"

He turned from the easel and regarded the bottle of Smirnoff. He would take a drink. Just one. Maybe two. How lovely to relieve his worries with a slight buzz. No use making a case for abstinence, not with Tate around. Tate would only deride him.

"Just a second," he said, heading for his refrigerator. "I'll find something to mix it with."

Connor did not plunge in. His free fall into unconsciousness on Liberty Lake was still fresh enough in his memory to slow him down. Instead of gulping spirits like a man dying of thirst, he sipped and savored, assuring himself that this was simply a cup taken for old times' sake, that his near-death experience had made a wise and moderate man of him, and that he would stop after the next drink, or surely the one after that. Let Emerson Tate get plastered without him.

But by six o'clock Emerson Tate, having been slightly inebriated most of the day—indeed, most of his adult life—was not noticeably impaired, while Connor felt a binge coming on. They had gone from bar to bar, exploring the liquid resources of Rookery and hoping to find a place as congenial as the Lock and Dam in Minneapolis. Their requirements were few but quite specific. They were looking for a quiet interior with dark wood paneling, stools with padded backs, and a bartender who would keep their glasses filled without being summoned.

Mick's Joint had an attentive barmaid, Lefty's had comfortable stools, and the Jolly Corner offered blessed relief from jukebox noise, but they found none of these virtues in combination with each other, and nowhere in Paul Bunyan's hometown, apparently, had wood been milled for paneling.

"What in hell becomes of all the wood in these woods up here?" Emerson Tate asked Mick's efficient barmaid. "Why don't you use some of it to panel your walls?"

"Sawmills turn it into second-grade lumber for house construction," he was told. "Not much hardwood around here for finishing work. Mostly pine and popple."

He asked the same question again from his padded stool in Lefty's, where the barman replied, "Most of it goes to the fiberboard factory. These woods around here ain't good for much but fiberboard."

Later, the man behind the bar at the Jolly Corner said, "Paper. It all goes to the paper mill."

"Paper!" exulted Tate, by this time a bit slap-happy. "Where would we be without paper? Academe runs on paper the way trains run on rails."

"Paper," echoed Connor, smiling blissfully into his glass of gin. He was arriving at that most pleasant state of inebriation where the yoke of everyday worries is lifted from the shoulders and nearly every thought has a humorous implication. "Isn't it funny, Em, how you never think of a sheet of paper starting out as a tree?"

"Oh, I do," Tate protested. "I continually think of paper starting out as trees. Seems awfully shortsighted of you never to think of that."

"Yes, narrow and shortsighted," Connor agreed, laughing quietly. "I'll try to do better."

"It'll give you a greater appreciation for paper, Connor, taking it back to its origin as wood pulp."

"I *will* do better," Connor happily resolved. "I'll take it back *beyond* wood pulp. I'll think of it in the seed of the tree."

"That's better," Tate told him.

Gin, as usual, was opening up a pleasing distance between Connor and the problematical people in his life. Marcy immobilized by gloom. Laura smelling of pot. The Ashbys unhappy with the portrait they'd commissioned. Free now of Marcy's suffering, free of the Ashbys' disapproval, free of his concern for Laura (driving her home from campus last night, she'd promised to stop smoking), he was feeling very confident, much the way he felt when the quintet was onto something hot and smooth and his string bass was part of the reason for it. He also felt very hungry.

"Let's eat, Em. I'll telephone my daughter and tell her I won't be home, and then let's go find us a meal somewhere."

Tate, the picture of undernourishment, advised against eating. "Interferes with drinking, eating does. Takes the edge off. You always were one to eat a lot, Connor. For a drinker, I mean. You really ought to get control of your addiction to food." Nightfall was bringing out the lecturer in Tate.

Connor asked the bartender, "Where do you recommend we look for a meal?"

"Culpepper's," he was told. "Go east on Division, it's on the river, by the bridge."

While Connor left his place and crossed the room to use the telephone, Tate explained to the bartender his policy regarding food: "I always avoid eating except as a lifesaving measure."

Connor dialed two wrong numbers before he reached Laura.

"Daddy, where are you?"

"Tied up. Emerson Tate's in town."

"Emerson Tate? How come?"

"He's trying to get me to go back to my old job at Cass."

"Oh, do it, Daddy. Please do it."

"You'd like that, wouldn't you?"

"I can't wait. Please, Daddy, do it."

"It's possible."

"I hate Rookery. I hate school. I hate this house."

Her desperation penetrated his armor of gin and tore savagely at his heart. "Well, we're talking it over."

"Do it, Daddy."

"You're okay out there alone if Em and I grab a bite to eat somewhere?"

"I'm okay except there's nothing for supper, remember."

It dawned on him, then, that he'd promised to shop on his way home. Apologizing, he drew from his shirt pocket the list she'd given him. "Give me half an hour, Laura, I'll be home with the groceries."

"Or you could take me out to eat with you."

This struck him as a bad idea. He lowered his voice. "You've never cared much for Em."

"That's why I want to go with you. If I'm there, he might not make you drink so much."

"Laura," he said as calmly as possible, concealing his irritation, which in turn concealed his guilt. "I'm not having a lot to drink."

"Oh, Daddy." Her voice sounded despairing.

"Look for me in half an hour."

Leaving Tate at the bar, he crossed the street to buy groceries. It began to snow while he was shopping, large feathery flakes dropping thickly out of the black sky and shifting like goose down in the breezes under the streetlights. Coming out of the grocer's, he stopped to take in the beauty of it, the sidewalk carpeted with it, the air opaque with it, the Jolly Corner sign across the street an indecipherable blur of neon. The scene struck him as intensely pristine and magical, and he wished he could hold back time, for as surely as this snowy purity would tomorrow be slush and grime, so his present euphoria would be an aching head and a darkened spirit. Relish the moment, he instructed himself.

Opening the tailgate of his station wagon to put in his grocery bag, he saw lying there the envelope containing Peggy's photograph. He stood for a long moment—*relish the moment*—with the envelope pressed to his face, his eyes closed, the image of Peggy filling his mind and warming his heart. The snow descended upon him like a blessing, dusting his head and shoulders. Then he tucked the envelope down into the bag, flat between the breakfast food and the laundry soap. He would slip it into a drawer of his dresser when he got home.

He extricated Tate from the Jolly Corner, and they traveled east on Division. When Tate caught sight of Culpepper's, he said, "Let's stop for a quick one."

"I've got to run these groceries home to Laura. It's only another mile."

"No, I mean just a quick one. Check the place out."

A quick one was exactly what Connor felt the need of right

now—he'd lost a little of his edge in the grocery store—so he drove down through the parking lot, stopped at the river's edge, and sat staring at the snowflakes in his headlights.

"You coming?" asked Tate, getting out.

Connor didn't answer. He wasn't feeling so hot. An ache in his stomach, a pain in his temple. Was this the downside of his binge already? Had he already passed the crest, with nothing ahead but the hangover?

"Hey, let's go, it's cold out here."

He switched off the headlights and followed Tate between the cars and up a slope to the brightly lit, garish green facade of the supper club, his shoes crunching wetly on the snowy asphalt.

Culpepper's had no walnut paneling, no padded backs on the stools, and only occasional moments of peace between the numbers on the jukebox, but it did have Sammy Culpepper, a restaurateur so eager to attract the lucrative trade of academics that he shook their hands effusively at the door, and he went behind the bar himself in order to personally wait on them. He knew them to be Rookery State scholars by their soft hand and their careless way of dressing. Common laborers, his typical patrons, had calluses, while lawyers, CPAs, and other professional types always wore ties.

"What do you gentlemen think of the strike?" he asked, ready to take whichever side they preferred. He set doubles before them, gin for Connor, vodka for Tate.

"Crazy," said Tate.

"Not our finest hour," said Connor.

"Never could see striking myself. You end up better paid, so what? You probably never make up what you lost by walking out."

"Precisely," said Tate.

"I don't want to be reminded," said Connor.

"Gotta strike!" called a man from several stools away. "Can't let management keep screwing you year after year. We never got unionized at the paper mill till we went out on strike in 'sixty-one."

Sammy Culpepper diplomatically changed the subject. "Say, you gentlemen know my ex-wife, Helen Culpepper? She's taking classes at the college."

Tate said he wasn't from Rookery State. Connor said no, he guessed he didn't know her.

"Oh, you wouldn't have to guess if she was in your class. She's a real fruitcake."

"Ever since 'sixty-one, we've been writing our own ticket," said the mill hand.

"Maybe you've seen her around campus carrying a sack of rope. She makes things out of rope."

" 'Man may escape from rope and gun,' " quoted Tate. " 'Who takes a woman must be undone.' John Gay, born 1688."

"This is a very strong drink," said Connor.

"Thanks, thanks a lot," said Sammy, hugely gratified. "Doubles for the price of singles—what you might call an introductory offer. You professors like your booze, I know that."

The mill hand called out, "Hell of a wise move, you guys going out on strike. You guys'll be writing your own ticket after this, wait and see."

"God, did I get blitzed in here the other night with a couple of professors," said Sammy. "Absolutely clobbered. Two gentlemen from the English department."

"Who?" asked Connor.

"Smith was one. I forget the other one's name, a tall heavyset gentleman. You know Smith?"

"No," said Connor, who had recently seen a list of division members with no Smith among them. He suspected Sammy of lying.

"Could you put a little tonic in this?" asked Tate. "Straight vodka's not to my taste."

Straight gin, on the other hand, was doing the trick for Connor, at least for the moment. He felt his pains diminishing, his spirit lifted back up to the crest. Things were beginning to look rosy again, conversation recovered its amusing twist.

"Our good man down the way here says we'll be writing our own ticket," he reported happily to Tate.

"You better believe it," said the millworker.

Tate rubbed his eyes and said, "Before we're too far gone, what do you say we get Novotny down here and talk about his manuscript?"

"Good idea," said Connor.

"Hey, don't I know Novotny?" said Sammy. "Don't he write storybooks?"

"That's him."

"Sure, he used to sit right where you're sitting and work on his storybooks. My ex-wife's in one of his classes."

"I'll propose my proposal and you back me up," said Tate.

"Good idea," said Connor. "I'll go get him."

"Don't go get him. Call him up."

"He doesn't have a car. I've got to take those groceries home anyhow."

"Well, finish your drink, it's cold out."

"That's three nights in a row I was absolutely clobbered," Sammy boasted. Having steered the talk around to his area of expertise, he was reluctant to leave it. Upon closer inspection Connor realized that unlike Emerson Tate, whose symptoms were thus far limited to an unwholesome complexion (he was probably crumbling from the inside out), Sammy Culpepper, though younger, displayed every sign of boozy demolition: the pallid face with its ruddy areas of broken veins, the painfully overhearty demeanor, the nervous twitch of a smile, the neglected teeth, the tremor in the hands. "God, were we bombed. I mean just absolutely wiped out." He came at them with the gin bottle in one hand, the vodka in the other. "Don't hold back, gentlemen, this is on the house."

If this was generosity, thought Connor, it was the perverse sort he recognized from his own history as a drinker. Because you found such happiness in drinking, such relaxation, comradeship, forgetfulness, and joy, you wanted to share it with everyone in sight.

"Drink up," Sammy repeated, carefully and shakily filling their glasses to the brim.

There was no way Connor could drink it up. His body was in revolt. The pain was returning to his temple and advancing across his forehead. He was dizzy. His eyes were watering. Patsy Cline on the jukebox was singing painfully loud. He turned his glass around and around, judging whether he was too far gone to drive. He decided to risk it. He had to. Laura was starving.

"I'm going to run those groceries home, Em. You want to come along?"

Tate, engrossed with Culpepper in a discussion of vodka, its origin in the potato, its meritorious effect on the brain, waved him off.

He drove through the snow at his customary drinking speed, between five and ten miles an hour, ignoring the honking drivers creeping along behind him. He nearly slid into the ditch as he turned off the highway and onto the slippery approach to his house.

Entering the front door, he heard Laura on the phone in the kitchen. She handed him the receiver in exchange for the bag of groceries.

"Connor, I did a dumb thing."

"Who's this?"

"Neil. I did a dumb thing."

"So I heard."

"I gave your editor friend the brush-off."

"He told me."

"How can I get back in touch with him? I didn't know who he was. I thought he was a book salesman."

"Easiest thing in the world. I'm coming to pick you up in about ten minutes."

Neil sighed. "Thank God. He must like my book, to come all this way. Has he said?"

"Said it's got possibilities."

"Will he buy it?"

"He hasn't said."

"Oh, God, I hope so."

"I'm coming to get you."

"Hurry up."

Emerson Tate removed himself from the tiresomeness of Sammy Culpepper and went to sit in a large booth. The millworker followed, and sat down opposite him. Soon they were joined by a fifty-year-old, wiry-haired woman who thrust her hand out to Connor when he arrived and said, "Hi, I'm Vangie." She wore a black satiny jacket with yellow lettering on the back.

"Hello, I'm Connor."

"You're new here."

"Not exactly. I was here an hour ago and left."

"An hour ago I was soaking in the tub. It was a crazy day at the bait shop."

"You work in a bait shop?"

She turned and hunched her shoulders forward so he could read her jacket: CRUSTY'S BAIT AND TACKLE. "You a married man?" she asked.

"I am."

"Hi, I'm Vangie," she said to Neil, who had followed Connor over to the booth. "You're new here."

"Actually not. I used to come in here quite a bit a couple years ago."

"Couple years ago I was selling Avon. You a married man?"

"No."

"How come?" she asked, but instead of waiting for an answer, she introduced the man who sat beside her. "This here's Roy from the paper mill. He's a married man."

Neil and Connor both shook the millworker's very large hand. He was a pockmarked man wearing a fleece-lined denim jacket. His hair was white. "You teachers get yourselves unionized and you'll be writing your own ticket," he said.

"Sit down," said Vangie. "Make yourself at home."

Connor and Neil continued to stand. "Shall we take another booth?" said Connor to Tate. "This is your author."

"I know, we've met." Tate tipped his head up at Neil and gave him an unattractive smile. He appeared unwilling to move.

"Sorry about this afternoon," said Neil. "I was at the end of my rope."

Tate raised his glass, signaling his acceptance of the apology. "Forget it, son—sit down." He moved over to make room for Neil beside him.

On the table before them, Connor set the black briefcase he'd brought in from the car. "We've got some business to take care of," he told Vangie and Roy.

"Go right on ahead," said Vangie. "Don't let us stop you." She pressed Roy tight against the wall to make room for Connor to sit.

"Well, first we need drinks," said Connor. "Neil, what'll it be?"

"Beer."

"And you two?"

"Sammy knows," said Vangie.

Connor stepped over to the bar and ordered two of everything, though he could ill afford it, then he returned to sit next to Vangie and listen to Roy's account of the paper-mill strike of 1961.

Then Neil began the editorial conference, at Tate's request, by recounting the plot of his novel—Lydia running away from her family, meeting Zastrow, working for the Flandreaus, running from the plantation, meeting Randolph on the riverboat, Alphonse catching up with her in St. Louis.

Tate noticed with satisfaction that Vangie and Roy were captivated. "How do you like it?" he asked them.

"Was this a movie?" said Roy.

"Why did she run away in the first place?" asked Vangie.

"But the important, overall question is, how did you like it?" Tate repeated. "Would you buy this book?"

"My wife would," said Roy.

"How much?" asked Vangie.

Connor quickly downed his first drink and began his second. By going out to drop off the groceries, he'd again lost altitude.

Tate told Neil he had a few suggestions. "First let's consider the story line. I foresee several twists in the plot that you haven't written yet."

"I swear I saw this in a movie," said Roy.

"Why did she run away?" Vangie asked again.

Tate went on to say he hoped Neil envisioned a book much longer than its present size because readers wanted romance, and at this point, with the appearance of Randolph, the love story was just beginning.

"Oh, yes, romance." Vangie reached across the table and patted Neil's hand. "That Randolph's a real stud, isn't he, honey?"

Connor emptied his second glass.

Tate said further that the name Lydia was too old-fashioned for a book written in the 1960s. He suggested other names.

"Call her Vangie," Vangie pleaded, fondling Neil's hand. "And make that Randolph guy real studly, would you, honey?"

Tate said the author's name, too, needed improvement. "You can't sell a romance with a name like Novotny on the cover. I'm partial to Niven myself. Doesn't Niven have a nice ring to it?"

Neil, who'd been nodding agreeably yet nervously to all of Tate's suggestions, said softly, "Neil Niven," trying it out.

"Not *Neil* Niven," said Tate. "The reader's got to think you're a woman."

This caused Roy the mill hand to explode with laughter.

Connor exploded as well, but not with mirth. "Listen, Em, this is Neil's book, not yours! You've got no business making demands like this!"

"Who's demanding?" said Tate in a soft, even tone. "These are just some ideas I'm setting forth, and he can take them or leave them."

"He can take them or not get published, you mean." These last two drinks, for some reason, were not fueling Connor's sense of amusement. He felt a balloon of rage expanding in his chest.

"What's your problem, Connor?" Tate's voice, though still subdued, had an edge to it. "Just because you lost your commission from the power-and-light tycoon, do you suddenly think every artist is above constructive criticism? Well, let me remind you that our young friend here is a beginner, and beginners need editorial assistance."

"I'm not saying they don't need assistance, I'm saying you go too far when you distort Neil's vision by trying to make his book a cheap romance."

Tate turned to Neil. "Am I distorting your vision?"

Neil, who had been scowling at Connor as though warning him not to interfere, turned his furrowed forehead on Tate, as though he were thinking it over.

"Look, Em . . ." Connor paused to cough. "Take, for example, the girl's name. Lydia won't work, you say, because it's not fashionable. Well, just remember the setting is a hundred years ago when Lydia probably *was* fashionable. Change her name and you make the book less authentic." He coughed again and again. "And as for Neil's name . . ." More coughing. "I suppose you want to call him . . ." A long, choking series of coughs.

Tate said, "Editors have needs too, Connor," and turned his attention back to Neil, advising him to choose a woman's name he was particularly fond of.

"Peggy," said Neil. "Peggy Niven."

"No, no, for God's sake, not a nickname."

Tate's arrogant manner was beginning to irk Neil. He said he hated to give up the name Neil. He liked the name Neil. What was wrong with the name Neil?

"Nothing's wrong except nobody's going to buy a book about a woman written by a man. How about Cornelia? It's got Neil in it."

"Cornelia Niven," cooed Vangie. "I love it."

Roy the mill hand, quivering with laughter, reached across and shook Neil's hand. "Pleased to meet you, Cornelia."

A group of snow-covered snowmobilers filed in the door. Connor followed them to the bar, demanding another drink and watching carefully as Sammy mixed it because he suspected him of making them weaker than before. Gin wasn't having its desired effect. Nothing was amusing; his worries were returning.

What with Marcy's hospitalization infringing on his thoughts with greater and greater urgency, he carried his drink to the telephone and called Victor to ask about health insurance. Victor wasn't in, so he tried Leland. He got Lolly, who spoke to him at length about her plans to put the quintet on the radio—most of which he didn't hear, racked as he was by a silent coughing fit. By the time Leland got on the line, Connor was weak and gasping for air, and only able to say, in answer to Leland's inquiry, that yes, he could be counted on to work against the strike by crossing the picket line.

"Are you all right, Connor? You sound out of breath."

"I'm fine, Leland." He hung up and was seized by more coughing, this time a paroxysm so deep and extended that he sank to the floor, choking. He finally caught his breath, but remained sitting on the dirty carpet with his back to the wall, depleted and half asleep, until a snowmobiler came over to use the phone and helped him back to his booth. There, Vangie wiped the saliva from his beard and Tate ordered him a medicinal shot of brandy. His eyes were so frighteningly red and moist that Neil couldn't look at them.

When Sammy brought the brandy, Connor was rumbling and shaking with a renewed round of quiet coughing. Roy the mill hand suggested that he go easy on the booze until his breathing cleared up. Connor slid the shot glass aside. Vangie took a sip and passed it along to Roy, who was lifting it to his lips when Connor reached over to retrieve it, deciding that if he was going to die, he wanted to be drunk when it happened.

He downed it, and felt better. He gave everyone a bright, pleased look.

Tate said, "See, I knew a shot was all you needed," and he called to Sammy for another.

"How about a lift home?" said Neil, his eyes still averted from Connor's.

"Hang around, my boy," said Tate. "We've got more work to do."

"Yeah, hang around, honey," said Vangie, "and tell us why she ran away in the first place."

"Yeah, hang around, Cornelia," said Roy, giggling and gesturing to Sammy that they were all in need of another round.

Sammy came with a full tray. "When you get around to your next storybook," he said to Neil, "I'll tell you what it's like to be married to a fruitcake."

They drank until midnight. Sammy steered Connor and Tate outside and through the snowy parking lot to the station wagon, with Roy and Vangie trailing behind to bid them farewell. Neil walked the fifteen blocks home rather than risk dying in a car crash. Connor drove safely home with Tate, though the next morning he didn't remember doing so.

Alex Bolus wasn't the only deserter.

As the bad news spread concerning strike pay and health insurance, an epidemic of cold feet broke out that would have scuttled the strike if Victor and Annie hadn't come up with a reassuring mixture of preaching and blueberry pie.

Victor, skipping his classes, spent half of Monday and all of Tuesday evangelizing. When he wasn't on the phone, he was darting in and out of offices or collaring colleagues at the front door of

McCall Hall, inviting them to his house for pastry and coffee and planning sessions. Almost everyone accepted. Though many were losing their courage, they hadn't quite lost the remnant of what their courage had felt like—the same enlivening thrill that children feel in naughtily defying their elders—and they wanted to get it back. Moreover, not only was Victor a hard man to say no to, Annie had proved herself on Sunday to be a happy and generous hostess.

Annie's optimistic nature was infectious. Both days, late afternoon and through the evening, a stream of professors tracked snow into her little kitchen on Trillium Street, consumed gallons of her strong coffee and enormous portions of her blueberry pie, while rekindling in one another the spirit of the Alliance. The lament of the unaffordable bicycle was somehow more touching with Annie telling it in her whimsical, half-humorous fashion, and that story gave rise to their own tales of hardships past, poverty present, and deprivations likely to come. Victor showed them charts of typical incomes proving that professors made less than electricians, plumbers, nurses, carpenters, insurance adjusters, and unionized garbage haulers. They arrived in the kitchen, many of them, looking worried and beaten, but hardly anyone left without renewed determination. Taking up a second list Victor handed around, most signed up for duties over and above picketing.

Though Victor was not known for lengthy premeditation, he'd put quite a lot of thought into this list, having come to understand the importance of titles in academia. Those on the main trunk of the Telephone Tree, for example, became Communication Directors. Whoever agreed to deliver coffee and doughnuts to the picket line was called a Provisioner. Old Professor Shea, overseeing the assembling of picket signs in the Dashes' garage, a job consisting of stapling rectangles of tagboard to three-foot lengths of lath, took great delight in being named (and insisted on being addressed as) Chief of Construction.

On Tuesday night, the last guest gone, the children put to bed, the last pie tin scoured and dried, Annie and Victor cuddled on the couch and watched for mention of the strike on the ten o'clock news from Duluth.

"Victor, do you know how many cans of blueberries we went through?" she asked sleepily.

"Plenty, I bet."

"Twelve cans."

"Wow," he said softly, nearly speechless himself with fatigue.

"That's the big cans, not the small ones."

"Wow," he said again, and then yawned.

"It took a big chunk out of our food budget."

"Don't worry, the Alliance will cover it."

"And sugar and flour and butter, be sure you bill them for that."

"Will do." His enormous yawn left him teary-eyed.

"There's blueberry stains on the oilcloth. Do you suppose the Alliance would buy us a new one?"

"Sure. What are we talking—coupla dollars?"

"Six ninety-five. There's a nice red-check one at the five and dime."

"Sure, we'll send the bill to Milwaukee."

They watched the weather forecast. Clear and cold. Maybe warmer by the weekend.

"Clear and cold we can take. At least we won't we picketing in a goddamn blizzard."

"Victor, do you ever think you're in a funny line of work?"

"Work? Who said it's work?"

"I mean professors are such worrywarts. They're so serious about little things."

"Yeah, how long do you think they'd last on the pipeline?"

"Kimberly, for instance—she's all het up over what to wear on the picket line. If it's cold, can a professor get away with wearing slacks, she wanted to know."

"Half a shift on ditch work, say four hours, and they'd probably keel over." Victor, amused by the thought of Accountant Cardero ditching, pressed his face into Annie's hair and chuckled softly.

"And they talk about promotions all the time. Who's going to make full, who's going to make assistant? What does that mean, Victor?"

"Not who's going to make assistant, Annie. Assistant's as low as you can get and still be a professor."

"But *you* aren't assistant."

"That's because I'm not a professor, I'm an instructor."

"Why aren't you?"

"I'm not working on an advanced degree."

"What's Peggy?"

"Assistant."

"How about Leland?"

"Full."

"Would you like to be full?"

"Sure, who wouldn't want to go around acting like a big cheese? Oberholtzer, he's full—you see how he treats me and Peggy and Neil." Victor laughed a short laugh. "Neil calls him Dad."

"To his face?"

"No, not to his face."

"How about associate? Would you like to be one of those?"

"Naw, associates don't get to be dads. They're more like uncles."

The newscast ended without word of the strike. Victor mumbled a few curses as Annie led him off to bed. Lying in his arms in the dark, she asked, "Victor, how do you think it'll all come out? I mean really."

He shifted positions, sighed a long sigh, and admitted he had his doubts. "Noon tomorrow's the soonest we'll know. How a strike starts is usually how it comes out. Either the picket line gets crossed or it doesn't. Either the picketers carry their signs with pride, like soldiers on parade, or they slouch around like they're embarrassed. I mean, so much depends on our attitude. Either we flinch every time management accuses us of shirking our jobs, or we tell management to kiss our ass. You can see all that in the first three, four hours of a strike. By noon I should know if I've got to go looking for another job."

"Another job!" She sat up. "Victor, we just got here."

"I know, but the way it works, unless you got tenure, they can lop you off anytime. How long do you think it would take Zastrow to lop me off if the strike fails?"

"He'd do that—actually fire you?"

"Sure," Victor purred. "He hates me."

"That's terrible, Victor." She straightened the quilt and lay back down in his arms. "Donnie's just now getting used to school. Moving again would be real hard on him."

"Whereas if the strike's a success, I'd have all this credibility with the faculty, and he wouldn't want to go against that."

She pondered this, then said sleepily, "You'd be their hero, wouldn't you?"

"Yeah, more or less, so he'd wait a year before he fired me."

"Victor!" She sat up again.

"Can't be helped, Annie. That's life. I'm screwed either way."

She sat staring out at a streetlight. After a time she asked quietly, "Where would we go?"

Half asleep, he answered in the same hushed tone, "Who knows, Annie?"

She lay down again. They talked in whispers.

"Would you look for another teaching job?"

"Hard to say."

"Do you like teaching?"

"Beats work."

"Do you like the people you teach with?"

"They're okay . . . all except the dean."

The clock downstairs struck eleven.

"What would you like to do best, if you didn't teach?"

"Organize strikes . . . have Jack Short's job."

"Move to Milwaukee?"

"If need be."

There was a long pause before Annie, drifting off to sleep, mumbled tenderly, "Your dean's a real shit-ass, isn't he, Victor?"

PART 4

Don't Blame Me

Victor was up at the break of dawn, eating leftover pie while shouting encouragement into the phone to his Viceroys. By sunrise he was standing at the corner of Sawyer and Eleventh, deploying his early shift of eight picketers. He was a little disheartened to see how pale and sheepish they looked in the early morning cold. Alex Bolus, who had returned grumbling to the cause, was looking particularly sour under her gray curls and her yellow stocking cap. She wore a voluminous purple coat hanging down to her ankles. On her feet were a pair of red basketball shoes, and she was already complaining of painfully cold toes.

"Don't bunch up, spread out, look alive!" Victor instructed them. "Challenge everybody who comes to work. Remind them you're not walking the line just for the hell of it, you're out here freezing your posteriors off for their welfare as much as your own."

"How about students?" he was asked.

"Turn them back. Here's where your skill as teachers comes in. Educate these kids in the main fact of your life—you're a peon working for peanuts. With the student body on our side, I guaran-goddamn-*tee* we can put the College Board in its place, and that place is a step *below* the state legislature, not above it. Now look sharp and don't let me see any passive picketing."

"What in God's name is passive picketing?" asked Alex Bolus.

"A passive picketer leans his sign against a lamppost or a tree and sits in his car to warm up. Now look alive."

Watching his platoon spread out along the sidewalks, four along Sawyer, four along Eleventh, he felt his fiery spirit rekindle itself. He was beside himself with pride. Here at last, for all the world to see, was a goddamn strike. He hadn't felt this gratified since the day he'd gotten up out of his wheelchair and taken his first steps following the pipeline explosion. That was the day his life turned around. He hadn't planned to become a teacher, but his head injury precluded a return to manual labor, and as soon as his social worker and his rehab counselor learned that he was able to walk again and his skull would hold his brains in, they studied the job market and prevailed on him to become an educator. So he went back to college at thirty to finish the degree he'd given up on at twenty, and was hired by Dean Zastrow the minute he graduated. Holding merely a B.A., however, he was not given a tenure track position, thus making him easier to dismiss when enrollment stabilized. He didn't complain. It was a job, however temporary, and he rather enjoyed teaching. It gave him more time off than the pipeline ever did. It was fun to be able to lecture people for fifty minutes at a time. It was warm in winter.

But teaching never caused him to inflate with almost unbearable excitement, as he was doing now, watching the first professor approach campus on his way to work. It was Reginald Fix, the fingernail-collecting fertilizer expert, a mousy little man with poor eyesight. As the picketers converged on the corner to confront him, he halted before crossing the street and squinted to read the large red letters of the signs they held up.

Faculty
Alliance
of
America
•
ON STRIKE

In a rare moment of restraint, Victor retreated from the encounter, climbed a short way up the snow-encrusted slope leading to McCall Hall, and took up a position behind a prickly little bush, giving his troops the chance to prove themselves. Which they did. When Chemist Fix turned and headed back the way he had come, Victor let out a series of whooping, loonlike cries of glee.

He had occasion to repeat these sounds a few minutes later when a column of drowsy students, glad of the excuse to go back home and resume their night's sleep, did just that. But his cries of happiness were tempered this time by his realization that well over half the student body lived in campus dormitories and thus would not come into contact with strikers on their way to class. Dean Zastrow had declared, and Jack Short had made Victor agree, that picketers had no business anywhere on campus except along the perimeter of Sawyer and Eleventh. (There was no need to patrol the third side of the triangular campus, for surely no one ever came to class across the frozen river.)

A few minutes later three cars pulled into the faculty parking lot across the street. Victor tensed up. Here, arriving for their eight o'clock classes, were three professors known to oppose the Alliance. Two of them—Georgina Gold of Speech and Henry Henderson of Languages—were the outspoken sort, and the other one—Barry Skeffington of Geography—was their silent but devoted disciple.

Victor, by force of will, remained behind his prickly bush and watched a nasty little scene unfold. The insurgents advanced. The picketers converged. Someone was pushed. Someone shouted. Georgina Gold grabbed a picket sign and broke it over her knee. The most insistent and angriest shouts came from Alex Bolus, who kept pumping her fists in the air like a cheerleader and calling out, "You stupid jerks!" Then, quite suddenly, the cluster disbanded, Linguist Henderson proceeding to his office while Professor Gold and Geographer Skeffington retreated across the street.

Victor gathered his troops around him. "Don't feel bad," he told them. "When you turn back two of those three clowns, you've really done something."

Alex Bolus corrected him. "One out of three. Georgina's not

going to her car, she's going down the block to tattle on us to Lolly Edwards."

"She wants Lolly to come and see how unprofessional we are," added a picketer whose name Victor didn't know, a tall woman with ruddy cheeks and a runny nose. "She wants Lolly to tell about it over the air."

"I say call the cops and arrest the bitch," muttered Alex Bolus, displaying her broken stick, her eyes agleam with anger.

They watched Geographer Skeffington pull out of the parking lot and drive away as another car arrived. This was Historian Quinn's little Opel, but without Quinn inside. His wife, Rachel Quinn, was driving, and beside her on the front seat was a large thermos of coffee and a box of Danish pastry. Her husband was unwell this morning, she explained, and she was serving as his substitute provisioner.

Victor allowed half his cohorts ten minutes to stand around the car and take nourishment while he and the other four challenged a number of students and professors hurrying to class at the last minute. The results were not encouraging. Only about half the students were turned away. Many of the young men who crossed the line expressed their need to be in class so as not to be forced into the United States Army. Not a single professor was deterred.

When it was Victor's turn to stand at the car window and drink coffee, he studied the red hair and mysterious eyes of Rachel Quinn and wondered how it felt for a woman of such robust health and beauty to be married to a man so chronically pale and sickly as Larry Quinn. Hers he recognized as the sort of sculpted, dramatic beauty a lot of men fell in love with. Not Victor, though. Victor had married the girl of his dreams and that was that. Nothing dramatic or sculpted or mysterious about good old Annie Dash. Everything about Annie was ordinary, except the devotion she inspired in her husband.

This meditation on comparative wives was interrupted by the tall woman with the runny nose, who said, "Here comes Edwards." They turned to see Leland on his way to work.

"Watch and see if he doesn't try to ignore us," said Alex Bolus. "Smile and not say a word and try to sail right on by."

"Might as well let him sail," said Victor regretfully. "He's in deep with management."

But he didn't pass them by. Desperate to keep the quintet alive, Leland felt oddly fortified, felt himself suddenly filling up with the same heady self-confidence he'd experienced at Mount of Olives on Sunday afternoon. He veered over to the cluster of chilly strikers standing at the car and said, "Good morning, everyone."

They regarded him, he sensed, with contempt. One or two muttered a greeting.

"Victor, promise me one thing," he said.

Victor swallowed the last of his coffee and asked harshly, "What's that?"

"Promise me this won't come between us as musicians."

Victor looked as though he'd never heard such an asinine proposal in his life. "And why shouldn't it?"

"Well, isn't it obvious? Some things are more important than salaries and striking and all this sort of . . ." He held back the word *foolishness*. He swept his arm to include Provisioner Quinn near at hand as well as the picketers across the street. "All this sort of confrontational activity."

"Who says?"

Spurred by an unfamiliar twinge of anger, Leland blurted, "Connor says." He wondered if the drummer was too dense to understand what the quintet meant to the other four musicians. He hadn't intended to refer to Connor, who had sounded drunk on the phone last night, but the artist, he felt, was his highest card. "He asked me to make sure we stay together."

"Connor?" Victor raised his eyebrows in surprise. The picture painter was the last person he expected to go all sentimental over music. "Whose side is he on, anyway?"

"Look, Victor, my point is that with the quintet there *aren't* any sides. We all want to play right through the strike, twice a week, as before."

"Be a little hard for me, won't it? Crossing my own picket line?"

"No need for that. We can play at my house. We have this big room upstairs, our enclosed sleeping porch. Mother says it's okay with her. Just this morning I moved a portable heater in, to get it warmed up for tonight. Mother's scheduled us for her Saturday show and we really need to rehearse."

Victor tried to picture himself on enemy turf. Lolly Edwards and her radio guests had been predicting ruin for strikers. But mightn't it be a good idea to meet the woman face-to-face? He could try appealing to her sense of fairness, and maybe get a spot of his own on her show.

"Drums," he said. "What do we do about drums?"

"Leave it to me, I'll take care of drums." Leland's face brightened with hope. "Will you come?"

Victor turned and looked at his thoroughly chilled picketers. One of the men kept picking up his numb right foot and shaking it. Others were red-nosed and teary-eyed from the cold. The tall woman was staring at her watch as though in disbelief that her three-hour shift was scarcely half over. Alex Bolus, for fear of frostbitten toes, had gotten into the Opel and was sitting beside Rachel Quinn, with the bakery box on her lap.

"No," he said. "A captain's place is with his troops."

"But there's no picketing after four o'clock, is there?"

"Listen, Edwards, this is day-and-night work I'm into here." He raised his voice, hoping to enliven his picketers. "Maybe you think running a strike is all fun and games, like teaching. Well, it's not. I've got the future of this whole goddamn faculty in my hands. You think that's something I can walk away from at four o'clock? Maybe next week it'll be all over and we can go back to playing love songs in the band room, but right now your drummer's got *work* to do."

Leland tried to summon up a fitting response, something about the vividness and excitement of music in a life otherwise gone colorless without it, but the word "music" was all he could think to say. "Music . . ." he said sadly, studying Victor's darting eyes and sensing the man's nervous vitality. He could practically hear the pulsing of Victor's heart.

"Music . . ." he said again, shrugging, turning, leaving the parking lot and crossing to his office, despairing, imagining the breakup of the quintet, himself playing solo piano for the rest of his life, perfecting the same old pieces over and over, no one to play with, Mother his only audience.

"You're sure you can fly now, Em?"

"Absolutely. Fit as a fiddle. Full recovery."

"It's a bouncy airline, so if you're the least bit queasy . . ."

"No worry there. I'm a new man." Emerson Tate, delayed a full day by drink, was being driven to the airfield by Connor. He spoke with pride, as though surviving a hangover were noble work. "I'm ready to fly home and resume stamping out ignorance."

Connor turned to study his friend's face. Tate's complexion was a shade or two paler than when he'd arrived on Monday, but it was much improved over last night's green-gray death pallor. By last night, after twenty-four hours together, both men had drunk themselves into a paralytic state. Connor was still in pain. His lungs hurt. The sun on the snow intensified his headache, he was dizzy, and his hands shook. Worse, he was ashamed. He'd lacked the fortitude to fend off Tate and his bottle. He'd disgraced himself in front of any number of people, including probably his daughter and Neil Novotny. Worse than that, though he'd searched the house, he couldn't find Peggy's picture. He could only assume that Laura, who'd already left for school, had found it Monday evening in the bag of groceries.

"Call me as soon as you check into insurance, would you, Em?"

"The very minute."

"Because if Cass will cover me—"

"Cass will cover you. We're desperate to have you back." As part of his recruiting effort, Tate had promised Connor health insurance, beginning immediately.

Connor was skeptical. "I'll need to hear that from your personnel office."

" 'Promise him anything.' That's a direct quote from the vice president."

"I'll believe it when I hear it from personnel."

He parked beside the airstrip and adjusted the mirror to compare his own sickly appearance to his friend's. As usual after drinking, the seams of his face resembled scars. His eyes were puffy and pink. His beard seemed to have turned grayer overnight. But he was breathing without effort—that was the main thing. Yesterday's second round of drinking, again at Culpepper's, had brought on no recurrence of Monday night's choking cough.

"And if I come back, remember your promise."

Tate laughed and said, "Sure," in a tone that promised nothing.

"I'm serious, Em. You won't ever again open a bottle in my presence."

"Cross my heart." Tate went on laughing happily. "I'll let *you* open it."

Connor flared. "Damn it, don't scoff." Turning his anger away from his friend, he looked out his side window at dead weeds standing up in a field of snow. Beyond the field a row of tarnished pines stood tall against the cobalt sky. "I'm done being drunk, Em. You've got to believe that."

"And haven't I said the same thing time after time." Tate couldn't seem to stop laughing. "Over and done with, I've said, it's nothing but tea with a twist of lemon from now on."

"Em, let me tell you something. In January, seven weeks ago Sunday, I just about died of drink. I mean, I came within that far of falling over the edge. Somehow I was spared. I resolved not to drink anymore." He turned from the window, glaring at Tate's gleeful expression. "What the hell's so funny?"

"Nothing's funny. It's just that I'm so Christly happy that you'll be moving back where you belong."

"I haven't said definitely."

"Oh, come on, admit it, Rookery was a terrible mistake."

"Look, I've got to weigh the dangers of going back into the company of drinkers."

Tate renewed his laughter.

Connor bristled, but said nothing.

When the little airplane came into view over the trees, they walked to the gate in the chain-link fence, Connor shielding his eyes from the cold sunshine.

"Em, I'm sorry you worked things out with Neil."

"I knew he'd come around. Boy like Neil needs to be in print so bad he can taste it."

"You're probably ruining his novel."

"Nonsense, I'll make it a best-seller."

"Forget sales, Em. Think of the novel itself."

"I do. I think it's mostly crap."

They stood watching the plane touch down and roll to a stop.

"Thanks for the fun, Connor. Take care of yourself."

"I will."

They shook hands.

"Come back to Cass."

"I might."

Tate crossed the tarmac and climbed aboard. Connor returned to his car. He sat waiting for takeoff, weighing whether for the sake of his art he could afford to return to the city where he'd learned to be a drunk. Not that leaving the city had taught him *not* to be a drunk, but despite this latest debacle, or rather because of it, he was more determined than ever to reform. His coughing fit at Culpepper's had done it, those few moments fighting for air reminding him how it felt to look death in the face.

The plane bounced to the end of the runway and lifted itself into the air. He watched it wobble up over the forest. It made a wide circle, was caught by the wind and swept south, a dark speck against the blue. He wanted to follow it south, wanted to put Rookery behind him. Tate was right—he owed it to his public to introduce them to his mothers and daughters. He owed it to himself. He owed it to his mothers and daughters.

Acheson was a bandleader with a drinking problem and no first name. His Melody Misters played the Arcade Ballroom every third weekend, and therefore he had a standing three-night reservation at Mrs. Connor's rooming house across the street. More often than not, Acheson would show up sober on Fridays, in time to eat supper with the family and whoever was occupying the other guest room.

A marvelous storyteller, Acheson regaled his supper companions with funny tales from the small-town dance halls, taverns, and school gymnasiums he'd played in since his last visit to St. Paul. He had the gift of aping facial expressions by rearranging his features in a hundred different ways, and he made Sonny Connor laugh till his ribs ached when he described the fistfight that broke out in the Kellogg Dance Hall between a midget and a giant, or, better yet, when he told about the herd of cows that broke out of their pasture and followed a farmer to the dance in Dorset. Acheson could imitate not only the farmer's expression of amazement and chagrin, but also the stupid determination on the faces of the cows. Connor, in later years, came to realize that his study of Acheson's delightful face across the supper table was his introduction to the art of portraiture.

Connor's mother was a complaining woman with more talent for cooking than cleaning. Roomers were more than happy to pay the extra fifty cents for one of her meals, but the sitting room smelled of soot, and when they opened a window for a change of air in their rooms, dust puppies came rolling out from under the bed. Connor's father, an itinerant construction worker known as a mud man (he specialized in the mixing of mortar), was seldom present, afflicted as he was with a severe case of wanderlust. Occasionally a ten- or twenty-dollar bill would arrive in the mail from Texas or Montana or Alaska.

The two Connor girls, Sally and Millie, were so much older than Sonny that they were gone from home by the time he turned ten. Finding himself suddenly bereft of their slapdash but sincere solicitude, mostly ignored by his impassive mother, and scarcely remembering what his father looked like, Sonny fixed his attention on Acheson.

"Don't you have a first name?" he asked him one evening after supper, accompanying him to the Arcade. This was a Friday night ritual for Sonny, carrying the bandleader's trombone case across the street. He was eleven.

"Have one but never use it."

"Why?"

"Don't like it."

"What is it?"

Acheson paused in the doorway of the dance hall, a barnlike build-ing with stylized dancing couples painted over the door. *"It's a secret. You'll tell people."*

"No I won't."

"Promise?"

"I promise."

"My name is Guy."

Sonny tried it out, saying softly, *"Guy Acheson."*

"Shhh." Acheson put his finger to his lips.

"I don't think it's so bad."

"One bandleader named Guy is enough. There's this guy in Canada."

"I don't like my name either," blurted Sonny.

"Can't say I blame you."

"I just want to be called Connor."

Acheson relieved the boy of the trombone case. *"Thanks, see you later,"* he said, then added, *"Connor's a good name."*

Just then, two other Melody Misters arrived, the bassist and the drummer. *"Hi, Sonny,"* said one. *"How you doin', Sonny,"* said the other. Whereupon Acheson made a face for Sonny, an exact representa-tion of what the boy was feeling—abject humiliation—and yet so rub-bery and funny that he laughed all the way back to the house.

When he was twelve, his mother allowed him to follow Acheson inside and hang around the dance floor for an hour or so before bedtime.

When he was thirteen, his mother lost her persistence where bed-time was concerned, and he stayed till the place closed up. This was the year he learned to smoke and play the drums.

When he was fourteen, the bassist began teaching him to play his in-strument as well, and he was allowed to sit in for a couple of numbers each evening, a slow blues number on the string bass, and then some-thing a bit peppier on the drums. He'd never felt so gratified in his life. He was no stranger to art; for some time, he'd been drawing the occa-sional comic strip and mailing it off to his father, but he hadn't known the thrill of applause, never felt himself essential to a team, never been *so downright happy. Begging to play more, he gradually worked up half a dozen pieces, but Acheson said that was the limit; there were laws against minors working where drinks were served, and he was forbidden to speak of his playing outside the ballroom.*

The three weeks between engagements were an eternity. The stringed bass intrigued him more than the drums, but when could he practice his bass playing except during warm-up time and intermission? He was at least able to practice his drumming at home, when his mother was out, using sticks of kindling on various tables and pie tins. "Blue Moon" became his specialty on the bass, "Walking My Baby Back Home" on the drums.

His fourteenth year was also the year when Acheson thought it would be fun to get the boy drunk. He was right. It was amusing for all the Melody Misters, particularly his friends the bassist and the drummer, the biggest boozers of all, to watch the boy weave and mug and say hilarious things off the top of his head, and of course it was fun for Connor to be the center of their attention—so much fun, in fact, that he got drunk every third weekend thereafter for several years.

In the hospital, he went directly from the elevator to the nurses' station to find out if Marcy's spirit was still seriously overcast. A sour old woman all in white—white hair, white complexion, white uniform, white fingernails—told him to wait while she summoned the nurse in charge of Marcy's unit. Waiting, he imagined the colorless daughter this woman might have produced and the ethereal, bloodless portrait he might paint—four eyes of pale gray staring out of the bony white and off-white planes of their faces.

She returned and handed him over to a woman with "Nathanson R.N." on her name tag, who seemed to have his wife confused with somebody else. His wife, said Nurse Nathanson, was a sweetheart, a dear soul everyone would miss terribly when she went home tomorrow. Not only had she been helping to feed her roommate, a stroke victim, she'd been going from room to room bringing cheer to everyone on the second floor.

"Marcy Connor?" he asked, needing verification.

"Such a dear sweet soul," she said, with a brisk nod of her head.

He could only assume that Marcy had turned her display of false cheeriness up a few degrees since Sunday. Either that or by some miracle it wasn't false. Could she be genuinely happy? He opened his mind to this possibility, but not very far. A small glimmer of hope was as much as he dared allow himself.

"She's going home already tomorrow?" he asked.

"Oh yes, it could have been today, she's that wonderfully stabilized, but Dr. Hyde put her on a new little something to raise her spirits, and he wants to make sure it agrees with her before he releases her."

"A little something? You mean medicine?"

"Two a day, morning and afternoon."

"And it has side effects?"

"Sometimes. Not very often."

"What's it called?"

"I can look on her chart. It's a little blue capsule—very uplifting."

"A pep pill, do you suppose?"

Nurse Nathanson smiled and put a finger to her lips as if to say, *This will be our secret.*

"And the side effect would be . . ."

"Very infrequent."

"Yes, I realize that, but exactly what is it we're watching for?"

"Well, some people flip out."

But not Marcy. Far from flipping out, Marcy appeared absolutely self-possessed when Connor followed the nurse into her room and found her smiling in her chair with a pillow behind her head and her feet on a stool. It wasn't the tense, wide-eyed smile he imagined a pep pill might produce; it was the demure, lowered-eyelid smile he'd fallen in love with when she was twenty. Furthermore, she looked rather pretty. She'd taken some trouble with her makeup. Her hair had been tended to; it was washed and combed and pinned in a style that took him back to their days as students together in art school. He tried to suppress the urge to throw his mind open to happy possibilities, tried not to let more hope come pouring in than he could stand losing. She might still be acting a part for the hospital staff. No hope was better than dashed hope—he'd learned that over the years.

And yet there were about five minutes when he couldn't help feeling lucky to have the woman he'd married returned to him. Bless Dr. Hyde and his little blue capsule, bless Nurse Nathanson, bless the old woman lying flat on her back in the next bed, her mouth open apparently in sleep but possibly in death—the very woman Marcy had actually helped to feed at mealtime. What an incredible turnaround: that his wife should actually feel compelled to nourish someone in need. He suddenly felt like rushing off to his studio and taking up his palette and brush. Hope always worked this effect on his creative spirit, made him optimistic and energetic enough to begin a new portrait. Indeed, several portraits. Canvas after canvas flashed through his mind—the faces of women and girls, some of whom he'd never seen before. He glimpsed the colors, the shadows, the highlights, the expressions, the moods.

These five provocative minutes ended when Nurse Nathanson, having fluffed Marcy's pillow and replenished her ice water, sang a farewell and left the room. Instantly he felt a change of atmosphere. Even the recumbent figure on the other bed must have sensed it, because she gave out with a throaty little sigh and turned her drowsy head toward the window, away from Marcy, away from Marcy's eyes, which were rising to meet her husband's, away from Marcy's smile, which was turning into the bitterly ironic expression he was used to seeing at home, away from Marcy's words, which began softly and slowly with the observation that Connor was a shit.

"God, what a shit you are. A job might improve my state of mind, you tell me, but what kind of job can a woman find with a degree in art in this godforsaken town?"

It was true. He had suggested she look for work.

"Cleaning houses and offices, that's all there is in the want ads. What kind of shit wants his wife cleaning houses and offices? Is that your idea of how a woman improves her state of mind—cleaning houses and offices?"

With this as her preamble, Marcy went on in a somewhat louder voice, causing Connor to pull the door shut and the old woman in the other bed to twitch and groan. She spoke without pause, grinding steadily along with amazing articulation, her sharp words flying at him like sparks off a grindstone.

"God what a shit. You smell like booze. Didn't you tell me you'd stopped drinking? I swear you said that. You stood beside my bed day after day, bragging about what a great and holy and enlightened human being you'd become since you put booze behind you. Listen, I know yesterday's gin when I smell it. It's the one thing you've brought to our marriage—this whole body of knowledge about gin. It's the one thing you've taught your wife and your daughter to appreciate, the effect of gin on a really serious drinker. We've learned when to expect you to start slurring your words and when you'll fall down, and when you'll throw up and when you'll pass out. Sometimes you fool us. Sometimes it's the other way around, you pass out *before* you throw up, and if you don't mind my saying so, I really do wish you wouldn't do it in that sequence. I mean, if there's one part of the drinking process I can't seem to learn to appreciate, it's watching a man throw up when he's unconscious."

Here concluded part one. She paused for water, holding Connor in her gaze as she drank. He said nothing. He felt dizzy, as though her words had blown him off balance. He felt flooded with shame, for drinking again. And of course he felt hopeless. He tried steadying himself by returning her level gaze. Her eyes, he noticed, were dilated. Her movements with the plastic tumbler were jerky.

Part two had to do with Laura, and the tragedy of watching a girl with Laura's brains go to the dogs.

"I don't think she's going to the dogs, Marcy."

She insisted that Laura was turning out to be heartless and disobedient and there was little hope she'd be able to live a normal happy life. She hated to think of her daughter going through life a crabby bitch.

Connor pointed out that she was only thirteen.

"Listen," said Marcy, "anybody as stubborn as Laura, with her perverse habits, is doomed to a life of frustration."

Granted, said Connor, she did seem perverse in her choice of friends and she did seem to know her own mind to a surprising degree, but thirteen was too early to write her off as a lifelong crank.

Marcy had much more to say on this topic, and hadn't finished when the woman in the other bed opened her eyes and moaned, perhaps in protest against what she was forced to listen to. Marcy rose and went to her bedside. She apparently read something needful in the woman's expression, for she rang for the nurse. The three of them waited in silence until Nurse Nathanson swept into the room with her smiley high spirits, and Connor asked Marcy if she wanted to go to the lounge to talk further about Laura.

She spoke as though to a very tiresome guest. "Why don't you just leave?"

"Glad to," he said, and did.

Victor remained with his picketers hour after hour, overseeing the changing of the guard at ten o'clock and keeping careful count of professors crossing the line. Near noon he guessed that less than twenty percent of the morning's classes had been in session, and since this was an incredibly better estimate than he'd expected, he sent Aaron Cardero, his eager lieutenant, on a spy mission.

"Make a quick trip through McCall, Aaron. See how many classes are actually meeting. It could be we've got this college by the short hairs and not realize it."

When Mrs. Kibbee caught sight of Accountant Cardero bounding happily up the walk, she threw open her window and warned him, "The dean's on the warpath, stay out of sight."

Undaunted, Cardero climbed the steps, telling her, "Victor Dash sent me, Lorraine."

"Tell Victor Dash the dean's mad as hell. Every time he looks out and sees a picket sign going by, he has a fit. None of you Alliance people will go near him if you know what's good for you."

Cardero paused on the top step, not ten feet from her window, and gave her the disarming smile he used on his financial advisees who didn't understand money, an expression that said, *Now, now, I realize this is complicated but let me lead you through it.* He said, "I'm not coming in for very long, Lorraine. I just need to see how many classes are meeting."

"Don't be a fool," she said. She was wearing a pink print dress and warming her upper arms by rubbing them briskly. "Come back in twenty minutes and I'll tell you what you need to know. Now make yourself scarce."

Cardero went back and reported this exchange to Victor, who had gone to his car to warm up. "You want me to try again?" he offered.

"No, that dame knows what's up." Victor sat at the wheel speaking over the coughing noise of his engine.

Cardero, standing at his open window, turned and looked longingly at the building. "I could sneak in the back door."

"Forget it, that dame's worth ten spies. We had one like her in the pipeline office, Adeline Stoltz, she knew more about laying pipe than all the field men put together."

Cardero went off to join the picketers. He stamped his feet and waved his arms for twenty minutes—the noonday sun hadn't raised the mercury more than a degree or two—and then he returned to the entrance. Mrs. Kibbee put her arm out the door, handed him a sheet of paper, and quickly disappeared. This he delivered to Victor, getting into the convertible and sitting beside him. He saw that Mrs. Kibbee had gone generously beyond his request, had apparently phoned all the buildings on campus and listed all the professors who had met their classes thus far.

"Nice of her," said Cardero.

"Nice of her, yeah, but look at this, for Chrissake." Victor was jabbing his forefinger at the paper, aiming at the percentage Mrs. Kibbee had worked out. "Forty-seven percent," he sputtered. "She's got to be wrong. Hell, we turned away Fix, Mackensie, O'Connor, Bushill, Carlson . . ." Victor flung his door open and got to his feet enraged, calling out the names of others who'd been turned away. "Andrews, Keating, Farquarson, Carlson—did I say Carlson . . . ?"

His recital was interrupted by Leland, who was passing through the parking lot on his way home to lunch. "Victor, I've arranged to have the drums from the band room brought to my house for the evening."

" 'Preciate it," he shot back, turning red with the effort it took to be civil. " 'Preciate it, but I can't make it. Lots of things to tend to."

"I talked to Peggy and Neil. They'll be there. Neil's got good news to tell us about his book."

"Edwards, how many classes do you guess actually met this morning—any idea?"

"Almost half. The dean's keeping track."

"But Jesus Christ almighty, who's teaching them? I haven't seen more than twenty people go in to work."

Leland looked quickly away, adjusting his hat and his silk scarf and searching his soul, mulling whether to reveal what he knew. There was the Ship of State to keep afloat—better not tell. But there was the quintet. He told.

"They're coming in by the north gate."

Victor's mouth dropped open, and something like panic appeared in his eyes.

It was a hidden, seldom-used driveway, Leland hastened to explain, at the far end of the campus where Sawyer Street came to an end in a dense stand of oak trees. It had once been the main entrance, but was more or less abandoned years ago when the major new buildings were put up facing Eleventh.

"Show me," Victor ordered. "Cardero, stay here and keep an eye out for more invaders."

Cardero stepped out of the car with alacrity. Leland and Victor got in.

Sawyer Street narrowed as it dropped into the trees near the river. The oaks were red oaks, hanging on to their rusty, dry leaves through the winter. Stirred by the breeze, they made a sound like rushing water and cast shadows over the car as it came to a stop near two squat pillars of crumbling brick.

"See?" said Leland, pointing to a trail of packed snow between the pillars. "They never bother to plow here, but people have been driving through nonetheless."

A car, in fact, came up behind them, the driver sounding his horn.

Victor opened his door and leaned out, craning his neck back and shouting, "Drive around me, and lay off your goddamn horn."

"Sorry," the driver called out his window. "Lack of room."

Victor sprang out of his car and shouted, "How much room do you need for this crummy little Falcon?" It wasn't until he stood at the driver's open window that he realized he was speaking to his chairman, C. Mortimer Oberholtzer. He felt slightly chagrined to have spouted off to someone as harmless and impossible to despise. By way of explanation, he added, "I've never cared much for Falcons."

The chairman, too, sounded an apologetic note. "I hope you won't think ill of me for going to my office, but I have to water Honey's violets," he said, implying falsely that he wasn't going to work. "Should have taken them home yesterday, of course, but I forgot."

So revoltingly craven was this excuse that it called up in Victor an emotion quite foreign to him—pity. Instead of stating how much he hated snivelers and sneaks, he said simply, like a sentry, "Carry on, sir," and moved his car off the beaten track.

The chairman, driving past them, saw Leland in the car and gave him a bewildered smile, to which Leland responded with a pained expression and an energetic wave of his hand, hoping to confirm, despite appearances, his anti-Alliance state of mind.

They watched the Falcon bounce through the gate over humps of ice; then Victor turned his car around and headed out of the woods.

"I'll post a picket there," he said. "That won't leave two-faced cowards anyplace to sneak in, unless they want to swim the river."

Both men avoided mention of what was in their hearts, Victor feeling grateful to Leland, but he didn't want to admit it, "Thank you" being too tender an expression to convey to an enemy; and Leland, for his part, praying that Victor would show up for evening practice, but not wanting to seem overly eager. "Please" would have sounded like begging.

A car approached them as they drove out from under the oaks. "Goddamn, look who's coming in now," Victor said. It was Connor in his station wagon.

"Mnnnnh" was Leland's noncommittal reply.

Connor passed them looking neither left nor right; he seemed to be concentrating on his hood ornament. Victor, through his mirror, watched him pass through the gate.

"Funny," said Victor. "I never thought of Connor as a chicken-hearted sneak."

Connor wasn't sneaking in. The north gate, when passable, was the normal route to work for most of Rookery's artists and manual training professors because it was close to Industrial Arts, one of the oldest buildings on campus.

He parked in his customary spot, in the shadow of the football bleachers, and crossed the practice field to his building. He was struck by the diminished foot traffic along the campus walks, also by the silence in his building—no screaming hacksaws in the metal shop, just one solitary hammer tapping away in the wood shop. He climbed to the second floor, and there, as expected, he found Mr. Ashby of Rookery Power and Light standing at the door of the art studio with his overcoat draped over his arm. He was a large, muscular man with short gray hair and thick glasses. The fabric of his shiny blue-brown suit looked to Connor like snakeskin. His first words were, "Well, did you fix it?"

Connor, reluctant to answer, said, "Hello." Let the man see for himself.

Ashby made impatient, huffing noises as Connor unlocked the door—apparently no other art professor had shown up for work—and led him across the studio to the easel standing near the north wall of windows.

Seeing at a glance that nothing had been altered, Ashby glared at Connor. "What the hell?" he said.

Connor studied the canvas. Tate had been right, this was incredibly good. The light and dark tones of the faces seemed not to be laid in by the artist; they seemed like sunlight and shadow falling across two distinct souls. Mother Ashby was looking even more vigilant as the paint dried—menacing, actually. Her daughter was looking more vacuous.

"You didn't fix it!" said Ashby, as though addressing an automobile mechanic.

"It's the best I can do."

There was a flash of anger in the man's eyes. "That's not my wife."

Look again Connor would have told him if he didn't feel sorry for the man, didn't feel partly responsible for drawing him into aesthetics beyond his depth. He'd sensed from the start that the Ashbys would be hard to please. He'd acceded to their entreaties not because he'd foreseen the intriguing result on canvas (he hadn't), nor to keep his eye sharp (sometimes his motive), nor to keep his paints from drying up. He'd done it for the fifteen hundred dollars.

"And look at this, it's out of focus." Ashby was pointing to his wife's right cheek. "You ought to be able to fix this fuzziness."

"No," said Connor softly, shaking his head, trying to hide his satisfaction behind an expression of regret.

"But look here." Ashby unpinned from the corkboard nearby one of the snapshots Connor had been working from. "There's nothing out of focus in this picture."

"Painters aren't cameras, Mr. Ashby."

"Hell of a lot more expensive than cameras, that's for sure." He handed Connor the photo and then shook out his overcoat and put it on. "I can't, in good conscience, pay you until you fix it."

Connor sighed. He wasn't surprised.

A bright, hopeful expression ran suddenly across the man's face. "Tell you what. I'll give it to her for Mother's Day instead of her birthday. That gives you two months."

"Sorry." Connor unpinned the remaining snapshots. "Here, I won't be needing these."

Ashby took them and turned, grimacing, to look out a win-

dow. Following the man's eyes, Connor saw a red car parked at the
north gate, and someone standing beside it with a picket sign.

"You teachers," said Ashby with loathing. "You're never
satisfied."

It was hard to tell at this distance and with one of the brick pillars standing in the way, but it looked like Peggy's car.

Ashby slipped the photos into his pocket and went to the door,
where he paused to look back. "It's your move, Mr. Connor. Let
me know if you decide to fix it."

Lifting his hand in farewell, Connor watched fifteen hundred
dollars walk out the door. Then he turned back to the window and
saw the woman move out from the shadows and into a beam of
sunlight. Her hair was as black as Peggy's.

He unclamped the Ashby portrait and carried it into his office,
where he slipped it carefully into the rack over his desk. At the refrigerator he opened a bottle of soda and stood there sipping and
straining to call up the creative impulse he'd felt during those few
hopeful minutes in the hospital. The impulse was gone. He felt defeated, empty, aimless. He resolved to go through the motions anyhow—maybe the impulse would come. From the supply room
adjacent to the office, he picked up his roll of untreated canvas and
a rectangular wooden frame nearly as tall as himself. These he carried out into the studio, where he unrolled the canvas, sheared off a
six-foot piece of it, and stretched and stapled it to the frame. He
then opened a can of gesso and began applying a thick coat to the
canvas with a large housepainting brush.

"No class today, Mr. Connor?"

He looked up to see a pair of young men in the doorway—
Lloyd Johnson and Chuck Lucking, two of his drawing students.
"Up to you," he said. "Come in and work if you want."

They came in, not to work, apparently, but to watch *him*
work. From across the table, their eyes on the glistening gesso,
they quizzed him for a couple of minutes about canvas preparation, then shifted to current events.

"How come you aren't out on the picket line?" asked Lloyd
Johnson, a thin, balding boy with a thin, reedy voice. "Aren't you
for the strike?"

"Not really."

"Us neither. It's got us worried."

Chuck Lucking spoke up. "The draft, you know. For us, it's either school or boot camp."

"You're in school," Connor pointed out.

"Not for long," said Lucking. "They're closing down the college."

"Who is?"

"The dean. It just came over the P.A. in the student center."

"Locking everybody out at five o'clock," added Johnson.

Connor groaned. Good-bye studio.

"Can they do that, Mr. Connor? Can they just lock the doors and not let anybody even study—not even in the library?"

"Apparently."

"Well, cripes, what about our deferments? We'll get drafted."

Connor saw the anxiety in Chuck Lucking's face. "It's not your fault if there aren't any classes to go to."

"Tell that to my draft board."

"I'm sure they'll understand."

"No, that's the thing—they won't. They're desperate for draft-age guys in my county."

Connor turned to Johnson. "You too?"

He nodded. "We're both from Loomis."

Connor applied more gesso. "Maybe you should explain that to the dean."

"The dean," muttered Johnson. "We just came from the dean. He says don't blame him, blame the strikers. He says take our case to the strikers and maybe they'll quit striking."

"We're telling the governor," said Lucking. "We're getting two school-bus-loads to go down to St. Paul Friday and have a rally on the capitol steps. Profs and students both. Will you come with us?"

"Five hundred miles round-trip on a school bus? Sorry."

"You could go in a car. Some profs are going down in cars."

"No, sorry. My wife's in the hospital."

There was a minute's respectful silence before Johnson asked, "What's the matter with her?"

"Some nerve problem. Until she gets out I'll have to be home with my daughter."

"Not on Friday," said Lucking. "Your daughter's going with us."

"Hardly." Connor chuckled. "My daughter's a freshman in high school."

"Laura Connor? Isn't that your daughter?"

Connor stopped painting.

"She and Gary Oberholtzer. They both signed up to go along."

Twenty minutes into her shift at the north gate, no cars having entered or emerged from campus, Peggy began to feel foolish patrolling an unpopulated thicket of oaks, and so, despite Victor's instructions, she became a passive picketer. With her car parked perpendicular to the trail and her picket sign standing against the front bumper, she sat listening to the radio and feeling lonesome. She'd begged Victor to give her a partner, but he was shorthanded this afternoon—two of his troops had failed to show up—and he claimed to need all the others on the front lines of Sawyer and Eleventh. How depressing to be sitting alone in your car under a canopy of dead leaves and snow spread out where the sun never shone.

Suddenly a car came careening toward her through the gate, spinning its wheels and knocking down her sign as it passed in front of her, narrowly missing her bumper. This was Connor's white station wagon, and it came to a stop in a drift of snow. She saw that it contained an easel and a large, blank canvas.

"Sorry if I scared you," he said, walking over to the window she eagerly rolled down. "I didn't see that icy spot."

"Who's scared? I thought you were showing off."

Standing at the window and taking her hand in both of his own, he decided this was the way she ought to be painted—looking lovely in her navy pea coat with a green plaid scarf at her throat and smiling this joyous smile. He drew his eyes away from her and glanced about at the trees, the snow, the sky. He said, "Cold job, picketing."

"Frigid. And lonely as well—get in."

He went around to the other door, propping up her sign on the way, and sank into the passenger seat. The car was hot. It smelled faintly of perfume and chocolate. Joni Mitchell was softly singing "Both Sides Now."

"Here, before I overdose," she said, handing him half a candy bar.

He ate hungrily. His only food today had been breath mints.

A car left campus. The educator at the wheel kept his eyes straight ahead, avoiding eye contact.

"Who's that?" asked Connor.

"Cavanaugh," said Peggy. "Sociology."

"Oh."

"Victor sent me down here to stem the incoming tide of professors, but everybody's going the wrong way."

"Rats off a sinking ship," said Connor. "At five o'clock the place closes down altogether."

"It does?"

"A lockout."

She laughed gleefully. "Now we're getting somewhere."

"Where, exactly?" He didn't understand her delight.

"A standoff. The lines drawn. The worst possible thing would be if the semester went limping along at half speed without any showdown."

"But what good does a lockout do the dean?"

"It covers up his inability to hire enough scabs to keep the place operating. It's also a strategy to cause dissension. He figures those who want to teach will pressure the rest of us to call off the strike."

He nodded seriously. "It's all such a mystery to me."

"You're not supposed to be aware of these things, Connor—you're an artist."

"Without a studio."

At this, she leaned into him and kissed him, and he felt instantly feverish and weak, his scalp and shoulders tingling, his arms virtually paralyzed, scarcely able to return her embrace.

She dropped her head and pressed it to his chest.

"How long is your shift?" he asked in a husky voice.

"Till four. You'll come home with me?"

The invitation made his head swim, actually blurred his vision. "Yes, yes," he whispered, squinting at the clock on the dash. Well over an hour remained. Eternity.

At the sound of an approaching car, she sat up and studied him and was amused to see the effect of the kiss. He looked at once expectant and deflated. "What's the matter?" she said in a teasing tone.

He gave her a helpless little shrug and asked, "Do you have another candy bar?"

"It just so happens." From her purse she produced a peanut bar.

He tore off the wrapper, broke it in two, and put half in the palm of her hand.

The car leaving campus belonged to Brooks Dumont of Manual Training. He greeted Peggy and Connor as effusively as it was possible to do with two panes of glass between them—slowing down, waving, smiling, nodding—and then he gunned his little Chevy II and spun his wheels up through the woods, kicking up shards of ice.

They ate the candy bar.

"Can you paint at home?"

He shrugged. "I'm going to try."

"Have you seen her today?"

He nodded.

"How is she?"

It took him a moment of chewing to find the right word. "Difficult."

"The doctor couldn't help her?"

"The doctor gave her a happy pill."

"And?"

"It made her nurse happy."

Another car left campus. This was Chairman Oberholtzer, smiling politely, as if to say, *No hard feelings.* Peggy made a small hissing sound and Connor chuckled.

They finished the candy bar.

Another car appeared. This was the custodian of Industrial Arts. He grinned going by, no doubt anticipating several days of easy maintenance in an empty building.

"How long before she comes home?" asked Peggy.

He frowned. "Tomorrow."

She studied him. "You don't look thrilled about it."

"No," he said, envisioning the stormy weather ahead. Involving himself with Peggy was sure to compound the sorrows pervading his household. How overwhelming the power of romance, he thought, that a man should become so reckless with the lives of the people in his care. That he should be sitting here desiring this woman, not his wife. That he should take her in his arms and kiss her eyes and lips and throat. Which he did as soon as the custodian's car disappeared.

At five-thirty she rose from his arms and stepped across the tiny bedroom and into the kitchen to answer the telephone. He lay there for a minute, studying the flowered wallpaper, then went to the window to investigate a sputtering-engine noise in the alley. The weather had changed. Below him, through a thin veil of sleet, he saw a truck pull up to the refuse bin behind the JCPenney store. A man got out of the cab and unfastened and dropped the front panel of the bin while the driver backed the truck up close to it; then they both threw the refuse—mostly flattened cardboard boxes—up over the tailgate, chattering as they worked, one with a cigarette hanging from his lip, the other with a strong voice that carried disconnected words up to Connor through the sleet. "Took her out . . . best-looking . . . see what she could do . . . she was fast . . . I drove it home—pow." The power of romance, thought Connor, until he realized the man was describing a car. "Eight seconds from zero to sixty . . . she'll do ninety on the straightaway." But yes, romance after all, he thought, for this man was clearly lovestruck. "What a honey . . . everything in perfect shape, body, crankcase, even her fan belts. . . ."

"Connor."

He turned from the window, shivering in his nakedness.

"Please stay." She'd returned and was lying facedown under the quilt, her voice sleepy and soft.

"Who was it?"

"The Telephone Tree."

He slipped back under the quilt and they entangled themselves, warming each other.

"What's the news?"

"The lockout. Please don't go."

"Laura," he said, and felt her nod of understanding.

"Will you bring her to Leland's tonight?"

"I'll have to. I don't like to leave her out there in the sticks alone."

"Come back tomorrow," she said. "We've got to make up for lost time."

"Lost time?"

She whispered in his ear, "A semester and a half of not fucking."

He chuckled. Then he abruptly turned away. "I'd better not. Marcy comes home tomorrow."

"What time?"

"Around noon."

"In the morning, then, as soon as Laura leaves for school."

His eyes filled with tears. He would not come here again. Talk about Neil Novotny being unfaithful to his novel, here in this bedroom was infidelity on a grand scale.

She rose to a kneeling position and leaned over him, wagging her breasts across his beard. "I'll give you breakfast."

Peggy was first to arrive at the Edwards house, first to sink into Lolly's pillowy embrace on the doorstep, first to be forced upstairs to examine the wallpaper samples under consideration for Leland's bedroom.

The choices had been narrowed to a plaid, a stripe, and a design of green fish against a faint background of seaweed. The room itself was small and charming, with photos on the walls from every stage of Leland's boyhood. Peggy was fascinated by those portraying father and son. Their resemblance to one another was striking, and so was their attachment. Historian Edwards had been a handsome, long-faced man. Leland had been lanky and serious from infancy onward. Lolly had been much less fat before her husband's death.

From downstairs came the sound of Leland welcoming the next guest and sending him up to join them—Victor Dash, of all people. He came to a halt in the bedroom doorway, his hand to his mustache, smoothing it, his eyes full of expectancy, as though he were about to witness a meeting of titans, and he one of them.

"My stars, how tickled I am to finally meet you," said Lolly, removing his hand from his mustache and lifting it gracefully high, as though in a minuet. "Leland said you'd be too busy with strike business to give us the pleasure."

"I figure making your acquaintance *is* strike business. I need radio time."

"And you shall have it," was Lolly's immediate reply. "I have openings next week."

"No, tomorrow," insisted Victor.

Laughing at his impertinence, she said, "I'm sorry, Mr. Dash, tomorrow's cosmetics and Friday's birdhouses, and of course Saturday's the combo. But next week I can get you on for half the show Monday or the whole show Wednesday. Let's say Wednesday, for the full fifteen minutes."

"Strike could be over by Wednesday."

"Well, it's entirely up to you, but I thought rather than sharing the Monday show with Mrs. Carruthers—she sews doll clothes, and I promised her at least six minutes on Monday."

Victor looked uncertain. "I'll let you know."

"Do that. Meantime, we're choosing paper for Leland."

There was nothing uncertain about Victor's wallpaper opinions. "Not pink!" he exclaimed with horror when Lolly held up the sample of plaid, which was mostly gray and blue with only a trace of rose, not pink. "You can't give a guy pink!"

Lolly laughed and unfurled the fish, which had curled up on the bed. "How about this one?"

He tipped his head, studying it. "If that isn't just the goddamnedest wallpaper I've ever seen. You trying to drive your boy nuts, or what?"

More laughter from Lolly—fond, excited laughter: this guy was a stitch. She unfurled the stripe. "And this."

Again a moment of thought. "Yeah, that he could live with. At least it wouldn't wake him up nights."

Neil Novotny then appeared in the doorway, carrying his clarinet case and wearing a clean shirt.

"My stars, Neil, how wonderful to see you—it's been ages." Again the lifted hand, this time accompanied by little pats on the cheek. "Leland tells me you have scads of students wanting to study with you—surely the sign of a well-loved teacher."

"My teaching days are over," Neil declared, his eyes trained on Peggy. "In case you haven't heard—I called the dean a warty little tyrant."

"What?" exclaimed Peggy and Victor together. Neil's explosion had gone unremarked on the faculty grapevine, strike news taking precedence.

"Mrs. Kibbee says my job might be secure till June if I lay low, but why would I want to stay? I've got a publisher for my novel."

"A publisher—why, that's wonderful," said Lolly.

"No shit!" said Victor. "Who?"

"T. Woodman Press of St. Paul. A top-quality house. Very well thought of in the industry."

"Oh, how lovely. Radioland will want to know all about it. I have openings next Monday or Wednesday."

"Just a minute," said Peggy. "You said *what* to the dean?"

"I said he was a warty little tyrant, and he was standing in my way of succeeding as a teacher." Neil's laugh was a couple of nervous yelps. He looked wild and overheated. "I told Oberholtzer off too, while I was at it. Something about his wife and her everlasting violets, I can't remember exactly."

"Jesus!" said Victor. "You can't go saying stuff like that to management. They'll chop off your head."

"For shame," said Lolly, turning icy. "Honey and Mortimer don't deserve that. You'll have to apologize immediately or—"

Here she was distracted by the appearance of a young girl in the hallway, peering into the room, taking everything in with hard, ungiving eyes. Sweatshirt and jeans. Shoulder-length blond hair and shoulder-length strings of beads hanging from her ears. A cynical twist to the lips. Lolly's first thought was that a hippie child had wandered in off the street, but then she saw the bearded artist take up a position behind her and recalled seeing them together at the Christmas party. Lolly had been dying to meet the artist because he was said to be so many things that intrigued her— a recluse, a genius, and a drunk. If only she could lure him onto the airwaves, he'd be the first genius and recluse, if not the first drunk, that "Lolly Speaking" had ever presented to its listeners.

Peggy introduced them, avoiding Connor's eyes for fear of revealing the ecstasy flooding her heart at the sight of him.

"And how do you like our fair city?" Lolly gushed at the girl.

"You call this a city? I'm from Minneapolis."

Lolly, chortling, seemed genuinely amused by this reply. Patting the girl's cheek, she turned again to the matter of wallpaper. By this time Leland had hung up all the coats and joined them. The stripe was the unanimous choice of the visitors, although Laura Connor liked the fish but didn't say so. It was no use being contrary if you couldn't get the fat lady's goat, if she responded only with chortles and pats on the cheek.

Leland, who was destined to look at it for the next decade or two, was not consulted about the paper, nor did he express an opinion. Knowing his proper place, which was that of the crown prince in a powerful matriarchy, he stood at his mother's right hand looking agreeable and keeping his mouth shut.

Next they were ushered along the hall to the sleeping porch. This was a good-sized room with three walls of windows and woodwork of knotty pine. The temperature was a bit chilly, but the reading lamps gave off a cozy, golden light. A pair of Peggy's students, delivering the instruments this afternoon, had laid the bass fiddle on a wicker couch and set up the drums in the middle of the room. The Edwardses' second piano was a parlor spinet.

While Victor settled in at his drums, Connor moved about the room, looking down at the lights emanating from several kitchen windows and falling into several backyards. He imagined what a superb painting studio this would make.

Neil uncased his clarinet, Peggy her sax. Leland sounded chords on the keyboard. It lacked the resonance of the piano in the band room.

Lolly took Laura by the hand. "Come along, Miss Minneapolis, you can keep me company while I put a snack together for these merrymakers."

Laura snatched away her hand. However, being a willing student of food preparation, she did follow the fat lady down the back stairs to the kitchen.

There was a good bit of settling and resettling before the quintet made comfortable use of the wicker chairs and stools, a good bit of tuning and retuning before they grew accustomed to the brittle acoustics. In this strange new venue, they seemed to be much closer to the sounds they were making. The bass and sax and clarinet bounced back at them off glass; Victor's drumbeats ricocheted around the room like bullets.

Neil had a request. "Could we start with 'Don't Blame Me'? Do you all know it?"

"We'll start with 'Your Feet's Too Big,'" proclaimed Victor.

"But I've been practicing 'Don't Blame Me.' Here, I'll play you the melody."

But Peggy had an agenda. She interrupted Neil's tooting to announce, "First, 'Goody, Goody.'"

"In here?" said Connor. "We'll blow out the windows."

"That's the point."

There was a moment of silence, marking the first time the lovers' eyes met since he left her apartment less than two hours ago, and Neil, though not ordinarily clever with insights, saw their soulful look and suspected that something serious had developed between the two of them. He wasn't shocked or even a little surprised—he'd seen it coming—but it made him sad all the same.

This time the noise of "Goody, Goody" was as stupidly chaotic as the first time they'd played it, but louder; the sax a ruptured muffler, the clarinet a blown gasket, the piano an overturned load of slate. The snare drum popped and rattled, the kick drum boomed like a bomb, and the bass produced a grinding sound like that of mismatched gears. When Peggy put down her sax and screamed out the words, the phone rang in the kitchen and the elderly Mrs. Severson from across the alley asked if Lolly was aware that someone was crying for help in her upstairs window.

"Oh, it's only some of Leland's friends come in to play with him."

This remark confirmed Mrs. Severson's view of Leland as a thirty-five-year-old case of arrested development. Next she phoned her neighbor to the south, Mrs. Cook, who sent her husband out to investigate, and her neighbor to the north, Miss Corrigan, who went our herself. They were joined by others as the voice in the high window grew more desperate-sounding, the accompanying din more deafening.

The mad volume couldn't be sustained for more than ten minutes. "Goody, Goody" ended with a toot and a crash and laughter all around.

Peggy said, "There, we've taken possession of the room."

Connor added, "Of the neighborhood." He was pointing down at five figures huddled together in the alley with upturned faces.

Peggy cranked open a window and called out, "Don't Blame Me," this being next on the agenda, and cranked it shut again.

Here Neil took the lead. His playing was unusually sweet and controlled. He'd practiced. Having made his publishing deal, his method of celebrating had been to put his recording of "Don't Blame Me" on the phonograph the moment the construction workers had left for work this morning and to play it three or four dozen times until he'd memorized every nuance of Benny Goodman's clarinet. Leland was familiar with this version; this was apparent in the easy precision with which he now and then came forward and backed away. Peggy and the rhythm section, less sure of their parts, attempted nothing fancy. They faded further and further into the background—yes, even Victor—as the piano and clarinet addressed one another in lucid conversation, all the more intriguing because Neil and Leland had never before been featured together. Now they were playing like a pair of old veterans, old friends. With every phrase, Peggy saw Neil expand with pride. Every phrase being soft and inaudible through glass, Connor saw the onlookers in the alley disperse.

"Again," Peggy said when they finished, and they played it again, even better.

And that's how "Don't Blame Me" became one of the five numbers planned for Saturday's show. The program was drawn up over pie and coffee, Lolly making pleasurable remarks as she jotted the titles down on a card. "Oh, 'These Foolish Things,' how exquisite." "My stars, it's been ages since I've heard 'Mood Indigo.'" "Oh, I simply adore 'I'll Get By.' How Leland's father and I used to dance the night away." "Isn't 'My Blue Heaven' simply the darlingest thing you ever heard? I tell you, these pieces mean the world to me."

Leland was dismayed to realize that she'd made no such re-marks when he practiced these very same pieces on the baby grand in the living room. He'd been playing "Mood Indigo" and "Stormy Weather" at least once a day for weeks, to no apparent effect.

Their snacks consumed, the group went to their instruments once again, but Lolly delayed them. "Now in preparation for Sat-urday's show, I want to find out in what direction each of you wishes fate to lead you." This was her rather overblown way of in-quiring about their professional aspirations. She'd got the idea years ago from a *Good Housekeeping* article she'd seen in a beauty parlor—celebrities talking about where they wanted their careers to take them—and she'd been asking the question over KRKU ever since. The musicians, watching her wiggle herself deep and immov-ably into her cushions, despaired of getting back to their music.

"I'll bring it up on the program, so think of this as a kind of re-hearsal," she said. "Now who will start?"

Neil started, eagerly, full of confidence. "It so happens I'm on the verge of seeing my dream come true. I'll be getting a contract from T. Woodman any day. They're known for their scholarly books, so I'm not being paid thousands, but if this novel makes any kind of splash, my editor tells me the sky's the limit for future books. My working title, as some of you know, is 'Losing Lydia,' although my editor is talking about changing it to something more upbeat and also possibly giving me a pen name because he says Novotny isn't catchy enough, and possibly changing the story line here and there in order to make it more dramatic, but overall it will go to press pretty much as I conceived it. They're real eager to get it out. You might see it in bookstores as early as September."

Laura Connor was all ears, all admiration. So was Leland. Lolly listened unmoved, her mind on the dastardly insults Neil had di-rected at the Oberholtzers. Peggy saw Connor hang his head, and she knew why. He'd told her, in bed, about the editorial confer-ence at Culpepper's. This book of Cornelia Niven's was going to have a good bit of theme-destroying violence done to its plot.

Lolly moved on to the drummer. "And you, Mr. Dash? Where would you have fate lead you?"

Victor said he wanted to be a strike organizer. "I'd like to make my living leading slaves like us out on strike and telling management to shove their jobs where the sun don't shine. The College Board is a collection of stupid tightwads and the chancellor is a stuck-up idiot. They never consulted us about a wage freeze and they never gave us a chance to negotiate—how come you never bring *that* up on the radio, Mrs. Edwards? How come you always come down on the side of the robber barons?"

"You shall have your say, Mr. Dash."

"I've been listening lately. About the only people you interview are rednecks like Ron Hunsinger and old ladies with recipes for brownies."

"Monday or Wednesday," she blithely told him. "And now, Peggy dear, where exactly would you have fate lead you?"

Oh my, how tedious, thought Peggy. Didn't this woman, with her years of broadcasting experience, understand that by rehearsing conversations you robbed them of all spontaneity? Nevertheless, she indulged her hostess, and felt her convictions gathering strength as she uttered them. "All through graduate school I thought I wanted to end up teaching at Middlebury or Brown. Brown because it's where I got my undergraduate degree and it's all so familiar, and Middlebury because the one time I saw it, there was sunshine on the hilltops, ground fog in the valleys, and students strolling to class under bright red and yellow maples. It looked like heaven. So where do I end up? In a place I never heard of until Neil called up and told me there was an opening in music, a place where women are paid two hundred dollars less than men because they're women, a place where half my choir never learned to read music and three-fourths of my Music Appreciation students never heard of Mozart or Haydn, a place where I'm told this was the mildest winter in twenty years because there were only fourteen nights of fifteen below zero."

Peggy looked about at her listeners. She caught all of them looking apprehensive, as though fearing she was about to announce her resignation. Except Laura. Laura looked gratified.

"But on the other hand," Peggy continued, hoping to mollify them, "there's the quintet, which we have to thank Leland for getting started. The quintet means the world to me—it feels so much like family. I mean even if we never take it any further, even if we break up before we find our audience, I can truly say I've never in my life had so much fun playing music."

The faces around her brightened for a moment, until she added, "But . . ." Here she paused for a long time, smiling a faraway smile and fondling the big glass beads of her necklace. Then she gave her head a little shake as though clearing it of dreams. "But I still long to teach at Middlebury or Brown."

No one but Laura appeared to approve of this aspiration. Connor grimaced. Leland and Neil looked sad. With his kick drum Victor began sounding dull thuds with long pauses between them—a tolling farewell.

Lolly's reaction was to dismiss Peggy's longing with a wave of her hand and declare, "You are too well loved in Rookery, Peggy dear—you can't possibly leave." She turned then to Connor, purring warmly, "And the artist? Where would the artist have fate lead him?"

He looked up rather darkly from under his bushy eyebrows and said, "Anywhere there's ample time to paint."

Lolly laughingly pointed out, "Now you're on strike, you ought to have all the time in the world."

He smiled and held his tongue, not wishing to specify the exact nature of the time he longed for—time free of anxiety, no conversations about suicide, no fretting about his daughter, no classes to teach; open-ended time with room for his mind to move around and ponder and paint and paint out and paint over and finish each canvas to his satisfaction before starting the next; time to go on painting mothers and daughters without interruption until death took his brushes away.

Lolly pressed him. "Where, exactly, would you like to have all this time?"

"Paradise."

They all stared at him, mystified.

"You mean heaven?" his daughter asked, amazed to think her father might have suddenly come to believe in an afterlife.

"Yes."

"Now explain that," demanded Lolly. It was quite an adventure, following the twisted thoughts of this alcoholic genius to their shadowy sources.

"I can't," he said. "What do you say we get back to our music?"

"No, wait," Lolly insisted. "What do you see when you picture heaven?"

It took Peggy to subdue her. She did this by playing the opening notes of "Mood Indigo" on her saxophone, and the others joined in. Victor set the pace, repeating the slow, tolling beat he'd started earlier. Leland's deep, unhurried chords were suitably somber. The saxophone carried the melody because Neil was sitting this one out. Neil, having spent the day overdosing on "Don't Blame Me," could concentrate on nothing else for the time being—except his imagined book displayed in store windows. Connor, too, was imagining. Ponderously plucking his strings, he closed his eyes and imagined paradise. He saw a studio as roomy and amply windowed as this sleeping porch, he saw a canvas-in-progress as interesting as the Ashby portrait he'd just finished, and he saw Peggy as his lifelong companion.

Day Two. A thawing breeze at sunrise. Victor again took up his post and deployed his early shift, which today included half a dozen unscheduled volunteers. Behind him, except for Administration Row, McCall Hall stood dark and all but empty. Dean Zastrow sat at his window, fretting and fuming, not wishing to believe that instead of causing a reaction against the Alliance, his lockout seemed to have increased the number of picketers. He counted fourteen in all, nearly double yesterday's force. While several of them moved back and forth along the street, others stood warming themselves at a smoky fire they'd built in a big oil drum in the parking lot. He saw Shopman Dumont and Geographer Skeffington among them, the traitors.

In his outer office, meanwhile, Mrs. Kibbee was fielding phone calls from a disgruntled variety of students, parents, professors, and businessmen. Reginald Fix, the chemist, phoned to say his latest compost experiment would come to nothing if he wasn't allowed to observe the organic changes in the fingernail clippings in his laboratory. The mayor of Rookery phoned to say it was a dark time for the city's reputation. A young woman scheduled to take her state nursing exam in sixty days phoned to say her entire class of nursing candidates would be joining the caravan to St. Paul tomorrow. She said her class was divided about the strike, but not about the stupidity of the dean for shutting down the campus, and she would say that to the chancellor and the governor and whoever else would listen. Even President Gengler's wife phoned, from Clearwater Beach, but not concerning the strike. She asked Mrs. Kibbee to renew one of the president's prescriptions for ointment, and to send it along to the house with the week's mail. They'd be arriving home Saturday night.

Victor watched a car leave campus, four students with their duffel bags and laundry bags, waving gaily at the picketers, glad of the unexpected vacation. A second car, a few minutes later, apparently contained men with lower numbers in the draft lottery, for they glowered as they sped past. An arm was thrust out a window and Victor was given the finger.

Even more professors showed up for the ten o'clock shift, many of whom had voted against striking. Had they not been locked out, they would have gone to their offices, as yesterday, to fuss over their footnotes and syllabi, their grade books and committee reports, but now with time on their hands, they thought striking looked interesting, particularly on this first truly fine day of spring, a day to throw open your jacket, stuff your scarf in your pocket, and watch the snowbanks shrink and dribble downhill to the river. The climbing sun made the fire in the barrel unnecessary, but fire in a barrel, too, looked interesting, and they fed it throughout the day with cardboard boxes and fireplace wood fetched from home.

By noon the number of picketers had swelled to two dozen or more, and Victor was ecstatic to discover that he'd run out of signs. He went to Leland's house and phoned Milwaukee, ordering a dozen more to be sent special delivery. He phoned Annie, his backup provisioner, and ordered more coffee and rolls. He phoned St. Paul and told the chancellor his goose was cooked.

Neil was not among the strikers. Neil was toiling away at his Ping-Pong table, rearranging his plot to suit Emerson Tate. He brought Zastrow, the courthouse clerk, downriver to St. Louis and set him on Lydia's trail again, only now her name is Lynda. By an incredible coincidence, Zastrow happens to be walking down the very street where Lynda's hotel is located just as she is stepping out onto the boardwalk with her brother, whose name is now Clark instead of Alphonse, and her lover, whose name is now Rhett instead of Randolph, and he trails them through the streets of the city with more than seduction in mind. Rape and murder, advised Editor Tate. He also requested more breathtaking emotion on Lynda's part, whatever that meant. Neil had been rather proud, given his meager experience with women, of how fully he'd portrayed his heroine; she was innocent, beautiful, fearful, stubborn, and now she was falling in love. What more could he possibly add? He needed to talk to a woman about this. He went to his phone and called Peggy's apartment, but she didn't answer.

Peggy was out walking off her disappointment, trying to defend herself against the lonesome blues. At noon she'd given up and cleared the table she'd set for two, aware that he'd be at the hospital by this time, to pick up his wife. From the cars going by on Division Street came the hiss of tires on water, the sound of winter unlocking its iron doors and allowing the sun to beam down heat as well as light. She could actually feel its warmth on her face. When had she last been overdressed for the kind of day it was? It seemed like years. Stopping to look at her reflection in a store window, she took off her tam and shook out her hair, arranging it with her hand. Then, proceeding aimlessly along the street, she used her tam to wipe away tears. How stupid of her to think a man like Connor could sustain an affair. He was too principled for an affair. As principled as she had been before she met him.

At the hospital it took twenty minutes to draw Marcy down from the second floor, where all along the hallway there were kisses of farewell and promises of everlasting friendship from patients and nurses alike. There was talk of her returning for volunteer work, as well as a weekly counseling session with her doctor. She bestowed her smile on one and all, the demure smile Connor had fallen in love with. This was the Marcy of old, the woman he'd married, the mother of his daughter. He allowed his hope to blossom again. He couldn't help it. An inner voice told him he was setting himself up for disappointment, but another voice said that if he couldn't trust today's smiles and laughter and sunny nature, if this woman turned on him the minute they were alone and said something crude and insulting, then her hate for him was too strong ever to overcome, and he wasn't ready to believe that. Or, given the intense light and darkness of her shifting moods, she was insane, and he didn't want to believe that either.

Driving her home, he kept glancing at her. She continued to smile in a hazy, unfocused way, her thoughts perhaps directed back to the warm farewells on the second floor. Wait till she comes out of this one, said the inner voice, she'll really let you have it. No, it's all right, said the second voice, this time is different because of her doctor and her medicine and the sense of usefulness she acquired in the hospital. Was it too much to expect her to visit with him over a cup of tea instead of closing herself up in her makeshift bedroom? To this end, he'd set out the teapot and her favorite kind of tea—rose hip—and had bought what used to be her favorite snack—poppyseed hard rolls with apple butter. They would talk about next year, Cass College, which part of the city to live in. They would talk about Laura.

He parked the car and followed her across the sunny yard to the house, carrying her bag and vowing to resume his fidelity—if fidelity, once violated, could still be called fidelity. He should never have weakened and gone to bed with Peggy. How could he be critical of Neil for selling out as a writer when he himself was a faithless husband? It wasn't hard to envision the bliss of living with Peggy, but of course this was a shortsighted and wrongheaded vision. He had a family in need of his care. Peggy was an addiction. He must give her up, like alcohol.

"Marcy, how about some tea and rolls?" he asked, following her inside.

She said nothing. Her sour expression was her answer. As though magnetized by her bed, she paused only long enough in the living room to regard his painting equipment and to say, "Don't tell me you're going to stink up the house with turpentine," and then she closed herself in the dining room, pulling the curtain across the doorway and adding stridently, "Tell Laura to keep the volume down on the TV when she comes home."

Connor was suddenly sick with grief. He went into the bathroom and threw up. Then he bathed and shaved off his beard. Then he sat in the living room and searched though his sketchbooks for a subject absorbing enough to lift him out of his misery. If he could find it, he'd force himself to paint it. But he found nothing. His sketchbooks were filled mostly with landscapes from his preportrait days, and landscapes no longer intrigued him. The few faces he'd drawn looked soulless. With faces, for some reason, he did a better job painting directly from life or from photographs, bypassing the sketching stage. Whereas he used to enjoy doing landscapes in pencil, rearranging the elements this way and that, faces never came alive for him in pencil or charcoal; the eyes seemed unfocused, the expressions vacant.

He put aside the sketchbooks and sat looking out the window. He watched the cars go by. He ran his hand over the unfamiliar contours of his beardless face. He'd worn the beard for ten or twelve years. He didn't know why he'd shaved. Perhaps by changing his outward appearance he hoped to exorcise the inner man who was living such a forlorn and comfortless life. Or perhaps his bare face was an aid in giving up Peggy, who said she loved his beard.

He continued to gaze at the highway and reprimanded himself for setting so much store in Marcy's recovery. He hadn't been able to help himself. Hope had engulfed him the way depression engulfed Marcy. He'd struggled against it, but lost. Lost his hopelessness first, and now lost hope. What was a man to do without hope if he couldn't paint or drink or go to see Peggy? Music? His string bass lay on a bed in the Edwardses' sleeping porch.

Whom could he talk to, other than Peggy? He had nothing in common with Victor but music. Leland, though sympathetic by nature, seemed to have lived the sort of antiseptic, trouble-free life that left him unfamiliar with anguish. Neil was a self-absorbed dreamer, lost in his novel.

He would talk to Laura. He would take Laura shopping when she got home from school, and they would talk, not about his anguish, just talk. She needed a new spring jacket. He would buy her that, and maybe some earrings if he had enough money. She was crazy about flashy earrings. He recalled the days when he'd enjoyed her opinions and little jokey observations about the life she was leading. That was in the city. There'd been no such conversations since they'd moved north. Was that his fault, or was it the father-daughter chemistry transforming itself as she grew into adolescence? He must work to reformulate it, recover the chemistry they'd had.

Waiting for the school bus to bring her home, he continued to sit by the window in the silent house, his eyes following the cars and trucks that now and then went by. The silence, he realized after a few minutes, was unnatural. Always, when she slept, Marcy's breathing was audible behind the curtained doorway. This stillness told him she was either awake or dead. He imagined her dead, and was swept by a momentary sense of relief. Which he quickly suppressed. He went to the doorway and drew aside the curtain. Her eyes were open, directed at the ceiling. She lay perfectly still. He felt the same bowel-churning alertness he'd felt when he was seventeen and discovered his mother dead in a chair. She'd sat there with her head tipped back and a newspaper folded neatly in her lap. The silence told him she was dead. He was shocked. He felt confused for weeks and months afterward, but not primarily as a result of her death. What confused him was his father's apparent lack of emotion over the death. To this day, it wasn't clear to Connor whether his father's impassive reaction was manly stoicism or a genuine lack of feeling for the woman he'd been married to for thirty years. They'd lived much of that time apart, his father gone on construction projects. Like father like son, thought Connor—he and Marcy leading separate lives, though under the same roof.

"Marcy?" he said softly.

"I'm thinking," was her immediate reply.

"What about?"

"Never mind."

He retreated.

She was thinking about her happiness in the hospital, how useful and appreciated she'd been. She was thinking about her four-day freedom from the down-pulling weight of gloom she always felt in her husband's presence—in her husband's house even when he wasn't present. She'd forgotten what it felt like not to be tired all day, not to be worn-out with hatred for the man she'd married. The traveling psychiatrist, Dr. Hyde, had recommended marriage counseling, and he gave her the name of a counselor in Rookery who had saved a lot of marriages. Marcy laughed in his face. If she thought her marriage to Connor was going to be saved, she told him, she'd kill herself for sure. How did he think she was able to maintain her happy nature in the hospital if not by imagining divorce?

Speaking the word had sent a surge of energy though her. She'd never said "divorce" aloud before. She'd been afraid to because of Laura. Also because she had no income of her own and no prospect of a job beyond cleaning houses or operating a cash register in a grocery store. Her degree was in art, she told Dr. Hyde. Nothing as practical as art education or graphic design, just art courses across the spectrum—papier-mâché and painting and pottery—which left her not particularly accomplished in any one medium.

Saying the word aloud, however, had made the act irresistible. Other women divorced, though none of her acquaintance, and so must have found relief and happiness. She would talk to Laura about it, be honest with her, hide none of her feelings or intentions. Laura was strong enough to take it in stride. Her daughter, as Dr. Hyde had pointed out to her, was at this point perhaps the strongest Connor of the three.

At the window, he watched the school bus roll to a stop and discharge the several students who lived in the small houses and mobile homes along this section of highway. Laura wasn't among them. Had she gone to the hospital, forgetting that Marcy was being released today? Was she at school, getting involved finally, as he'd advised her, in something extracurricular—the newspaper or stagecraft?

He drove into town, stopping first at the hospital and then at Rookery High School. He didn't find her. He drove next to Culpepper's, intending to use the phone and maybe break down and have a drink. One drink would do him a world of good right now—only one. He went directly to the phone, bypassing the bar, and dialed his house, but to no avail—Laura wasn't home and Marcy wasn't answering. He then stood at the bar making small talk with Sammy Culpepper as he watched him mix a martini. "On the house," said Sammy, setting it before him with a flourish. He thanked him, but instead of drinking it, he turned the glass around and around on the bar, and then abruptly walked out the door.

He drove to the college for no good reason, perhaps out of habit, perhaps to confirm that the library was closed and Laura was not studying there. It was and she wasn't. Driving through the intersection of Sawyer and Eleventh, he rolled down his window for fresh air. He saw a dozen picketers standing around a smoking oil drum in the faculty parking lot. They were drinking coffee and engaged in animated conversation, Victor among them. Victor's excited voice and laughter told Connor all he needed to know about the contest between labor and management. Today had gone to labor.

He crossed the Badbattle and drove downtown. He parked in front of the JCPenney store and climbed the stairs to Peggy's apartment. She knew him by his footsteps and flung open the door and was about to throw her arms around him, but hesitated, shocked to see him clean-shaven. It made him look younger and thinner; also less commanding, less mysterious. He looked chastened.

"Where's your beard?"

"Gone," he said, smiling.

"Good," she said. She put her arms up around his neck and clung tightly.

"But you liked it."

"I loved it," she said in his ear, "but I love the way your smile looks without it."

He followed her inside and shut the door.

"Shall we . . . ?" she asked. "I mean right away?"

He answered by helping her off with her clothes.

Laura was standing on a boulder under the Eleventh Street bridge. She was shivering. Beside her, on an adjacent boulder, stood Gary Oberholtzer, who was smoking a homemade cigarette while eating a candy bar. He was beginning to feel snaky. He kept offering the joint to Laura, but she kept refusing. One of the reasons she'd agreed to meet him after school was to demonstrate her superiority by not smoking pot. Driving her home from McCall Hall the other night, her father had smelled it on her and said she mustn't smoke anymore, so of course she wouldn't. It was her policy to do what her father said. That was the reason for her transgressions—so he'd forbid her to continue. But she didn't tell this to Gary. She told Gary that smoking pot was childish. This angered him, but it was an anger that was soon lifted away from him like the smoke he exhaled, and he giggled.

Another reason for meeting him was her eagerness to hear what he had done with the photo of Dr. Benoit in the nude. Having found it in the grocery bag on Monday night, she'd put it in her dresser drawer and waited twenty-four hours for her father to ask her about it. She'd rehearsed in her mind how she'd hand it over without a word. That was her way—immediate conformity to her father's wishes. His wish that she not go to St. Paul with the strikers was another example. "Don't skip school to go down there, Laura," he'd said. "Okay," she'd replied.

"Where's the picture?" she asked Gary. She'd shown it to him yesterday, saying how much she despised the woman, and Gary had promised to bring it to the attention of his father. Maybe his father would fire her.

"I put it on their dresser after he went out so she'd find it first," said Gary, speaking of his parents. "She raised holy hell with him when he got home. I was in my room, listening." Gary paused to laugh a dreamy, silent laugh with his jaw hanging open. Laura could see the candy in his mouth.

He mimicked his parents. "She said, 'For the Lord's sake, Mortimer, what's this?' and he said, 'Why, I believe it's Dr. Benoit,' and she said, 'It's Dr. Benoit without a stitch of clothes on, is what it is, and what's it doing in our bedroom?' "

More silent laughter, more food exposed on his tongue.

"So they called me in and showed it to me, and of course I made like the picture got me all excited, and I said something like,

'Hey, wow, who's the babe?' and I turned to my dad and said, 'Hey, where can I get one of these?' " Gary looked very pleased with himself for a moment, but then his expression changed to a frown and he shuddered, as though he'd just now discovered how chilly it was in the shade of the bridge. He swallowed the last of the candy bar and said, "But I wonder if we did the right thing with it. I mean, if we couldn't have got more fun out of it, maybe, by getting copies made and leaving them around."

"Around where?" asked Laura.

"Just around, you know, all over town." He laughed again. "You know, make her famous, with her tits hanging out."

"So why don't we?"

He frowned. "Well, Jesus, don't be stupid. Where is it?"

"You can't find it?"

"I figure my dad took it to campus. He's probably showing it around."

So much the better, thought Laura. "Come on, it's cold," she said. "Let's go to Claudia's."

"What for?"

"Get a Pepsi or something. Warm up."

"You got money?"

"Enough for a Pepsi."

"Buy me a hamburger."

Climbing up from the river, Gary fell on the rocks and hit his head. She heard the sound of it—skull against stone—and thought it might have killed him, but he got to his feet, and with her help he was able to climb to the street and walk unaided, though not very straight, in the direction of Claudia's Lunch.

Seeing her chance to be noticed by Victor Dash, who would perhaps worry her father about the spectacle they made, she guided Gary along the edge of the campus, gripping him tightly by his open jacket and leading him among the picketers with blood trickling down his face. The professors who knew Gary called him by name and asked what was wrong, but they got no response because he was too woozy to answer and Laura's lips were clamped shut in hard determination.

———

On Friday, Day Three, listeners to KRKU at midmorning heard Lolly Edwards achieve a raspy telephone connection with Kimberly Kraft at the state capitol. Kimberly's voice was breathless and high-pitched with excitement.

"Three busloads of students on the capitol steps, Lolly. I'm so proud of them out there with their homemade signs and banners. Maybe you can hear them calling for the governor to come out. They've got a foghorn."

"Bullhorn," a man's voice prompted.

"I mean bullhorn."

"Who's there with you, Kimberly?"

"Six of us from the faculty. I'm calling from Senator Steadman's office. We're all going shopping after the rally."

"Shame on you, Kimberly. The merchants of Rookery aren't going to be at all happy to hear that."

Testily came Kimberly's reply, "What have the merchants of Rookery ever done for us?"

"Oh, come now. Among other things they've been sponsoring my airtime since Hector was a pup, and I've broadcast a lot of campus news for you over the years. Now tell me, what do the signs and banners say?"

"There's one says 'Pay our profs a living wage.' They're mostly like that."

" 'Make love not war,' " the man's voice put in.

"Oh, yes," said Kimberly. "Quite a few protesting the war. Another one says 'Give peace a chance.' Two or three say, 'Equal pay for women.' "

"Well, I should hope so," said Lolly. "Is Peggy Benoit with you?"

"No, she didn't come down. She was planning to come, but then couldn't, for some reason. Maybe she's on picket duty."

"Not today," said the prompting voice. "She's not on again till Monday."

"Who's that talking to you?"

"Aaron Cardero. Here. I'll put him on."

"Hi, Lolly, how's the weather up there? Can you hear the bullhorn?"

"I can hardly hear *you*, Aaron. The connection comes and goes."

"Kimberly, open the window so Lolly can hear the bullhorn."

"Is the senator there?"

"He's outside on the steps. It's a beautiful day down here. St. Paul hasn't got any snow."

"Do you think the governor will come out?"

"No telling, Lolly. You know how governors are."

"I've been told the College Board is not going to give in. If everybody's not back on the job Monday morning, they're going to stop all paychecks, even for the nonstrikers. They're going to let Rookery State wither and die before they'll compromise. Have you heard that, Aaron?"

"You hear a lot of things."

"But this I heard from the chancellor himself. I called him this morning."

"Doesn't surprise me. Victor Dash says people always talk tough during a strike."

"Put Victor Dash on the line, would you, Aaron? I want to know what he thinks about this."

"He's not here. He stayed home on the picket line."

"How about the senator? Could you get him on the line?"

"Kimberly, would you ask the senator to come in and talk to Lolly? Say, Lolly, what's the weather like up home? We left in the dark."

"It's nice again today, Aaron. Do you know if the senator is taking a stand on the strike?"

"I'd be surprised—you know how senators are. Can you hear the bullhorn now?"

"This is really a poor connection, Aaron."

And it got worse, fading into a squeal and a hum before the senator came on the line.

"Well, so much for our friends in St. Paul, dear listeners. Stay tuned to KRKU for more about the rally, and don't forget next Monday I'll be having Victor Dash as my guest, president of the Rookery chapter of the Faculty Alliance of America, so we'll be getting that side of things from the horse's mouth, so to speak. On my Saturday afternoon show, dear listeners, you're going to hear the Icejam Quintet playing the music of the thirties and forties that you all love so well, Leland on the piano, accompanied by four of his friends on various other instruments. We'll devote the full half hour to them, and I promise you you'll love every minute of it. Now, in the meantime, don't forget to order your five-day chicks from Munson's Feed and Seed before the fifteenth of March if you want chicks in your brooder by the middle of April. And now it's recipe time, dear listeners, and I've asked Mary Ellen McGuire to join us with her ideas for leftover spaghetti sauce. Mary Ellen . . ."

"Turn it off," said Dean Zastrow, who was sitting at the Edwardses' kitchen table snapping his watchband and glowering into his empty coffee mug.

Leland, who stood at the avocado-colored stove waiting for the percolator to finish its work, reached over and turned the volume down, but (out of respect for his mother) not quite off.

"Well," sighed Chairman Oberholtzer, his pipe clenched in his teeth, "that doesn't tell us much, does it?" He was standing at the bulletin board scanning Lolly's notes and clippings. "Doesn't tell us much at all."

Zastrow muttered, "It tells us the governor isn't breaking any speed records rushing out to greet them. At least it tells us that."

"True," said Oberholtzer. "Hard to say if that's good or bad."

Zastrow's tone was defiant. "They'll get no satisfaction. Mark my words, they'll come home from St. Paul with their tails between their legs."

"I don't know," Oberholtzer ventured. "Governor Gunderson comes from a labor background."

"It isn't up to the governor. It's up to the board."

"But the governor appointed them."

"So what?"

The vehemence of this remark confirmed Leland in his dislike of the dean. Never before had he heard anyone say "So what" to his chairman. He was mortified to think that it was up to a man as uncivil and contentious as Dr. Zastrow to steer Rookery State through troubled seas. Yet there he was at the helm, the only administrator Leland could turn to with this morning's frightening news from the chancellor, relayed by his mother—the board was threatening to shut down the campus for at least the rest of the semester. Since the lockout prevented him from setting foot on campus, he'd invited the dean to his house for coffee, and the dean had fairly flown down the street, as though he'd been just waiting for someone to confer with. The board's ultimatum was news to the dean—Leland could tell by the way he pretended not to be shocked. The board and Chancellor Waldorf had obviously lost confidence in Zastrow, and hadn't bothered to keep him apprised of their decisions.

Leland's news did not endear him to the dean. On the contrary, the dean had turned instantly icy. Anticipating this, Leland had invited Chairman Oberholtzer to act as a buffer.

"Here we go," said Leland, referring to the climactic noises emanating from the percolator. "Only be a minute now."

The dean's lockout strategy had backfired. The college had limped through Day One with at least half its classes in session, but now, on Day Three, it was immobilized. Instead of turning the loyalists against the Alliance, the lockout had turned most of them into traitors. Even Bernard Beckwith and Reginald Fix—Leland never would have guessed *they'd* go over to the other side.

"It's the nice weather working against us," said Oberholtzer. "Another cold day like Wednesday, with sleet, and I assure you there'd be a great falling off of picketers."

"Foul weather won't help us," said the dean, "and the governor won't help us. Rookery State's in a hell of a bind. Between the strikers and the College Board, do you realize we could go out of business permanently?" He appealed to Leland. "Tell him, Edwards."

"Mother called the chancellor this morning. He told her the board wouldn't compromise no matter what."

Oberholtzer held out his cup as Leland poured. "That doesn't surprise us, does it?"

"And they decided none of us will be paid unless everybody's back to work on Monday morning."

"Oh my, that *does* surprise us. Is that legal?"

"Mother didn't say."

———

After waiting two and a half hours on the capitol steps, the Rookery delegation cheered as Governor Gunderson came strolling out into the balmy sunshine. He was the sort of politician who inspired cheering and goodwill, a tall, lean man with a warm smile and a firm handshake and looking a little like Jimmy Stewart in midcareer. He waved and squeezed hands left and right and listened first to Aaron Cardero's plea for intervention and then to the nursing students'. After five minutes of this, he raised his hand to indicate he had a good grasp of their troubles and asked if he might borrow the bullhorn from Chuck Lucking, who happened to be holding it. Chuck stepped forward and showed him how the switch worked, whereupon the governor put it to his mouth and said, "Find yourselves another college to go to," and went back inside.

The crowd was stunned. They milled about for a time in silent disbelief before boarding their buses for the long ride home.

Meanwhile, Victor was delivering this oration to three dozen professors on the corner of Sawyer and Eleventh:

"If we'd been in St. Paul for the latest meeting of the College Board, ladies and gentlemen, we'd've seen an amazing sight. We'd have seen six people shitting in their hats! They're out of their minds. Can you picture them closing down the college for the rest of the semester? The minute they try it, I promise you there'll be such a public outcry across the state of Minnesota that they'll be eating crow before the goddamn sun goes down."

Neil was among the listeners. He'd planned to work all day on his novel, but the mailman had destroyed his concentration by delivering a contract from T. Woodman Press. As soon as he opened the envelope and saw what it contained, he threw on his parka and hurried to the college to mingle with the strikers and proudly display its four pages of legalese.

"Can you imagine the merchants and parents and taxpayers sitting still for a complete shutdown of higher education in this city?" asked Victor. "Just wait till our elected officials, including the governor, start feeling the heat of public opinion—all six members of the board will have to resign and go into hiding."

Behind Victor, and detracting somewhat from the impact of his words, two workmen with a shovel, a pickax, and a bag of cement were planting the wrought-iron legs of the college sign in the frozen ground. When they stripped the sign itself of its wrapping and stood it up, the intake of breath was audible among those who hadn't been told of the motto.

ROOKERY STATE COLLEGE
PAUL BUNYAN'S ALMA MATER

On a less worrisome occasion, the jokers in the crowd might have carried the day, with remarks like "What year did Bunyan graduate?" and "I'd like to see his transcript," but the mood today was one of general unease, and the chuckling died quickly away.

"Their ass is grass, my friends. There'll be demonstrations in St. Paul that'll make today's rally down there look like a Sunday school picnic. And the beauty of it is, it won't take any effort on our part. The College Board, by being such idiots, will have brought it completely upon themselves."

Nor could the crowd spare much enthusiasm for Neil's contract. Some looked upon it with envy, some despised Neil for his careless ways in the classroom, and still others, because he spent so little time on campus, didn't know who he was. Among the last was Reginald Fix, the fretful old chemist, who took one look at the document and tried to lose himself in the crowd, mistaking it for a court summons.

"Over the weekend, my friends, while you're out along the highways and byways spreading the word about the bullies on the College Board, make sure somebody stays home close to the telephone, because you'll be hearing plenty from the Telephone Tree, probably two, three times a day, is my guess. Now on Monday, Day Four, we'll start over with the same picketers we had on Day One. If you're in doubt about your schedule, call my house and Annie will tell you. She's got the schedule hanging over the sink. Anybody got any questions?"

No questions. Only an uneasy silence. The professors glanced furtively at one another and then cast their eyes at the ground or the sky or the bare branches of the campus elms, avoiding Victor's penetrating examination of their faces. He didn't like what he was seeing: the same injured and frightened expressions he'd witnessed before the strike began, when the Alliance was swept by a sudden loss of heart. Well, why shouldn't they be afraid, with the board hitting them below the belt? The Alliance would emerge triumphant, of course—if not by striking, then by means of its lawsuit—but for the time being, these poor devils needed coddling.

"Now one last thing," he impulsively announced. "Annie and I are holding open house again tomorrow and Sunday, so I hope each and every one of you will drop in any time of the day or evening, just come on over for a cup of coffee and a good, old-fashioned visit."

He left them then, shaking hands and slapping backs as he went. Neil followed him across the street to the parking lot, trying to show him his contract, but Victor said later, he was in a hurry. Neil stood back, thwarted but too high on his success to be offended, and watched Victor start his convertible, which had recently suffered an ear-shattering split in its muffler. Careening out of the parking lot, Victor waved at him, and sped home to tell Annie to start baking pies.

When the phone woke them from sleep in the late afternoon, Connor urged her to ignore it, but Peggy replied, as before, "It might be my brother," and slipped out of bed. She went into the chilly kitchen with a blanket wrapped around her.

It was indeed her brother.

"Hi, Kenny, any news?"

"I haven't located Benoit yet, but at least he got my letter—I know that."

"How do you know?"

"I sent it to him at the *Globe*, registered, and got the receipt back."

"What did you tell him?"

"Let's just say if he plays any more tricks after reading my letter, we'll know just how deranged he really is. I threatened him with everything short of execution."

"He's not deranged, Kenny. He's simply angry."

"Matter of opinion."

"We'll just let it ride now."

"Like hell, I'm determined to find this pervert."

"Listen, I know you still think of me as your helpless little sister, but it's up to me to say, Kenny, and I say your letter will take care of it. We'll just let it ride, okay?"

A long pause. "Okay, if you promise you'll call me the second he tries anything new. So help me, I'll track him down and—"

"I promise, but I'm sure he's history."

Her brother growled and mumbled.

"How's the family?" she asked.

"Family's fine. Are you coming home for Easter?"

"I can't, we're on strike."

"Yeah, so I hear. I talked to Sue." He laughed. "You're striking over two hundred dollars, she says." He laughed harder. "God, you teachers."

"There's more to it than that. The state legislature appropriated money, you see. . . ."

He continued to laugh his full-throated, infectious laugh. Peggy laughed too, and stopped trying to explain.

"Easter's not for three weeks," he said. "You aren't striking all month, are you?"

"I hope not, but I'm losing all this rehearsal time with my choir. The concert's the weekend after Easter."

"Your mother's coming for it. Did she tell you?"

"No."

"She's writing you about it. Couple days in Minnesota, couple days in Wyoming."

"Tell her to bring a dress she'd like to be remembered in."

"What's that supposed to mean?"

"I want her to sit with me for a double portrait."

"By who? A sidewalk artist?"

"A portrait painter."

"In Rookery?"

She was irked by his scorn. "Don't bother. I'll tell her myself."

———

Winter returned on Saturday: rain graduating to sleet and then to large bouncing pellets of ice. COUNTDOWN TO CRISIS, said the lead headline in the *Morning Call*. Two photos appeared side by side, one portraying several unidentified strikers huddled around the fiery oil drum in the parking lot, the other showing Governor Gunderson on the capitol steps with a bullhorn to his lips. AL-LIANCE CHILLED BY ST. PAUL was the subhead, referring to the board's threat to shut down the campus, as well as the governor's terse message to the demonstrators.

"A governor with backbone," said the front-page editorial, be-seeching the faculty to get down off their high horses and let the experts decide where the taxpayers' money could best be spent. The governor was to be congratulated for his integrity, the board for its swift retaliation. If the faculty didn't cut their ties with the hapless Faculty Alliance by Monday morning, all of them would be out of work at least until summer school, some of them forever. "What's become of the days when a teacher's primary desire was to teach like a professional rather than behave like a common la-borer?" asked the editorial in conclusion.

Victor threw down the paper. Shouting curses, he stomped around the living room, scattering his children, who were playing football there—the new cat was the football. Annie suggested he take out his rage on the editor instead of his kids. He did that. He went to the kitchen and telephoned the editor. He said he hadn't earned a living wage since his days as a common laborer, and it was hard to behave like a professional when you were so underpaid you couldn't afford to buy your kids a bicycle. He said that the Faculty Alliance, far from being hapless, was attracting more and more sup-porters among the faculty now that the College Board had gotten up on *its* high horse. Victor recommended, in conclusion, that the editor stick his newspaper up his ass.

Peggy, alone in her apartment, read the paper with alarm. She called Kimberly Kraft, who told her that the demonstrators had come up against a stone wall at the capitol, but she was still full of hope. "Have you seen the Twin City papers today, Peggy?

We're all over the front pages. The Alliance is making this huge impression. It's all so exciting—our strike could go on for six months."

"But Kimberly, if the semester stops, how do I pay my rent? I'd have to give up my apartment and move home to Boston."

Kimberly, a professor of independent means, said, "Oh my, I hadn't thought of that."

"Because strike pay won't do it. Who can live on thirty dollars a week?"

"Oh, I know, it's an insulting amount. I spend nearly that much on dry cleaning."

"Can't Victor get the Alliance to increase it?"

"Oh no, haven't you heard? After next week there won't be any more strike pay. Milwaukee says the fund is drying up fast. I told Victor it was just as well—thirty dollars is such an insulting amount."

Peggy sighed, "Oh, Kimberly," and hung up.

She called Victor, who verified the bad news, quoting his message to the editor.

"Victor, it's getting scary."

"Nobody said striking was easy."

Next she called Georgina. Georgina said she was glad she had the appliance business to fall back on. Ron's father was turning all the book work over to her. "I know you don't think much of Ron," said Georgina in a syrupy, ironic tone, "but he's a steady, reliable man, and he's not married to another woman."

Peggy didn't immediately catch on. "Who said he was?"

"I'm referring to the man going in and out of your apartment at all hours."

"Some other time, okay, Georgina?"

She hung up, took several deep breaths to overcome her fury, and then called a number she'd memorized but never dialed.

Connor answered.

"Can we talk?" she asked.

"Sure."

"Have you seen the paper?"

"Just now reading it." His daughter, sitting across the room from him, did not look up from her library book.

"I have this feeling, Connor."

"Yes?"

"Like everything's going to turn out bad."

"It already has, if you ask me."

"I don't mean just the strike. I mean you and me."

Waiting for her to expand on this, he heard his wife moving around behind the curtained doorway. Laura continued reading.

"Connor, are you alone?"

"No."

Laura turned a page.

"I'll see you at Leland's, then?"

"I'll be there." Anything more he could think of to say—I love you, I'll follow you home after practice, I dream of living with you—was unsayable at the moment.

"All right, then," she said. Both of them held the connection open for a while before hanging up.

"Was that Dr. Benoit?" asked his daughter.

"Yes."

"I thought so." She laid aside her book. "I want to go to the show this afternoon."

"What is it?"

"Hot Rods from Hell."

"Sounds awful."

"Gary wants to see it." She held her father in her steady gaze, expecting him to forbid her to see Gary Oberholtzer—hoping he would, in fact, for Gary was proving to be very stupid and tiresome.

He said nothing. He put down the newspaper and listened to the sounds of Marcy getting back into bed. Last Sunday I was handing her over to nurses, convinced she'd never recover, he thought, and tomorrow she's going off to work as a volunteer at the hospital. What a reversal, he thought, what a week: Marcy's suicide threat followed by a strike, a drinking binge, a commission withheld, a lockout, visits to Peggy Benoit's bedroom, and tomorrow a musical performance on the radio. To say nothing of the invasion into Laura's life by this Oberholtzer freak. He would say nothing to Laura about young Oberholtzer. You couldn't dictate one's friends without causing a backlash.

Marcy spoke from behind the curtain. "I'm on duty at two to-morrow, so if you need the car you'll have to give me a ride." As a new volunteer, she'd been assigned a Sunday shift in the hospital gift shop.

"All right," he said. He went to the doorway and looked in at her. "I'm going to drive Laura in to the movie. Then our quintet's on the radio at two, if you'd like to hear us."

Marcy's face was tight with medicated intensity. "I really don't mind working Sundays and holidays," she said brightly, "because that's when you're home most of the day."

He said nothing. He was arrested by a sudden twinge along his upper spine, where an animal's hackles were, a feeling of rage that he'd striven to suppress all his married life. It felt hot. It burned his neck and ears. It speeded up his heartbeat. This was anger in its pure form, anger so intense he was nearly blinded by it. He wheeled around and returned to the living room, where he awkwardly snatched up his easel and canvas and stumbled out to the car with them. He came back inside, his shirt wet, his forehead glistening with sleet.

"Let's go," he said to Laura.

They put on their coats. Laura helped him gather up his paints, and followed him out to the car.

Leland sensed an ominous new mood among the players as they gathered in the sleeping porch and began warming up for their debut on "Lolly Speaking." An argument erupted, quite surprisingly, between Neil and Connor. They had just finished running through "Mood Indigo."

"What's going on with you, Connor?"

"I'm trying out something." Connor turned to the others. "Could we go over the last couple phrases again?"

"I can't play with you on this," Neil whined. "Your rhythm is off, you keep tripping me up."

"Take your beat from Victor, then."

"I can't, not when he's diddling around with his brushes like that."

"What do you want, a goddamn marching band?" asked Victor.

He struck his cymbal, struck it again and again, in a slow, irritating cadence.

"Don't get huffy. All I'm asking for is a beat I can hear."

Up to this point the tiff was not unprecedented. Neil was never shy about venting his unhappiness. What *was* astonishing was Connor's sudden anger, his shouting, "Novotny, grow up!"

Neil flinched. He turned for solace to Peggy. "Is it too much to ask for a beat I can hear?"

"All right, boys, settle down," she scolded.

"Connor, are you jealous because I sold my novel?"

"Oh, for God's sake!"

"You've been acting funny ever since I sold my novel, like you're jealous or something. I mean, right from the start, at Culpepper's the other night."

"You sold more than your novel, Neil. You sold your vision."

Peggy spoke up. "Save it for recess, you two. And Victor, would you stop that god-awful noise?"

Victor put down his sticks. Boom, from the kick drum.

"I did not sell my vision. It's called editing, in case you never heard of it."

This exchange was making Leland very nervous. He got to his feet, opened the lid of his spinet, and put his head down into it, searching for the faulty hammer of a weak key.

Boom.

"You're a great one to talk about selling out, Connor. Painting mothers and daughters."

Peggy abandoned her neutral role and took up Connor's cause. "I'll have you know he's lost the commission for his new portrait because he refused to make it pretty."

"Well, what about the strike? He voted for health insurance instead of the strike. What kind of integrity is that?"

"That's not the same," said Connor.

Victor jumped in. "The hell it isn't." Boom.

Leland closed the spinet lid and risked a glance at his friends—Peggy giving Victor a murderous glare, Victor answering with a defiant shrug, Connor rubbing his three-day whiskers and looking sour, Neil gloating.

"Look," said Leland, speaking to his piano, "I'm guessing it's the strike that's bothering us all. We're trying to keep the lid on our anxieties, and we can't seem to get past it, so I have a proposal to make. I think there should be a kind of summit meeting."

"Yes, a summit meeting," said Lolly, sailing into the room clutching a sheaf of program notes. She was heavily bejeweled and richly dressed in a loose-fitting pantsuit of brown velvet. She had applied bright patches of blush to her cheeks. Privy to her son's idea, she expanded on it. "At a neutral site," she said. "Say tomorrow afternoon—the Genglers will be back from Florida."

"Honey and Mortimer have volunteered their house," added Leland. He turned to Victor. "Is there any reason the Alliance and the administration can't sit down together in good faith?"

"Why not?" replied Victor magnanimously. He was calling to mind the great surrenders of history. He pictured himself in Grant's role at Appomattox. He was MacArthur on the battleship *Missouri*.

"Surely the Alliance will accept less than the full appropriation?" Lolly suggested. "For this year at least?"

"I don't see why not," Victor said. Why not let the board have a few bricks and a load or two of cement. Hadn't Grant permitted the rebels to keep their horses? MacArthur didn't hang or behead the emperor.

"Oh, my goodness," said Lolly, "we're on the air in thirty seconds." She rushed over to a corner of the sleeping porch and settled behind a card table on which stood a microphone and a portable radio. She switched on the radio in time to hear herself introduced by the announcer, and then she switched it off and greeted her listeners in a voice not quite her own—a breathy, speeded-up delivery with lots of swooping changes of pitch. She introduced her guests by telling where they wanted fate to lead them.

"Our saxophonist and vocalist is the extremely young and talented and beautiful Dr. Peggy Benoit of the music department, who wants to forsake us and go and teach in New England, where she comes from, which is very, *very* upsetting to us, because she is without a doubt the most talented and beautiful product of last year's crop of Ph.D.s, and it will be a sorry loss for Rookery State

College if and when fate finds her a position out east. I want to thank you for being on my show this afternoon, Peggy."

"You're welcome." Peggy rolled her eyes at Connor. She understood now why Lolly had wanted to rehearse this discussion. It wasn't going to *be* a discussion. It was going to be a recitation by Lolly, who jealously hoarded every moment of airtime.

"Mr. Victor Dash wants to leave us too, I'm afraid." Lolly spoke with her eyes slightly crossed, keeping them focused on the microphone an inch or two from her mouth. "He wants to leave teaching altogether, in fact, to become some sort of labor-relations worker, and judging by the way he's set the faculty strike in motion, I'm sure he'll enjoy success in that field. Mr. Dash is our drummer. Thank you for being here, Mr. Dash."

Rat-a-tat-tat, crash, boom. Victor, wielding his sticks, nodded agreeably, pleased that despite the woman's aristocratic sympathies, she hadn't sounded derisive of his ambitions. Stilted maybe, but not derisive. Boom, boom, crash.

"Mr. Connor plays the string bass and teaches in the art department, but he's best known as Rookery's foremost portrait painter. He tells me his aspiration is to find sufficient time to paint his adorable pictures of mothers and daughters." Here she uncrossed her eyes and directed them at Connor across the room. "I understand you're working on a new one of Lois Ashby and her darling daughter Belinda." Here was a man she could safely engage in conversation—he had so little to say. She asked him how it was coming.

"It's finished," he said.

"Already! My, if you aren't the speedster. Now all you listeners out there with daughters in your families, if you want the perfect personalized picture for over your fireplace, just call our very own resident artist, Mr. Connor by name, and make an appointment. You don't come cheap, I understand."

"Well, no, I don't come cheap."

"And you won't do fathers and sons, I'm told."

"No."

"How about fathers and daughters?"

"No, I don't care to do those either."

"How about mothers and sons?"

"No."

She laughed heartily. "So it's tough cookies for Leland and I. Tell me, Mr. Connor, do you have a first name?"

"I do."

"And would you tell us what it is?"

"Joseph," he lied.

"Oh, the father of our Lord. I just love the name Joseph. Did you know Leland's middle name is Joseph?"

"I didn't know that."

"Why is it, then, that everyone calls you by your last name?"

"I dislike the name Joseph." He put his head down and thrummed a couple of strings to indicate that he wished to get on with the music.

Lolly turned her attention to Neil, but scant attention it was. "Our clarinetist is Mr. Neil Novotny, who teaches English and writes novels."

Sitting eagerly forward on his chair, Neil was prepared to answer her questions about breaking into print, but there were no questions. She was still indignant over his hysterical attack on C. Mortimer in the corridors of McCall Hall. Honey Oberholtzer, in telling her about it, had nearly wept when she came to the part about her violets.

"And my son Leland, of course, needs no introduction. Who can forget those wonderful recitals of Miss Carpentier's piano students, rest her soul? We'll never forget the recital where one of the Skoog sisters broke her finger playing something wild, will we, Leland?"

Extended laughter from Lolly, while Leland played scales to remind her that precious minutes were being lost.

"Well, there you have the Icejam Quintet, my friends. They're going to start with their lovely, *lovely* rendition of 'These Foolish Things' right after this message from Thorvold Lincoln Mercury."

This being a one-way transmission, Lolly had to turn up her portable radio in order to resume on cue. Thorvold's message (free floor mats with each purchase) lasted nearly two minutes, and the weather report (sleet and snow today, rain tomorrow) one more. Thus, ten minutes of their half hour were gone by the time the quintet began "These Foolish Things," and half the show was over before they finished it. Lovely wasn't the word for today's rendition. Their playing was mechanical and brittle; the transitions weren't smooth. During the next commercial break, Peggy pointed this out to the group, and the second piece, "Stormy Weather," they played much better, nearly as well as in rehearsal, though there was no telling what it sounded like over the air, what with all their colors and harmonies funneled through the single microphone on Lolly's card table.

It was during "Stormy Weather" that Lolly's bedside phone began to ring in the next room. She went to answer it. In a minute she was back, and it rang again. She answered it again. She returned to her place as the musicians were winding up their piece. It rang a third time and continued ringing as she read advertising copy. She interrupted her praise of LuJean's Boutique to remind her listeners that this wasn't a call-in show today, but the ringing continued, and Leland went to answer it. He left the receiver off the hook and hurried back to provide the lead-in to "Don't Blame Me."

Here they finally hit their stride, Neil's sweet Goodman imitation out front, the drum, piano, and bass blending nicely in the background, the saxophone coming forward only when Neil needed a rest, the melody wistful, the tempo dreamy. They weren't half finished when Lolly signed off.

The music continued as she gathered up her notes and went into the next room to call the station and ask how they sounded. She was told by the manager, a young man named Mel, that he'd been swamped with calls.

"Here too," she said.

"None in favor."

"Don't tell me."

"Let's face it, Lolly—Rookery isn't crazy about college profs these days. As station manager, I hope you aren't having them on again."

"We'll see." Lolly resented Mel's implication that he was *her* manager as well. She was, after all, part owner of KRKU. "There must have been at least a few who said they liked it."

"Not one."

"Oh, rats."

"I'm shorthanded here Saturdays, Lolly, so I'm telling callers to talk to you."

"But Mel, how did *you* think it sounded?"

"I'm not much for that old stuff. If I'm going to listen to old stuff, I'll listen to Bill Haley, that type of thing."

She fielded three more calls before the music stopped. The first caller said professors were greedy snobs. The second said the faculty ought to be home correcting papers rather than playing fast and loose with Benny Goodman. The third said she was disappointed in Lolly for devoting her Saturday show to that childish-sounding music played by eggheads instead of covering the arts and crafts show at the armory.

She was sickened by their animosity. Their resentment seemed to spill out beyond the strike, seemed directed at teachers for being teachers. Where did all this bitterness come from? Why were so many people so willing to bite the hand that fed them? The college pumped around a million dollars a year into Rookery's economy. She would research the exact figure and remind her listeners of it on Monday morning with Victor as her guest.

She emerged from her bedroom to find the musicians filing down the staircase. Trailing after them, she apologized for not fitting all their music in—how perturbed they must be.

They were all very kindly in their response, claiming not to mind. And they didn't mind. Still under the harmonious spell of their best playing, they were not easily perturbed.

Helping them on with their coats, Leland again brought up the summit meeting, and Victor said tomorrow at one o'clock would be a good time for it. That way, he could assemble his Alliance at, say, two-thirty and apprise them of developments and still get back here for the Sunday jam session. He asked Peggy to be a delegate and speak for women's salaries.

"At Oberholtzer's?" she inquired, reluctant to face her leering chairman.

"Neutral ground," Leland reminded her.

"Don't worry, I'll be there too, Peggy dear," said Lolly, with absolute faith in her own magnetism. She let the four visitors out the door, kissing Peggy and shaking Victor's hand and Connor's and Neil's (the last very briefly) and not mentioning the disapproving phone calls. "I'll have the five of you on my show again," she promised.

Alone with Leland, she spoke of the calls. He said that the one he answered had been equally scathing. "I'm not surprised," he added, recalling that, as a boy, he'd been ridiculed by his fellows for his scholarly tendencies.

"You're not surprised? I'm flabbergasted."

"Rookery's always been uneasy about having a college in its midst, Mother. It probably goes back to its days as a lumbering center."

"What's lumbering got to do with it, pray tell?"

"You know what I mean—it isn't as though our main industries have required a college education, or even high school for that matter."

"But the heat in those voices, Leland. It was frightening."

"I know," he said sadly. "It's the strike."

"But it seems to run deeper than that—as if the strike only ignited what was already there."

"I know," he repeated. "That's why the strikers are doomed."

"You really think so?"

He nodded slowly, grimly, taking no pleasure in his conviction, nor in his mother's rare inquiry into his mind.

"Leland, I sometimes wonder if your father might have joined the strikers."

"Mother, don't say that!"

"He was a fair-minded man, you know."

"But loyal to the college, first and foremost."

"What's disloyal about fighting for a salary that's rightfully yours, Leland? Or giving women equal pay?"

Her son looked panic-stricken. "Don't tell me I've chosen the wrong side."

"Maybe not wrong for you," she said.

"I'm only following Mortimer's lead."

"Maybe not wrong for Mortimer either."

He looked relieved. "Then who could it be wrong for?"

"Me."

His laugh was tense. "Oh, Mother, you're not going to say that over the radio."

"I'll see how I feel on Monday."

He tried to look amused.

"I'd like to take the measure of Rookery's loyalty to the college, Leland. I'd like to put out the call to all those who think the College Board's too big for its pants. I'd like to ask them to join me on the picket line."

"Mother, don't say that!"

"If she was my real mother, maybe I could have some sympathy for her, but she's not. She's my stepmother."

Gary Oberholtzer, sitting across from Laura in a booth, chewed ferociously and appeared unaffected by this revelation. With his elbows on the table, he held his half-eaten hamburger in both hands, at eye level, planning his next bite. He had catsup on his chin.

"It was something to see, how mad he got. I was in the front seat with him and I could tell how mad he was by the way his right ear turned red. I was hoping he'd turn the car around and go back and shout at her—she's been treating him like scum for years and it was getting worse and worse—but he didn't. He was holding it all inside."

Gary closed his eyes and swallowed, then opened them and sank his teeth into his hamburger. They were the only diners in Claudia's Lunch. They'd walked from the movie, and their jackets and hair were wet. Claudia was sitting in front, at the window, picking her teeth and watching it snow.

"So I said to him, 'Let it all hang out, Dad. Don't hold it all inside, you'll have a stroke.' But he didn't say anything. He just gave me this smile I hate because it breaks my heart. It's like he's in a coma or something, and he can't communicate but he wants to. All he can do is give you this helpless little smile. Well, if he isn't talking to me, who's he talking to?"

Gary stopped chewing. He extracted some meat from his mouth and examined it for bone. Finding a tiny piece, he wiped it on the front of his jacket. He then chewed gingerly and experimentally for a time, his eyes on the ceiling.

"Well, we know who, don't we? He's talking to Dr. Benoit. And I wouldn't be a bit surprised if he's been talking to her in *bed*."

This engaged Gary's interest like nothing she'd told him so far. "You mean he's humping her?"

"He's been real late getting home this week, and the campus is shut down and he's not picketing, so what am I supposed to think?"

He swallowed and nodded thoughtfully. "He's humping her."

"I mean I can't say for sure, but they've got to be, don't they?"

"You want me to find out?"

She said "No!" without thinking, before she realized that the satisfaction of knowing the truth would outweigh her disgust.

"How would you find out?" she asked.

"I get around." By which he meant he spent a lot of evenings looking in windows. "I've seen people humping."

"Geez, Gary, you're horrible, you know that?"

"Where does she live?"

"Downtown, over JCPenney's."

He frowned, trying to imagine how he might get up onto neighboring roofs. "She in the front or back?"

"How should I know?"

Gary, shifting his attention back to his hamburger, said nothing more. Laura heard Claudia emit a long sigh in her booth by the window. The snow was falling more thickly now, out of a darkening sky.

Laura leaned across the table and spoke in a whisper, her forehead nearly touching Gary's hamburger. "I mean, if he's actually having an affair, I guess I wouldn't mind knowing."

Claudia heaved herself out of the booth and lumbered back toward the kitchen, muttering, "Finish your eats, you kids. I'm closing up."

On Sunday afternoon Peggy was greeted by Honey Oberholtzer and shown into a room where ten chairs had been arranged in a circle, seven of them already occupied. Her chairman, purring with pleasure, stood up and beckoned her to a place next to his own, near the fire, and guided her into it with a hand roaming up and down her back. "Thank you," said Peggy, steeling herself against his touch.

"You're most welcome. Will you have one of Honey's muffins with your tea?"

"Just tea, thanks."

He went into the next room for the teapot, but not before giving her shoulder a painful squeeze.

The room was large and well appointed and smelled of damp wool, for all the delegates had arrived in a rainstorm. Everyone was chattering noisily to a friendly neighbor while eyeing an enemy across the way. The wall behind Peggy was a vast bookcase, filled with the literature of the Western world. The large windows on the opposite wall were partially darkened by vines which Honey had trained across them. Logs burned hot and bright in the fireplace.

"Dr. Benoit, we're in for an early frost next fall," said President Gengler, who was sitting in the rocking chair on her right and looking as if his vacation had done him some good. His neck was still rough as tree bark, but dry and scaly, not inflamed; no new patches of rash. He wore a rich-looking necktie of red and brown stripes and a figured vest that might have been satin. "The first frost follows the first thunderclap by exactly six months," he explained, "and there was thunder this morning." Adjusting his heavy-rimmed glasses on his large nose, he turned to his wife on his right and said, "That means you'll have to cover our tomatoes by the twelfth of September, Justine."

"I didn't hear any thunder," his wife replied sharply. "How do you do, Dr. Benoit."

"How do you do. You had a pleasant time in the South?"

"Pleasant enough, but we're apprehensive."

"Oh, I'm sure compromise is possible." Peggy wasn't at all sure of this, but the woman seemed in need of an encouraging word.

"What I mean to say, we're sitting as far as possible from the Dashes because they have a cat. If Herbert has a reaction, we'll have to leave."

Mrs. Gengler today was a study in gray and black. A handsome gray shawl was draped over her left shoulder and across the lap of her ankle-length black dress. Her earrings were polished black stones. Holding Peggy in her gray-eyed, expressionless gaze, she raised her elbow to the arm of her chair, cupped her chin in her jeweled hand, and said, "I checked Herbert's mail when we got back."

Peggy caught her breath. Oh, no, please God, not another eight-by-ten glossy.

"Nothing," said Mrs. Gengler, with the hint of a smile.

Her husband looked slightly offended. "What do you mean, nothing, Justine?"

"Never mind."

Annie Dash, seated next to Victor and facing Peggy across the room, greeted her with a wave and a giggle, and when Peggy responded with a smile, she burst out in a full-throated laugh, as though anticipating a performance of great hilarity. She wore a red and yellow dress with a scalloped collar. On her feet were sneakers and anklets. She looked about seventeen.

Her husband, also in sneakers, and looking sloppy in threadbare sweater and slacks, was in conversation with Lolly Edwards. Leland, wearing a new pinstripe suit, sat between them, listening and nodding his head. Lolly was engulfed in a tentlike garment of a prison-stripe design: wide bands of black and mustard. Her complexion was highly colored with anticipation or hypertension or both, and she was directing fond glances at Peggy out of the corner of her eye.

Peggy had learned last night, by way of the Telephone Tree, that it was the Oberholtzers' idea to invite the spouses and Lolly Edwards. Victor had objected on the grounds that business was hard to conduct in a social setting, but Honey and Mortimer had insisted—for the Genglers' sake, Peggy assumed, the president being such a zero without his wife close at hand to speak for him.

"Justine grows tomatoes," the president confided.

"How nice," said Peggy.

"Yes, it *is* nice. Now tell me, Dr. Benoit, would that be where the steel plate is, where I see the bare spot?" He was peering across the room at Victor.

"I've always assumed that, yes."

"Ah, I see." The president turned to his wife. "Dr. Benoit says I'm right about the steel plate, Justine. It's that spot over his ear."

His wife appeared impervious to this verification. Her eyes were on the doorway, and Peggy's eyes, too, were drawn to the stranger—a woman—entering on the arm of Dean Zastrow. This would be Mrs. Zastrow, who after nearly a year's delay had only recently followed her husband to Rookery. All the guests fell silent, unable to conceal their curiosity. She was a manicured, heavily braceleted, blond-rinsed woman who had spent so much time under a sun lamp and worked her face over with so many layers of makeup that her color, meant to be tan, was more like the dead amber Peggy had seen on mummies in *National Geographic*. Her eyes were adorned with long false lashes, wet from the rain. She crossed the room with the studied movements of a model or a convalescent. Her raincoat, also wet, she kept tightly buttoned and belted as she sat carefully down in the chair her husband designated, next to Lolly Edwards.

Lolly broke the silence with a gushy greeting—"Oooooh, how lovely," and so forth—but the woman responded with nothing more than a foggy smile, and she turned her eyes toward the fire.

Dean Zastrow, emitting little gasps and snorts of pleasure or anxiety or disgust (who could tell?—Peggy couldn't), got his wife to stand up again, and he helped her out of her coat, which he handed to Honey, who took it away. Mrs. Zastrow's body was lean and bony under her cream-colored suit. She was older than the dean, Peggy guessed. Much older, judging by her wrinkled hands and the stiff way she lowered herself into the chair.

The dean sat down, not beside his wife, but next to Peggy, in the chair Mortimer Oberholtzer had vacated. "I've been charged with representing the board," he told her in a loud, important voice meant to be overheard by the Genglers.

Peggy nodded as though she approved. An expression of anger crossed Mrs. Gengler's face. The president said it was early for thunder.

Chairman Oberholtzer, returning with a teapot and cups on a tray, was visibly disappointed to find his place occupied. Honey followed him in with a plate of muffins. The dog, Boots, pranced in behind her and went friskily about smelling everyone's knees.

The chairman poured tea for Peggy and the Zastrows, and then went around offering refills. Mrs. Zastrow snatched a muffin from the plate and ate in quick, squirrellike nibbles while feeding morsels of it to the dog. Peggy, trapped between the president and the dean, moved her chair slightly backward, so as not to interfere with their discussion of thunder and frost and tomatoes. Her eyes were caught by four large, tinted photos standing on the mantel, apparently the four Oberholtzer sons as high school graduates. They all resembled one another in a blondish, Aryan way, and because they wore suits and ties and short hair and smiled agreeably, she couldn't tell which one was Gary. How astonishing, thought Peggy, that in a mere three years a person could change from one of these comely young men into the mess that Gary was today.

Leland attempted to start the meeting, raising his voice above the chatter and saying, "Well, we're all here. I suppose we might as well get down to business."

Business was delayed by his mother, who laid a restraining hand on his arm and called out, "Peggy dear, how *are* you? I didn't get a chance to say hello because your colleague here"—she pointed at Victor—"is such a marvelous storyteller."

"Let's get this show on the road," said Victor.

Rising rather stiffly from her chair, Mrs. Gengler stepped over to Mrs. Zastrow to introduce herself.

Lolly continued, "Peggy, I must tell you about the phone call I got from the Van Buren Hotel."

Leland cleared his throat and tried again. "I think now that everyone's here . . ."

"The manager of the Van Buren said he'd heard your combo on the radio and it was simply *marvelous* and he wondered if you were available for engagements—*wedding* dances and the like, and I said I'd see if you had any open dates. I told them I was your *agent*, no less, I hope you can see the humor." Lolly laughed at her own audaciousness. "I mean I don't in any way expect a commission, but I thought for the sake of expedience—"

Victor leaned across her son and clapped his hand over Lolly's mouth. She was momentarily stunned, but recovered quickly, taking the hand and kissing it, and then laughing louder and flinging it away. Annie laughed too, in harmony.

Victor repeated, "Let's get this show on the road."

Leland got to his feet and said, "We'll get started, then."

Mrs. Gengler said, "First I'd like to introduce Mrs. Zastrow."

"That can wait," roared Victor. "Everybody sit down."

Mrs. Gengler, speechless with indignation, returned to her place. Mortimer hastened to the last remaining chair, on the dean's left hand, and sat down. Honey, calling the dog, left the room. The dog remained, having found a friend in Mrs. Zastrow. He cocked his head and sighed, beseeching her for more crumbs.

Leland said, "Mortimer, if you would," reminding the chairman, who still hadn't given up the pretense of being neutral, that he had volunteered to preside.

"Oh, yes. Well. Why don't we begin?" He drew a few note cards from the pocket of his tweed coat and read a tedious, Oberholtzian statement of welcome. Peggy could tell he was very proud of it by the way he glanced up for approval after each sentence. "When in the course of college events," it began, and it ended with ". . . for God and our country." He paused for agreement, which was expressed here and there by murmurs and head-nodding, and then he asked each delegate for an opening statement, beginning with the president.

An alert look came into Herbert Gengler's eye, such as the others were not used to seeing there. He leaned forward in his rocking chair and clasped his hands tightly across his vest. "I'll be honest with you, I haven't come here with an agenda. I am not predisposed to approve or disapprove of either side in this conflict. My only wish is that we walk out of this room today with the conflict resolved."

For a silent moment he was stared at by one and all. They were astonished less by his failure to take management's side than by his speaking cogently on the subject at hand. They'd expected something off the wall. His wife nodded approvingly and reached over and took both his hands in her own. Peggy was impressed by this gesture of conjugal solidarity, but it wasn't that at all, she soon realized, for no sooner had attention shifted to the next speaker (Dean Zastrow) than the president began struggling to get his hands out of her grip, and when he did so he raked his neck and jaws most horribly, drawing blood.

Dean Zastrow said, "Chancellor Waldorf is under the weather and can't be here today, and so he asked me to speak for the board. He said to me, and I quote him, 'Lay out our offer to compromise and the Alliance can take it or leave it.' " Here the dean paused for dramatic effect, sniffing and snorting and tapping his nose. Peggy sensed how tightly wound he was, sensed his body straining at the seams of his tight suit. "Their offer is this, that instead of withholding salary increases for the entire biennium, 1969 and 1970, as previously announced, they will consider providing a certain amount of money for increases in 1970, that is, for the school year beginning a year from next fall."

"How much?" asked Victor.

"How much what?"

"How much of an increase?"

"That's to be determined."

"But there *will* be an increase?"

"They'll consider it."

"If we could delay discussion until after the opening statements," said Mortimer.

"Increases for all the colleges, or just Rookery?"

"That will be determined," said the dean. "Now, as for the secondary issue, that is, the discrepancy between the women's salary schedule and the men's—"

"Who said it's secondary?" blurted Peggy.

"Please, my friends," said Mortimer.

"As for this discrepancy, the board has decided it will look at it next year."

"Look at it? What do they mean, look at it?"

The dog evidently heard something appealing in Peggy's voice, for he went straight over to her and drooled on her skirt.

Victor asked, "What's all this next-year bullshit?"

"Please, Victor," said Mortimer. "Abiding by the order of seniority, if the dean is finished, we'll move right along now and hear from Leland."

"Excuse me," said Mrs. Gengler, standing up and helping her husband to his feet. "Herbert needs to go home now and tend to his dermatitis." She set their empty cups on the mantel.

"Oh for God's sake," said Victor and the dean together, the latter under his breath.

The president's shirt and tie were bloody. "You'll excuse me for not shaking hands," he said, crossing to the door with a sad, defeated smile and displaying his bloody fingers. "Good luck to you all."

Mrs. Gengler, following him out, glowered at the Dashes, obviously holding their cat responsible.

Leland's opening statement was full of optimism. "I'm encouraged by what Dr. Zastrow has told us. I knew the board would be decent about it."

"What's so decent about nothing?" Victor wanted to know. "Didn't you hear what he said? The board is offering us exactly nothing."

"This year, yes," Leland agreed, "but not next year. Next year we'll realize an increase—"

"In a pig's ass! Next year the board will *consider* an increase— didn't you hear him? All that means is they'll vote to put us in the toilet again."

"Please, gentlemen, we haven't concluded our opening statements. Leland, do you wish to add anything more?"

"No, that's all," he replied darkly, his optimism dimmed under the cloud of Victor's skepticism.

"All right, well said, Leland, my boy. And now Victor will elucidate for us the concessions the Alliance is willing to make."

Victor took a few moments to give his mustache a brisk and thorough brushing with his fingertips while drilling the dean with his most penetrating look, and then he said, "The Alliance will accept a raise in pay that's less than the legislature intended for us, but not a year from next fall, this *coming* fall."

"How much less?" asked Leland, looking guardedly hopeful.

"That's negotiable, but not, I repeat, a year from next fall, this *coming* fall."

"Well, we're off to a tremendously fantastic start, I'd say." Mortimer then turned to Peggy. "And now, perhaps the young lady . . . ?" He chuckled, as though doubting a young lady capable of an opening statement.

"I'm here not as a compromiser," she said. "I'm here to make sure we don't negotiate away our demand for equal pay for women. The women of Rookery State, all eleven of us, want a single salary schedule, and we want it, not a year from next fall, this *coming* fall."

Victor's admiring look said he was in proud agreement. So did the breathy sound coming from Lolly Edwards—a kind of blissful, admiring sigh.

Boots, meanwhile, was trying to nuzzle up under the hem of Peggy's skirt, and Honey Oberholtzer, having returned from seeing the Genglers out, came to her aid. "Shame, Boots, shame." She gripped the dog by the collar and hauled him over to a bench by the door, where she sat down a little apart from her guests and roughly massaged his ears.

Mrs. Zastrow, having finished her muffin, licked her fingers.

Mortimer said that a discussion could now ensue.

Dean Zastrow said that an increase in salary for next fall was out of the question. All the money had been designated for construction and supplies.

"Then you better *un*designate it," Victor shot back, "otherwise there'll be no compromise."

The dean, having conveyed the board's message, fell silent. He cast a look of supreme confidence left and right, giving Peggy in particular the full benefit of his slit-mouth smile. He wished he could go on to convey the reasoning behind the board's decision, but Chancellor Waldorf had warned him not to. "No use rousing the natives to anger," the chancellor had said. "No use explaining anything to that Dash fellow—he's too dim-witted to understand anyhow. Let them think the money's already been spent, and let it go at that." The board couldn't very well raise salaries in Rookery without doing so on the other three campuses. If that happened, the other three faculties would surely embrace the Alliance, and the dear old Congress of College Professors, with its high professionalism and its low expectations, would be a thing of the past.

Victor, angered by the dean's silence, raised his voice. "Tell your board and your chancellor that they'll have to do better than that, and they'll have to do it before three o'clock, because the Alliance is meeting to vote on your offer, and if I tell them what it is—not a goddamn thing—they're going to be so goddamn mad, let me warn you—"

His gruff intensity aroused Boots to a state of sexual excitement. Bounding over to Victor, the dog attached itself to his

crossed right leg, stood on its hind feet, and threw itself into a copulating frenzy, drooling all the while on Victor's knee.

"Oh," screeched Mrs. Zastrow excitedly, her first utterance of
the afternoon. Everyone in the room was embarrassed, particularly
the Oberholtzers. "Give his balls a kick," said Mortimer urgently.

Victor couldn't believe his ears. Though tempted to do exactly
that (it was a method of proven effectiveness he'd used on other
dogs), he assumed he'd misunderstood. He tried pushing the dog
away, but to no avail.

"Just give his balls a kick," said Honey. "That always distracts
him."

What's this, both Oberholtzers condoning it? Then I'll do it,
thought Victor, and with great pleasure—I'll distract this goddamn
dog into lifelong impotence, and he brought his foot up and
planted it so swiftly and firmly in the dog's testicles that the animal
flew yelping across the room and sped out the door in a crippled,
crouching run.

"Oh you horrible man!" cried Honey, and she dashed away after her dog.

"Now see here, what's the big idea?" Mortimer was out of his
chair and out of patience with Victor. He came at him, pipe stem
first, and Victor, afraid of being impaled, rose to defend himself.

Peggy, too, stood up, eager to leave this useless meeting now
turned suddenly insane. Leland stood because Peggy stood. Lolly
stood because her son did. Dean Zastrow stood, hoping everybody
would clear out, so that his wife, not a natural mixer, could get to
know Honey Oberholtzer. His wife continued placidly sitting
there, her eyes turned to the fire but unfocused, the fingers of her
right hand absently tracing her necklace.

Mortimer, without laying a hand on Victor, somehow pro-
pelled him out of the room. Peggy found her coat, said good-bye to
Lolly, thanked Honey for the tea, and as she fled out the door into
the rain, heard the laughter of Annie Dash raised to a new, hysterical level.

Annie, convulsed with mirth, was still in the living room,
pointing at the chair where Victor had been sitting, under which
were two well-chewed tennis balls.

Calling the meeting to order in Mount of Olives, Victor beheld the solemn, deflated spirits of his colleagues, who by this time had all been apprised of the board's threat to shut down their campus—forever, if need be. They sat gazing up at him in virtual silence. Aaron Cardero and Kimberly Kraft sat together in the front pew, trying to maintain smiles of encouragement. Victor saw Peggy and Connor sitting together at the back. He saw Leland and Mortimer conferring in whispers in the baptismal alcove. He didn't see Neil. He didn't see Alex Bolus. Rain was drumming loudly on the roof.

He wasted no time in reporting the bad news. Maybe a small rise in salary a year from next fall, but only maybe. An adjustment in the women's salary schedule at that time as well, but only maybe.

His listeners appeared unmoved to anger or defiance. They continued to sit there, lumpish and discouraged. This called for more than a pep talk, thought Victor; it called for the most crucial exhortation of his life. So he launched into it, charging up and down the middle aisle preaching defiance and resolve and promising the widespread support of the general population. He might have been talking to stone. He saw no one catching his fire, saw no change in expression except on the faces of certain cowards like Professor Reginald Fix, who added a look of fright to the dark pessimism already there.

"Nobody said striking was easy, my friends, but if we're ever going to get the respect we deserve and make a decent living for our families, then we've got to see this through, we've got to make these slave drivers in St. Paul feel the heat of public opinion."

His listeners grew restless and stopped paying attention. They pictured their bank statements and the numbers representing the very thin line separating them from insolvency. They turned to their neighbors, muttering, asking how they could have fallen for this crazy scheme in the first place. They'd known all along where the power was. Why had they gone up against the College Board with no more weaponry than cardboard signs on three-foot lengths of lath? It was easy to imagine what the board was thinking—if they put down the Rookery strikers, collective bargaining would be set back a decade or more among midwestern academics. As for the public outcry Victor promised, who besides the students and faculty really cared if this campus at the edge of nowhere went out of business? Apparently not even the citizens of Rookery cared. The call-ins on "Lolly Speaking" were running ten to one against the strike. The *Morning Call* was making a mission out of trashing the Alliance.

A vote was called.

"Stand up for yourselves and call the board's bluff," railed Victor, as Kimberly and Aaron distributed the ballots. "There's no way in hell they can shut down Paul Bunyan's alma mater." But his voice was giving out, his words all but lost under the drumming on the roof, which was growing louder and causing the faculty to imagine the misery of getting out of bed tomorrow morning to picket in the rain.

Besides Victor, there were only five other professors who voted to continue striking. There were two abstentions—Peggy's and Connor's. There were 106 votes in favor of going back to work.

Kimberly wept as she announced the results. Aaron, standing at her side, looked stupidly amused, as though the voters were joking. Victor covered his eyes. When he uncovered them, he saw Georgina Gold waving her hand in the air, and he gave her the floor. "Take it away," he said, striding down the aisle and out the door, leaving her in charge, and with those words the brief ascendancy of the Faculty Alliance of America, Rookery chapter, came to an end.

Georgina stood up at her place, raised her voice over the sound of the rain, and announced that she'd been authorized by the Congress of College Professors to welcome everyone back into the fold, membership effective immediately, dues deferred until fall. She would distribute application blanks around campus within the week.

"That's more like it," shouted someone at the back, and there was a small scattering of applause and a collective sigh of relief. Connor and Peggy joined the stream of professors making their way to the door. How close they had come to drowning in labor strife, said C. Mortimer Oberholtzer, how comforting to think of themselves back in the safe harbor of the dear old C.C.P. Connor saw the relief in the faces of his colleagues. They were free once more to wallow in the small, murky pond of academe, free to take up the familiar old obscurities of their lecture notes and scholarly articles, free to indulge in the safe little jealousies and triumphs inherent in promotions and committee appointments. By the time they reached the door, somebody was telling Connor that they'd gone along with the Alliance only to humor Victor, and they'd gone on strike only for the fun and adventure of it and never really expected to succeed. Leaving the church, he watched the faculty spring happily through the cold rain to their cars like fugitives breaking out of prison.

Having sold two get-well cards, a stuffed toy, and a sprig of dried flowers in a plastic vase, Marcy Connor was so tired she wanted to die. She hadn't realized how much energy was involved in maneuvering between the display shelves and card rack and counters of the tiny gift shop and smiling all the while at customers. Having spent the last six months either in bed or within a few feet of it, she'd grown very heavy, and now, less than an hour into her three-hour shift, she was woozy with fatigue and weak in the legs.

Deciding to look for help, she left the shop unattended and went over to the receptionist's desk in the lobby to ask if someone could be called to take her place because she wasn't feeling well. The receptionist, a thin young man wearing a suit coat and jeans, frowned up at her from behind a bouquet of daisies and said he wasn't responsible for assigning workers. She went next to the coffee shop, but found no one behind the counter because Sunday was self-serve day. She took the elevator to the second floor and looked for her new friends among the nursing staff, but today's shift included no one she knew. Afraid that she might not make it back downstairs without collapsing, she approached a smiling young nurse and asked for a pep pill. The nurse said sorry, she wasn't authorized to give out prescription drugs. "I think they sell No Doz in the gift shop," she said.

Marcy returned to the first floor and considered going to emergency and lying down on the first flat surface she came to, but emergency was at the far end of the building, and here she was within twenty feet of the gift shop. Luckily, she found no one shopping. She shut the door and turned the OPEN sign around to CLOSED. It wasn't pep she needed, but sleep, she decided, blessed sleep. She sat in the straight chair at the back of the shop, out of sight from the windows, and ate a Milky Way and several sleeping tablets.

She sat there for a long time before realizing that the sleep she was about to fall into would be long and deliciously deep. There was a numbness in her mouth and throat and all the way down into her stomach, and she was losing some of the feeling in her fingers and feet. If she was ever going to take her own life, ever going to sleep undisturbed into eternity and not feel a thing, this would be the time and the place. She struggled to her feet and staggered over to the counter for a bottle of aspirin. She uncapped it with the last of her energy. Unable to stand, she lay down on the floor behind the counter with a teddy bear for a pillow and tried to think of a reason to stay alive and go back to her miserable life with her hopeless husband in that squalid little house by the side of the highway. Laura was the only reason that came to mind, and Laura was beyond reach, lost to bad moods and barbaric friends. Laura would likely end up like her mother, and her mother didn't want to be around to see it. She brought the aspirin bottle to her mouth, spilling most of them, and was able to swallow only six or eight tablets before she fell asleep.

Mortimer and Leland returned from Mount of Olives to the Oberholtzer house and what would have been a victory party if the Zastrows weren't such wet blankets—the dean so mean-spirited and his wife such a zombie—and if Lolly Edwards didn't keep saying how sorry she was that the Alliance caved in.

Having drunk a good deal of hard liquor while awaiting their return, Dean Zastrow grew vehement in his declaration that all the strike leaders, tenured or not, would pay a heavy price for tampering with Minnesota's finely tuned mechanism of higher education. Lolly said surely not Kimberly Kraft, surely not Peggy Benoit, but the dean said yes, Kimberly Kraft along with the rest of Victor Dash's conspirators would not soon forget the disgrace they'd brought to this normally peace-loving campus. Others might espouse letting bygones be bygones—the chancellor, of all people, advised forgiveness if the prodigals showed up for work Monday morning—but that wasn't the way you ran a college.

Lolly got her dander up. "You'd better be careful, you'll drive away some of your best teachers. Peggy Benoit is building up the music program to what it was years ago. She has her choir singing like angels."

The dean took a large swallow of scotch and then, directing his grim smile at Honey Oberholtzer, expressed his special pleasure in the way the summit meeting had ended, Victor Dash proving what a savage he was and how deserving of dismissal. "Man like that needs to be gotten rid of," he said.

"I couldn't agree more," said Honey. "What a perfectly horrible man."

"Bad influence on the younger professors," added the dean.

Leland shook his head mournfully, feeling already the loss of his drummer.

"Wrong sort of fellow for a campus like ours," Mortimer pointed out. "Wrong sort entirely."

"But that business with Boots was all such a *mistake*, don't you see?" said Lolly. "Honey, when you referred to Boots's . . . you know, his . . . playthings . . ."

Honey didn't get it. Lolly turned to her son for help, but Leland was incapable of saying "balls" to Honey and could only shrug and turn red.

Mortimer, too, was incapable. Avoiding his wife's eyes, he nodded knowingly at Lolly and turned to the sideboard to busy himself with the ice bucket.

But Mrs. Zastrow wasn't incapable. The zombie suddenly came to life, giving off the sound of convulsive chuckles. She drew her eyes away from the fireplace, peered over the rim of her glass, and directed her second utterance of the day to her hostess. "You told him to give the dog's balls a kick, and he did."

Honey's eyes went to the ragged tennis balls lying under the chair, but it was impossible to tell if she finally understood.

The dean prevented his wife from being of further help by changing the subject. "Once we're up and running again, Mortimer, I'd like to have a ceremony in front of McCall, inaugurating the new sign."

"Capital idea. Fantastic."

"It's a great piece of work, that sign."

"A fantastic piece of work."

"You can't beat varnished butternut for signs. I learned that in North Dakota."

Now it was Lolly's turn to have a chuckling fit. She trembled and snorted and said, " 'Paul Bunyan's Alma Mater'—I can't believe it." She pulled a hankie from somewhere in her tentlike garment and wiped her eyes, quaking as she said, "What sort of student was Mr. Bunyan, I wonder. What was his major?"

"I can have Mrs. Kibbee look it up for you," said the dean, causing a hush to fall over the room. He wondered why everyone including his wife was suddenly gaping at him as though he'd said something brilliant. "It's not fair to the alumni as a whole to single out one in particular who's become famous," he said.

Peggy arrived at four on the dot, furling her umbrella and declaring, "I'm warning you, Leland, I'm feeling blue as hell."

"I was afraid of that." He stepped gingerly back from her, as though her emotion might be contagious.

"The Alliance is no more—don't gloat," she said.

"Peggy, I'm not a gloater, you know that."

"The women of Rookery State, Leland—we've been told to go jump in the lake."

"I'm sorry about that too." He reopened her umbrella and set it on the living room carpet to dry.

"It's such a helpless feeling, having our strings pulled by Big Brother in St. Paul."

"It could all be reversed, Peggy. By the courts, I mean."

"I'm not holding my breath."

"Let me fix you a drink."

"Maybe later—let's get right to the music."

On their way upstairs he said, "Mother stayed on awhile at Honey and Mortimer's. The Zastrows will give her a ride home."

"She's one of a kind, Leland. I actually believe she would have turned up on the picket line if the strike went on one more day."

"Yes, she was serious about that."

"Would that have embarrassed you?"

"Yes."

"I'll bet she's embarrassed you a lot in her day."

"Oh, yes, a lot. But one has to admire her at the same time."

"Her spunk. It's wonderful."

In the sleeping porch, Peggy flopped onto a wicker couch and asked him to play the song he wrote for her.

He sat down at the piano and did so, but stopped after a few measures. "Why not join me on the sax?" he said.

"No, it's too lovely," she said. "I'd rather listen."

So he went further into the piece, slowly at first, losing himself on a meandering path through its melody, tracing and retracing its autumnal theme, making it sad, making it sweet, filling the sleeping porch with its minor-key mood, and then, nearing the end, he felt a strange sensation overtake him. He felt as though the bottom were dropping out of his heart. He felt like weeping. Ashamed to do so, he began to rush the piece, coming down hard on the final chords and avoiding the wistful fadeout he'd imagined when he wrote it. Upon finishing, he whipped out his handkerchief and went to work dusting the keyboard.

"I'm touched whenever you play it, Leland. I never had a piece dedicated to me before."

"I'm glad you like it." He did not turn to face her.

"My sax would only detract—can you see that?"

"Yes, I suppose."

"I think you ought to trail it off more at the end, make it more bluesy."

"I know."

"More of a dying fall, like the first time you played it for me."

"I remember."

"I'd love to hear it that way again. Would you try it?"

"I don't think I can."

She laughed. "What do you mean? Of course you can."

Still he didn't look at her, afraid she'd see his anguish, afraid he'd have to admit his devastation over the breakup of the quintet, which was bound to happen now that Dean Zastrow was bent on massacre. He couldn't talk about it. He hadn't known the words for heartbreak when he was fourteen and his father died, and he didn't know them now. He couldn't tell her how much of his life he'd spent dreaming of just this sort of musical friendship, and how far, thanks to Peggy, the real thing exceeded the dream. Maybe other people could talk about matters like that; he couldn't.

"Why can't you play it?" she wanted to know.

He finished dusting the keys and ran up and down a scale. He swallowed his sorrow and tried speaking brightly. "I have this idea, Peggy. How about if we work up 'Your Feet's Too Big' and surprise Victor with it?"

"Oh, this is no day for 'Your Feet's Too Big.' I wouldn't be up to it."

"No, you're right," he agreed, glancing about at the rain-streaked windows. "It sure is gloomy."

"The weather has nothing to do with it," she said impatiently. "Don't you realize this is the day we found out how weak we are as a faculty? We're like characters in Kafka, at the mercy of people whose names we don't even know. Who *are* the people on the board, Leland? Do you have any idea?"

"I used to know their names."

"No women, I suppose."

"Not that I recall."

"Of course not. I imagine six men smoking cigars. Who are they? Where are they from?"

"From all walks of life, supposedly, and appointed by the governor. I think there's a stipulation that four of them be citizens of the four college towns and two are chosen at large."

"Who's from Rookery, then, and why haven't we been in touch with him?"

"Well, actually, there isn't anybody from Rookery. There's one each from Moorhead, Winona, and Mankato, plus three at large."

"So why is Rookery left out? Are we too small to count?"

"No, that's not it, we always used to be represented. Harry Steadman was on the board for many years before he went to the legislature. The way it works, each college president submits a list of names for the governor to choose from, but I understand that President Gengler, for some reason, never got around to it."

"That ass."

Leland flinched.

"But he is, Leland. He's a lazy ass."

"He has that itch, Peggy. It's hard for him."

She raised her voice. "So he's an *itchy*, lazy ass."

Leland had to chuckle in spite of himself.

"And our dean is a warty tyrant and our chairman is a lecherous dolt."

He stiffened. "No, Peggy. That's going too far. I really have to object to that. Mortimer and Honey are particular friends of Mother's and mine."

She sighed and fell silent.

He ran up and down a few more scales as rain continued to lash the windows.

"Leland, I don't think the others are coming."

He continued playing softly, while turning his wrist to see his watch.

"Maybe I should call them," she said. "I'm worried how Victor's taking it."

"Yes, I wonder too. He left the church without a word. You could use the phone in Mother's bedroom."

"And Connor ought to be here by now. He had to give his wife a ride home from the hospital."

"She's sick again?"

"No, she's doing volunteer work." She rose from the wicker couch and left him fiddling around with Gershwin.

Lolly's bedroom was done up in light pastels and heavy antiques. Peggy sat on the bed, a four-poster of carved walnut, and dialed Connor's house first. There was no answer.

Next she tried the Dashes and got Annie's happy chirp: "We're on our way out to eat pizza, Peggy. Why don't you join us?"

"I can't, Annie, I'm at Leland's, and we're wondering if Victor's going to show up."

She heard Annie call at the top of her voice, "Victor, did you forget about practice?" His reply was a bark.

"I don't know, Peggy. Maybe after we finish eating."

"How's he taking it, Annie? Is he okay?"

"Oh, he'll be fine." She laughed. "He's just mad as hell right now."

Suddenly Victor was on the line. "Get busy and look for another job, Peggy Benoit, we're belly-up in Rookery."

"What?" She was startled. "Why, what have you heard?"

"I've heard the voice of my pipeline experience, and it says our ass is grass."

"Whose ass is grass, Victor?"

His words were a series of explosions. "Everybody who had a role in the strike."

"I didn't have a role."

He shouted, "Don't act so goddamn innocent, Miss Crusader for Equal Pay!"

"Victor, listen—"

Louder: "Just get busy and start looking for a goddamn job."

"Listen, Victor, come over to Leland's after—"

"Because we're all dead in the water."

"You need to beat your drums, Victor. Come over to Leland's."

"Leland's! Are you out of your mind? What are *you* doing at Leland's? He's the enemy, for Chrissake. You and Neil and I get thrown out in the street, and what's pansy-ass doing about it? He's sitting there dusting off his piano with his hankie."

"Victor, if you—"

"Admit it. How long have you been there?"

"Twenty minutes."

"And how many times has he dusted off his piano with his hankie?"

Peggy shouted into the phone, "Victor, shut up!"

Silence for a moment, then quietly: "What?"

She closed the bedroom door before continuing. "Leland is nobody's enemy and you know it. He's one of the best friends you've got in this town, and you haven't got very many. Now get over here as soon as you can, and beat your drums."

"Fuck my drums!" The line went dead.

Sitting on the bed, boiling, she phoned Neil, who sounded only vaguely interested in the demise of the Alliance, and when she asked him to come and jam with them, he yawned and said he'd been losing sleep over his novel and he thought he'd better go to bed early so he could bring a fresh mind to his art in the morning.

She boiled over. "Don't give me that self-pity crap, Neil. If you were a real artist, you'd know what this music means to the rest of us at a time like this. Now get over here and pretend you're Benny Goodman and we'll all feel a whole lot better."

"Peggy," he whined, "it's raining."

"I'll ask Connor to pick you up. Good-bye."

She tried Connor again, but again there was no answer.

Connor, for the second consecutive Sunday, was watching nurses install his wife in a hospital bed. She was scarcely aware of what was happening. Despite the grueling stomach-pumping procedure they'd put her through, she was still drowsy from the sleeping pills.

Lolly came home at five o'clock and was gratified to hear her son and Peggy working up a passionate rendition of "After You've Gone." She slipped into her bedroom and listened while she eased herself out of her prison-stripe dress, her tight shoes, and her brassy clip-on earrings and slipped into a more comfortable garment of red jersey that clung around her neck and knees and billowed in between.

There was a low-down quality in Peggy's voice that Lolly had never noticed before, an unladylike sort of burr or growl that put her in mind of a smoky tavern that she and Leland's father had once gone into during a convention of historians in Chicago. Tired from shopping in the late afternoon, they'd dropped in off the street, attracted by the music of a three-piece band and the rather raspy voice of a pretty young woman on a high platform singing "Cheek to Cheek." They paid an exorbitant price for a glass of abrasive wine and were shocked when the singer's rendition became raspier and jazzier and she began to bump and grind and shed her clothes. This she did fairly quickly, perhaps because there were so few men to tease, only four or five morose-looking types standing at the bar gazing up at her pelvis, and she was down to her tassels and G-string before the Edwardses had quite gathered up their shopping bags and left. Why would dear Peggy want to imitate the disgraceful style of a vamp?

When it became apparent that there was to be no break in the music, Lolly stopped it by coming out of hiding.

"Peggy dear, I'm told the Alliance is a thing of the past."

"Dead as a doornail, Lolly."

"Oh, rats. And here I was ready to get on the bandwagon. It's hard to believe how quickly things turned around. Why, on Thursday I thought you people had the upper hand, and now, just like that . . ." She snapped her fingers.

"You know what irks me, Lolly? Being controlled by six people in St. Paul whose names we don't even know."

"Well, you know their spokesman's name, Chancellor Waldorf. He's such a blowhard."

"But the board members ought to be made to understand what they've done to us."

"The court might rule against them," Leland reminded her.

"I'll be surprised," said Peggy.

"And there's the court of public opinion," he added. "I mean, as Victor said in church, people might begin to criticize the board for its impunity."

She wheeled on him. "I don't believe *that* for a minute."

Leland lowered his eyes and nodded. He didn't believe it either.

The doorbell interrupted them. Leland went down to answer it, expecting Connor and Neil.

"Laura," he exclaimed.

She stood there with rain dripping off her straggly hair. She'd walked the several blocks from the hospital.

"Does your mother need any help in the kitchen?" she asked.

Later, when it was apparent that no one else was coming to play, when they'd done all they could with a piano-sax rendition of "Bye Bye Blackbird," and when the aroma of spice cake was beginning to drift up the back stairway from the kitchen, they took a break from their music. Leland shook out his handkerchief and applied it again to the keyboard. Peggy stood at the window grieving for Connor, yearning for Connor, and watching droplets of rain gather on the twigs. The rain was letting up as the light faded. It was nearly six o'clock.

"Peggy."

"Yes?"

Leland said nothing. She turned from the window. He was looking at her with wrinkles in his brow she'd never noticed before. She stepped over to the piano and saw his sorrow.

"What's the matter?" she asked. There was a boyish, supplicating aspect to the face he turned up to her.

"Can you stay for a while?"

"Are you okay, Leland? You don't look so hot."

Smiling required a great deal of effort. So did his confession: "I just want you to stay. I mean, we're doomed as a quintet, aren't we?"

"Hard to say. Neil's all tied up with his book right now, and who knows if Victor will get over being mad?"

"Because . . ." He groped for words. "If we're doomed, I don't think I could stand to stop playing these songs all at once. I mean if you and I could just . . ."

She hugged his head to her breast. "Don't worry, my friend, tonight you and I are going to play till we drop."

Then there was cake and hot chocolate and a stilted, four-sided conversation about movies, which ended when Connor stopped by to pick up Laura. He didn't come in. Having materialized on the doorstep out of the rainy dark, he quickly faded back into it. His daughter trailed after him, promising Lolly she'd be back soon for a bread-baking lesson.

Peggy threw on her raincoat, grabbed her umbrella, and hurried out to the station wagon. He was starting the engine when her face appeared at his side window. He rolled it down.

"Is there anything we can do? Laura told us about Marcy's relapse."

"No, thanks," he said in a weary, defeated voice.

"Will she be okay?"

"She says so, the nurses say so, but who knows?"

"It's not too late to come in and join us. It's only eight o'clock."

"Dad, I've got homework," Laura reminded him.

"We've got to get home." The flatness of these words alarmed her. Ever since he'd gotten interested in her, she'd been aware of her power to lift his spirit, aware of a heightened tone of voice when he spoke to her, an expectant look in his eye. Now the tone was gone. The look was gone. He seemed spiritless.

"Will I see you tomorrow?" she asked, aware that Laura was nudging him with her elbow.

He said, "Sure." It sounded like a brush-off.

She backed away then, telling herself not to crowd him, not to be difficult. He already had two complicated women in his life. She slowly walked backward, keeping the car in sight until it turned toward the bridge. She paused for a minute on the doorstep, looking down the dark street and listening to the rain beat down on her umbrella. Then she stepped inside and found Leland gone. Lolly was gathering up the plates and coffee cups.

"He just went out the back way, Peggy. Come keep me company while I clean up the kitchen."

"Where's he going?"

"Honey and Mortimer's. He said he'd be right back."

"I thought he wanted to play longer."

"Oh, he does. It just occurred to him he had to see Mortimer about something. He'll be right back." When she saw Peggy looking indecisive, she set down the plates and cups and came up to her, gushing, "Here, let me take your coat, Peggy dear. You can't be thinking about leaving so early, not in this downpour. My, doesn't poor Connor have his problems. I daresay his wife is a lost cause. I know he's concerned about his daughter, but he doesn't have any worry there. Laura's smart as a whip. Smart ones make their way in the world—have you ever noticed? It's the stupid ones that get into trouble." She reached into the closet for a coat hanger. "Here, take off your coat and tell me what you know about his wife. Don't you think she's a lost cause?"

"I want to go home, Lolly."

"Oh, no, I'm so disappointed. Do stay, Peggy dear, you said you wanted to play and sing far into the night."

"The mood passed."

"Leland will be so disappointed."

"Tell Leland it will have to be some other time. I don't think we could get it back tonight."

"Can I tell Leland it will be Wednesday night, as usual?"

"Yes," said Peggy, thinking, Tell him anything, just let me go.

Lolly released her then, suspecting that she was following Connor to a rendezvous. "Ta ta, Peggy dear. I'm sorry he left like this, but whatever he's saying to Mortimer, I'm sure you'd approve."

Peggy left with this odd statement echoing in her head. She went home and quoted it to her sister in Maine, as part of a two-hour conversation by phone. Her sister said Lolly sounded like a nutcase.

Odd as it sounded, Lolly's statement was true: Peggy would have approved. Leland had gone to the Oberholtzers' to defend her honor.

Peggy had no sooner followed Connor out to his car in the rain than Lolly had asked Leland, "Did you know Mortimer keeps a nude picture of Peggy in his den?"

Leland had been speechless. He closed the door and turned to her looking incredulous.

"I am furious about it, Leland. I couldn't very well let on with Peggy here, but I'm absolutely furious. Can you imagine anything so crude? Mortimer of all people! He brought it out to show the dean."

A look came into her son's eyes that she'd never seen there before. Intense anger.

"And he wasn't even drunk. The dean, I think, was drunk—he'd been knocking back liquor like it was going off the market in the morning—but Mortimer wasn't even tipsy. He was just acting silly, you know how he gets sometimes, and he said, 'I've got something to show you,' and he went into his den and came out with this picture of Peggy in the altogether."

Leland clenched his teeth.

"And Honey just sat there smiling—can you believe it? There's no telling what Mrs. Zastrow was thinking, she's off in her own world, but the dean said something about Peggy's body and Mortimer laughed and Honey just sat there smiling. What I should have done was snatch the picture away from him and tear it up in tiny pieces, but I was paralyzed with shock. I turned to Honey, expecting— Leland, where are you going?"

He'd taken his coat from the closet and was heading across the living room with fire in his eye. She followed him through the kitchen and back porch and forced an umbrella upon him. "Hurry back," she called excitedly. She'd never known him to act on impulse. Nor to look so wild-eyed. Anger, she thought, made him very handsome.

He'd left the umbrella in the car. He rang the doorbell and drew his raincoat up over his head. He tried to compose himself. If he were to burst in on the Oberholtzers angry and agitated, he'd never get his hands on the picture. He must pretend to have other business in mind. Could he bring it off? Dissembling was not one of his skills.

Honey came to the door. "Hi, Leland, your mother already left."

"Yes, I know. I'd like to talk to Mortimer."

"I'll put on the teapot," she said, leading him into the living room, where embers glowed in the fireplace. Boots followed, sniffing his wet shoes. "He'll be right up, he's down in the basement stoking the furnace."

Alone for a minute, Leland scanned the room for the photograph. He peeked into the drawer of the lamp table that stood next to Mortimer's favorite chair. He was down on his knees searching through the Sunday paper scattered on the rug when Mortimer came into the room full of jovial bombast. He was wearing slippers and a tattered cardigan and wiping his hands on a dirty rag.

"Leland, my boy, if only you'd stayed longer and heard the fantastic things Dean Zastrow said about you. I told him about your fabulous work in behalf of right reason, what an example you are to the younger faculty, and he agrees with me there's no better professor at Rookery State than you, my boy. What can I do for you? How about a nightcap?"

"Just a cup of tea will be fine."

They sat in chairs near one another. Mortimer tossed the rag into the fireplace.

"Glad you came back, Leland. Gives me a chance to say, just between the two of us, just how thankful I am that you're in my division. I mean, where would Languages and Fine Arts be without your reliable presence? Have you ever considered how diminished we'll be without you, if the dean goes ahead with his plan?"

Leland was startled. "What plan is that?"

"Your mother didn't tell you?"

"No."

There was a soft "woof" from the fireplace as the rag went up in flames.

"Well, the day is coming, he says, when he's going to need an assistant dean, and I said to him, 'Dean,' I said, 'let's not bring in an outsider for a job like that, let's promote one of our own,' and I'll let you guess, Leland, whom I suggested."

Leland, quailing, said, "Not me."

"Who else? Best detail man in the division, that's you. I told the dean that, and I could tell he was impressed. Sorry to get in ahead of Lolly with the news, but we're going to groom you for higher things. Sky's the limit, my boy."

"If you don't mind, I'd rather just teach."

His chairman thought this wonderfully funny. He laughed and shouted in the direction of the kitchen, "Did you hear that, Honey?"

"What I came about, Mortimer, I wonder if Neil is really being let go, if somebody should see about freshman textbooks for next fall."

"Ah, there you are. What a fabulous man for details. Take the ball and run with it, my boy." Another call to the kitchen: "Bring this man some tea, Honey." Turning back to Leland, he saw his face undergoing a change—a crimp-mouthed, narrow-eyed look that struck him as strange. "What is it, my boy, a stomachache?"

Actually, it was Leland's attempt, based on Fred MacMurray's example in *Double Indemnity*, to look lascivious. He hesitated before speaking, afraid his chairman would sense his outrage and not play into his hand. But he had to go forward for Peggy's sake, and so he said, finally, "I was just wondering, Mortimer, I hear you've got a picture you've been showing of Peggy."

"Have I got a picture!" Suspecting nothing, he rose out of his chair and left the room. It would never occur to C. Mortimer Oberholtzer that any man wouldn't take supreme delight in feasting his eyes on the naked flesh of Dr. Benoit. He returned to the living room and proudly presented the large white envelope to Leland.

"Take your time, she's a great beauty," he said. "I'll go see if your tea is ready and mix myself a little nightcap."

What luck. Leland had imagined himself tearing up the picture in Mortimer's presence and thereby risking his exasperation, indeed perhaps his lifelong animosity. But no, with Mortimer and Boots gone from the room, he calmly drew out the photo, stepped over to the fireplace, and laid it facedown on the burning rag. In a moment it was ash.

PART 5

My Blue Heaven

Monday morning, Peggy picked up her campus mail, which included three memos from Administration Row, and carried it to the student center, where she joined Leland at a table near the window. Classes had resumed without incident. The student body felt refreshed after their long weekend, and most of their professors, relieved at having avoided unemployment, were spinning out droll stories having to do with the Alliance. They analyzed the strike with humor and mock gravity, as though their dispute with management had been a melodrama staged for everyone's amusement. Leland and Peggy, however, took a more sober view.

"It's like the strike never happened," said Leland, sincerely wishing it hadn't.

"Oh, it happened all right." Peggy was sipping coffee and reading Memo One, in which President Gengler promised no recriminations. The strike was in the past, he said, a beautifully rebuilt campus was in the future, and everyone would soon be invited to a dedication ceremony at the site of the new college sign at the corner of Sawyer and Eleventh.

"Oh, God, Leland, I feel another Signage meeting coming on."

"Yes, as a matter of fact, the dean would like us to get together

403

and plan the ceremony," he said. "Nectar and cookies on the lawn, that sort of thing."

Memo Two was full of surprises. For one thing, it was signed by both the president and the dean, an indication of unprecedented accord. For another, the secretary's initials "lk" were replaced by "dv," indicating that Lorraine Kibbee had been replaced between memos by Deelane Villars. Also, it announced that the College Board, "in an act of good faith and generosity, and in an attempt to eventually rectify the gender discrepancy, will include in the next paycheck a bonus of twenty-five dollars to every faculty woman statewide."

"What does he mean, 'an act of generosity'?" fumed Peggy. "There are exactly eleven women teaching at Rookery State. That'll cost the board less than three hundred dollars."

"Two hundred and seventy-five," Leland agreed.

"What an insult!"

Georgina Gold came in then, and asked if she could sit with them. Leland said, "Of course." She wasn't surprised that Peggy said nothing.

"Did you notice Deelane's taken over from Mrs. Kibbee?" asked Georgina. "What a stupid move *that* is."

"Mrs. Kibbee was given the option of staying on as a member of the secretarial pool, but she quit altogether," said Leland. "She told the dean she'd rather go home to her pigs."

"How do you know that?" asked Peggy, amazed as usual by Leland's inside information.

"She told me."

"The only brain on Administration Row," lamented Georgina.

Leland, examining Memo Two for grammatical flaws, found one. " '. . . to eventually rectify'—Mrs. Kibbee would never have let a phrase like that get by her. I don't understand why she was fired."

Leland might have the facts, thought Peggy, but not a grasp of the vengeful side of human nature. "Mrs. Kibbee's downfall was her proletarian sympathies," she told him.

"But Memo One says no recrimination."

Both women looked at him as if to say, *You poor sap.*

"Don't tell me you've forgotten our meeting with Chancellor Waldorf," said Georgina. She laughed a rare little laugh. "Who can forget the way Mrs. Kibbee kept pressing on his chest with her pencil?"

"But what qualifies Deelane to take over?" he asked. "I mean, what does she bring to the job?"

Again he was given the poor-sap look.

"Youth," explained Peggy.

"To be more exact, she's wiggly," said Georgina.

Leland grimaced and looked at his watch. "I'm off to class," he said, gathering up his books. They watched him hurry away, buttoning his suit coat and checking the knot of his tie.

Memo Three was from the dean alone. It was all about punishment. Neil Novotny's appointment had been terminated for insubordination, it said, and Honey Oberholtzer (B.A., English, University of North Dakota) was taking over his classes until the end of the semester, at which time a permanent replacement would be found. Aaron Cardero had resigned as chairman of Accounting and Office Procedures in order to return to full-time teaching. Kimberly Kraft was giving up her advisership to various student clubs such as Future Teachers of America in order to return to full-time teaching. Alex Bolus had resigned as women's athletic director in order to return to full-time teaching.

Georgina shifted around in her chair to face the wall of windows. "I want to apologize," she said.

"It's okay," said Peggy.

"What you and Connor are up to is none of my business."

"It's okay."

"But you asked for it, you know."

"I did?"

"You called Ron a jerk, remember."

"So I did."

Georgina waited for Peggy to complete the matching set of apologies, but Peggy said nothing. She too had turned to the windows, and was trying to suppress the feeling of panic that had been set in motion by Memo Three.

Georgina turned and saw her distress. "Hey, what's the matter?"

"The quintet's as good as finished, Georgina. Neil's out of a job, and Victor won't last very long."

"What did I miss?" said Georgina, picking up the memo. "It doesn't say anything about Victor."

"It's between the lines. First his Viceroys get demoted, then . . . Memo Four."

Georgina considered this. "Well, there's still Connor and Leland."

"Connor's quitting, going back to the city."

"Really? Well, Leland, then. He's a good musician, you told me."

Peggy didn't try to make her understand how abandoned she felt, how bereft of friends. Even Georgina was forsaking the profession for Rookery's foremost redneck and his kitchen appliances.

"I'm sorry, Georgina—what I said about Ron."

"It's okay."

They both sat with their arms crossed, staring out the window. A strong south wind was bending the pines and drying up the puddles along the walkways. Warm sunlight made a mirror of the ice-covered river.

"Georgina, don't resign your position."

"Are you kidding? I'm out of here."

"But selling refrigerators . . ."

"I can adapt."

How true, thought Peggy. How quickly, during the strike, this woman had taken up the stolid position of the local reactionaries, and now, the strike over and the Alliance dead, how quickly she'd resumed her sardonic carping.

"Peggy, I love a dare."

"What do you mean?"

"Would you dare me to go to our dean and ask him to invite Paul Bunyan back to his alma mater as commencement speaker?"

At first this struck Peggy as a joke too weak to be funny, but then, thinking it over, she realized that Zastrow might actually fall for it. This made her smile. Then she chuckled. Laughing, she leaned into Georgina and gave her a hug.

"I dare you," she said.

"And will you sing at my wedding?"

Earlier that same morning, Marge Nathanson, R.N., had come on duty, read the list of weekend admittances, and went straight to Marcy's room to wake her up for breakfast and a bath. "Oh, Marcy, Marcy," she sang, "why have you come back so soon?"

Marcy opened her eyes and growled.

"I'll bet it's that little blue pill acting up on you. We'll ask Dr. Hyde to put you on something else, and we'll have you back to normal in no time."

Marcy closed her eyes and turned her face to the wall.

"Oh, oh, what's this? Marcy's a trifle glum this morning. Well, just wait till we get her some orange juice and a nice bath and she'll be her sunny self again."

"I don't need a bath. I need sleep."

"Now, now, we can't be grumpy on such a glorious, glorious morning. Here, let's open the blinds and let the new day come shining in."

Sunlight flooded the room. Marcy covered her eyes.

Laying a hand on her shoulder, the nurse felt Marcy stiffen. "Where is the Marcy we had here last week, bright as a new penny? Where did she go, where did she go?"

"She needs a decent meal," said the woman in the other bed, an elderly, crotchety woman named Bennett, being treated for heart disease. "Who wouldn't be grumpy, eating the hog slop you feed us?"

The nurse shook a finger at her. "We're giving you meals that are good for your heart, Mrs. Bennett. From now on, you're just going to have to get used to eating different food. Marcy, I'll be back in a little bit when you're feeling better."

Marcy, still facing the wall, heard her leave. She dozed off and slept for an hour or more. She was wakened by a cleaning woman swabbing the floor, carelessly banging the mop handle against her bed. Marcy scowled up at her; then, seeing who it was, she smiled weakly.

"God, don't tell me you're back," said the cleaning woman, peering sternly down at her.

Marcy sighed.

"She's mental, I heard," said Mrs. Bennett.

"You heard wrong," said the cleaning woman. "Her husband's

the mental case. He's a drunk, just like my husband Bushman. Last week we had talks about it, didn't we, sweetie?"

Marcy nodded. She followed the woman with her eyes as she moved along the bed; then she craned her neck in order to keep her in view as as she moved over to mop under the window. Last week, this large, ungainly woman, Eldora Sparks by name, had energized Marcy every time she showed up with her cleaning cart and her bucket on wheels. She was so marvelously outspoken on the subject of drunken husbands, and so refreshingly blunt about her bitterness, that Marcy felt a kinship with her such as she'd never experienced before. Here was somebody who thoroughly understood the trouble she'd seen.

"Held you responsible for his boozing, didn't he, sweetie. Said you were at fault."

"No, actually—"

"That's always the way they do." Eldora Sparks paused in her work to give Marcy a penetrating look. "They claim they never would've touched a drop except they got married and their happiness flew out the window."

"Well, that's not exactly—"

"My husband Bushman always used to blame me like that, used to say marriage was a trap that left him nowhere to turn but to booze."

Marcy was on the verge of saying this particular detail wasn't true of Connor, but then she reminded herself that he wasn't worth defending.

"Bushman finally lost track of right from wrong, he did, made up so many excuses for himself he got so he couldn't tell truth from lies anymore." She dipped her mop in the bucket and went sloshing around under Mrs. Bennett's bed. "Like the time we were coming home from the fish fry at the Legion Club—that's about the only thing we ever went to as a couple, fish fries and funerals—and a highway cop stopped him for weaving over the center line, and Bushman told him it was because I kept grabbing the wheel as he drove, told him it was a habit I had that if I took it into my head to go somewhere other than where he was headed, I'd grab the wheel and try steering us off in a different direction."

"It wasn't true, was it," Marcy prompted eagerly. She'd heard this same account last week and loved the conclusion it was leading to.

"Hell, no, it wasn't true. I never touched a steering wheel in those days—I didn't know how to drive."

"But you didn't tell the policeman that."

"What good would that do? By that time I was so used to being Bushman's scapegoat that I never bothered to contradict him no matter what kind of bullshit he was spreading, not even when the cop started agreeing with him about what a loony wife he had, telling him he'd better get help for me before somebody got killed. All the while I just sat there like a dunce."

"But you were thinking."

"You bet I was thinking, sweetie." Eldora Sparks was now beyond the other bed, and calling loudly across the recumbent Mrs. Bennett. "I was having this breakthrough thought, saying to myself, 'This cop is absolutely right, I *do* need help. Look at the way I've stayed living with this lying bastard all these years. Why, if I don't get myself out of this fix I'm in, somebody *is* liable to get killed, and that somebody is going to be Bushman.' That's the thought that came to me."

Marcy's eyes lit up with excitement. "You actually thought you might *do* it!"

Eldora Sparks nodded thoughtfully, first across at Marcy, then down at Mrs. Bennett, who had drawn her covers up tight to her chin as though in fear of what was coming.

"Might've, is all I'm saying. What I mean, it suddenly struck me as possible. Not that day or the next, but eventually I might just possibly take it into my head to go ahead and do it, because even though I was born with the patience of a saint, I was feeling this buildup in my belly and head and all over, and if I didn't find a way to let off some of that pressure, why—who knows—I might take a hammer to Bushman's bald little skull while he was sleeping some night."

A squeal of delight from Marcy. How intoxicating to picture Connor dead instead of herself. She'd never imagined such a thing. Free at a stroke, without the disgrace or turmoil of divorce. Oh, such joy—to be a widow. She watched Eldora Sparks return to her bucket and dip her mop.

"I never heard such crazy talk in my life," said Mrs. Bennett.

Eldora Sparks wrung out her mop. "So that was the turning point for me, right there. Bushman put the car in gear and we drove away from that cop with our marriage entirely changed around, and just about over besides."

Marcy loved everything about this woman, her portly build, her queenly bearing, the surehanded way she used her housekeeping tools, and most of all her unwavering confidence. She wasn't the first disenchanted wife Marcy had met, but the others always seemed so rigid with anger. Eldora was so *relaxed.*

"Crazy talk," Mrs. Bennett repeated.

"You didn't murder him," said Marcy, eagerly reaching out to take the woman's arm and keep her nearby. "You didn't actually *do* it."

"No, of course not, sweetie." Her tone grew softer as she turned to explain to Mrs. Bennett. "I'm not a killer. I simply went and got myself a divorce."

This was as much of the story as Marcy had heard. At the word "divorce," her face clouded. "What about your children?" she asked.

"We never had any. That was the one total blessing of that marriage, sweetie, Bushman being too drunk at bedtime to make a child. Many a time I thanked the Lord God in heaven for that. Being the kind of patient dope I was in those days, children would've made me think twice about getting free. I've seen it with other women. Children holding them back from getting on with their life."

Eldora Sparks made a move toward the door, rolling the bucket ahead of her, but Marcy tightened her grip.

"I have a daughter. If it wasn't for her—"

"See that's where you're wrong, sweetie. If it's bad for you, why isn't it just as bad for the kid? Maybe worse for the kid, growing up with a drunk for a dad. Bust out of there and take the kid with you. One divorce will do it for both of you. It's like two tickets to freedom for the price of one."

Releasing the woman's arm, Marcy sat up and dangled her feet off the high bed. She looked out at the wet street. The sun was bright in puddles that rippled in the wind. "He was very sick in January," she said of Connor. "I thought he was going to die."

"Yeah, they usually do that, get your hopes up and then recover." Eldora, though free to move, remained beside the bed, apparently sensing how intensely Marcy needed her. "That's because drunks are tough. I swear there's a pickling agent of some kind in booze that acts as a preservative. How many times have you seen some old bird on a bar stool shaking so bad he can hardly get the glass up to his mouth, and yet there he is, year after year, sucking it down like it was mother's milk."

She moved off then, steering her bucket out into the hallway. After a moment she returned with a dustcloth.

"You know the old Legion Club downtown? I don't mean the new one out by the shopping mall. You been in it?"

Marcy said she hadn't.

"You?" she asked Mrs. Bennett, who shook her head as well.

"It's called the Jim Durken Post, and inside you'll find eight bar stools reserved for the same eight drunks. You see them perched there week after week, year after year, and once in a blue moon one of them'll kick the bucket and somebody else'll step in and take their place, some newcomer just moved to town, or some younger guy just learning to get serious with booze. Bushman held down the second stool from the end all those years we were married, and he's still there as far as I know—I never go in there anymore. I like a good fish fry as much as the next person, but there's other places almost as good. The VFW isn't half bad, although their batter's sort of flabby when it cools off. The Catholic parish on the south end of Sawyer gives you a real good fish fry, but they only do it four times a year."

The woman fell silent when Nurse Nathanson breezed in, singing, "Oh, good, good for you, Marcy, sitting there so bright-eyed and bushy-tailed. Get into your clothes now and take a nice walk up and down the hallway before your breakfast comes. It's important to be up and doing."

"Can I go home with you?" asked Marcy, looking past the nurse at Eldora Sparks.

"Sure," the woman replied with no hesitation. "I'm off at three. Get your duds together and come on over. You won't be the first woman I sheltered from some drunken bum."

"Now, now, Marcy," said the nurse. "Tomorrow Dr. Hyde comes, remember."

Marcy stood up, took a moment to steady herself, and went over to her locker in the corner of the room. "I'm going to leave at three."

The nurse turned to the cleaning woman and said angrily, "Eldora, I don't want you making trouble. Marcy has to stay and see the doctor."

Mrs. Bennett rose up on one elbow and said to Marcy, "Could you bring me in a steak and french fries for supper?"

Eldora Sparks said to Marcy, "Two years ago, I partitioned off the laundry room and had a room fixed up for my niece when she came to live with me. You can have her room."

"Eldora, just mind your business and leave Marcy alone. She's under doctor's care."

"If you know Claudia's Lunch, you could get it there," said Mrs. Bennett. "Claudia makes up a real nice five-ounce steak and fries for two ninety-five."

"What would you like to drink?" Marcy asked her, feeling once again like the capable caretaker she'd been last week on this floor. Her stomach was no longer queasy and her head was clear. She felt light on her feet.

"Marcy, come to your senses," said Nurse Nathanson. "I can't let you leave till you've seen the doctor."

"A chocolate malted," said Mrs. Bennett.

"Back later," said Eldora Sparks, waving her dustcloth at Marcy as she moved her cart out of the doorway to make room for the breakfast cart.

A young woman came in with a tray and said, "Connor?"

Marcy pointed to her bedside table.

As soon as the tray was set down, Nurse Nathanson lifted the cover off the plate and said, "English muffin and scrambled eggs—yummy."

When the young woman brought Mrs. Bennett's tray in, the nurse examined that plate too. "Yummy," she said. "Fresh fruit and wheat toast."

"Wouldn't feed it to a hog," said Mrs. Bennett.

After breakfast, Marcy got dressed and went off in search of Eldora Sparks, to help her with the dusting.

"Mr. Dash," said Deelane Villars, standing in Victor's office doorway, "the dean's been trying to get you on the phone."

"What's he want?" Victor sat at his desk in his shirtsleeves, the receiver pressed to his chest.

"Wants to give you the dickens, is my guess." Deelane laughed, presenting him with her flirty, sidewise look.

"Tell him I'll be there in a minute. I'm on the phone."

"Better hurry, he's hell on wheels when he's mad." She batted her eyes and sauntered away.

He went back to his phone conversation, his third of the morning with Jack Short in Milwaukee. "Okay, I got it all settled," he told him. "Our lease is up June first, and the semester ends the day before, so I can be on the job the third. What did you find out about salary?"

"Ten thousand."

"Jesus, I'm making almost that here, and I've got summers off."

"That's just to start. It can go up fast if you do the job."

"*If* I do the job. Listen, you're talking to the guy who shut down this entire goddamn campus for three days last week. What do you mean, *if* I do the job?"

"You'll do fine, Victor, I know. You could be up to fifteen in three years."

"Okay, send me the contract and find me a house."

"I can mail you the contract this morning."

"What's my title?"

"Strike organizer."

Music to Victor's ears. He squeezed his eyes shut and popped them open to prove he wasn't dreaming. "Say again, Jack."

"Strike organizer."

"That means no office work, right?"

"Not much. You're mostly out on the road."

"Jack, listen, I gotta warn you." He made his voice low and confidential because the door was standing open. "If you send me that contract and find me a house in Milwaukee that suits Annie, I promise you this—the next time teacher contracts come up for negotiation, the Faculty Alliance of America, Midwest Section, is going to have so goddamn many strikes on its hands, you'll have double your staff of lawyers."

"I like your spirit, Victor, always have."

"I'm talking college professors, high school teachers, grade school teachers—hell, before I'm done we're going to have Catholic sisters walking off their jobs."

Jack Short laughed.

"Now make *me* a promise, Jack." His voice dropped even lower, became more secretive. "When the time is right, promise me—and I'm talking about the not-too-distant future—just promise me that we'll come back and take on the Minnesota State College Board again."

"You bet, Victor."

"Say in two years."

"Let's say four, Victor. Two bienniums."

"But we'll do it, right? That's a promise?"

"You bet, Victor. Your board hasn't heard the last of the Alliance."

"Jesus." He squeezed his eyes tightly shut again, this time to prevent tears of ecstasy from running down his cheeks. Emotion choked off his voice. "Jesus, Jack . . ." he squeaked.

"Victor, you okay?"

"Gotta run, Jack." He got this off before his voice broke, and he hung up. He sat for a minute, limp, his hands hanging down between his knees. Then he got up and went to the window. He looked out at the prickly bush where he'd stood as president of the Alliance and deployed his strikers in their battle for decent salaries, equal pay for women, and professional respect. He felt pangs in his heart, pangs of failure and pangs of hope. What a joy this strike had been. What a disaster. What heroes his picketers had been, every last one of them, marching up and down the street against impossible odds. He'd be back someday, by God, and next time the odds would be reversed. He'd come up from the south, and he wouldn't talk strike in Rookery until he made sure he had Winona, Mankato, and Moorhead in his pocket.

He continued staring out the window at the crowds of students hurrying along the walkways between classes. Across the street in the parking lot, he spotted the rusted oil drum where his heroes had warmed themselves. The sight of it set off fresh pangs of emotion. Some said he'd acted too soon, he'd been stupid to think he could fight the state of Minnesota from this single little campus without the support of the three larger colleges. Bullshit. Rookery had sounded the alarm. Introduced collective bargaining to the egghead community. Made St. Paul sit up and take notice. He imagined returning in two years, or four, and walking into the board office and saying to the new chancellor, whoever he was, and to the six board members, whoever they were, "Hello, my name is Victor Dash," and watching them blanch with fear. God, he couldn't possibly wait four years for that. He'd prevail upon Jack Short to turn him loose the very next biennium.

This prospect elated him so thoroughly that he made up a little song about it, and he tried out a tap-dance routine around his office chair. A pair of students passing his open door—a young man and woman—came to a halt and watched. Being unacquainted with Victor, they thought it curious that this man with a sinister grin on his face should be stomping around his office while singing, "They're going to shit their pants in St. Paul!"

"I wonder if boxing might be the answer," said the principal of
Comstock High School, conferring with Victor's parents for the purpose
of determining the length of his suspension. Victor, a freshman, had at-
tacked a sophomore boy in the schoolyard and punched him nearly
unconscious.

"Boxing?" inquired Victor's mother. *"You mean you condone boxing in your school?"*

"The manly art of self-defense," explained the principal, an athletic
young man recently hired for his reputation as an innovator. *"Boxing
matches in the gym during noon hour. Give boys like Victor a healthy
outlet, and the student body something to amuse them. Keep them from
going downtown and swiping merchandise."*

"It'll also break a few noses," said Victor's father, a farmer whose
nose had once been broken while roughhousing with his son.

*"Not with boxing gloves, Mr. Dash. There's a special eight-ounce
glove for boys. It's like getting hit with a pillow."*

"A healthy outlet is what he's needed all his life," said Mrs. Dash.

"Victor's always been a handful," her husband agreed.

*Since birth, actually. Victor was only a day old when, lying on his
stomach in his hospital bassinet, he'd lifted up his head and uttered a cry
like nothing the doctor on duty had ever heard from a newborn, a howl
so urgent and demanding that it silenced the other babies and brought
nurses running to see if he'd been pricked by a safety pin.*

"You've got a hyperactive baby," the doctor said to Mrs. Dash.
*"You seldom see one strong enough to lift his head off the sheet like that.
You're going to have your hands full for the next fifteen or twenty
years, unless he finds a proper outlet for his energy."*

*Victor's outlets, from the start, were mostly improper. As a barrel-
chested three-year-old, he knocked over lamps, tables, and dozens of
other children his size. In his kindergarten there was an epidemic of
people sitting on tacks. In the primary grades, he bent for the first time
to social pressures, learning not to fill every minute of the schoolday
with loud talk, but he couldn't master sitting still for more than twenty
minutes at a time, and so his teachers allowed him a brief stroll around
the classroom two or three times each period. In the fifth grade, summoned to the principal's office for spitting, he spat on the principal's hot
radiator and watched it sizzle.*

And now most recently, in the schoolyard, he'd taken on this large, lumpish tenth grader named Raymond Sandburg, bloodying his nose, cutting his lip, and leaving him dizzy and limp. Victor came away with nothing but a slight bruise over his eye, and proved, to his satisfaction, that Raymond Sandburg's reputation as a bully was entirely undeserved. Victor was suspended for a week.

By the time he returned to school, boxing had been introduced to Comstock High. The ring was a wrestling mat dragged out to the middle of the gymnasium, and three noon hours a week—Tuesday, Wednesday, and Friday—the student body filled one whole section of bleachers, calling for blood. The principal served as referee. A fight consisted of three rounds of two minutes each, unless a boxer called for mercy before the bell. The bell was a steam pipe which a janitor, serving as timer, hit with a hammer.

Victor, in the ring, was a merciless dervish. He wheeled and danced and shot punches left and right almost faster than the eye could follow them. He quickly became the crowd favorite, boxing at least twice and often three times a week, until he'd beaten all challengers, even upperclassmen much bigger than himself, but without his speed of hand or elusive footwork or fanatical desire to flatten people. One such opponent, the son of a prominent farmer named Hanrahan, he actually knocked unconscious with a right hook to the ear.

The principal was gratified by the effect: Victor lost his interest in schoolyard mayhem, and fewer merchants called up complaining of noon-hour shoplifters. He conveyed this to Victor's parents, who in turn admitted that his idea had proved successful. It had been weeks, they said, since their son last tipped over an outdoor toilet or climbed the village water tower.

Over time, however, it was Victor's skill more than anything else that destroyed the program. He was such an unstoppable fighting machine that his challengers one by one lost heart and quit boxing. As for the cheering section, spring came, and it was more interesting to stroll downtown and steal things once again than it was to watch a fight with a predictable outcome. Furthermore, there was a growing movement among influential parents to ban the sport, indeed to seek the principal's resignation before he could inaugurate any more of his bright ideas. (He'd been talking about a girl's track team, a course in human sexuality, and on-the-job training for boys interested in tractor mechanics.) The parents' movement had started with the Hanrahans, whose son, knocked out, had taken a frightening twenty minutes to come to, and another day and a half to get rid of his headache.

The following September, when Victor set fire to the small tree he'd helped plant the previous Arbor Day, his parents were once again summoned to school, where they found the new principal replaced by a newer one. This man's interest lay not in sports but primarily in the arts, and to the Dashes he looked rather too meek for his job. His idea for the reformation of their son struck them as foolish and hopeless, but of course they went along with it and laid out the money for the phonograph and the drums because they'd tried about everything else to no avail. And it worked like a miracle. What with band instruction in school and his own set of drums and his Gene Krupa records at home, Victor spent the rest of his schooldays beating the mischief out of himself.

Victor's dance around his office chair was interrupted by his ringing phone.

"Dash, this is your dean."

"My dean, ah, yes."

"Dash, C. Mortimer and I need to see you."

"Need to see me, ah, yes." His agreement with Jack Short had elated him to the point of silliness.

"Right away!"

"Right away, ah yes, of course. Come on down. Bring C. Mortimer with you. Bring whoever you want." He felt as if he'd had a shot of laughing gas. "Any friend of my dean is a friend of mine."

"In *my* office, Dash."

"In my dean's office, ah yes—why not?"

His dean hung up.

Victor, humming and snickering, dialed his house. He told Annie to call the dean's office in five minutes and ask for him.

"What's up, Victor? Is it about Milwaukee?"

"You bet."

"You got the job?"

"Give me five minutes, Annie."

"Tell me now."

"If his secretary puts you off, tell her it's urgent."

"Hey, Victor, you got it, didn't you? You sound like you got it."

"Ninety days and we're history here, Annie."

He put on his sport coat and strutted down the hallway, smoothing his mustache.

Deelane Villars, looking entirely incompetent behind Lorraine Kibbee's desk, batted her eyes at him and said, "Go ahead on in."

Neither his dean nor his chairman shook his hand. They were sitting at the small conference table in the inner office, Oberholtzer nervously stoking his pipe, Zastrow indicating by gesture that Victor should sit opposite them.

He chose a leather easy chair instead, which faced them from some distance away. Sinking into it, he said, "Sorry about your dog, Mortimer."

His chairman did not reply. He blew smoke at the ceiling.

"Honest mistake. Your wife said, 'Give his balls a kick,' so that's what I did. Probably do him a world of good in the long run, break him of climbing up on people's legs like that."

"Let me ask you something," said Zastrow, who seemed about to pop all his tight buttons.

"Shoot," said Victor.

The dean, having dealt what he assumed were crippling blows to the Viceroys and a crushing blow to Neil Novotny, was prepared to deliver his knockout punch. He pictured himself relenting little by little as Victor groveled to save his job. He would permit him back next fall, but first he must sign a statement promising never again to foment dissension among the Congress of College Professors. Moreover, he must issue an apology to the faculty, staff, and student body, regretting the trouble he'd caused. Also, he must agree to tutor Deelane Villars in matters of written composition and telephone etiquette. Miss Villars had the habit of answering the phone with, "Dean's office, hi, how ya doin'?" and her spelling was atrocious.

"Dash," said the dean, "who has shit in his own hat now?"

"Ah, that's a good one," said Victor, genuinely amused.

The chairman emitted a little cough, a little chuckle, a little more smoke.

"Dash," the dean continued, "about next year, do you plan—"

Victor raised his finger to silence him, calling his attention to the phone ringing in the outer office. "That could be for me," he said.

"I've told my secretary not to interrupt us."

"It might be urgent," said Victor.

They turned to see Deelane get up from her desk and approach the doorway with her swivel-hips in motion.

"It's your wife, Victor. She says it's urgent."

"I'll take it in here, Deelane." He popped up out of the easy chair and picked up the phone on the dean's desk. "Sorry," he said to the two men, and waited a moment for the call to be transferred.

"We got ninety days to pack and get the hell out of here, Annie. June third I'm on the Alliance payroll in Milwaukee with the title of Strike Organizer. . . . You're goddamn right, Annie, not the first year maybe, but Jack says in two, three years I'll be up to fifteen thousand easy, and all expenses paid. . . . You bet I did, Annie, I told him it had to be a place you liked. Gas range, washer-dryer hookup, window over the kitchen sink, walking distance to a grade school—I went down the whole list with him. . . . Sure, I'll miss the quintet, but that's the beauty of it—I'm going to be on the road a lot, and I'll be back through here every so often and get together and play with them. And then of course next biennium the Alliance'll want me back here to test the waters for another strike."

Glancing at the two men, he was disappointed by the dean's impassive expression. The chairman was pacing away, blowing smoke into a far corner of the office.

"I already did, Annie. I told him I was sorry. . . . Sure, he's no dummy, he knows it was best for the dog in the long run, teach him not to do that to people's legs. . . . Okay, Annie, talk to you later."

He put down the receiver and returned to his chair. "Now what was it you were asking me?" he said.

"Later," said Zastrow, "I've got other business to see to at the moment."

Victor popped out of his chair. "So have I," he said on his way out. "I've got to get started on my letter of resignation."

Eating dinner at a posh restaurant in St. Louis, Lynda Harker (formerly Lydia) and her brother Clark (formerly Alphonse) decide that instead of returning to their family in Pennsylvania, they will accompany her newfound lover Rhett (formerly Randolph) to his ranch in Oregon, where they will become his partners in the raising of horses and beef cattle. Her brother Clark, it turns out, has quite a lot of money to invest in this enterprise. Lynda, it is understood, will become Rhett's wife.

But first there's the problem of this evil Zastrow fellow, who has sneaked into Lynda's room and waits for her there, hidden in the armoire.

Neil, writing this, didn't believe a word of it. He left his Ping-Pong table and went to his bedroom to phone Emerson Tate and convey his misgivings. He asked him why Clark, for example, after

searching far and wide for his sister, would suddenly decide not to
return home with her, but choose to set off on the Oregon Trail
with a stranger.

"Because the book needs more drama," was Tate's reply.

And how likely was it that after days of running barefoot
through the forest, Lynda would be turned out in a fancy dress and
eating dinner in elegant surroundings in St. Louis?

"Have her brother take her out shopping beforehand," said
Tate. "Women like to read about people dressing up."

"Where does all this money of Clark's come from?"

"It's family money."

"But they're a family of poor immigrants."

"Not anymore. Make them rich."

"And another thing, aren't they ever going to look back with
longing at the life they left behind?"

"No, they're not the type. They're brave and forward-looking
young people."

These glib solutions were followed by a lecture on the book's
target audience. Neil's readers would be women between the ages
of seventeen and thirty-five who hankered for excitement and romance and weren't troubled by dubious little details. They read
books like this in order to be distracted from the irksome elements
in their own lives, such as parents and poverty and the urge to look
backward with longing.

"So what do I do with Zastrow in the closet?"

"It's obvious, isn't it? He springs out at her when she comes
back to the room."

"Then what?"

"She's rescued by what's-his-name, the stud she's in love with."

"Rhett."

"Rhett, right. Only not right away."

"What happens in the meantime?"

"They struggle."

"How long?"

"Page and a half, two."

"Then what happens to Zastrow?"

"Dispose of him, at least for now. Maybe he'll turn up later."

"Dispose of him, how?"

"You figure it out—it's your book."

Because a mighty wind was sweeping a drizzling rain across the campus on dedication day, March twenty-first, the ceremony took place not at the site of the new college sign, but some distance away, in the lee of McCall Hall. President Gengler and Dean Zastrow, bundled in coats and scarves, stood side by side on the steps and shared a microphone. Mrs. Gengler stood on the step above the president, holding a black umbrella over his head. The swirling wind snatched their words out of the loudspeaker and shredded them over the meager gathering of about twenty professors and three or four students, all of whom were straining to catch enough syllables to make sense out of what the dean was reading to them.

It was a rundown of the campus improvements. This beautiful new sign made of wrought iron and butternut was merely the first campus improvement, he said, in an ongoing effort to improve this campus to the point where it would be the most improved-upon campus in the state of Minnesota. Here he paused like a politician for applause, but who can clap while holding caps on their heads and umbrellas? He went on, then, to list the facilities to be built or improved upon during the next several bienniums—the dormitories, the science hall, the power plant, the hockey arena— and then he introduced the president, who commented on the nasty weather and recommended that everyone get back indoors and dry off. "Thank you for coming out for this fine . . ." he was heard to mumble as his wife turned him around and steered him through the door. The dean followed them in.

"Damn, they were supposed to mention refreshments," said Peggy under the pink umbrella she shared with Georgina. "Refreshments in the corridor," she called out, backing up the steps. "Come in, everybody—refreshments inside."

Inside, she found Connor waiting for her. "Are you lost?" she asked, rushing up to him and resisting the impulse to touch his face, his young beard stiff as a brush. She read happiness in his smile. She hadn't seen him in fifteen days.

"Can we talk?" he asked.

"Wait till I uncover the cookies."

She fussed over the refreshment table for a minute, then invited the small crowd forward to help themselves. She beckoned to Connor to join them.

"Could we go up to your office?" he asked.

"Sorry, I promised Mrs. Gengler I'd keep my eye on her crystal and silverware." She didn't want to be alone with him just now. If he was here to call off their affair forever, she wanted to hear about it in a crowd. She'd save her emotions till later, alone.

Georgina came between them for a minute, expressing her disappointment at Connor's plan to leave Rookery. "I'd been imagining the portrait you'd do of me and my daughter when I have one."

"I didn't know you wanted children," said Peggy.

"Ron and I have decided a boy and a girl would be nice."

"What if you don't get one of each?"

"Oh, we will—Ron's very systematic." Leaving them, Georgina gave Peggy a squeeze and said, in her ear, "Good luck," for she knew what this rare appearance of Connor's in McCall Hall was all about. *When are you going to start dating healthy men?* she'd asked Peggy the other day. *I know I risk offending you, but I have to say you get hung up on the weirdest specimens.* Peggy hadn't been offended. She'd been telling Georgina about the nude photo taken by Gene Benoit and lost by Connor during his binge at Culpepper's. *Gene was weird, I'll grant you,* Peggy had replied, *but Connor's a wonderful man.*

So wonderful, in fact, that he'd been breaking her heart by pulling away. Georgina knew that these two weeks apart had been his idea. A moratorium, he called it, while he figured out where his duty lay.

"Well?" said Peggy, her eyes not on Connor, but on Georgina climbing the stairs.

"It's over," he said. "For now."

"It's over? Then why are you smiling?"

"I'm not."

"You were."

"It's a disguise. I feel like hell. Let's talk somewhere else."

"Let's talk here. Is she moving back home?"

"No, it's not about Marcy. It's about Laura."

"Laura hates me."

"Not 'hates,' Peggy. 'Envies' maybe, not 'hates.' "

"She hates me."

"She needs time to get used to us."

They stood side by side in the corridor, each of them holding a cup of strawberry punch and looking blankly at the refreshment table. They might have been two academics discussing a dissertation.

"Get used to us? Are you saying it's *not* over?"

"Well, I can't expect you to wait, but I love you, and—"

"You're right, no woman in her right mind would wait."

"Ideally, we would go our own directions for a while, and then . . ."

"What's ideal about going our own directions?"

"I mean just for a while."

"How long?"

Here he stalled.

"How long?" she asked again.

"Two years."

There was a hitch in her breathing. "Jesus," she sighed.

"Until Laura's out of high school."

A woman's voice interrupted them—"Dr. Benoit, aren't you feeling well?" It was Mrs. Gengler standing at her side nibbling a cookie on a napkin. "You look pale."

"Just chilly from the rain, Mrs. Gengler."

"Take care of yourself, there's flu going around."

"I will."

"I understand you're leaving us, Mr. Connor."

"Yes, going back to Cass College."

"You're too good for Rookery."

He thought at first that she was being sarcastic, but she looked sincere, and added, "You'll be missed. Herbert and I saw the Steadman portrait and we think you're very accomplished."

"Well, thank you."

"I suspect Dr. Benoit will be gone too, before long. And so will Herbert, thank God. He has one more year until he retires, then we can put this outpost behind us. Come over here, if you would, Mr. Connor, I'd like Herbert to meet you."

She took Connor away then, reminding Peggy, "Take care of yourself, there's flu going around."

He devoted five minutes to the president, listening impatiently to his description of various vacation spots in Florida, and when he turned back to Peggy, she was gone.

Eldora Sparks had a car too small to carry much, so it was three weeks before Marcy got all her clothes and bedding moved, along with the few other things she didn't want Connor to have, such as the good china that they'd received as a wedding gift from her parents.

Connor, respecting Marcy's determination to live with her newfound friend—indeed, seeing how invigorated she'd become since meeting her—offered to move her belongings in the station wagon, but Marcy said no, she had to do it herself, for the sake of her self-respect. She said this on the first Saturday in April as she and Eldora were lugging the pasteboard wardrobe she'd bought from Sears out the front door.

Connor was puzzled. "How would my help damage your self-respect?" he asked.

Eldora answered for her. "She needs to do a few things for herself in life."

"But *you're* helping her."

"That's different," said Eldora and Marcy together.

Watching them tie the wardrobe on top of the car with ropes through the windows, he thought how lucky he was that Laura hadn't abandoned him. True, Laura did occasionally spend a night with her mother in town, sleeping on Eldora's couch, and he couldn't very well object to that. She'd done it, she said, in order to take part in the drama program at school and to avoid the tedious bus ride in the morning. He'd stopped seeing Peggy at Laura's request. He thought he understood her dislike of Peggy. Didn't a child have the right to expect her father to be morally upright? Of course. Did a father in turn have the right to expect his child to reject her mother entirely in favor of him? Of course not.

Marcy and Eldora tied their knots awkwardly tight, and then

Marcy went back inside for a few things in the kitchen. Eldora came and stood beside Connor on the stoop, facing the highway and the pasture beyond. The sun was warm and intoxicating. This was the first day of the year for going outdoors in shirtsleeves.

"Will you call me if she acts suicidal again?"

"She won't be suicidal," said Eldora decisively. "Not with you out of the picture."

He couldn't help chuckling a little. He found it impossible to dislike this large, brusque, humorless woman, despite her man-hating remarks. This was the fourth time she'd brought Marcy home for a load of belongings, and she called up in him a kind of grudging respect. She was vigorous, straightforward, and fluent on the subject of marriages gone bad. Her case-hardened opinions were shocking, certainly, but delivered in a voice so flat and unruffled that she might have been reading them off a page. He could see why his wife liked her. On her first visit, she'd introduced herself by saying, "Hello, Mr. Connor, I'm your wife's new landlady. I'll shake your hand because you haven't done anything to hurt me yet." She'd said this without a trace of guile.

"Take a good look at your little woman," she said now, shading her eyes against the sun and squinting out across the pasture. "You won't be seeing much of her anymore. She's fed up, and there's no way she'll ever come back and live with you again. It's like me when I got my dander up over Bushman—I was about ready to knock in his skull with a hammer, I was that worked up, but then I thought, hell, there's an easier way out of this—I'll just pack up and leave and never come back. Lucky for Bushman. Not that this little sweetie of yours is the type to ever take after you with a deadly weapon."

"Lucky for me, I suppose."

"Sure, lucky for you, but not for her. What I mean, she'd be better off if she could've blew up a few times before she got to hating you so. She could've died of those pills, you know."

"Yes, I realize that. That's why I'm asking you to watch her and not—"

"But that's water over the dam. She's not going to try that silly stunt again."

"How can we be sure of that?"

"Because she's finally got somebody to listen to her. Why, last night we were sitting there with the TV on and I don't think we saw five minutes of it, she was carrying on so about you." Eldora took her squint off the land across the highway and directed it squarely at him. "I mean, two straight hours of hate. It was really something to hear."

"How could you stand it?" he asked.

"It was music to my ears, Mr. Connor."

Marcy came out carrying her overshoes and a bag of food from the refrigator. She said, "I think that's everything." They got into the car. Eldora started the engine.

Connor felt nothing, neither regret nor relief, until Laura dashed out of the house and squeezed into the backseat. He watched the car rumble off down the highway, feeling severely betrayed.

Concertgoers, leaving their cars and strolling across campus, stopped and said, "Listen. A robin." They scanned the bare branches overhead, but were unable to see the bird singing its broken song of good-night. They went on at a slower pace then, savoring the warm air, gazing at the faint coppery light dying in the western sky, pointing out the earliest stars lighting up over the river. They carried word into the auditorium that a robin had been heard in Rookery.

"Ah, how wonderful," said those already seated. "How lovely." Another month would pass before the first tree put forth its first leaf, and no lawn had yet sprouted a green spear of grass, but the robin's song erased all doubt that the seasons were still arranged in their correct order. Summer would come again.

"We heard a robin," said Leland, following his mother and Peggy's mother into a row near the front, where the Oberholtzers were seated with the Genglers.

"A robin, well, well, that *is* good news," said Mortimer.

Honey, his wrenlike wife, nodded her head and smiled.

The imperious Mrs. Gengler, seated next to Honey, appeared unmoved.

"Much later than last year," said President Gengler. "Last year we had a robin in our yard the first week in March, didn't we, Justine?"

"I have no idea," she said with disdain. Not being a native of the North, Mrs. Gengler had not, like her neighbors, spent the last several weeks going around with her ear cocked for the return of this bird.

"This is Mrs. Martin, Peggy Benoit's mother," said Lolly, lowering herself into a seat and presenting her houseguest, a wrinkled, white-haired woman wearing an expensive moss-green coat over a suit of gray flannel. Introductions were awkward, given the seating arrangement, the Genglers and Oberholtzers leaning forward to smile down the row and say how pleased they were to meet her, and Mrs. Martin attempting to shake the only hand within reach, President Gengler's, and finding it wrapped in gauze.

Senator Steadman, from the row behind, said there had been robins in St. Paul already three weeks ago.

"This is Harry Steadman," said Lolly. "Harry is our state senator."

Mrs. Martin, twisting arthritically around in her seat to look at him, appeared duly impressed.

"And his wife Veronica."

The elderly visitor turned farther in her seat and said, "How do you do," to a ruddy-faced woman with high-piled red hair.

"Mrs. Martin has come all the way from Boston for her daughter's concert," Lolly proclaimed in her public voice to a large section of the audience. "Leland and I invited her to stay with us because Peggy's apartment is so awfully tiny. From here she's going to Wyoming to visit another daughter, who lives on a ranch."

"Wyoming is so pretty," said Mrs. Steadman, who'd never been there.

"Do you think so?" said Peggy's mother. "I was out there a few years ago, and it struck me as awfully barren."

"Depends what part of the state you're talking about," said the senator diplomatically.

"Near Laramie is where my daughter lives."

The subject of Wyoming was dropped, and Mrs. Steadman

opened another, asking Lolly if Victor and Annie Dash were in attendance. Because of the strike, she'd heard a great deal about the Dashes and wanted to see what they looked like.

Leland looked around, searching the audience, knowing he wouldn't see them. Except for his duties in the classroom, Victor had divorced himself from Rookery State.

"Mr. Dash is the most horrible sort of person," pronounced Honey Oberholtzer, recalling Victor's savage kick to the underside of her dog. "We're all very happy he's resigning."

Lolly chortled quietly, recalling the same thing. "Annie Dash is such a sweetheart," she said. "Whenever you see her with her three little ones, you can just tell she's full of the milk of human kindness."

"*Macbeth,*" called out Mortimer—a professorial reflex.

President Gengler adjusted his heavy glasses on his scaly nose and said, "Did you know Dash has a steel plate in his head? Up close you can see the spot."

"What about the clarinetist—is he here?" asked Mrs. Steadman of Lolly. Since the quintet's appearance last month on Lolly's radio show, learning to identify musicians had become something of a citywide game or contest.

"Novotny's the name," Lolly told her. "Is Neil here, Leland?"

Her son scanned the audience. "I don't see him."

"I've taken over Mr. Novotny's classes, you know, and I've made the most devastating discovery," said Honey. "He promised every student an A! Well, you can imagine the awkward position that leaves me in. I wouldn't think of giving everyone an A, but I've decided not to tell them until the end of the course, otherwise I'd have a revolt on my hands."

"He's working night and day to finish his novel," said Lolly, whose opinion of Neil had softened since he was so abruptly dismissed from the faculty. "It's a love story that could make him famous."

"We're not surprised he's not here, are we, Mortimer?" Honey was showing everyone her sourest face. Not only was she rankled by the A he'd promised, she was still wounded by his blowup in McCall Hall—the awful things he'd said about her husband and her violets. "Anybody that inept in the classroom has to be ashamed to show his face on campus."

Mortimer's response was a smile, a shrug, and a mumble. His wound had healed.

"How about the artist?" asked the senator humorously. "Suppose he's sober enough to make it?"

Leland half turned and gestured for silence, his finger to his lips. "He's two rows behind you."

The senator glanced around for a glimpse of the bearded man who'd done the high-priced portrait of his daughter and granddaughter.

Mrs. Steadman thrust her head farther forward, between Honey's and Lolly's, and confided that she'd removed the portrait from over the mantel and hung it in the family room in the basement. "It was just too bold for the living room. You couldn't look at it day after day."

"I'd give anything to have a painting of Connor's in *my* living room," said Lolly. "Bolder the better, is my belief."

"Not if you had to look at it day after day," insisted Mrs. Steadman, while giving Honey a secret little nudge on the shoulder. She and Honey, among many others, were troubled by Lolly's change of attitude, her general air of mindless goodwill, her espousing exotic causes and people until you had to wonder about her sanity. Like most of Rookery, the Steadmans and the Oberholtzers had been severely scandalized the day Lolly came out in favor of the Alliance, announcing over the air her willingness to join the strikers on the picket line. Luckily, the strike ended before she embarrassed her son and herself by actually going out and *doing* it, but she continued to harp on the salary issue and the women's equality issue until you were sick of it.

"Oh, there's Neil coming in now," said Lolly excitedly. She had turned to face the back of the hall.

Another nudge and a knowing glance between her two friends. They thought it very tiresome the way she kept extolling these chums of Leland's as though they were God's gift to higher education when in fact one was a drunk, another was a foulmouthed rabble-rouser, a third had been fired midterm for insubordination, and the woman among them had the instincts of a whore—going to bed with the drunk and having her picture taken without any clothes on. Any number of men had studied the photograph before it disappeared, and told their wives and friends about it. As for her affair with the artist, this had been verified by Ron Hunsinger's fiancée, who despite having two strikes against her as a citizen of Rookery—she was a non-native and a professor besides—was proving to be a trustworthy source of gossip.

Silence fell over the house as the choir filed out from the wings and took their places on risers. President Gengler sat forward in his seat and lifted the tail of his suit coat. "Justine," he said softly, and his wife reached up under the coat and scratched.

There was applause as Dr. Benoit, the fallen woman, followed her choir onstage looking the picture of virtue in her plain, off-white, ankle-length dress with a deep blue scarf at her throat, her black hair cut in a prim pageboy, and her small blue earrings sparkling brightly when they caught the light. Honey and Mrs. Steadman clapped in spite of themselves, for even if you were repelled by the affair and the naked picture, you had to admit that this was perhaps the most beautiful woman ever to grace this stage, and you could sense, even without knowing much about music, even before they opened their mouths, that she was doing miraculous things with the choir. Under their previous director, a likable but undemanding old contralto named Olga Hatfield, the choir never looked so well scrubbed and spiffy as they did tonight, the young men in tuxedos and the young women in black velvet dresses.

Nor had they ever performed with such discipline. All voices began a section of Handel's *Israel in Egypt* precisely on the downbeat, wove their way flawlessly though its harmonies, and came out together at the end. The applause was warm and long. Peggy bowed demurely and then announced a change in the program because one of her soloists was down with the flu. Instead of songs from *The Sound of Music*, they would perform a medley by Jerome Kern.

Listening to "Where and When," Leland thought it a wonder that these same youngsters who came to class in ragged clothes and long hair and flaunted so abrasively their clumsily held opinions should appear tonight so neat and self-possessed, should be so eagerly obedient to their director's every signal, be capable of producing such beautiful sounds. At their winter concert they'd been good, but not this good. Peggy was obviously a marvelous director. How curious, he thought, the way some professors toiled away year after year without making much of a reputation for themselves, while others were branded good or bad from the start. Leland himself was one of the former. Twelve forgettable years in the classroom without inspiring much fondness or dislike for either himself or his subject matter. Well, thank God he hadn't earned an out-and-out bad reputation, like Neil's. You knew from the start Neil would never be a teacher. Neil had decided to move to St. Paul and devote himself full-time to writing. Peggy, on the other hand, had the teacher's gift. If tonight's concert ended this very minute, before intermission, her reputation would be made.

As a professor, that is. Her private life, Leland knew, was not what it should be. Did she and Connor have any idea what a scandal they were causing? Two months and Connor would be gone—maybe that would take care of it. Peggy was staying on. Just this past week, before the April first deadline, she'd signed her contract, saying publicly that she owed the music program at least one more year, while confiding to the quintet that nothing had opened up in New England.

What a blessing—her staying on. With three-fifths of the quintet leaving town, what would he do if Peggy went too? "Don't worry, Leland," she'd assured him. "From now on it's the Icejam Duo." This was in reference to Georgina Gold's wedding reception, where they'd been asked to provide the music, as well as the two dates next fall Lolly had booked for them in the dining room of the Van Buren Hotel. Peggy hadn't been enthusiastic about playing the Van Buren. She'd been of the mistaken notion that it was a fleabag. But then Lolly took her on a tour of the place, showing her the exquisite restoration of the lobby, lounge, and dining room, and describing the plans for restoring the facade. Peggy was won over, and Leland was relieved beyond words. He prayed that next year's crop of newcomers would include another musician or two, so that he and Peggy could rebuild.

———

Next on the program was something very old, sung with deep feeling in a language Neil didn't understand—Latin or Norwegian, he guessed. Neil was leaning against the doorpost at the back of the auditorium engulfed in his parka. He was hot, but couldn't very well open the zipper and reveal nothing underneath but a dirty undershirt. He'd refused the offer of a seat because he intended to dash home to his novel after a couple of numbers, his head being full of erotic encounters between Lynda and Rhett.

In their latest editorial phone call, Emerson Tate had prescribed more intensity in the love scenes, and Neil discovered he had a talent along those lines. He had his two lovers copulating day and night, on riverboats, in hotels, and in a covered wagon on the Oregon Trail. He found that writing about sex produced a kind of literary tumescence that minimized the rest of the story. The death of Lynda's brother, for example, was related in one short paragraph. "Better get rid of the brother, he's getting too interesting," Tate had advised, and so Neil had him die in a dark alley, defending his sister against Zastrow. Zastrow died too, in the same encounter, but Tate insisted he be brought back to life in order to follow Lynda out west. "Think about it, Neil—Rhett has to be the one who kills Zastrow. How can Rhett be the hero if you don't make him more heroic than her brother?" Tate was blessed with this incisive kind of artistic vision, and Neil was flattered that so much of it should be directed his way.

"*Gadiamus igitur,*" sang the choir, and Neil wondered if Peggy would someday regret his leaving town, would regret that she never truly warmed up to him, regret not marrying him. He imagined her someday pursuing him to St. Paul, where he planned to find a room near T. Woodman Press and keep turning out novels until he won so many literary awards that McGraw-Hill or Simon & Schuster lured him to New York. She'd come to him then, and admit her foolishness in falling for Connor. She'd confess that as soon as Connor left Rookery, she saw the light, saw that Neil was her ticket back to the East Coast, saw how proud she could be as the wife of a distinguished novelist. But she'd better make it quick if she hoped to find him still in St. Paul. His career was about to blast off.

———

Despite Connor's attempts to avoid them during intermission, the Steadmans and the Oberholtzers caught up with him in the lobby and commented on the music, the weather, the robin. His celebrity was such—both as painter and adulterer—that they experienced a kind of dangerous thrill in talking to him, or rather, in being *seen* talking to him. He politely answered their questions about his plans for next year. Yes, he expected to move in the early summer, his family wanting to settle again in the city as soon as possible. He didn't tell them that this was Laura's desire alone, no longer his wife's. Yes, his wife was much better, her illness greatly alleviated, thanks to the specialist who came to town on Tuesdays. Thanks to Eldora Sparks, was the truth he held back. No, he had no intention of buying a house in the city, unless something irresistible turned up at the ridiculously low price he could afford. Unless Marcy joined him in the city—that was unspoken as well.

Marcy appeared to be permanently estranged from him. "Home is where you're comfortable," she'd told him, "and my home is with Eldora." So be it, and damn his bad luck. He wouldn't miss the Marcy she'd been for the past eight or ten months, but he'd sure as hell miss the woman he'd originally married. Apart from companionship, he was bound to need a woman's help in steering their headstrong daughter through her adolescence. Laura was dividing her life about equally between three houses—Eldora's, Connor's, and Lolly's.

Having gathered up his few morsels of information, the Oberholtzers and Steadmans moved on, fanning out through the tightly packed lobby to relate them to their many friends, to point Connor out to those who didn't know who he was, to pair him with the pretty choir director in the minds of those who hadn't yet heard about the affair.

Connor stood listening to the chatter around him, hoping to hear praise for Peggy, but heard instead more about the robin, the weather, and a couple of inane jokes. Then suddenly Neil was standing beside him, relaying greetings from Emerson Tate.

"He says you're driving down to the Cities next month."

"Right," said Connor. "I've got to find an apartment."

"He says for an opening night."

"Or afternoon." Cass College was making a big thing of his return, honoring him in May with an exhibit and reception. There
would be wine and snacks in the college gallery, and his old colleagues would doubtless be amazed by his abstinence. There would
be handshakes and polite conversation and talk of many new commissions, a few of which would actually come to fruition. There
would be students he remembered from last year and students
whose names he'd forgotten. He dreaded it like the plague. He'd
never before endured an opening without getting as high as he
could as quickly as possible. His old friends at Cass, heavy drinkers
to a man, would be made very awkward by his sobriety, and so
would he.

The old friends he *truly* looked forward to seeing were the
eight or ten drawings and oils the college owned, along with perhaps twice that number of oils gathered from private collections
around the city. He'd been sent a list. Picturing them in his mind,
he had his doubts about two or three, but most of the work, particularly the six mother-daughters he did before leaving Cass, he'd
surely be pleased to see again.

"The family going down with you?" asked Neil.

"Just Laura, as far as I know."

"How long you staying?"

"Overnight."

"Mind if I hook a ride with you? Tate wants me to meet with
the T. Woodman board of directors."

"Not at all."

"They've been reading my early drafts piecemeal. By that time
I'll be able to deliver the whole thing revised."

"Congratulations."

Neil looked away then, because Connor, despite his congratulations, was studying him with a suspicious look in his eye.

"Tell me, Neil, why do you have to meet with Tate's editorial
board?"

"They want to welcome me into their stable of writers." Neil
glanced at Connor, and added, "Tate says."

Connor appeared to chew this over, extracting something

distasteful from it. "You're not submitting your book for their approval?"

Neil laughed nervously and said, "No, I already have Tate's approval. What the hell are you getting at?"

"Just that I've never been sure how influential our friend Emerson is in their eyes. I mean I'd hate to see you trying to please all those board members, and come home with all kinds of suggestions on how to improve your book."

"No worry there," he replied, wondering if he should worry.

"I know when I did some work for them a couple of years ago, gratis at that, the board picked over each illustration real petty-like until I threatened to withdraw the whole lot."

"Can't happen. They're paying me. I've already signed the contract."

"Have *they* signed it?"

"They will. Tate promised."

Connor shrugged as if to say, *Okay if you're satisfied . . .*

"I've got to get back to work." Neil pulled the hood of his parka forward and down to his eyebrows and tied the drawstring tightly under his chin. "See you later."

"Neil, it's warm out."

"Oh, yeah, I forgot." He untied the string. "Nice concert."

"The best," Connor agreed.

Talk about petty, thought Neil, stepping out into the spring evening, Connor's turning into a real fussbudget.

At the other end of the lobby Leland overheard interesting conversations about Peggy, about the quintet, about the left turn in his mother's thinking, and about Connor. He heard the quintet defiled for playing new music, and for playing out-of-date music, and he also heard it praised for the same reasons. He heard that Marcy Connor had gone crazy and left her husband, having fallen under the spell of a harridan named Eldora Sparks, and he heard, conversely, that Connor had driven her crazy and into the comforting arms of the kindly Eldora Sparks.

About Peggy, the topic was primarily the outrageous cost of the tuxedos and black velvet dresses, which she had asked her choir members to buy or rent for the concert. Ron Hunsinger raised his voice to remind his circle of listeners that dozens of perfectly good choir robes were hanging forgotten in a closet somewhere in the music department. They were blue and white, the school colors, and made of a shiny material guaranteed not to fray or come apart at the seams for fifteen years, and if they were good enough for Olga Hatfield, why in God's name weren't they good enough for Peggy Benoit?

It was Lolly Edwards who came to Peggy's defense, laughingly telling Ron that Olga Hatfield had had no taste.

"She sang grand opera," said Ron, as though this made her unassailable.

"Listen, Olga Hatfield might have been an opera singer, but she had no style, and by the time she took up teaching, her voice was shot." Lolly then turned to Peggy's mother and explained that her daughter's predecessor was not only a hopeless director, but she used to devote part of every choir concert to a solo of her own, and her voice was like a rusty radiator. She laughed, turning to her son for corroboration. "Didn't she, Leland?"

"She did."

"Remember how shot her pipes sounded?"

"I do."

"So, you see, it's no wonder Peggy's job is so demanding," Lolly broadcast to the crowd. "Peggy's had to build this choir from the ground up."

"That's still no reason to spend money on tuxedos," said Ron. He turned to his fiancée for support. "Is it, Georgina?"

"No reason at all," said Georgina, looking bored.

"Remember how great they looked in those robes, Georgina, all blue and white?"

Here she deserted him. "I thought they looked pretty tacky."

"Tacky!" His eyes flashed with anger.

"Tacky isn't the word," said Lolly, hugging Georgina's upper arm in gratitude as the lights dimmed in the lobby.

Riding to Minneapolis in Connor's station wagon, Neil fed his manuscript, chapter by chapter, to Laura in the backseat. Dressed for her father's exhibit, and hoping to impress her girlfriends, she wore her best outfit, a yellow print dress with white stockings and sandals.

"What do you think?" asked Neil each time they exchanged a sheaf of pages.

"Super," she said. Separating the chapters were pages of letterhead stationery from Grandpa's Fruit Basket. She asked Neil to autograph one of these pages, which he did, and she carefully folded it and slipped it into her purse.

A quick and avid reader, she finished the entire book in less than three hours and pronounced it "super" in its entirety. Neil, stashing it back into its Red Owl grocery sack, pressed her for a more considered judgment. "What did you like best about it?"

She smiled an inward sort of smile, imagining Gary Oberholtzer's response—if Gary could read. The humping, Gary would say.

"Did you like Lynda okay?" Neil prompted.

"Sure."

"How about the fight at the end—were you excited?"

"Sure."

"How about before the end, though—did the plot keep your interest?"

"Hey, what can I say? It was super."

They arrived in the city at noon. Neil was taken in hand by Emerson Tate, who drove him to a refurbished warehouse in St. Paul, where they rode a freight elevator to the third floor, followed a twisting hallway of exposed Sheetrock, and came to a door labeled T. WOODMAN PRESS INC. Entering a cluttered, chilly room, they found two men sitting at a table ignoring a ringing telephone on a nearby desk. The men had their overcoats on. One of them, a very old man with a freckled face and a shrewd look in his eye, stood up and gave Neil a solemn handshake. He said his name was Truehart and apologized for the lack of heat, explaining that this building's heating season had ended on the first of May and today was unseasonably cold. The other man, younger but afflicted with some sort of spine-bending deformity, remained seated and invited Neil to sit beside him. This man's name was Lenzen. He asked Neil about the weather in the North—had it actually been snowing in Rookery this morning, as the radio claimed?

Neil tried, without success, to remember. "No," he said, guessing. "Only a little rain." He resolved then and there to be a more observant person. His novel finished, he could now afford to notice things. He looked out through the room's only window, which was nearly opaque with grime, and saw whitecaps on the Mississippi. He looked about the room and saw dozens of cardboard boxes of a uniform size stacked along the walls, presumably containing books. He noticed that Lenzen and Truehart were wearing dark suits and silk neckties, while Tate had on the same drab corduroy suit he'd worn to Rookery, and over it the same threadbare black raincoat. He then looked down to see what he himself had on under his parka. Sweatshirt and jeans, he discovered.

Lenzen, as chairman of the board, opened the meeting by apologizing to Neil for the absence of two of its members, one of whom was home with a broken collarbone. The other, he said, was dead.

"Oh, I'm sorry," said Neil. "What did he die of?"

Heart disease was Lenzen's guess. Truehart said cancer. Tate spoke up and said no, it was something other than heart disease or cancer, but he couldn't recall what. By inquiring further, Neil learned that the man in question, a member of the Woodman family, had died two or five or seven months earlier and never been replaced on the board because the Woodmans were distancing themselves from this publishing enterprise.

"That's where writers like you come in," said Tate heartily. "Our plan is to replace the Woodmans and their financial support with our new line of fiction. 'An Emerson Tate Novel,' it will say across the top of each dust jacket."

Neil, seeing the dust jacket in his mind—indeed, imagining himself the savior of the firm—did his best to look modest as he drew his completed manuscript out of its paper bag and set it on the table. He nudged it toward Lenzen, causing the deformed man to lose his smile and replace it with a worried frown. Truehart looked askance.

What followed was a tactful discussion meant to convey the board's misgivings about the chapters they'd read so far. "A formulaic book," said Lenzen, by which he meant predictable. "Full of words," admitted Tate, by which he meant it was stilted from beginning to end. He added, however, that most problems along this line were easily fixed by a good editing job. "Gamy" was the old man's opinion, by which he meant pornographic.

Neil lowered his eyes and smiled, humbly absorbing what he took to be praise. Carried away by his vision of literary success, and woozy from a series of sleepless nights devoted to the final chapters, he scarcely heard the rest of the discussion, which grew steadily more pointed and antagonistic and led finally to an outright skirmish in which Tate had to marshal his best arguments against his fellow directors, had to defeat Lenzen's stuffy reluctance to publish popular fiction, while at the same time he had to fight a rearguard action against Truehart's old-fashioned aversion to gaminess. The battle raged on with Neil sitting there staring out through the grimy window and blissfully imagining jacket blurbs. He settled on "A gamy, formulaic book full of words" as the most fetching.

When at length he heard his name spoken and found Lenzen sliding a copy of the contract toward him across the table, finalized with Lenzen's signature as well as Truehart's (and the advance adjusted only slightly downward: six hundred dollars instead of eight), he was unaware of the heroics Tate had performed on his behalf, unaware of how close he'd come to losing his publisher.

He asked the directors to recommend a neighborhood where he might find a nice but inexpensive apartment. They spoke exotic names, Crocus Hill and Frogtown, and Tate said he'd drive him through those areas after lunch. Neil stood up then, and shook hands with the freckled man and the deformed man and allowed himself to be steered dreamily out of the building and down the street to the car.

Tate started the engine, but before driving off he opened his briefcase and took a nip from his flask. "Congratulations, Cornelia," he said, "we're in business."

"What?" Neil had momentarily forgotten his pen name.

"Cornelia Niven."

"Oh, yeah."

"Congratulations."

"Well, what can I say?" Neil replied, quoting Laura Connor. "It's a super book."

Tate chuckled and offered him a swig, but he declined. The bottle was put away, and they drove off to have lunch and look at apartments.

By the time they arrived at the college gallery, a long, thickly carpeted room with padded benches down the middle and "The Blue Danube" playing softly from a hidden speaker, they found Connor alone among his paintings.

"Where is everybody?" asked Tate, shedding his black raincoat and heading for the refreshment table, where the wine bottles were mostly empty. "Where are all the VIPs?"

"Been and gone," said Connor, his voice sounding flat and far-away because it was that ambiguous and difficult hour of the late afternoon and he was fighting off his thirst by meditating deeply on his work. He was studying the wife and teenage daughter of Lawrence Flory, president of Cass College. The portrait was darker than he remembered it, the faces more chiseled and pol-ished, but quite successful overall, due in large part to the interest-ing sidewise glance of the daughter as her mother gazed straight out at the viewer. *What's going on in Mother's head?* the girl seemed to be wondering. *Countless preoccupations, but none to do with you,* ap-peared to be the answer. This was how Connor read their relation-ship a year ago when he painted it, and read it again today when they accompanied President Flory to the reception, the young Miss Flory trailing behind her parents, studying their every move, the parents meanwhile paying her no attention.

Tate read the label on a half-empty wine bottle. "A good turnout?" he asked.

"Big crowd."

Neil, removing his parka, saw the evidence of this in the guest book. He added his name, and in the space for comments, he wrote *Super.*

Connor moved on to a work commissioned by Eva Czarnecki, the good-humored proprietor of the neighborhood grocery near the Connors' former apartment. Eva, at fifty, was the daughter in this portrait. At her side, nearly cheek-to-cheek, was her eighty-year-old mother, a woman so well preserved they might have been of the same generation. Both of them shared the same round, Slavic face, the same bemused smile full of teeth; indeed, they seemed to be entertaining the same passing thought. Their hair, white and black, was the single marked difference between them. Being very proud of the portrait, Eva kept it on display in the store. Connor had seen it there, above the spices, jellies, and coffees.

A quartet of chattering college students entered the gallery and signed the guest book as Emerson Tate sidled up to Connor with two glasses of wine. "No hard liquor, but this isn't bad. Here, try it."

"No thanks, Em."

"You'd rather I went and got my briefcase?"

"No, I'm not drinking."

"Oh come *on*." Tate's face turned ugly with the expression of someone whose worst fears are confirmed. He stalked away and offered a glass to Neil, who quickly drank it down.

Next to the Czarneckis hung the Ashby portrait, which Connor had brought down today in his station wagon. The ornate gilt frame he'd chosen enhanced Mrs. Ashby's aristocratic demeanor, made her even more imposing and protective than before, made the child beside her utterly inaccessible. He hoped this piece might find a buyer before the exhibit ended—the Rookery hospital was pressing him to pay up. He considered it one of the two best paintings in the room, and he'd expected it to arouse more interest this afternoon than it did. No one had paused very long to study it.

"Here, allow me," said Tate, pleased to see the four students heading for the wine table, and he rushed over to pour out glasses for them. They were three young men and a young woman. They made a long ceremony of tasting and approving, before turning their attention to what hung on the walls. They moved up and down the room, at first murmuring self-conscious judgments to one another, and then eventually relaxing as one of them tried out funny remarks. This comedian was a very short young man, scarcely five feet tall. From his deep chest he produced an extremely resonant voice. "Small, but I like it," he said, pointing to the thermostat on the wall, and his companions doubled over with laughter.

"Jesus, look at this, would you," said another of the young

men, a lanky Native American wearing a long suede coat. He had replaced Connor in front of the Ashby portrait.

"Hey, sick!" exclaimed the young woman. She appeared to be the most sophisticated of the group. Her mismatched clothes—a fur jacket and cowboy boots—looked expensive.

"Jesus," the comedian echoed, his comedy deserting him before the Ashbys. The fourth visitor, a frail young man, brought his long woolly scarf up to his face, shuddered, and turned away.

Connor was intrigued to witness Mrs. Ashby's powerful effect on this foursome of innocents. Small wonder the power-and-light tycoon was repelled. Who would want to admit this fearsome face was the one you'd married?

"Hey, how about this?" said the lanky one, moving along to the next canvas. "A movie star."

"Hey, wow," said the scarf.

"Those eyes," said the young woman, smiling and nodding her approval of Peggy.

"Why's she with that old bag?" asked the comic. He reached up and was about to cover Mrs. Martin's face when the young woman snatched his hand away.

"That's her mother, you jerk," she scolded. "These are all mothers and daughters along here."

"How do you know?"

"It says in the program." She lowered her voice, but not too low for Connor to hear. "And that's the artist himself standing over there."

The men were silenced by this information. Between glances at Connor, they scanned all the double portraits, looking for family resemblances, while the young woman remained in front of Peggy, responding to Peggy's smile with a dreamy smile of her own.

Connor stepped up beside her, in order to see Peggy freshly through the young woman's eyes. Though sketchier than his other portraits, this one he considered his strongest work to date. Because Peggy's mother was eager to leave Rookery, she'd given him only one sitting. He'd intended to invite Peggy back for a second and perhaps a third sitting, but then sensed the risk in adding any more detail.

It was the wonderfully mysterious depth of Peggy's eyes that anchored the painting to the canvas. The background was rough, the faces were incomplete, and the source of light was confusing, and yet there was no mistaking the message. It gave a disturbingly evanescent quality to Peggy's beauty, and to her mother, and to the entire concept of a parent's bond with her child. Peggy, coming into her prime, was looking intently off the left-hand side of the canvas, engrossed in what lay ahead. Her mother, whose wrinkles seemed to be multiplying as you watched, was looking right, at her past, and not entirely pleased with what she was seeing. It was a painting in progress, two lives in progress.

Neil came up and stood beside him. "Say, Connor, I never knew you did Peggy and her mother."

"The day after the concert."

"Never had time to finish it, huh?"

"It's finished."

"It is?"

"Of course it is," blurted the young woman in the fur jacket and boots. "What more could he add?"

Neil studied it. "Well, more detail in their chins and their hair and their ears and the background . . ."

The young woman appealed to Connor. "Don't listen to him, okay?"

"I won't," he assured her. "It's finished."

"I love it. How much does it cost? Would you take installments?"

"It's not for sale." He intended to hang it in his city apartment, unless Laura objected. If she did, he'd hang it in his campus studio. He thought of Peggy day and night. Distancing himself from her had done nothing to weaken his dependence upon her. He loved her.

"Well, someday I want one of your paintings," said the young woman.

"How about this one?" he said, stepping over in front of the Ashbys. "I can let you have this on installments."

She shook her head and made a face. "Sick!" she said. She joined her companions at the refreshment table for a last swallow of wine, and then they departed.

There was a last minute influx of viewers at closing time, several of them being Cass College professors with heartwarming things to say to Connor about his work and his return next fall to the fold. "Eager to have you back where you belong." "Not a clinker in the bunch—you're playing at the top of your game." "You were too good for Rookery State, I thought when you moved north, and now I see you're too good for Cass."

These generous remarks intensified his longing for gin. He left the gallery with Tate and Neil, but didn't follow them to Tate's car. "I'll have to forgo supper with you guys," he said, not trusting his resolve. "I'll grab a bite in the dorm and turn in early." He and Neil had been assigned a campus guest room.

"Who said anything about supper?" asked Tate. "Our novelist here needs a thorough introduction to the Lock and Dam Saloon. We may never get around to supper."

"That's the problem," said Connor.

Again his friend's face took on the look of a man betrayed. "Connor!" This was a reprimand.

"I'm pretty worn-out myself," said Neil meekly. "I wouldn't mind doing the same thing."

"Not you too!" said Tate, clutching Neil by the arm and leading him off toward his car. "We'll be at the Lock and Dam after your beauty nap," he called back to Connor.

"See you soon," called Neil, unable to resist his editor. "I won't be late."

Waving them away, Connor was overcome with an astonishing wave of emotion, a surge of pride and satisfaction much like that brought on by completing a really fine painting. He turned on his heel and took a roundabout way to his dormitory, reacquainting himself with the campus, savoring the chill, city-tainted air, and wondering how losing a close friend like Tate could feel so rewarding.

The next morning the college housing director took Connor and Laura around to look for lodging. Laura rode glumly in the backseat of the director's car and dragged her feet in and out of apartment buildings. At their last stop, Connor took her aside and asked what was wrong.

"I'm not going to move back here with you."

"Not move back to the city?" He was shocked. "It's what you wanted."

"Not anymore."

The housing director, a brisk little woman in a navy blue suit and necktie, had gone ahead to the car, leaving them standing under a budding maple in the courtyard of the Hiawatha Arms. It was warmer today, sunny and still. Spring, judging by the birdsong and the fragrance of lilac, was making a comeback.

"Laura, why?"

The girl shrugged, her eyes riveted on the top button of her father's shirt. Her dress looked wilted, for she hadn't brought along a change of clothes. "My friends really bug me!" She delivered these words with force.

"What happened?"

"Nothing *hap*pened." She raised her anguished eyes to his, as though she were on the verge of explaining, but quickly dropped them again, adding only, "They're just such creeps."

He laid a hand on her shoulder. "Tell me, Laura."

At the touch of his hand, she began to weep.

"Take your time," he said, leading her over to a stone bench, where they sat for a while in silence. He suspected at least part of the trouble. Two of her friends, Cheryl and Barb, had come to pick her up at yesterday's exhibit. They were to take the bus downtown to shop, to eat, to see a movie, and then Laura would stay with Barb overnight. Connor remembered the two girls as the least sinister of Laura's city crowd. He knew Cheryl's mother, a faculty member at Cass. Barb's father held an office in city government. But they'd changed a great deal. Both girls, having shown up wearing the briefest of miniskirts, were clearly developing the bodies of women. They'd learned to use makeup in subtler ways than beginners. They'd begun to carry themselves with the teenager's false yet bold assurance. In their desperate race to maturity, in other words, Cheryl and Barb had outdistanced Laura.

After a few minutes, Laura overcame her weepy state and said, "Let's go." Returning to campus, she seemed more composed. She entered into the discussion of what they had seen, preferring, she said, the Hiawatha Arms. The rooms there were of ample size. In the other apartments, she disliked the tiny second bedroom.

"My choice as well," said Connor, though the Hiawatha Arms was miles from the college.

"I suggest you sign a lease, then," said the housing director, "before somebody else snaps it up."

He did so.

The semester ended with a boycott of Mrs. Oberholtzer's final exam. Honey Oberholtzer had managed to antagonize nearly everyone in her classes—the men and the women, the dull and the brilliant, the draftable and the undraftable—with her tiresome lectures, her meaningless quizzes, and her rigid adherence to an outdated syllabus. How many poems by James Whitcomb Riley could you recite aloud in class and still keep your self-respect? Why was it important to remember the publication date of every story by O. Henry? Why, in fact, did you even have to *read* O. Henry?

But it wasn't for these reasons that Chuck Lucking and Dickie Donaldson led the boycott. It was because of her announcement, a day earlier, that she would not grant A's to all students. Neither her conscience nor her teacher-training would allow it, she said. Of her ninety-odd students, fourteen showed up for the exam.

She went to Dean Zastrow for advice.

"Flunk them all," he said, drawing a finger across his neck in a throat-cutting gesture. Then he smiled his salamander smile and said, "Or, if you're too softhearted to do that—as I expect you are, being a woman—then you can give them a second chance, and flunk only those who refuse to take advantage of your kindness."

Next she consulted her husband Mortimer. "Opt for the charitable course of action, Honey," he advised.

This she did, announcing a date and time for a makeup exam.

Chuck Lucking, Sandy Hupstad, and Dickie Donaldson sought the advice of Chuck's adviser, Dr. Benoit. Because Dickie was so large and Peggy's office so tiny, they conferred in the hallway. Peggy told them that Neil had been stupid to promise A's across-the-board, but still, Mrs. Oberholtzer was obliged as his substitute to be fair and play by his ground rules.

By using this analogy from the playing field, Peggy won the immediate trust of Dickie Donaldson, who said, "Yeah."

Chuck Lucking said, "I doubt if fairness will have anything to do with it. Mrs. Oberholtzer's a dictator."

"She's on her own wavelength," Sandy Hupstad explained, wrinkling her pretty nose in disapproval. "We thought Mr. Novotny had no sense of his audience—that's what we're taught in playacting, a sense of our audience—but Mrs. Oberholtzer acts like she's teaching in her sleep."

"Would you talk to her for us?" asked Chuck. "I mean, we're real worried. She says she never gives more than ten percent of her students A's."

"Yeah," said Dickie, articulating his anxiety.

"All right," said Peggy. "We'll go and see her together."

Mrs. Oberholtzer had left campus for the day, so the four of them walked down Sawyer in a thin, warm drizzle and called at her house. The door was opened by a carpenter installing bookcases in the entryway, but they were prevented from entering by Boots in a foul mood. The dog stood on the threshold, growling and salivating, with its head lowered, its eyes on their ankles.

C. Mortimer finally came to their aid, smoking his pipe and chuckling and quieting the animal with a handful of dog biscuits. He led them into a small room containing a couch, a beanbag chair, and a television set tuned in to a show promoting hair replacement.

"Make yourselves comfortable," said Mortimer, "I'll fetch my better half."

With the sound of crushed beans and ripping seams, the mammoth Dickie Donaldson sank onto the beanbag. Peggy left the couch to Sandy and Chuck, preferring to stand because surely her chairman would return and want to sit there beside her. A doctor appeared on TV, saying, "Baldies miss a lot in life," and this principle was borne out by a series of shots portraying activities enjoyed by men with lots of hair, most of them involving breasty women and small red automobiles.

Soon Honey Oberholtzer appeared in the room looking beaky and bilious and greatly aged by her three months in the classroom. "Well?" she snapped defensively, stepping over to the TV and turning off the sound but not the picture. Chuck and Sandy got to their feet, explaining why they had come, while Dickie remained sprawled on the leaking beanbag with his hands clasped behind his head and his eyes on the before-and-after pictures on TV—pallid, unhappy-looking men becoming more robust and cheerful as hair grew lower on their brows.

Honey turned to Peggy and asked in a chilly tone if she was taking the students' side.

"They kept up their part of the bargain, Mrs. Oberholtzer. They never skipped class."

"A grading system is nothing to tamper with, Dr. Benoit. The bell curve calls for seven percent A's. I decided to be lenient and promise them ten."

"What's the bell curve?" asked Chuck Lucking.

"It's the basis for all grading," said Honey. "You learn it in teacher-preparation classes."

"I never heard of it," said Peggy.

"Seven percent A's, seven percent F's, twenty-one percent B's, twenty-one percent D's, the rest C's—ask Kimberly Kraft."

"But how were they to know that?" asked Peggy. "You never told them until yesterday."

"They never asked." Honey examined an African violet on a windowsill, snapped off a dying leaf, felt the soil for moisture.

Peggy pressed on. "These are special times, Mrs. Oberholtzer. The draft, I mean. These days, a poor grade can send a boy into battle."

"Tell me about it!" The woman wheeled around and shot Peggy a ferocious look; then she left the room.

Mortimer appeared in the doorway, wearing a raincoat and a benevolent expression. "Would anyone like a cup of coffee?"

All declined.

"Cheerio, then, I'm off with Boots around the block."

Honey returned with one of the framed photographs Peggy had seen on the living room mantel. "My Gary," she cried, displaying her unrecognizably clean and wholesome son. "Don't tell me about sending a boy into battle. Gary was inducted into the army at Fort Leonard Wood a week ago Monday."

Peggy was able to get in only a brief reply—"I'm sorry about that"—before Honey became strident in praise of her precious son and in condemnation of Presidents Johnson and Nixon. She said there would be no compromising the bell curve, and she asked her guests to leave. Boots, aroused by her heightened voice, broke away from his master and came running in, trailing his leash, and dived teeth-first at Dickie Donaldson, who for all his size scrambled desperately to his feet and ran out the front door with his shirt ripped.

The others followed him, Honey calling after them in the rain—not unreasonably, it seemed to Peggy—"What's the use of trying to put men on the moon if we can't keep our babies off the battlefield?"

Hurrying back to campus in the rain, Peggy promised the students she would lead them through a study session. "Too bad Mr. Novotny moved to St. Paul," she said. "I'm no authority on literature."

"Neither was Mr. Novotny," said Chuck Lucking.

"But he was kinda cute," said Sandy.

"Look," said Dickie. Finishing what the dog had begun, he tore off his shirt pocket and held it out for them to see.

"Do you have to know how to swim to join the navy?" asked Chuck, considering his military options.

The Dashes' moving day was sunny and warm. Connor and Neil helped Victor load his rental truck. Leland would have helped as well, but was wary of Victor, who hadn't spoken to him since the strike ended. Peggy and Kimberly showed up to help Annie clean house. Alex Bolus went around with a can of paint, touching up the scuff marks on the walls, while Aaron Cardero came with his power mower and tended to the neglected yard.

It was midafternoon when Annie climbed in behind the wheel of the truck to follow Victor to Milwaukee. The three children, shouting and squealing with excitement, climbed in beside her. Victor checked the oil in the convertible, slammed down the hood, and was inspecting the tires when Peggy said, "One more thing before you leave town, Victor, you've got to say good-bye to Leland."

Victor smiled and shook his head.

"Oh, Victor, please," said Annie, putting her head out her high window. "We'll say good-bye to Lolly too. I don't think I missed a single one of her programs all year."

While Victor retracted the convertible top and secured it with snaps, Kimberly pointed out that Leland was kind and sensitive and would love the chance to wish Victor well. Alex added that Victor was a grouch. "Do it," said Aaron Cardero. Peggy entreated him again and Connor added his encouragement.

"Screw them both," said Victor. He got into the car and silenced everybody by starting his thunderous engine.

With a grinding of gears and a chorus of squeals and shouts and honking horns, the Dashes pulled out of town. "Good-bye, good-bye," called those left standing in the blue cloud of their exhaust.

The next day it was Connor, Laura, and Neil departing, again a rental truck trailing a car out of town, but with no one to see them off. It was very hot. Halfway to the city, they stopped for refreshment, and Neil told Connor about his desperate financial state. Because he couldn't afford to rent an apartment, Emerson Tate had promised to put him up for a few nights in his bachelor pad while they worked on the book together, but after that he'd have to go home to Ohio. He'd borrowed a hundred dollars from Peggy for food and bus fare.

Reluctant to get back on the road in the heat, they spun out their conversation for an hour or more, with Laura sitting silently at Connor's side, making a mental note of all the facts. Dr. Benoit was leaving next week to spend the summer in Boston. She would return for a couple of days in July for Professor Gold's wedding. Dean Zastrow had offered Dr. Benoit a summer school class to teach, but she'd declined. Leland, on the other hand, would be teaching a remedial summer course to freshmen trying to make up for the poor grades Honey Oberholtzer had given them. Most were young men whose draft boards had extended them a three-month reprieve.

After a few days in the Hiawatha Arms—time enough to confirm that Peggy wasn't going to move in with her father before she went to Boston—as well as enough time to find that Cheryl and

Barb were more stuck-up than ever because now they had boy-friends—Laura took the bus back to Rookery, promising her father she'd return to the city for school in the fall.

Connor began work on two double portraits—four generations of a family of Cass College alumni.

A week or so later, Neil moved home to Ohio.

On the day before she left for Boston, Leland called on Peggy upstairs over the JCPenney store, and they went across the street to confer with Georgina and Ron in the appliance showroom. Peggy and Georgina hiked themselves up to sit on the lids of adjacent General Electric washers, and Leland bent over a Hotpoint range, writing in his notebook. Ron called his old father out of his glassed-in office to take care of customers.

They determined that at the wedding itself, Peggy would sing, a cappella, two of Georgina's favorite hymns, as well as Ron's favorite ballad from World War Two, "Coming in on a Wing and a Prayer." At the reception Leland would join her for an hour and a half of mostly instrumental pieces.

"I wish the quintet could be there to stay on and play for the dance," said Georgina, and then added with uncharacteristic tenderness, "It's a shame, considering all the practicing you did, that you never got to play in public."

"We were on the radio once," Leland reminded her.

"But I mean out in front of an audience."

"We've got plenty of records for the dance," Ron hastened to remind her, as though fearing the other three musicians might be willing to return from Minneapolis, Milwaukee, and Dayton. Clipped into Ron's shirt pocket were half a dozen ballpoints and a tire gauge.

"Do you hear from Neil?" asked Georgina.

"Neil's broke," said Peggy. "No paycheck since March. When and if royalties come rolling in, he might find a place to live in St. Paul, but until that happens, he's gone to live with his parents and sell apples for a living."

"Have you heard from Victor?"

"No, but Kimberly heard from Annie. She says they're crazy about Milwaukee."

Georgina's inquiry ended here, because she thought it indiscreet to ask about Connor. Ron, however, was too curious to resist:

"I saw the Connor girl around town this morning. I thought she moved away with her dad."

"She'll probably be back and forth all summer," said Peggy.

"She'll probably be at our house quite a bit," said Leland. "She and Mother like to try out recipes together."

"Shiftless kids nowadays," said Ron.

Gary Oberholtzer, home from boot camp in mid-July, looked to Laura like a plucked chicken. By cropping his hair, the army seemed to have stretched his neck, and she noticed for the first time what a chiseled face and beaky nose he had.

"Well, how was it?" she asked him across the table in Claudia's Lunch. It was a hot afternoon. They were both perspiring. Claudia sat at the front window with a fly swatter at the ready.

"You learn a lot," he drawled. He wasn't in uniform. He wore a Hawaiian shirt, and his arms were still very scrawny-looking. Instead of building muscle, the army seemed to have merely tightened him up, made him wirier.

"What did you learn?" asked Laura without much interest. She wore a T-shirt and tattered cutoffs.

"A lot."

"Like what?"

The army hadn't taken away his nasty smirk. "Guys eat their wives."

She knew what this meant but pretended not to. "I got this idea, Gary. I want you to help me."

"Some guys even eat their girlfriends," he said.

"It's about my dad and Dr. Benoit," she told him.

It took a few moments for this to register, and when it did, his smirk broadened and he asked, "They still humping?"

She shook her head. "She's gone to Boston for the summer, and my dad and I moved to Minneapolis."

He frowned, then shrewdly pointed out, "This ain't Minneapolis."

"I don't like Minneapolis in the summer, so I came back. I'm staying with my mother and her friend."

"You mean your stepmother?"

"Yeah, her. I'll go back when school starts. Now, what I want is, I want you to make a phone call for me."

He rubbed his eyes. "You got any weed?"

"I don't smoke."

"You did."

"Not anymore."

"I could use some weed. Let's go find some."

"We just got here." Laura called to Claudia for another Pepsi, and then she drew from the pocket of her jeans the manuscript page she'd been carrying around with her since reading Neil's novel. She pressed it flat on the table so Gary could read the letterhead, GRANDPA'S FRUIT BASKET.

"Your name will be Emerson Tate on the phone."

"Who's Emerson Tate?"

"Never mind who. Just say that's who you are. Unless Neil Novotny answers. If Neil Novotny answers, tell him you got the wrong number."

Claudia brought the Pepsi, then returned to her place at the window, picked up the fly swatter, and waited.

"How do I know if it's Neil Novotny? I never heard his voice."

"I'll be listening. I'll dial the call and listen to who answers, and if it's okay to go ahead, I'll give you the phone."

She pointed to what she'd written on the page. "Here's what you say."

He put on his reading expression, a painful frown, and when he finished, he asked, "Why?"

"To keep Dr. Benoit away from my dad."

"She *is* away."

"She's coming back for a wedding this Saturday."

"Whose?"

"A speech professor. Your parents are probably going. Practically everybody from the college is invited."

He shrugged, put the cold bottle to his lips, and drained most of it. He burped and slid the bottle over to Laura. "Whose phone?"

"The Edwardses'. Tomorrow morning at ten-thirty on the dot."

She knew precisely how many minutes Leland's summer school class overlapped with Lolly's radio time.

The news of Connor's death reached Peggy in Boston at four o'clock on Thursday afternoon.

"Pneumonia," said Lolly on the telephone. "He checked into a Minneapolis hospital yesterday morning and died last night, shortly after midnight."

"No, no," Peggy moaned. She reached out to her sister-in-law for support. "No, not *Connor*!"

"Somebody phoned Neil in Ohio, a man named Tate, and Neil called here wanting to know if I had your phone number."

Peggy's sister-in-law drew up a kitchen chair for her to sit on and whispered, "What happened?"

Lolly continued, "I asked Neil if he'd mind if I called you before he did. I told him your first thought would naturally be of Laura, and I could at least put your mind at ease where she's concerned."

Actually, her first thought was not of Laura, far from it. Her first thought was of herself and Connor making love in the tiny bedroom over the JCPenney Store. That this hairy, virile genius, her true love, should be dead . . . it took her breath away. She couldn't get another word out.

"Isn't it terrible, Peggy dear? Isn't it unbelievable?"

Speechless, she shook her head at the phone to indicate no, it wasn't unbelievable. It was exactly what she'd feared ever since she left Minnesota. It was in June, on her first night in this house of her brother's, that she'd phoned Connor and thought he sounded high. Was he on a binge? Was he risking his life by falling in again with his debauched friends? She spoke with him two or three times a week after that, and although his voice was never quite so crazily effusive again, he kept talking in untypical terms of optimism. Everything in his life was satisfactory, he insisted, his health, his living quarters, his studio, his cooking, his painting-in-progress. She missed his edge of cynicism. What had dulled it? He sounded like someone striving too hard to be happy.

"You wonder, don't you, Peggy dear, if it was drink-related. I mean after what happened last winter on that fishing trip. Leland is just devastated. He's gone over to see Mrs. Connor. He had such a deep respect for Connor, and he was—"

"When's the funeral?" blurted Peggy, her voice returning to her at a higher pitch than normal. "I'm flying back tomorrow for Georgina's wedding."

"Leland will find out from Mrs. Connor, and I'll let you know the minute he gets back. Laura's right here at my side. We were mixing up an angel food cake when Neil called. Maybe you should talk to her, Peggy. She's trying not to seem affected."

"Later," said Peggy. She had nothing to say to the girl who'd kept them apart.

"You worry when somebody tries to hold it all inside."

"Not now, Lolly. I'll talk to her later."

"You'll stay with us, Peggy."

"I've already got a reservation at the Van Buren for the wedding."

"But you know how much room we have."

"Thanks, Lolly, the Van Buren will be fine."

"But if you have to stay on, for the funeral—think about it."

"Surely it won't be in Rookery."

"Well, with his wife and daughter both living here, who knows?"

Peggy replaced the receiver and stood staring at it until her sister-in-law, a sandy-haired bundle of energy named Joannie, guided her out of the kitchen and settled her on a couch.

"Connor died," Peggy murmured.

The phone rang. Joannie returned to the kitchen to take Neil's call. Peggy had just heard the news, she told him, and she needed a little time to recover. She'd call him when she was feeling up to it.

"Connor and Peggy used to be real close," Neil told her.

"I know all about it," said Joannie, in whom Peggy had confided. She knew more than Neil did. She knew Peggy and Connor had called their love affair to a halt because of his daughter's antagonism. A two-year moratorium with no promises or expectations, they'd agreed. And Joannie sensed Peggy's further promise to herself. Once the daughter finished high school, she'd fly back into his arms. There'd be no keeping her away from the man.

Neil said, "Tell her I'm sorry, will you?"

"I will."

"Has she told you about me—Neil Novotny?"

"Sure, your name comes up. You're cousins after all."

"Cousins by marriage."

"And I'm her sister by marriage. My name is Joannie."

"I've always been crazy about her, Joannie."

"Me too. Now I'll have to let you go, Neil. She'll be calling you."

Soon Peggy was back on the phone, arranging with the airline to delay her return ticket to Boston. Then she called Annie Dash in Milwaukee, asking her to convey the news to Victor and tell him that the quintet must convene once more. Connor deserved a jam session.

Annie, subdued by the tragic news, quietly conveyed her condolences, and said that Victor could probably be there if the funeral was the weekend, but he had appointments in Iowa on the days following.

"I'll call Neil and get back to you," said Peggy.

She called Neil, who told her it was the high season for apples.

"Apples! What do you mean, apples? We're talking about the death of a dear friend."

"Let me explain, Peggy. The harvest is about to start, and the price of apples fluctuates like crazy. My father has to be on the phone with his fruit brokers while I'm out in the schools setting up our fall meetings with students."

"Tell your father you need three days, one to fly out, one to play music, one to fly home."

"But, see, I've got all these meetings scheduled with student advisers."

"Not over the weekend."

"No, but Friday and Monday."

"Send your mother out to meet them."

"Mother doesn't like to drive."

"So put Mother on the phone with the brokers and send Father out on the road."

"I don't think they'd go for that."

"Listen, Neil, it's bad enough that you went back into the family business—"

"It's only temporary, till my book comes out."

"—but it's appalling that you went back as a slave."

"Jesus, Peggy, give me a break. I haven't had a paycheck since last March, you know that."

"You mean they aren't even paying you?"

"I mean except from my parents. Look, here's my plan. I work for Grandpa's Fruit Basket this one last season, until 'Paula's Passion' comes out in November, then I move back to St. Paul and live on my royalties until I finish my next novel."

" 'Paula's Passion'?" Peggy inquired.

"It's what we've decided to call it."

"What happened to Lydia?"

"Lynda, you mean. We changed her name so we could get passion in the title—the alliteration of it, you see. My editor says passion is big this year." He went on to describe the cover art, and then he started on marketing plans.

Peggy broke in: "Connor is dead and about to be buried, Neil. Be there." She hung up.

Joannie was brewing tea. She turned from the stove to see Peggy shuddering and weeping. "We'll go out on the patio," she said. "We'll sit in the shade and you'll tell me all about him."

Peggy swallowed and tried to keep her teeth from chattering. "Nothing to tell," she cried. "What's there to tell if he's dead?"

Peggy's family decided that Joannie must accompany her to Minnesota.

"One look at her and you know she can't go out there alone," said her brother Bill, Joannie's husband, a heavy man with sideburns down to the hinge of his jaw.

"I'd go myself if I didn't have my art lesson tomorrow," said her other sister-in-law, a rather self-absorbed young woman enrolled in a life-drawing class.

"I'll kick in a hundred dollars," said Peggy's brother Kenny. This was the attorney who'd written the threatening letter to Gene Benoit concerning the nude photograph, a man in the habit of gritting his teeth between statements. "Christ, the men she gets involved with!"

These two couples, along with Peggy's mother, were sitting on Bill and Joannie's patio drinking martinis. Steaks were smoldering over charcoal. Evening sunshine came slanting across the lawn.

"She has her grandmother Martin's temperament, only more so," said Peggy's mother. She turned around in her squeaky patio chair to make sure Peggy was still in the kitchen, still on the phone inquiring about funeral arrangements. "In her grandmother's case, it used to be called nervous exhaustion, to distinguish it from a nervous breakdown. More of a short-term kind of collapse."

"She calls it the blues," said Bill.

"I know. She called it that when she was twelve or thirteen and you older ones left home. The lonesome blues, she called it. Her grandmother used to go all weepy and get the same look in her eye that we're seeing in Peggy."

"Despair, it looks like to me," said the younger sister-in-law.

"Who can blame her?" said Joannie. "Her lover's dead."

Lover. The word silenced the family, causing their eyes to shift away from one another. As though on cue, they all brought their martinis to their lips.

Peggy sat at the kitchen counter, the phone to her ear, her free hand gripping her hair. "She's a very unpleasant person to talk to," Leland was telling her. "She won't even say where the body is. I went back a second time, with Mother, but she wouldn't speak to us. That woman she lives with, Eldora Sparks, came to the door and said we shouldn't disturb her, so I have no idea when the funeral will take place or where."

"Neil's coming, and so is Victor. Will you ask Georgina if she'd still like the quintet to play for her dance?"

There was a pause. "Come again?"

"It will be Connor's memorial concert, only we won't tell anybody."

"Well, I don't know, Peggy . . . in public like that. How about Sunday we have a private session?"

"Look, Victor has to leave for Iowa on Sunday afternoon, and Neil has to take off for home."

"Well, I can ask her."

"I want to get there and play music and get away—without having to see Connor's body in the custody of his wife. I've decided I can't go to the funeral."

There was a pause. "Peggy, isn't this awful?"

She choked back tears. "What about Laura? Is she still with you?"

"She went home to her mother and Eldora. She promised to keep me informed."

"Has she cried or anything?"

"No, she's a tough kid."

"I'm not so tough, Leland."

"Did I say how sorry I am, Peggy? I know you loved him."

Mute with grief, she had to hang up.

Neil speculated that Peggy, losing Connor, might now be ready to love him at last. His mother agreed ("Be there for her, Neil"), and so he flew into Minneapolis with a sack of apples and his clarinet case, the latter containing, in addition to his instrument, a toothbrush and a change of underwear. He arrived in the late morning on Friday, and was met at the gate by Peggy and Joannie, who'd arrived half an hour earlier. He handed Peggy the sack of apples.

"Joannie, this is Neil—we're cousins, more or less."

"By marriage," Neil hastily pointed out.

"The apple merchant," said Joannie.

"And novelist," Peggy kindly added.

Neil kissed her for that, then kissed her a second time because she seemed in need of consoling. Her face was drawn, her eyelids swollen.

"Sorry I gave you such a hard time on the phone yesterday," he said. "It's just that Grandpa's Fruit Basket—"

"Forget it," said Peggy. "You're here now."

"Yes, Mother said I should come."

"That's Leland's line," she told him. Neil had the vaguely plump and pampered appearance she remembered from his boyhood. He no longer looked like a derelict; his khaki pants and flowered shirt were new. Mother Novotny's coddling obviously agreed with him. That, and coming up out of that awful basement in Rookery, up out of that awful novel. "How's the book?" she asked.

"The type's being set as we speak. We hope to have it out for the Christmas trade."

"Peggy tells me it's a romance," said Joannie.

He scowled at Peggy, correcting her. "A historical novel, with psychological overtones."

They heard a loud, familiar shout, a loud, unfamiliar laugh, and they turned to see Victor scurrying down the concourse. He gave each of them a painful handshake and an open, sunny smile that Peggy didn't remember from his Rookery days. She was amazed by how glad she was to see him. She'd missed his candor, his energy, his irreverence. Neil apparently wasn't the only one transformed by leaving the North, for Victor's hair was longer, covering his pipeline wound, and his mustache was trimmed. He wore a stylish shirt with an expensive tie knotted loosely at the collar.

She introduced him to Joannie and inquired about his family. Annie was fine, he said. The kids were fine. The new bike was a Schwinn.

Neil was studying him. "You look so different, Victor. Less military or something."

"More like a strike organizer?" asked Victor.

"More like a professor," said Peggy, laughing.

She inquired about his new job, and all the way out to the parking ramp, he extolled the Faculty Alliance of America, its personnel, its objectives, its cafeteria. He had seven high school faculties in Wisconsin and Illinois primed to begin the fall term with a strike unless their school boards came across with a living wage. He'd already visited Mankato, Winona, and Moorhead, preparing a four-sided assault on the Minnesota State College Board. "Hate to mix business with pleasure," he said, unlocking a nearly new Dodge Diplomat, "but I'll confer with Aaron and Kimberly and a few others while I'm in Rookery—that way we get to use this company car."

"Not business with *pleasure*," Peggy reminded him.

"Oh, that's right—Connor's dead." His face clouded. "I keep forgetting because it's so hard to believe."

The two women got in back, Neil in front. Victor was pleased to find in Joannie a woman as opinionated and talky as himself, and because he had to keep taking his eyes off the road to address her, he stopped the car after fifty miles and demanded that she and Neil change places.

Side by side in back, Neil, reticent by nature, and Peggy, subdued by sorrow, watched the corn rows and fence posts go by. Because high, thin clouds dispersed the light, it was the sort of day when you had to squint wherever you looked.

At length, Peggy fell asleep. Neil pondered the plot of his next book. Joannie and Victor discussed labor relations, the Red Sox, the Braves, the moon launch, and defoliation as a wartime strategy.

They were a hundred miles from the city, and farmland had given way to dense forests and blue-green lakes when Peggy opened her eyes. She gave Neil a brief, careworn smile meant to quell his hope for romance.

He asked, "How are you feeling?"

"Numb," said Peggy.

"Time heals all wounds," he told her.

She shrugged.

He probed his meager imagination and wondered if Peggy's story might be turned into a novel. He himself would be the narrator, the rejected suitor turned wise adviser, helping a beautiful singer through her bereavement over the death of her genius artist. His fictional name would be Neil Butler. Hers would be Peg O'Hara. In the end he would win her favor. How ideal. But he could imagine Emerson Tate saying, *Not enough plot, Cornelia, you need a dramatic twist at the end.* Throughout the editing process, Tate had kept insisting on surprises. Well, say Neil Butler fell for someone else in the end, leaving Peg O'Hara bereft. No good—

Tate wanted happy endings for heroines. All right then, say the artist somehow came back from the dead . . .

"Piss call," said Victor, pulling into a truck stop. They got out and stretched and returned to the car with snacks. "A hundred miles in a hundred minutes," said Victor, pulling back onto the highway and flooring it. "Clock me."

Forty miles later, still musing over his plot, Neil turned to Peggy and said, "Maybe he isn't dead."

She didn't look at him, but closed her eyes.

"I mean, suppose it's a joke. All I know is somebody called up and said I should let you know he's dead and then hung up."

"Somebody!" She glared at him. "Don't put me through this, Neil! Surely you know your editor's voice when you hear it."

"But I didn't hear it. Mother took the call."

Clutching his hand, she narrowed her eyes and imagined for a split second the possibility that her ex-husband had perpetrated a horribly malicious hoax, that Connor was alive and well and at this very moment painting a portrait in Minneapolis. But before she could feel the elation of such a prospect, she realized that Gene Benoit couldn't have made the phone call. Gene knew nothing of Emerson Tate and his connection with Neil. In fact, he probably knew nothing of Neil. And besides, given Connor's alcoholic history and Peggy's innate pessimism where love was concerned, she found Lolly's theory altogether convincing: her lover had drunk himself to the point of suffocation. Neil was an idiot for suggesting otherwise.

Snatching her hand away from him, she found a dry hankie in her purse and spread it across her eyes as she laid her head on the back of the seat. Pretending to sleep, she listened to the conversation in the front.

"When you get right down to it, schoolteachers are a pain in the ass."

"They are not, Victor. Schoolteachers are some of the last idealists of our time."

"The ones I'm dealing with are mostly a pain in the ass, bitching and moaning all the time."

"The ones I know don't have time to bitch and moan. They're too busy trying to keep America educated."

"Then, when the chips are down, they turn timid. Someday I'm going to develop a trade arm of our union. I want to organize pipeliners."

"You'd just better *do* that, if you can't respect teachers."

He pounded the steering wheel and uttered a high-pitched cry of delight: "The Pipeliners Alliance of America! Hasn't that got the most beautiful goddamn ring to it?"

Peggy and Joannie had no more than checked into two rooms of the Van Buren Hotel when they were summoned to the lobby by the desk clerk. "You have guests," he said. "A man and a woman."

In the elevator Peggy told her sister-in-law it would be Georgina and Ron. "They've come to check me out before rehearsal—Ron is such a perfectionist. I must look like a tramp."

She did, thought Joannie. Travel had wrinkled Peggy's shirt and slacks and lined her face. Grief had deadened her eyes. "No worse than me," she said charitably.

That's bad enough, thought Peggy, for her sister-in-law was perspiring and her hair was out of control.

The elevator door opened and Lolly Edwards came rushing at them. Behind her was Leland, bearing in his arms an enormous bouquet of fresh-cut daisies.

"Peggy, dear Peggy, my stars, how we've missed you." A hug and a kiss. "And this would be Joannie, my my, it's wonderful to meet you, Joannie." A hug and a kiss. "I want you to meet my son, Leland. Mr. Ragtime, I've been calling him lately. He's been playing nothing but rags all summer, 'Johnson Rag,' 'Spaghetti Rag,' I don't know what all."

She relieved her son of the flowers so that he might give Peggy a hug and a kiss and Joannie at least a peck. He shook Joannie's hand and gave Peggy a peck. "Are you okay?" he asked her.

"No, actually."

"We're only here for a minute," he said. "To see if we can do anything for you."

"We'll sit down," said Lolly, hoping for more than a minute.

They moved over to the high front windows and sat on two couches, daylight filtering in on them through lacy curtains.

Lolly said, "I still don't see why you can't come and stay at the house. You could have the sleeping porch and we'd leave you completely alone. It's so summery and nice, and every morning the songbirds have been singing their heads off."

Leland laid a hand on her arm to silence her. "First things first, Mother."

"Of course," she said, deferring to him in a manner that surprised Peggy. "Tell them, Leland."

"Now Peggy," he said, "I don't want to raise false hopes." While he paused to clear his throat and straighten the handkerchief ears protruding from the pocket of his tan sport coat, Peggy thought, Thank you, Leland, for acknowledging my involvement with Connor, my grief.

He continued: "Nobody we've talked to has actually seen Connor dead."

Her heart beat faster with the elation she'd suppressed when Neil had broached the subject in the car. Please, God, let Leland say next that he doubts it's true.

"I don't say I'm doubting it's true, mind you, but it's all quite mysterious."

Lolly said, "We've had our friends at Anderson Mortuary canvass all the funeral homes in the Twin Cities, and nobody has a service scheduled for anybody named Connor."

"We've also been in touch with people at Cass College, including the president," said Leland. "They've uncovered nothing."

"Emerson Tate?" said Peggy. She held her breath.

"Gone to Spain," said Leland.

Joannie, who was a little nearsighted, sat forward for a closer look at the Edwardses. "Hasn't anybody checked with the Minneapolis coroner's office?"

"We did that too," said Lolly.

"Nothing," said her son.

Joannie took Peggy's hand and told her, "We can hope."

Peggy asked, "You've talked to Marcy?"

Here, Leland looked to his mother as though imploring her to take over, but his mother, from behind her profusion of daisies, nodded as if to say, Go ahead, Leland.

He cleared his throat again, straightened his tie. "Well, of course Marcy's very strange. When I went to her yesterday and told her the news, she replied . . ." Here Leland paused and lowered his eyes. He spoke to his hands in his lap. "She laughed and said, 'Finally my luck is changing,' and she called Eldora Sparks to the door and put her arm around her shoulder and said, 'Eldora, wait till you hear this. You said all along I'd get lucky, and now it's happened.' "

He raised his embarrassed eyes to Peggy. "I thought I should tell you that, so you know where she stands." He was relieved that Peggy was apparently not offended by Marcy's disrespect. She too was sitting forward now, anticipating his every word.

"Then I went a second time, with Mother, but to no avail. So I went again, first thing this morning, to ask what arrangements she'd made." He lowered his eyes again. "Well, she hadn't made any, presumably hadn't given it a thought. I told her she'd better get in touch with somebody about services and burial and all, and she said she'd wait to be gotten in touch with."

"And then . . ." his mother prompted.

"And then Eldora came to the door and said that assuming he's dead, he'd be cremated and the ashes buried in her cemetery plot. It's a grave meant for Eldora's husband, and Eldora said—I quote her now—'If I had to lie down next to Bushman for eternity, I'd refuse to die.' "

Lolly began to quiver with laughter. "You'd have to know Eldora Sparks to appreciate that. Excuse me for laughing, but I really don't believe our friend Connor is dead."

"Bushman's what she calls her husband," Leland explained.

"After the gorilla, you know," added Lolly. "In Chicago's Lincoln Park Zoo."

The others waited for Lolly's laughter to subside; then Peggy said, "But has anyone called *him*!"

"Who?" said mother and son together.

"Connor!"

"Oh, yes, we've tried his phone all along. No answer."

Peggy stood. So did the others. Leland said he'd deliver them to the wedding rehearsal at seven o'clock. Lolly said they must come for lunch tomorrow, before the wedding. They said good-bye, and Lolly was about to go out the door when her son said, "Mother, the daisies."

Laughing loudly, she settled the bouquet into Joannie's arms.

"Oh, thank you, they're beautiful," said Joannie.

"How is Laura taking it?" Peggy asked.

"Laura isn't talking."

Laura, lying on a flat rock with her feet in the river, gazed up at the underside of the Eleventh Street Bridge and said, "Get it into your thick head once and for all, Gary, you're not humping me."

Gary was sitting on a nearby rock, smoking pot. "Hey," he said as sternly as his tangled brain waves permitted. "You can't talk to a soldier in the U.S. Army like that."

She laughed. "What I'm talking to is a drug addict under a bridge."

"I'll tell people we made that phone call."

She said nothing. Silence was the safest course where the rumor of her father's death was concerned. She'd already tried out muteness on Lolly and Leland, and it worked perfectly. They thought she was wordless with grief.

"I'll tell your stepmother."

Silence. Her mother already knew about the phone call to Ohio. Her mother thought it was funny. She and Eldora had even started elaborating on the rumor, making up details such as where he died and who his doctor was.

"I'll tell Dr. Benoit."

Why not? Dr. Benoit would find out the truth eventually anyhow, and finally get it through her thick head how much Laura despised her.

"I'll tell your dad."

That would get his attention. A reprimand was better than no attention at all.

"I'll tell . . ." He inhaled deeply, trying to think of someone else to threaten her with.

She hoped he wouldn't tell Lolly or Leland. She might lose her open invitation to their elegant house, their interesting kitchen.

Lolly had announced the death over the air this morning, and the truth might make her mad as hell.

"I'll tell . . ." he repeated, but lost his train of thought. Closing his eyes, he passed her what was left of his moist, ragged cigarette, and she flicked it into the river.

Leland drove Peggy and her sister-in-law to rehearsal at seven o'clock. He intended to wait and drive them back to the hotel, but Peggy said no, they were expected to attend a groom's dinner afterward at Culpepper's Supper Club—they'd get a ride with someone. This was not entirely a lie. In June, Georgina had speculated about such a dinner, but Peggy had heard nothing further.

Rehearsal lasted twenty minutes. The minister instructed Peggy where to stand and when to sing, but said she needn't run through the songs, because his wife the organist wasn't there. Peggy agreed to arrive early the next day and rehearse with her.

She was relieved that no one in the wedding party—all of them strangers but for the bride and groom—spoke of Connor's death. Georgina kept giving her knowing looks, as though she might do so, but they had no private moments together. After rehearsal, Peggy and Joannie managed to lose themselves in the crowded vestibule and hurried out the door and down the street like a couple of guilty schoolgirls before Georgina could invite them to the grooms' dinner, if there was one.

Sitting on a park bench overlooking the Badbattle, they took off their pumps and put on the walking shoes Joannie had brought in a tote bag. In the soft light of early evening they crossed the river and strolled through the campus. Except for the ugly new dormitory, Rookery State had never looked better. Blossoms nodded in flower beds along the walkways. Pine trees cast long shadows down the lawns to the lapping river.

They sat on the steps of McCall Hall, and Peggy told the story of the strike, the faculty's high expectations, their swift and ignominious defeat.

"Neil was a striker?" asked Joannie.

"No, Neil was occupied with his book."

"Connor was a striker?"

"Connor was occupied too. His wife was going nuts."

"Tell me about her."

"I'll do better than tell you about her," said Peggy, abruptly getting to her feet and waving mosquitoes away from her hair, "I'll show her to you."

In the phone book outside the student center, she looked up the address of Eldora Sparks. She was on the point of phoning Leland and asking for a ride, but decided not to arouse Lolly's curiosity. She phoned Aaron Cardero's house instead, where Victor and Neil were staying.

"Joannie and I need a ride over to Mill Avenue, Victor. I need to talk to Connor's wife, can you see that? I can't sit around not knowing what's going on."

"At your service," he said. "Give me three minutes."

"I can take you right back to Aaron's, if you'll trust me with your car."

"Nope—company car. I'll drive you wherever you need to go."

They found Mill Avenue in a neighborhood where all the streets were gravel and the forest encroached on the city limits. They drove past small, old houses surrounded by hickory brush and jack pine. They passed an abandoned sawmill and came to a mailbox on a post leaning out of an overgrown hedge, its paste-on letters identifying the residence of E SPARKS.

Victor turned in at the narrow drive and stopped behind a small car with last year's HUMPHREY-MUSKIE sticker peeling off its rear bumper. It was dusk under the trees. A dim, gray light emanated from the front room of a one-story cube of a house. A black and white animal, doubtless a cat, stirred on the stoop and scratched on the screen door. Scattered around the sandy yard were a number of large stones painted white.

"Want me to go with you?" asked Neil, who shared the front seat with Victor.

"No, just Joannie." The two women got out.

"I'll go," said Victor, opening his door.

"No," said Peggy, closing it. "This won't take long."

Again, the cat scratched on the screen, and Eldora Sparks, coming to let it in, was startled to see the women picking their way among her stones and thorny bushes.

"Marcy Connor?" said Peggy in the half-light.

The woman laughed.

Peggy stepped up onto the tiny stoop. "I'm looking for Mrs. Connor. I want to ask her a couple of questions."

Eldora continued to chuckle. "First time I was ever mistaken for somebody good-looking."

Behind Eldora, a cattle drive was moving across a black-and-white television screen. There was movement in a dark corner of the room, a heavy figure rising from a rocking chair.

"Who is it?" asked the figure.

"Come in," invited Eldora, pushing open the screen door.

They entered. "I'm Peggy Benoit, and this is my sister-in-law, Joannie Martin."

But for the TV, there was no light in the room. The cattle were complaining loudly. Connor's wife didn't come forward from her dark corner. Peggy saw that she weighed considerably more than she had at the Christmas party.

"I'm wondering what you've heard about your husband."

Marcy lowered herself back into her rocker. "Heard he's dead, is all."

"But I'm told nobody's actually seen him dead."

"The undertaker has."

Peggy's hand went to her mouth in horror. "What undertaker?"

"In the city. The one where he's being cremated."

Peggy tried to make out the woman's expression in the dark. She made an effort not to sound shrill as she asked, "So it's true?"

Marcy, rocking placidly, nodded her head.

Peggy reached out to Joannie, who took over for her:

"How did he die?"

"Pneumonia."

"Where?"

"Abbot Hospital."

"When?"

"Yesterday morning, nine-fifteen."

Peggy broke in: "I was told it happened the night before, around midnight."

Marcy shrugged.

"Who did you talk to?" asked Peggy.

"His doctor."

"What's his name?" asked Joannie.

Marcy sighed impatiently and asked her companion, "Eldora, what was his name?"

"Wasn't it Vander-something?"

"Vanderkellen."

The four women stood for a moment in a kind of frozen silence, not quite looking at each other. Peggy became aware of the aroma of bread in the oven.

Marcy spoke up. "I realize you don't see it the way I see it—I mean you're his woman now, right?—but it's all for the best. He was a terrible drunk. He'd've ruined your life the way he ruined mine, almost."

"You're right," Peggy said softly. "I don't see it that way." She went to the door feeling unbalanced or disoriented. The woman's voice was amazingly clear and coherent. She'd expected to walk into a madhouse.

"You're sad and I'm happy," the voice continued from the rocker. "And do you know what the difference is? The difference is that you weren't the one married to him for fifteen years."

In the car, Victor and Neil urged them to come to Aaron's house and join the reunion of his Viceroys—Kimberly Kraft and Alex Bolus were there. Peggy and Joannie, claiming travel fatigue, declined.

In the elevator, Peggy also declined Joannie's offer to call Abbot Hospital and locate Dr. Vanderkellen.

"Tomorrow, Joannie."

"But I thought you wanted to know the truth."

"We know the truth, don't we?"

"But we need it confirmed. We heard he died at night, and we heard he died in the morning. Something's not right."

"Not now," said Peggy.

The elevator let them out near their adjacent doors.

"I think it's a mistake to put it off."

"Look, Joannie, for twenty-four hours I was convinced Connor was dead. Then I was made to think there's a chance he's alive. Let me still think there's a chance till the wedding is over, because if it's confirmed he's dead, I'll need to let myself fall apart, and I can't do that before the wedding."

She closed herself in her room.

Lunch at Lolly's made Peggy nervous. She kept expecting the phone to ring, a call confirming the fatal news. It rang only once. Leland answered, and, after a minute, returned to his Caesar salad flushed with pleasure. It had been Victor, he said, calling to say all was forgiven.

"What a self-important little man," said Joannie.

"Oh, isn't he the limit!" said Lolly, laughing. "Such a character."

"Did he apologize for his grudge?" asked Peggy.

"No, I was the one who apologized," said Leland. "He asked if I was sorry, and I said yes."

"Sorry! For what?"

"I have no idea." Leland laughed with his mother.

Soon after the meal, Peggy excused herself, leaving her sister-in-law absorbed in Lolly's recipe books. She went back to the Van Buren, changed clothes, and spent the afternoon walking along the Badbattle, following it far out beyond the edge of the city. It was hot and rather humid, but she felt capable of walking forever along the dirt roads beside fields of bearded grain, clover, and pasture grass, each field against a backdrop of pines so green they looked artificial. During her residence in Rookery, she'd never examined the surrounding countryside, never allowed her senses to take in its colors and contours, its smells and birdcalls. Beautiful, she thought, if only it weren't so bereft of humanity, so lonely. There were certain vistas of a mile or more where no house or barn was visible. Not even a telephone pole.

She climbed a path through a grassy field to a height affording a broad view of the river bottom. At the crest she found a boulder to sit on, under an oak tree for shade. Resting there, looking back over the way she'd come, she regretted the course she'd taken with

Connor. What she regretted most was not trying to dissuade him from pulling away. Given another chance, she'd have been more headstrong, harder to get rid of. Laura or no Laura, she'd argue for his uninterrupted love. What a joy it would be to return to Rookery in the fall if Connor were still here. Or even if he were still in Minneapolis—at least they could be together weekends.

A hawk rode the air currents high above her. Grasshoppers jumped about at her feet. She sat there for a long time, imagining the life she might have had with her genius artist. When she finally roused herself and came down from the height, it was much later than she thought, and she arrived back at the hotel with scarcely enough time to dress for the wedding.

Most of the faculty guests, being Georgina's colleagues, were seated on the bride's side of Mount of Olives, but Leland and Lolly, because they'd known him from childhood, sat on the groom's. Leland glanced at the notepad on his mother's lap. *Tufted organza with flowers of satin,* she'd written. *Veil of tulle—crown of satin roses.* Even more than recipes or interviews or news of disease and death from the nursing home, it was her florid wedding reports that Lolly was most famous for. He watched her write, *Bride's bouquet—baby's breath, fern, red carnations.* And then, *Peggy's "In the Garden" so sublime—a voice from on high.*

Indeed, Leland had never heard Peggy in better voice. Standing beside the organ, which was located at the side of the church near the baptismal alcove, she uttered sounds so clear and soaring and piercingly beautiful that everyone turned and gazed at her in wonder—Ron Hunsinger with his mouth hanging open, and Georgina Gold with an inward, blissful expression Leland had never thought her capable of. Even Pastor Langerud, a chronic sobersides, smiled a little, and so did the pastor's wife as she tastefully moderated the tones of the organ.

Leland watched Ron's father, the appliance tycoon, quickly touch a finger to the corner of his right eye, and then, a few moments later, to the corner of his left. Across the aisle, Kimberly Kraft gushed tears of joy, while at her side Alex Bolus looked untypically pensive. Alex, hopping mad since the dean had divested her of the athletic directorship, was going to leave at the end of the summer to take a job at North Dakota State in Fargo—so maybe her friend Kimberly's tears were not entirely joyful after all, thought Leland.

He saw Chairman Oberholtzer catch Peggy's eye and wink at her, while his wife Honey leaned over to whisper something to the mummified Mrs. Zastrow. Leland was amused to recall C. Mortimer's reaction to the disappearance of the nude photograph. The day after Leland burned it, his chairman had come to his office and humbly inquired if he'd taken it home with him. Leland said no, he'd laid it on the carpet beside his chair, and suggested that perhaps it got thrown out with the Sunday paper, which was scattered on the floor. It was virtually the first lie of Leland's life, and he was amazed by how smoothly he told it and by how clever rather than guilty it made him feel. His chairman, realizing that it was garbage-pickup day in his neighborhood, looked suddenly ashen, as though he'd lost a priceless heirloom. A few minutes later, from his office window, Leland saw his chairman's Falcon following a garbage truck across the Eleventh Street Bridge.

Next to Mrs. Zastrow sat her husband the dean, his eyes on his watch, as though timing the ceremony. In conference with the dean about becoming his assistant—a job he ultimately turned down as too lowly for even an associate professor—Leland had had the opportunity to look at a few résumés of the fall term's new faculty, wherein he found a bit of hopeful evidence. There was a man named Erkins in History who'd listed the U.S. Army Band under "Other Experience." Connor's replacement in Art, a man named Breitbach, had minored in music as an undergraduate.

"Psst," said Lolly. "What's she playing?" Peggy's song had ended and the organ was coming on strong.

"Joy of Man's Desiring," whispered Leland.

"Brahms?"

"Bach."

She bent to her notepad.

The reception and dance were held in the half-completed ball-room Sammy Culpepper was adding to the river side of his supper club. Sammy and his staff had been working feverishly most of the day, stashing the builders' tools out of sight, sweeping the concrete floor, moving in a piano, setting up tables, unloading bouquets of carnations and heavy green plants from the florist's van, and rolling out broad squares of red linoleum as a temporary dancing surface.

While the wedding was still in progress across town, Neil and Victor arrived with the college drums and saxophone, having used Leland's and Peggy's keys to get into McCall Hall and the band room. Neil was surprised to see the eleven-year-old Alison Culpepper wearing an apron and setting out silverware and paper napkins. She scowled at him, and he took renewed comfort in having put the classroom forever behind him. He asked, not that he cared, "How's your mother?"

"She got an A from Mrs. Oberholtzer," the girl seethed.

"Glad to hear it," he said, opening his clarinet case and laying his toothbrush and clean underwear on the piano.

"She earned it," said the girl.

"Glad to hear it," he repeated, putting the clarinet to his lips.

"Mrs. Oberholtzer's a *good* teacher."

He advanced upon her, blowing yelplike squeals from his instrument, and chased her from the room.

The unfinished walls of cement block were only three or four rows high, which was ideal for the kind of day it had been—sunny and muggy but with a cooling breeze now off the water. By the time the last guest arrived and went through the receiving line, the sun had gone down and the smell of fresh concrete was more or less replaced by the aromas of perfume, alcohol, sweat, carnations, turkey à la king, and the vaguely fishy scent of the Badbattle in July.

Leland and Peggy provided the dinner music. Then, after cutting the cake, Georgina gave them the high sign, and the quintet, minus one, arranged themselves around the piano, their backs to the low wall and the yellowish sunset glow in the river. They began with their show-off pieces, since no one appeared ready to dance. Victor got their attention with his drumrolls and tricky cymbal work and rim shots throughout "Walking My Baby Back Home"; then Leland and Neil teamed up on "Don't Blame Me."

After that, buoyed by the music and swept with a kind of wild abandon, Peggy dared them to play "Goody, Goody," and they went to work trying to build it up and hold it together, but once again their playing was too fast and crazy—what *was* there about this piece?—and the result was the same as before: screeching and crashing and moaning as the edifice splintered apart and came tumbling down. Peggy called out the next title from the wreckage, so that they left it without apology and moved without pause into a slow and controlled rendition of "My Blue Heaven."

Georgina led Ron to the center of the red linoleum, and Peggy watched them dance until it made her too sad and she lowered her eyes to her fingerwork on the sax, spilling tears on her fingers.

Next, they played "After You've Gone," and more dancers joined the bride and groom. Because Neil seemed to know what he was doing on this piece, Peggy backed off, backed away, sat down on the low wall and scanned the tables of the guests visiting over their after-dinner drinks. She saw Historian Quinn looking depleted and bilious while his wife Rachel carried on an animated conversation with old Professor Shea. She saw Bernard Beckwith yawning at something Brooks Dumont was telling him. She saw her sister-in-law sitting with Alex and Kimberly.

And then, for an instant, she saw Connor, or someone who looked like Connor, turning away from the doorway beyond the tables leading to the bar and lounge.

She put down her sax and ran across the dance floor. The bar and lounge were crowded, every stool and booth occupied. She looked into fifty faces before concluding that her eyes, in accord with her wishful thinking, had played her a savage trick.

Meanwhile, Connor was outside, hurrying around to the river side of the building to greet Peggy before she took up her sax again. Leland, first to see him materialize out of the sunset glow, which had darkened to violet, stopped playing. Neil nearly dropped his clarinet. Victor, assuming this unexpected opening in "My Blue Heaven" was his signal for a drum solo, went pounding and crashing madly along, unaware that his fellows had left their instruments to stand at the low wall to welcome their bassist back to life.

"Connor, my God," exclaimed Neil. "Is it really you?"

Leland put out a hand to touch him. "Did you know you were thought to be dead?"

Ignoring these mystifying greetings, Connor threw his arms open to Peggy, who came rushing across the dance floor and leaped at him and clung to him as he lifted her over the low wall and set her down on the sand. Victor dropped his sticks. The room fell silent. Lolly was heard to gasp. Joannie got up from her place and came forward for a closer look at the man kissing her sister-in-law. So did the Oberholtzers and the Steadmans. So did the bride, leaving the groom on the dance floor and clutching Leland by the arm and exclaiming, "It's him."

Victor, standing among his drums, noticed how puzzled many of the guests appeared, and so he rattled off a brief drumroll and shouted, by way of explanation, "Three days in the goddamn grave, ladies and gentlemen!"

Peggy and Connor disappeared around the corner of the building, and the remaining three musicians did their best with "Bye Bye Blackbird," which wasn't all that good. Next, they worked "Smoke Gets in Your Eyes" out to a ridiculous length, waiting for their singer and bassist to return.

In his station wagon, on their way to McCall Hall to pick up the string bass, Connor told her, between kisses, how he'd left the city on Thursday, fleeing his need for a drink. It was around noon on Thursday. He'd finished his third double portrait of the summer, and he ached to show it to Peggy. Cleaning his brushes and tidying his studio, he suffered pangs of loneliness so severe that he groaned with pain. Their separation was unendurable.

Another commission awaited him, he told her, but he needed a respite from work. He needed a life away from his easel, away from his solitary apartment. Emerson Tate, who was about to leave for a vacation in Spain, was expecting to meet him at the Lock and Dam for a farewell jar. Connor felt his will weakening, he said, so he went to his car and drove straight out of the city. He didn't even stop by his apartment for a change of clothes.

He took a meandering route north, crossing over into the lake country of Wisconsin, and kept driving until he came to Lake Superior. Instead of turning west, back toward Minnesota, he turned east, having forty-eight hours to kill. Peggy, he knew, would be back in Rookery on Saturday to sing at Georgina's wedding. He drove steadily through the afternoon and well into the night, his

thirst following closely behind, and ended up in a motel in Mar-
quette, Michigan, a mile or more from the nearest bar or liquor
store.

Two more days he drove, Friday and today, continuing in a
circle around Lake Superior. Here and there, where the road ran
close to the lake, he stopped to sketch the formations of iron-
colored rock rising up out of the water. He stopped and studied the
faces in coffee shops in Ontario. He stopped in Duluth and bought
a shirt and underwear. He arrived in Rookery in time to see the
wedding party leave the church. He checked into the Van Buren
and showered and changed clothes.

After half an hour, Connor and Peggy returned to Culpepper's, having determined to spend the rest of the summer together.
They lifted the string bass over the low wall and situated it next to
the piano.

"What'll it be?" Peggy asked as Connor tightened his strings.

Leland's reply was the opening chords of "These Foolish
Things."

They played astonishingly well. All the soloists, even Neil,
seemed to have a pleasing direction in mind and knew the smooth-
est route to get them there. No blind alleys, no wrong turns, no
running out of gas halfway home. To Peggy's practiced ear, they
were no longer a group of five malcontents thrown together by cir-
cumstance, but a single entity producing a sound so unified and reliable that their audience kept up an almost constant patter of
applause. She saw even those who'd drunk too much sit up and take
notice, sensing themselves in the hands of professionals.

How did you account for an ensemble's improvement, she
wondered, after months of not playing together? Was it that they'd
each gone off in pursuit of their *own* improvement, and then come
together again as more complete and satisfied people? That was
true certainly of Victor, who, after side trips through injury and rehab and a stint in the classroom, had found the job of his dreams.
She'd never before seen Victor manage his drums with such a relaxed, unforced self-confidence.

How come we're so goddamn good? mused Victor, his eyes on

Leland, watching for him to signal the next transition. Between them, the piano and drums were providing a peppy, staccato bridge between solos. Timing was everything. Rattle rattle, plink plink. Rattle plink. Ah, that Edwards knows his stuff—always has—and yet tonight he's doing something different, loosening up, letting his shoulders sway as he plays, acknowledging applause instead of hiding from it, looking up from his keys and actually smiling at the audience. Who the hell does he think he is—Liberace?

Actually, Leland was seeing himself as a youngster, performing in his twelfth consecutive recital of Miss Carpentier's piano students. In those days, he'd mastered not only the piano, but also the sort of stage presence that endeared itself to an audience. But then, having mastered it, he'd quickly lost it. At eighteen, just as he was coming into possession of his boyhood, it was suddenly over, and he'd been struggling ever since to catch up to his more mature contemporaries. Not once in the intervening years, until tonight, had he felt confident enough to communicate with his admirers with his eyes as well as his melodies. Such a small thing, he thought, to meet someone's eyes with your own. Such a wonderful thing to feel finally grown-up. It all started last January when he'd first run through "These Foolish Things" in Neil's basement. The strike seemed to have helped him along, though he didn't know exactly how; it was as though by taking a stand on the strike, he'd finally put a foundation under himself. But more crucial than the strike were these four friends surrounding him in Culpepper's half-finished ballroom—his combo, his team, his boyhood vision come true. Such a small thing, he thought, to meet someone's eyes with your own. And such an easy thing, when you're part of an ensemble. When he finished his solo part and teamed up with Victor to hand it on to Neil, there was an outbreak of clapping and whistling from a table of Leland's fellow professors—Beckwith and Dumont and Cardero—and he beamed them a smile meant to indicate how mightily warmed he was by their cheer.

Neil played like someone going deep into himself, for he was eating his heart out, aware that Peggy was lost to him forever now that Connor was back among the living. But instead of being diminished or discouraged by his sorrow, he was fascinated by it. He rather enjoyed eating his heart out—it seemed like such a useful thing to do. As a published author, he had to be alert for any expe-rience that might be turned into fiction, and so, probing his wound, he played phrases over and over, ever more somberly, and produced a murky effect that appealed to those who liked their jazz on the dark side. Peggy helped him along with some of the darkest colors she'd ever played on her saxophone, and Connor helped too, with the deepest chords he could find on his bass.

Connor, when it was his turn, came up out of the dark and made light of all these foolish things Peggy had been singing about. Connor was feeling euphoric. Peggy still loved him. She would re-turn with him to the city. He was dizzy with happiness. He felt lighter than air. He felt drunk.

And so the Icejam Quintet played until everyone had gone home, and they kept playing long after that, into the small hours of morning, Sammy Culpepper blissfully drinking himself uncon-scious in a booth in the barroom, his employees gone, his daughter Alison fast asleep in a booth nearby.

Their music drifted out over the water and across the railroad yards and flowed downtown by way of Division Street, faint strains of it heard by a policeman sitting on the steps of the city hall who would have ordered them to close down their concert if he didn't enjoy it so much, heard by a late night disc jockey lock-ing up KRKU and then unlocking it again to check his turntable and tape player because he thought the beautiful strains of "My Blue Heaven" might be coming from inside, heard by a man living in the apartment Peggy used to occupy over the JCPenney store, a solitary insomniac who wished he had a woman to turn to and say, "Ain't that music pretty?"

The next day, Connor drove to Eldora Sparks's house and spent an unfruitful half hour standing among the white-painted stones trying to make conversation with his daughter. She said she'd never return to Minneapolis as long as Peggy was in his life, and it was with mixed feelings—relief, anger, pity—that he left her there. He drove across town and discussed her with Lolly and Leland, eliciting their promise to watch over her to whatever extent she permitted. He expected by autumn she'd change her mind and return to school in the city. Lolly welcomed the chance, she said, to get to know the girl better. "Such potential," she told Connor. "Such intelligence, such a mind of her own, such a way with bread dough."

He left then, for Minneapolis, Peggy riding beside him, Joannie and Neil in the backseat.

Joannie flew home alone to Boston, Neil to Dayton.

Victor talked Aaron Cardero into accompanying him to Iowa.

On Monday morning, Lolly corrected her false report to radioland of Connor's death. When, at the end of her gushy account of the wedding, she took phone calls, she recognized one of the voices as the prankster's falsetto. She hung up before the voice uttered the obscenity it seemed to be aiming at. Since she hadn't heard the voice since before Gary Oberholtzer went to boot camp, her suspicions seemed confirmed. Later, at home, she confided in Leland that if it was Gary mimicking women on the air, couldn't it also have been Gary calling Ohio and claiming to be Emerson Tate? Leland said she was probably right.

Peggy and Connor spent Monday and Tuesday getting in and out of bed in the Hiawatha Arms. It was from bed, on Tuesday evening, that they watched Neil Armstrong walk on the moon.

On Wednesday, a district judge upheld the action of the Minnesota State College Board, ruling that it was within their discretionary power to redistribute public funding as they saw fit. Naturally, Dean Zastrow and the more stalwart nonstrikers were overjoyed. And so was Victor, for a less obvious reason. When the news reached them in Des Moines, he told Aaron Cardero, "Next time, without the courts to fall back on, you professors are going to have to depend on the Alliance as your only goddamn salvation!"

On Thursday, Gary Oberholtzer returned to active duty. By this time, Lolly's suspicion had gestated into a certainty, and led to her speculation that Laura might also have been involved. That afternoon, when the girl came to bake bread with her, she was about to confront her concerning the phone call to Ohio, but then realized that Laura's response would be stony silence. Better if her father handled it. Lolly would tell Connor of her suspicions and leave it to him. She was sure to see a good bit of Connor this fall, for he and Peggy intended to spend their weekends together. On the Saturdays Peggy didn't fly south to the city, Connor would drive north.

In September, registering for fall semester, Helen Culpepper stopped in at Leland's office to bat her eyes at him and say she was enrolled in his History of the English Language class. She introduced him to her dour-looking daughter and drew from a pasteboard box a bristly, uncomfortable-looking hammock she was knotting.

On that same day, Sandy Hupstad introduced Peggy to her new boyfriend, Dickie Donaldson. Dickie, she said, had spent the summer working in a snowmobile factory, waiting to be drafted, but his draft board seemed to have overlooked him, so he thought he might as well try college again and get back into football.

"Yeah," said Dickie Donaldson.

"He was all-state in high school," she told Peggy. "And he's got my Hudson Hornet running like a dream."

Peggy inquired after Chuck Lucking.

Sandy giggled and wrinkled her nose and said she guessed he was in Fort Leonard Wood, Kansas. " 'Least, that's where he left for in June."

At noon Peggy picked up her pile of summer mail at the campus post office and headed for the cafeteria, where she was to meet Leland for lunch. Crossing to the student center, she shuffled her envelopes and found a letter from Neil. It was, as she expected, the same message Connor had received a week ago in Minneapolis—an appeal for money in order to complete the printing and binding of his novel. T. Woodman Press had gone out of business, said Neil, but with $250 from each member of the quintet, Emerson Tate would help him get "Paula's Passion" published on schedule, and their reward would be several free copies of the book. She framed a reply in her mind. She would promise him money, but only in installments, and only if Neil's parents each contributed a like amount. She couldn't be so openhanded as Connor, who, to her astonishment, had mailed Neil five hundred dollars. Connor, feeling flush and magnanimous in the midst of his seventh double portrait of the summer, had said, "You can't give up on an artist until he's outgrown his childhood."

Leland, meanwhile, entering the student center from another direction, was approached by a young man with russet, shoulder-length hair. He wore jeans and a flannel shirt with a string tie, and an army fatigue jacket with ERKINS stenciled above the pocket.

"Are you Dr. Edwards?" he asked.

"I am," said Leland, rather put off by the man's appearance. It was unclear whether the hair under his nose was intended as a mustache or simply growing there by neglect.

"Erkins in History," the young man said. "I spent two years as a trumpeter for Uncle Sam."

"Oh, Erkins, of course," he replied, clapping the man on the shoulder, thrilled to remember where he'd seen the name before.

"I just saw your note on the bulletin board, Dr. Edwards, about playing some music."

About the Author

JON HASSLER was born in Minneapolis in 1933. He received degrees from St. John's University in Minnesota, where he is now an English teacher and writer-in-residence, and from the University of North Dakota. Jon Hassler is also the author of seven other widely acclaimed novels: *Staggerford, Simon's Night, The Love Hunter, A Green Journey, Grand Opening, North of Hope,* and *Dear James.*